The
CHAOS
FUNCTION

The
CHAOS
FUNCTION

Jack Skillingstead

A John Joseph Adams Book
Houghton Mifflin Harcourt
BOSTON   NEW YORK
2019

For information about permission to reproduce selections from this book, write to trade.permissions@hmhco.com or to Permissions, Houghton Mifflin Harcourt Publishing Company, 3 Park Avenue, 19th Floor, New York, New York 10016.

hmhco.com

Library of Congress Cataloging-in-Publication Data
Names: Skillingstead, Jack, 1955- author.
Title: The chaos function / Jack Skillingstead.
Description: Boston ; New York : Houghton Mifflin Harcourt, 2019. |
"A John Joseph Adams book."
Identifiers: LCCN 2018033155 (print) | LCCN 2018035449 (ebook) |
ISBN 9781328527875 (ebook) | ISBN 9781328526151 (hardcover)
Subjects: | BISAC: FICTION / Science Fiction / Adventure. |
GSAFD: Science fiction.
Classification: LCC PS3619.K555 (ebook) | LCC PS3619.K555 C48 2019 (print) |
DDC 813/.6—dc23
LC record available at https://lccn.loc.gov/2018033155

Book design by Margaret Rosewitz

Printed in the United States of America
DOC 10 9 8 7 6 5 4 3 2 1

For Ruby
My favorite daughter

I think of the future as branching probability streams.

— ELON MUSK

The dividing line between past, present, and future is an illusion.

— ALBERT EINSTEIN

Because you're a war reporter, and in the end you're always a head above the others, right? With that hero's aura . . .

— FRANCESCA BORRI

PART I

DEATH AND LIFE

ONE

OLIVIA NIKITAS SAT IN THE shade of an improvised awning, a canvas tarp that smelled like a dead goat. She checked her watch again, drummed her fingers nervously on the table. The hand-lettered HABIB CAFÉ sign hung crookedly by a couple of wire twists. Most of the buildings on both sides of the street lay in ruins, either bombed-out shells or pulverized beyond recognition. The proprietor, Habib, had dragged his coffee machine and generator into what was left of an antique shop. Olivia admired his entrepreneurial spirit. As a freelance journalist, she had been covering the carnage in Syria since 2023 — six years now. The spirit of Aleppo was pretty thoroughly annihilated, so the appearance of the Habib Café, barely ten weeks into a shaky postwar era, looked like a positive development.

Across the street a cat slipped through a mountain of wreckage, its movement so sinuous and fleeting that at first Olivia thought the cat was the shadow of something passing through the air, like a bad omen.

She picked up her coffee, a potent Arabic blend spiced with cardamom. Holding the cup in the fingertips of both hands, she brought it to her lips. The luxury of fresh coffee equaled a minor miracle after the deprivations of war. Even in the heat, with sweat trickling from her hairline and her shirt sticking to her body, Olivia savored the scalding jolt of caffeine.

A little girl, maybe seven years old, came running down the street, the ragged cuffs of her trousers whisking up dust. She called to the cat, grabbed a bent spine of iron rebar, and hauled herself after it, climbing a potential avalanche. Her arms and legs were bird-bone thin. Olivia winced, sitting there on her comparatively fat American ass. She put her cup down, feeling irrationally guilty for the indulgence.

The cat darted under a slab of broken concrete. The little girl peered after it, calling, "Qetta, qetta." The gap was just big enough that she might be tempted to crawl after the damn thing. Olivia lifted her sweat-damp hair away from the back of her neck and looked around, hoping for some adult supervision. Good luck with that. The city was overrun with orphans. Olivia started to stand.

In the distance, a gunshot popped.

Olivia went rigid. Technically, hostilities had officially ended. But that wouldn't prevent a rogue sniper from taking up position. The shot had come from the direction of the Green Zone. By now, Brian and Jodee had left and would be out in the open. Jodee Abadi was her escort into the Old City, and Brian Anker was her would-be escort into a different kind of hazardous territory: a relationship impervious to her usual strategies of detachment. Brian wasn't the first guy to take on that mission, but he had already gotten farther than most. If Olivia's heart was a door, then Brian was the pushy salesman who had wedged his foot in the gap when she tried to slam it in his face. For that, she resented him a little. He was good about the resentment. He was good about everything. It really pissed her off.

Another gunshot popped. *Where are you guys?*

Suddenly she felt it, the brittle substratum of the enforced peace. It could give way at any time. Foreign military forces led by the Americans barely held the city together. Soon something would break. A new insurgency, maybe. In the months since the end of the war, Olivia had gotten used to leaving her Kevlar vest in her room. She still brought her headscarf, though, even if at the moment she wore it loosely around her neck.

Two gunshots, and Brian (and Jodee) in the open.

By reflex, she reached for her phone, but there was no point. This district of Aleppo was a cellular dead zone.

The sound of something scraping and sliding pulled her attention back to the girl. A broken window frame surfed down the piled debris and cracked to pieces on the street. The little girl had her broomstick arm shoved all the way to the shoulder under the concrete slab. If the slab moved, it would crush her. Olivia quickly crossed the street. "Hey, kid! Be careful."

From the top of the mountain of rubble, the girl looked at Olivia and pointed down. "Qetta, qetta."

"Yeah, I get it. Your cat is under there."

"*Qetta.*"

Olivia looked east, *willing* Brian and Jodee to be there. Instead, a couple of old men crossed the street, their summer white dishdashahs seeming to float them above a haze of dust. Olivia hated that she worried about Brian. That's what you got when you let the salesman stick his foot in the door. She should have known better.

Olivia sighed and started climbing the rubble, muttering, "Qetta the fucking cat." The heat was causing her bra band to chafe, though she had caked on talcum powder. Blinking grit and stinging sweat out of her eyes, she reached the girl and put on a smile. In broken Arabic, she asked, "Where's your mother?" The kid stared at her with eyes too big for the bones of her face.

"Qetta," the girl said.

"Right. Look out, kid."

Olivia knelt in front of the gap. She felt off-balance. The whole mass of concrete, wood, sheet metal, and glass threatened to shift without warning. Under the slab, a pair of eyes winked like green sequins. Olivia took a granola bar out of her shirt pocket and tore the wrapper. She broke off a corner and held it for the cat to smell.

"Here, kitty."

The cat didn't move.

Hesitantly, Olivia reached under the slab. The cat crept forward, sniffing. Olivia thrust out her other hand, grabbed the cat behind the ears, and dragged it clear. Hissing and clawing, the cat wrenched out of her grip and leaped away. The little girl didn't even look at it. Her attention was one hundred percent on the granola bar. Olivia handed it to her. The child devoured the bar in three bites, then picked the crumbs from her shirt and sucked them off her fingers. Olivia unclipped the water bottle from her belt, pulled the nipple up, and offered it.

"That doesn't look safe," a familiar voice said.

Olivia looked around. Brian and Jodee were standing in the street watching her. "Jesus Christ, I was getting worried about you guys."

The little girl pulled on the water bottle. Olivia let go. "You keep it, honey."

Clutching the bottle, the girl hopped from one semi-stable spot to another and finally to the street. Jodee put his arms out to corral her, but she ducked past him and ran away, yelling, "Qetta, qetta!"

Olivia climbed down with considerably more caution. Brian and Jodee reached toward her, but she jumped the last three feet to the ground without their help and brushed her hands off on her pants. Brian's cotton shirt clung to his skin like wet rice paper. He held his arms open, and Olivia adroitly sidestepped him. Touching was part of Brian's vocabulary, but Olivia wasn't always in the mood for a language lesson.

Brian stuffed his hands in his pockets. "I was worried about you, too," he said.

"You're always worried about me."

"That's because you're always getting yourself into worrisome situations."

Olivia shrugged. "Comes with the job."

Jodee stood back, a half smile on his face. Olivia wrinkled her nose. Nice to know her antics amused him. Olivia had known Jodee for years, long before the current peace had stipulated that rebel fighters surrender their weapons. It was odd to see him without a gun. Stocky, balding, and middle-aged, he reminded her of her uncle Agata.

"That kid . . ." Olivia said.

"Somebody will pick her up," Brian said. "The Red Cross has gotten pretty organized in the city."

Olivia looked down the street. The girl was almost out of sight.

"You would never catch her," Jodee said.

Brian nodded. "If the Red Cross doesn't pick her up, she'll probably find her way to one of my water distribution stations. A lot of them do."

She turned to him. "More of your glass-half-full philosophy? That little girl doesn't have a chance."

"I think Olivia's glass is all the way empty," Jodee said.

Olivia rolled her eyes. "I'm realistic."

"Liv," Brian said, "just because you can't rescue everyone, that doesn't mean you can't rescue *some* of them."

Brian worked for a Portland-based NGO called Oregon Helps. At twenty-six, he was four years younger than Olivia, and—irrationally, in Olivia's view—an optimist. They made an odd couple, not that Olivia thought of them as a couple exactly. Brian was tall and Nordic-looking, his eyes blue behind the lenses of wire-frame glasses. Olivia was five foot four and decidedly non-Nordic. Her father, a second-generation Greek

American, had married likewise before moving to Seattle and opening his import business. After Olivia's mother died, young, her dad married Rohana, an export agent from Jaipur.

Brian hadn't said the L-word yet, but she knew he was itching to spit it out, maybe while his fingertips traced calligraphy on her bare shoulder. Love of the adult variety had never happened to Olivia, but everything else had. She knew this colored her perception. Okay, maybe Brian wasn't a pushy salesman but a charming one; either way, the result was the same: His damn foot was in the door.

"If we're going to the Old City," Jodee said, scratching the black stubble on his jaw, "we need to go now. It will be dark in a few hours."

"We're going." Olivia pulled her scarf up and arranged a proper hijab. There was a story in the Old City—a bloody one—and she wanted it.

✸

"SHAMEFUL," JODEE SAID, POINTING AT a ragged gap in the stone archway.

The Gate of Antioch stood as one of the oldest and best preserved of the nine original gates into the Old City. At least it had been, prior to the final year of the civil war.

"Mortar attack," Olivia said. The war had destroyed more important things than ancient architectural treasures. It had left a million dead. Three times that many driven away as refugees, flooding into Turkey and central Europe.

Which is not to say the destruction of historical sites wasn't bad, too —it *was*—and Jodee took it personally. Before the war, his business had arranged tours of the Old City and other ancient sites, and he had been a member of the Aleppo Preservation Corps. Jodee was fond of telling people that Aleppo was the oldest continuously inhabited city on earth. But when Olivia first met him, Jodee Abadi had been leading a heavily armed band of fighters, part of a moderate Islamist alliance called the Asala wa el-Tanmiya Front. War changed people. Or revealed who they really were.

A couple of bearded men in short-sleeved shirts loitered near the arch, watching them.

Olivia shaded her eyes. "Who are those guys?"

"I will find out." Jodee looked sober. "Both of you wait here. And try not to look like journalists until I discover what they want."

"I'm *not* a journalist," Brian said.

"Tell Olivia not to be one, either." Jodee walked toward the men.

Brian wandered over to the collapsing remnants of a makeshift and abandoned souk. He put his hands on his hips and appraised the empty vendor stalls, nodding thoughtfully. Olivia joined him. A scent of cinnamon and cassia bark lingered, trapped under the rusty corrugated roof.

"What the hell are you doing?" Olivia kept her voice low. She plucked her shirt away from her bra and flapped it, trying to generate a breeze underneath.

"Pretending I'm a tourist."

"Uh, great idea. Except there aren't any tourists."

"Liv?"

"What?"

"Would you call this one of your better ideas, coming here?"

"I don't have enough information to answer that."

Rumors persisted that a pro-Assad militia had recently used a fourteenth-century madrassa as a torture cell—the use of a school for this purpose managing to defile religion, education, and history at the same time. The war had ended, but not everyone was happy about coalition troops taking over. Assad supporters blamed the Free Syrian Army and its sympathizers for starting the whole thing. Discovering evidence of continued human rights violations on the part of the regime was a story Olivia very much wished to tell—and one Jodee Abadi very much wanted told.

"When do you think you'll have enough information?" Brian said.

"You sure ask a lot of questions."

"Don't you always say asking questions is good?"

"Was that another question?"

Jodee was talking to the bearded men. Olivia couldn't tell whether or not it was going well. In Aleppo, it was always safest to assume it wasn't. She put her hand on Brian's arm, trying for a moment to adopt the part of his vocabulary largely missing in her. "Hey."

Brian raised his eyebrows.

"Never mind," she said.

"Come on. What?"

"Nothing."

Brian removed his glasses, wiped the lenses on his shirttail, and put them back on. Despite his wide-brimmed REI sunhat, his nose and neck were perpetually sunburned and peeling. He shed more skin than a snake. "You were going to tell me I should go back to the Green Zone."

"You should."

"Liv."

"But I'm not telling you to, because what would be the point, right?"

"Right. Thanks for respecting my decision to not take the advice you didn't offer."

She grinned briefly. "Really, Bri, you don't have anything to prove."

"I know."

"What I said yesterday, it wasn't important."

"You mean about how you thought I might not be up to dealing with all the shit that goes on around here, like you and your hard-nosed pals?"

"I never said 'hard-nosed.'"

"Maybe not the actual words."

Jodee returned from speaking with the bearded men. Olivia pointed her chin in their direction. "What's going on?"

"They say it is not such a good day to visit the Old City."

"Why not?"

Jodee shrugged. "I don't know."

"Who are they?"

"I don't know."

"That wasn't a very productive conversation, was it?"

"Not on the surface." Jodee pressed the back of his hand to his forehead, as if checking himself for a fever. "It is very hot. Maybe we should not do this."

"It's always hot. Just point out the madrassa. I'm good by myself after that. You and Brian can go back."

"We could all go back," Brian said. "Right, Jodee?"

Olivia wished Brian at least would return to the Green Zone. Despite his protestations to the contrary, Olivia was confident he *was* there trying to prove something that she had more or less prodded him into thinking he needed to prove.

"By tomorrow there might not be any evidence left," Olivia said. She looked away for a moment. "Bri, I have to see it now. It's my job. But you—"

"Don't say it," Brian said.

She looked at Jodee. "Will those guys try to stop us?"

"I do not think so. They _like_ journalists."

Olivia squinted. "You told them?"

"I'm not a journalist," Brian said.

"I didn't have to tell them," Jodee said. "They recognized you. I already informed them that you would not leave. They did not seem overly concerned."

Olivia had been in and out of Aleppo for years. She had many contacts, and was probably known by more people than she knew herself. For a journalist, that was both a good and a bad thing.

Jodee cleared his throat. "It isn't far to the madrassa. If we are still going."

"We're going." Olivia started walking toward the gate. If Assad was orchestrating the torture of former enemies of the state — men like Jodee — and doing it right under the noses of Western occupiers, she _had_ to tell the story. Of course, the torturers could be acting on their own . . . probably _were_ acting on their own. But best to let the official investigators figure that one out. In Olivia's experience, it was rare that officials investigated anything before being embarrassed into doing so by the press.

As she passed the taller of the bearded men, he spared Olivia a measuring glance. A thick aroma of Turkish tobacco clung to him.

On the other side of the gate, a Syrian flag hung limply above the great medieval citadel. Many of the surrounding structures had been beaten into rubble. The streets were mostly empty, except for a few young men. Olivia's eyes widened when she saw one of them, armed with a machine gun, scurry around a corner.

"Not good," she said, and her heart beat faster.

"Do we need to get out of here?" Brian said.

Olivia turned to their guide. "Jodee?"

"This way." Jodee waved them into a cobblestone alley. He walked quickly, almost running. Olivia had to jog to keep up. They followed a crooked path, squeezing between walls thousands of years old, until they came out a couple of streets over. Three French soldiers, members of the peacekeeping force, walked by on patrol, their rifles shoulder-slung, soft berets instead of helmets covering their heads.

"This is your madrassa." Jodee pointed.

A single-story structure with a domed roof. Bullet holes pocked the sand-colored façade. Arabic letters, like contortionist stick figures, made a chain above the archway. Below the archway, a door wrapped in green copper stood open. At the sight of the madrassa Olivia stopped dead.

Brian, frowning, said in a whisper, "What is it?"

Olivia stared at the building, a strange sense of recognition resonating through her. "I feel like I know this place."

"Liv, are you all right?"

On the next block, gunfire erupted. Someone shouted in English, but the shout was cut off.

It was starting.

Instinctively, Olivia looked for cover. The French soldiers reacted to the gunfire, going for their weapons. But they weren't fast enough. Two men, their faces covered to the eyes by scarves, came out of nowhere and ran at them—or was one chasing the other? The second man did not have his weapon raised, and his empty hand reached out as if to catch the first man and pull him back.

The first gunman looked like a teenager. During the war she'd seen dozens just like him. Kids in flip-flops, armed with machine guns and righteous anger. This one shouted something about God and triggered his Kalashnikov. Heavy rounds racketed from the muzzle. The French soldiers danced briefly like marionettes and went down. A few yards from them, Jodee lay sprawled and bloody, unmoving.

The shooter swung his gun toward Olivia. The second man pushed the barrel down. "Antazar." He sounded angry. The shooter clearly wanted to kill Olivia, not to mention anything else that might be alive in the immediate vicinity. But for the moment at least, he didn't. Olivia's legs were shaking.

The man who had pushed the barrel down approached her. He was older, maybe thirty—same age as Olivia. A white scar cut through his left eyebrow and climbed his forehead like a jagged trend line. Olivia thought she knew him. Years ago there had been a man among a group of disorganized insurgent fighters. Olivia had embedded herself with them. Getting the story. She never knew his real name, but this man had been kind to her, intervening when some of the others had crowded her. In this place, kindness made an impression.

"Don't go back the way you came," he said. "Find shelter and stay low."

"I know you."

"Look to your friend now, and go."

He couldn't mean Jodee, who lay face-down in a pool of blood. Brian's hat rested a few yards from Jodee's body, and Brian himself stood near the madrassa, facing the wall, his head down and hands out of sight in front of him.

"Bri?"

He looked over his shoulder, his face curd-white above the sunburn line made by his missing hat.

"*Brian.*"

He half turned toward her, his arm braced against the wall. The left leg of his khakis was soaked dark, and drops of blood shone like glossy red enamel on his boot. Olivia started toward him. Behind her, a gunshot went off. She jerked around. One of the French soldiers lying on the ground held a 9 mm pistol extended. The man with the scar was still falling, a bleeding hole in his face. The kid in flip-flops unloaded into the soldier, the Kalashnikov rounds ripping across the soldier's chest. Then the barrel came up and pointed at Olivia and Brian.

This time there was no one to stop him.

TWO

THE WEAPON CLICKED — EMPTY.

The gunman reached for the replacement magazine holstered on his belt. Down the street an intense firefight broke out. The kid in flip-flops ran for cover. Bullets flew in every direction, or seemed to. Was any of it directed at *them?* Was it the coalition, a new uprising, Islamic State infiltrators? None of the above?

Olivia caught Brian as he staggered away from the wall. She pulled his arm across her shoulders, the weight of him almost dragging her over. Blood sopped his pants, so much blood. Olivia struggled to hold him up. *Oh, God, Brian.* She lugged him toward the door of the madrassa — the nearest place they could take shelter. A heavy explosion went off, so close the ground shook.

She and Brian staggered inside.

Hazy pillars of sunlight pierced the damaged roof and stood among the disarranged school desks. The air was hot and stifling. Outside, men shouted in Arabic. A crude door frame opened on a staircase plunging steeply down. She walked Brian toward it, struggling to keep him upright.

"What are we doing?" Brian sounded confused, weak.

"Hang on, Bri. We have to get out of sight."

She maneuvered him into the stairwell. Brian slumped against her. Awkwardly, they descended a dozen steps, then halted. It was too dark, but there was no going back. Gunfire rang out, so close it had to be coming from inside the schoolroom above them.

Good guys or bad guys? There was no way to tell.

Olivia pulled out her phone. It fit her hand like a carbon fiber playing card. The Gates-7 was the Swiss Army knife of phones, loaded with old-school apps like the LED flashlight she now tapped on. A dim circle of illumination appeared at their feet. Too dim. The battery no longer held a decent charge.

They continued down stone steps so worn over the centuries that they appeared to sag in the middle.

The sounds of fighting became muted, absorbed by the earth and by thick stones quarried around the collapse of the Mongol Empire. Underground it was cooler, but a fetid smell rose around them. Urine, feces, and the briny stink of terror. Olivia stifled her gag reflex, missed the next step, and fell to the ground with Brian. Her phone went skittering away, and she landed hard, striking the back of her head on the stone floor. For a few moments, the pain eclipsed everything. She squeezed her eyes closed and gritted her teeth, seeing stars. Next to her, Brian groaned.

"Oh, Jesus. Brian, Bri—"

Groping in the dark, she found him. Her fingertips came away oiled with blood.

"Hold on, Bri."

He made a sound then like a clogged drain. Emotion threatened to overwhelm her. Olivia tried to cut through it, find a detached place where she could think. Her emergency medical training came back, for all the good it would do her in the dark. She looked around but couldn't see the phone; the battery must have quit.

She felt for Brian's wounded leg. Blood pumped over her hands, hot and slippery, which meant a damaged artery. Panic lifted into her chest like a swarm of hornets. For a few seconds, she couldn't move. Then, using the heel of her hand, she pressed hard against his femur near the groin. Or tried to. Every time her hand slipped, more blood bubbled between her fingers.

She tore the scarf from her neck and tied it around his upper thigh, cinching it as tight as she could. Brian whimpered, too weak to scream. She doubted the tourniquet would work, but after a few moments the blood stopped spurting. Maybe it was helping, or maybe Brian was simply running out of blood.

He was trying to speak. "Tell my parents." His words were barely audible.

"Shut up. We're getting out of here."

He went quiet. She felt for his face, took it in her hands. "Brian, can you hear me? Brian?"

She put her ear to his chest, heard a faint, bubbling gasp — then nothing. Olivia picked up his wrist, tried to locate a pulse. There wasn't one. Next she found the carotid artery in his neck. No pulse there, either. She started CPR, keeping up the chest compressions and breathing until she couldn't keep it going any longer, until her arms and shoulders ached and her back cramped.

Above her, faintly, came the sounds of gunfire.

With every rescue breath, she knew he was gone. His lips, so sweet and yielding that morning, now were cold and rubbery.

She stopped CPR, panting now to get her own breath back. Across the room, so dim that at first Olivia wasn't sure she was seeing it, a pale ghost light became visible, like a tiny window in the floor — her phone, the screen grayed out to almost nothing.

Olivia rolled onto her knees and began to crawl. Her hand skidded in a warm puddle. She whimpered and kept going, reached the phone, and picked it up. The flashlight was still on, revealing a floor littered with a plastic bag, candy bar wrappers, a wrinkled sheet of newspaper featuring a grainy picture of Bashar al-Assad in his wheelchair, and a scattering of matchsticks and cigarette butts. *Lots* of cigarette butts.

Gathering herself, she got one foot under her and started to stand. Her head bumped something that yielded stiffly. She ducked away and turned the failing light on it. A human foot stuck out over the end of a table. "*Shit.*" The foot twitched, and someone groaned — a sound called up from hell.

She got on her feet and held her phone over the table. An old man, his shirt open, lay stretched out, his beard and hair biblically wild. Leather straps immobilized him. Cigarette burns made random constellations across his chest and neck, like eruptions of pox. A dark purple bruise spread upward from his groin. Someone had poked at his abdomen with a knife, leaving a dozen red dashes. Alligator clips attached to his earlobes trailed wires to a power box with a big-dial rheostat, like something out of Dr. Frankenstein's laboratory.

Olivia's gut clenched as if someone had slugged her. The old man's lips parted like one more wound. She leaned close. His breath smelled like rotten meat. The old man spoke, and the words were unintelligible, at least to Olivia. They sounded Arabic but without the modern intonations. There was also an English word, but it made no more sense to her than the Arabic. It sounded like "supers-potion."

Delirium and gibberish.

Olivia reached for her water bottle, but it wasn't there; she'd given it to the little girl. "Help's on the way," she said, not even trying to sound like she believed it. Even if help did arrive, it was already too late for Brian —and probably for this old man, too. Olivia's flashlight dimmed further, the battery nearly exhausted. The next sound out of the old man's mouth wasn't a word but a death rattle. Olivia pulled back, shook her head. "Fuck this place." She meant the torture cell, the city, the country —the world in its entirety. The whole disaster.

Something squirmed in the old man's hair. The wiry gray tangle twitched, and a thing like a beetle emerged. No bigger than a bean, its carapace cobalt-shiny where it wasn't smeared with blood. The bug emitted a minute clicking sound—

And flew straight at her face.

Swatting at it, Olivia stumbled back. Where did it go? She checked the front of her shirt. No bug.

She returned to Brian and flopped on the floor next to his body. The back of her head stung where it had hit the floor earlier. She carefully fingered the bump. It was tender and bleeding. What a mess, and it was her fault. Olivia fought the guilt that was trying to crush her, but there seemed to be no stopping it. "Brian, I'm so sorry."

Something twitched in her hair, tickled the back of her neck.

Click click click.

Pain like a hot needle jabbed into the base of her skull. Olivia clawed wildly at it, raking up a fresh wave of pain when her nails scraped the bump.

"*Fuck* this place."

She found Brian's hand and held it. For years Olivia had chased one crisis after another, freelancing between war zones and famines, tsunamis and violent protests. She had begun to witness the world as a single on-going disaster event. In the places where the event was particularly savage, particularly chaotic, she added a capital D. Reporting allowed her to stand aside, insulated her. Now she remembered something she'd once understood very well but had deliberately turned away from as a matter of survival: All disasters are personal.

She sat, knees drawn up, and bowed her head. *Be alive, don't be gone, be alive, Brian. I can't be the one who did this to you.* One foot in the door, but it was enough to let through a cyclone of pain. Her fault Brian was gone. Jodee Abadi, too. Why hadn't she done things differently? In her mind she saw Brian outside the madrassa, before he was wounded, saw him clearly in a suspended moment before he was shot.

A surge of dizziness rocked her. A wheeling light appeared, like a migraine aura, and she fell into it. For a while she lost herself. Then the world . . . *shifted.* Like an elevator that had stopped short and suddenly dropped the last six inches. Olivia grunted, as if the shift had been real and physical. She felt nauseated, confused. White stars briefly swirled in her vision, like when she had struck her head. Had she fainted? When she tried to let go of Brian's hand, *his* hand clamped down tighter.

Olivia gasped and tore free, as if she had been gripping a hot wire. Even as the rationalization sped forward—surely it was an involuntary muscle spasm—Brian said, "What's wrong?"

"Brian!"

"Whoa, take it easy. You sounded like you were going to be sick."

She threw herself at him.

"Hey, watch the leg. Christ, that hurts."

She held her fading flashlight over him. Brian blinked, his glasses missing; *they'd fallen off when she shoved him toward the madrassa, after the shooting started but before he took the hit.* Blood soaked through Olivia's scarf tied around his thigh. She clearly remembered doing that, yanking the scarf away from her head and making it into a bandage, applying pressure to the gunshot wound—a wound that appeared much less severe than the spurting arterial rupture that she also remembered.

She tried to concentrate through a murderous headache. Like a secondary memory laid over the primary, she saw the scene in the street. *This time the teenager in flip-flops was alone. He fired his Kalashnikov, wounding Jodee and two of the French soldiers before the third took him down. Jodee sat up, hurt but alive, yelling at them to get off the street. Then more gunfire, coming from multiple directions. Brian taking a hit. Yelling, staggering, clutching his leg, blood leaking between his fingers. A frantic retreat into the madrassa, down the stairs and into the stinking dark . . .*

Olivia couldn't process it. Couldn't think clearly.

Outside, the shooting had ceased.

"What is it?" Brian said.

"I don't understand what's happening. You aren't dead. I tried to save you, but I couldn't." She was babbling, and stopped herself. Brian looked confused.

"Liv? You're scaring me."

She controlled her breathing, but she couldn't slow down her heart or do anything about the throbbing headache, the nausea. "This is not possible."

"*What's* not possible?" Brian said.

"It didn't happen this way. I *wanted* you to be alive. But it didn't happen this way."

Boots came clomping down the stairs. She turned toward the sound. Bright lights attached to the barrels of assault rifles swept the torture cell.

The lights pinned Olivia and Brian.

"United States Marines! Show me your hands!" an American voice shouted.

They showed their hands. Olivia squinted, turned her head aside. The Marines were faceless behind the lights.

THREE

OLIVIA CLIMBED THE STAIRS, FOLLOWED by a young-sounding Marine who, when she stumbled, told her to take it easy. Others had already carried Brian away. Behind her, in the sewer-smelling chamber, someone said, "We've got another live one here." Olivia looked back. Shadows swooped and ducked away from the bright weapon-mounted lights.

Outside the madrassa, the heat struck her like a furnace blast. Across the square, two men helped Jodee into the back of an old bullet-riddled Peugeot—her friend resurrected, just like Brian, both wounded but alive in the second memory. In the real memory, she thought, reluctantly. Olivia had never before doubted her grasp of reality. But she had hit her head pretty hard on the floor of the madrassa, and right then she couldn't quite reconcile the competing versions of events.

"Jodee!" Yelling sent a hot needle into her temple, but at least the nausea had begun to subside.

He waved, grimacing in pain. The driver threw the door shut, got in, and drove them away.

"Where are they taking him?" Olivia asked one of the Marines.

He shrugged. "Whatever passes for a civilian hospital around here."

Marines lifted Brian into the back of a lightly armored transport. Olivia pulled herself into the vehicle and sat on the bench beside his stretcher. She looked at her hands. Bloodstained, yes, but not washed in gore to her elbows, as she had expected. She could still feel the blood —Brian's blood—bubbling and spurting between her fingers, but she must have gotten that wrong. Brian *had* lost a lot of blood, but nothing like what she had imagined in the dark.

A female Marine removed Olivia's scarf-bandage and used scissors to cut away Brian's pants. She tore the seal on an antiseptic swab and cleaned the bullet wound. It must have stung. Brian pulled a face and Olivia held his hand.

"Hang in there, Bri."

"I'm hanging."

Visible through the open loading door, two Marines — one a lieutenant — stood in front of the madrassa talking to a tall, bearded old man with pale skin, his shirt hanging open. It was the same old man Olivia had seen strapped to the table in the torture cell. Add one more to the resurrection parade, she thought wryly. He really was unmistakable; the old man was so tall, he towered over the Marines. As if he could hear Olivia's thoughts, his head turned slowly just then and he looked straight at her. Then somebody slammed shut the transport door, the engine started, and they rumbled out of the Old City.

❁

LATER, THE ADMINISTRATOR OF THE Green Zone infirmary arranged for the Red Cross to transport Brian to a state hospital on the western side of Aleppo, where they were better equipped to dig bullet fragments out of his femur.

Olivia was not allowed to ride along, and because of the new curfew, she had to wait for morning before she could cross the city.

The uprising had been disorganized. Not much more than a couple of car bombs, coupled with small-arms assaults like the one that wounded Brian and Jodee. A few RPGs. But the security crackdown hit the city like a steel tsunami.

At midmorning Olivia finally managed to beg a ride with a BBC video team. She wedged herself into the back of their van, where she bounced around on top of duffel bags, cables, camera equipment, and assorted junk. On this outing she wore her body armor with PRESS spelled out in block letters, front and back. The heat outside turned the back of the van into a convection oven. Sweat poured out of her, soaking through her clothes. She removed her Kevlar helmet and lightly touched the tender lump on the back of her head, and winced.

In her backpack she had stuffed her tablet, toiletries, a change of clothes, and her notebooks. She intended to see Brian at the hospital and then try to find a room nearby. The state-controlled side of Aleppo had reliable cellular service, and she planned to take advantage of it to file her latest report to *The Beat,* a London-based independent news blitzer. Olivia pitched a lot of stories to Helen Fischer, the editor in chief, and Helen commissioned many of them. Olivia considered *The Beat* home ground.

What took so long traversing the city were the checkpoints. At every one, soldiers in full tactical gear opened the back of the van, pointed M4s at her, and examined her credentials. Then they searched the vehicle thoroughly, opening all the bags and the cases of electronic equipment while Olivia and the BBC people stood around sweating, with whisper drones hovering above them like giant dragonflies armed with lethal stingers.

At every checkpoint.

After the last stop, once they were rolling again, Olivia said, "These guys are looking for something specific."

The reporter riding shotgun was a Londoner in her midforties named Toria Westby. Her red curls frothed out of her helmet, and her face glistened with so much sunscreen it looked like she had slathered herself with half a can of Crisco. She was new to Syria, a postwar video reporter, but she seemed competent despite her greenness. Olivia liked her.

"Right," Toria said. "Rumor is, somebody's trying to smuggle a hot biological out of the country."

Olivia had heard the same rumors but hadn't been able to substantiate them. She peeled a strand of hair off her sweaty cheek. "Any tips on what it might be?"

"Weaponized anthrax, I heard."

"Bollocks," the driver said. "It's worse."

"What's worse than weaponized anthrax?" Olivia asked.

The driver shook his head. He was a stubby little man, like the unlit cigar he kept corked in the corner of his mouth. His name was Mike. "I don't know. Something real bad."

Olivia touched the hard lump on the back of her head. Her fingertips came away slippery with clear fluid threaded with blood. Yesterday she had been so upset and focused on Brian that she had neglected to mention it to the medics. The whole thing with the contradictory memories felt surreal. If it had been happening to someone else, Olivia would have attributed the confusion to shock. But in her case that was ridiculous; Olivia had been in traumatic situations before—plenty of them—and it didn't work that way, not with her, shock or no shock. Most likely, she reasoned, hitting her head must have at least slightly concussed her, thus explaining her confusion.

She kept thinking about the old man and the one English word he had spoken before he died, or before she *thought* he'd died, the word that had sounded like "supers-potion." Back in her room, on a notepad, she had written down a list of possible words that sounded similar. After a while, something jogged a memory from her college days, and she carefully printed out the word: superposition. The word itself was as far as the memory went, though, and it didn't come up in her limited offline dictionary.

Now, in the BBC van, she crawled up to the seats. "Hey, Toria, do you know what 'superposition' means?"

"Uh, put one thing over another thing?"

The driver answered, talking around his cigar. "It's quantum physics." Toria and Olivia stared at him.

"What?" he said. "I've been to school."

Olivia said, "What's it mean?"

Mike took the cigar out of his mouth. "I think it's like that experiment where they put a cat in a box."

"You're thinking of Dr. Seuss," Toria said.

"Schrödinger's cat," Olivia said, remembering. In college, while working on the student newspaper, *The Daily,* Olivia had interviewed a quantum physicist who had arrived on a lecture tour. At one point he had described the thought experiment. A cat is sealed in a box with its life dependent on an observer collapsing the wave function of a sub-atomic particle entangled with the animal. Something like that. "Think of the cat as being both alive and dead at the same time," the professor had said.

Toria looked at her. "Oh, yeah. Schrödinger's cat." She winked. "I just like to give Mikey a hard time."

Mike said, "We're here," and plugged the cigar back in his mouth.

He meant the hospital. Olivia grabbed her backpack, thanked them for the lift, and climbed out, anxious to find Brian. *The cat is alive and dead at the same time . . .*

THE HOSPITAL SMELLED OF LYSOL and blood. An oscillating fan rattled in the corner of the postsurgical recovery room, pushing hot air around. Brian shared the room with three other patients, two of whom appeared unconscious. A morphine drip was attached to Brian's arm, and a drain was attached to his thigh alongside some ugly sutures. His leg was stained orange by the antiseptic splash. Absent was the array of vitals-monitoring equipment that would have surrounded him in a British or American hospital. By the end of the war, rebel factions had begun targeting hospitals on the state side of Aleppo in retaliation for bombing runs on their own facilities—all sides recklessly abandoning human decency and the rules of war. Though the government-controlled part of the city suffered less than the rebel-held districts, shortages of equipment, some medicines, and qualified surgeons abounded.

Brian looked like he was sleeping. Olivia stood by his bed, waiting —her backpack, heavy body armor, and helmet piled on the floor like a disassembled robot. She shifted her weight from foot to foot. Her back hurt.

The young Arab man—a boy, really—in the next bed, whose head was wrapped in yards of gauze, said, "I have a chair. For my mother who visits? Please, it is for you." He spoke with care, landing politely on the English syllables. The blanket below his waist lay flat where his left leg should have been.

"I'm okay," Olivia said, "but thanks."

Brian lifted his head. "Liv, for God's sake, take the chair."

"You're awake? You faker."

"I don't know how I'm supposed to sleep with all the talking around here." Brian rubbed his eyes. He sounded groggy but otherwise like his usual self. "You look good."

"You're not wearing your glasses." (*Lost when the firefight broke out and she shoved him.*)

"That has nothing to do with it. You're a beautiful blur."

She pointed at his leg. "Hurt much?"

He smiled tightly. "Ever pour vinegar into an open wound and whack on it with a meat tenderizer?"

"Only once. I didn't like it."

"Well. Then you know. Anyway, that was before the drugs. They got good shit in this place."

"Miss, please," the Arab boy said. "Sit."

Olivia gave in. "Thank you."

It was a red plastic patio chair, sun-bleached to pink, like what you might find at somebody's trailer park barbecue back in the States. Olivia pulled it around to Brian's bed. It felt good to sit. Bouncing around in the back of a van didn't count. Brian reached for her hand. Olivia's was sweaty, but his felt surprisingly cool, which she guessed was an effect of the morphine.

"How's Jodee?" Brian asked.

"I don't know. They were taking him away when we came out of the madrassa. I'm worried about him."

"He'll make it."

"And you know this how?"

"I guess I don't really know it."

Olivia took her hand back. "I called a couple of likely hospitals from a landline. One didn't have him. The other couldn't understand me and hung up."

"*Hey.*"

"I know. He'll make it. Bri, I should have listened to you when you said not to go into the Old City."

"I agree."

"Thanks for making me feel better."

"Feel better? I'm the one that got shot."

"That's my point," Olivia said.

"What happened isn't your fault. Jodee and I are grown men."

"Right."

They were quiet for a minute.

"Liv?" Brian said. "When I get out of here, I'm going home. Oregon Helps won't let me stay after this. Besides, there's stuff I have to deal with."

After a moment, Olivia said, "Ryleigh?"

"Yeah."

Ryleigh Magaw was Brian's girlfriend back in Seattle. Or maybe *had been*—that part was still technically TBD. Olivia lowered her voice. "What are you going to tell her?"

"I'm going to tell her the truth."

Olivia looked away, then back at Brian. "Maybe that's not a great idea until we figure it out for ourselves."

"I *have* figured it out for myself."

"Look, I don't want to wreck anything between you two."

"You're not wrecking anything," Brian said.

"Got it."

"Are you mad at me or something?"

"No," Olivia said. "But I'm not on the love train yet."

"So you've said. And you don't have to be. I'm telling you what it is for me."

"And Ryleigh thinks you're in love with her." Olivia watched a fly crawl across the cloudy windowpane behind Brian's bed. This kind of conversation drove her crazy. It would help if Brian's foot wasn't in the door. It would be *so* much easier.

"I'm not sure she thinks that," Brian said.

"Bri, come on." She felt like an asshole hashing this out while the boy with the amputated leg listened. Talk about First World problems.

"I thought I *was* in love with her," Brian said. "But—"

"But?"

"Why do you keep looking at me like that?"

"Like what?"

"I don't know. Like you're not sure it's me."

"Maybe I'm not." She was thinking about her conflicting memories. She hadn't actually seen Brian's femoral artery wound, but she *had* felt the spurting blood, *had* slipped in a puddle of it, *had* blown rescue breaths into Brian's dead lungs.

He looked confused.

"Can we talk about this later?" Olivia said.

"I'd rather talk about it now."

"Okay." Olivia suppressed her irritation, then changed the topic anyway. "Here's my advice. Don't break up with Ryleigh right away. Give yourself some time once you get back to the States."

"That's shitty advice."

"Brian, we're in a dangerous place. People hook up. It happens all the time. This is the Disaster. Back home, that's a different reality."

He stared at her like she'd slapped him. "That's what happened to us? We hooked up?"

"I'm not saying that."

"You just did say that."

She took a moment. "I'm sorry. Goddamn it, this stuff is too compli-cated."

"Unlike a hookup."

Words lay between them like bear traps.

"I have to go find a place to sleep tonight."

He patted the hospital bed. "There's room here."

"I don't think so." She leaned in and kissed him quickly on the lips, unable to forget how cold and rubbery they had been. "Your breath is terrible."

"You're complaining?"

"Just an observation. Get some rest. I'll check on you tomorrow."

"Liv?"

"Yes?"

"Thanks for staying with me when I got shot."

"That's okay. I didn't have anything else to do that day."

He laughed. "You always say the right thing."

"I really gotta go."

"You know what?"

"What?"

"You could come with me."

"Where?"

"Home. Seattle."

She rolled her eyes. "I'll see you tomorrow."

"Don't get shot or anything."

"I won't."

He closed his eyes, and she picked up the chair and returned it to the boy's bedside.

"Thanks."

He smiled at her, revealing perfect white teeth. "Be happy, miss. Life is good."

FOUR

OLIVIA WALKED OUT OF THE hospital, shouldering her backpack, and used her phone to find accommodations. It was a relief to have cellular service. The nearest hotels were clustered on Baron Street, six blocks away. She started walking, pushing through civilians crowding the sidewalks. Unlike the formerly held rebel districts, which largely lay in ruins, western Aleppo was battered but still standing, still functioning. She felt conspicuous in her body armor and helmet, but not enough to remove them. Snipers could as easily infest this side of the city as the other.

Sweat soaked through her clothes. Her boot rubbed at the start of a blister. She stopped and sat on the low window ledge of a pastry shop. The smells of honey and butter drifting through the window reminded Olivia of her mother's kitchen, of fresh baklava in the oven, and she felt an unwelcome stab of homesickness. Her mother was long dead, as was her father, and Olivia was estranged from Rohana, her stepmother, so the homesick feeling had no place to settle. The Disaster was her home, as much as anyplace else was.

She loosened the laces of her left boot, slipped it off, and peeled the sock down. A dime-sized spot on her heel glowed red. She rummaged a blister pack out of her cargo pocket and applied it.

A man stopped in the middle of the sidewalk a short distance away. Maybe a few years younger than her, he had wild, uncombed hair and was dressed in Western clothes: dark blue sport coat over a white T-shirt and black jeans. It looked like he wanted to approach her, say something. But when Olivia pulled her boot back on and stood up, he turned away and melted into the crowd.

Don't be shy, she thought.

Olivia stood and resumed walking. Dragonfly whisper drones patrolled the skies. Peacekeeping troops stood in pairs on street corners, fingers pointed outside the trigger guards of long guns, barrels angled down. Periodically, she looked back. Twice she caught sight of the man with crazy hair. A little worm of fear wriggled in her gut. Okay, *not* shy.

Olivia reported the truth about the war, its aftermath, and the atrocities committed — by all sides. So it goes without saying that a lot of people knew who Olivia was . . . and that some of them did not like her.

By the time she reached Baron Street she was limping. Despite the blister pack, her boot had rubbed the blister raw. Halfway down the block she stopped in front of the Hotel Baron, removed her helmet, and clipped it by the chin strap to her backpack. The hotel was three stories of traditional Islamic architecture, with balconies on the second floor. It had taken some war damage. Ropes secured a large black tarpaulin to one corner of the roof. The tarp heaved eagerly in the hot breeze, like a feeding bat. Olivia pushed her damp hair off her forehead and proceeded through the gate and into the lobby.

✳

IN HER ROOM — SECOND floor, with a balcony — Olivia cranked the spigot. After a moment the pipes shuddered and dispensed a stream of water, slightly more vigorous than a trickle, into the claw-footed tub. She dropped her smelly clothes onto the tile floor and felt sweat trickle down her ribs. Her bra had left a red crescent under each breast. Sighing with relief, she sat on the toilet and probed the blister on her heel, teeth gritted.

While the tub slowly filled, she retrieved a pocket mirror from her backpack and used it with the bathroom mirror to find an angle on the back of her head to investigate her wound. The lump didn't look as bad as she'd expected, considering how much it had been hurting. A little lower, just below the hairline, was a scar. She turned her head, tilted the pocket mirror. A seam of crusted blood made a vertical line.

She remembered the insect that had squirmed out of the old man's hair and flown at her. It had looked almost mechanical, with its cobalt sheen, like the "flies" some reporters used to grab video by zigzagging over crowds or into otherwise inaccessible buildings. But this thing hadn't been a video fly. This thing had *bitten* her. But shouldn't it be a simple puncture, not a slash? At least it didn't appear infected. Then again, maybe the scar had nothing to do with the insect; she'd certainly gotten banged around plenty otherwise.

After her bath she pulled on a fresh top and panties and drew aside the heavy curtain on the room's only window. In the dusk, three peacekeepers walked past on the street below. Two more slouched under an unlit streetlamp a block away. All the civilians had apparently dispersed, except for a woman in a full burka, who hurried into the Ramsis Hotel lobby at the other end of the street. In the alley across from the Baron, a man struck a match and held it cupped near his face.

But not just any man: It was *him*. Crazy Hair.

He shook the match out, and the tip of a cigarette glowed.

"Who the hell are you?" Olivia muttered.

SHE DRESSED QUICKLY, APPLIED A layer of moleskin to her blister, and limped down to the lobby. As she started to push through the outside door, the desk clerk called to her, "Miss, the curfew."

She stopped. The goddamn curfew. "I'm just having a look."

On the sidewalk, a couple of streetlamps had come to life. The peacekeepers turned toward her. Across the street, the alley was empty. Or the man had extinguished his cigarette and withdrawn into the shadows. Boots clicked on the pavement as one of the peacekeepers strode toward her. Olivia raised her hand, made a little wave, and retreated into the hotel.

The desk clerk followed her into the bar, where he magically became a bartender. A couple of men sat in the corner, drinking beer and speaking French. A lone fixture cast dismal illumination, which was absorbed by the heavy furniture. With the curfew, she wouldn't be able to see Brian again until tomorrow. Olivia ordered a gin martini. Some of the bottles on the backbar were empty and covered with dust, but what the hell.

"We used to be the best hotel in all of Syria," the bartender said. "Presidents stayed here." He shrugged. "But that's over now."

Olivia drank her martini fast and returned to her room.

She sat at the desk and booted her tablet, attached her report to an email, and sent it to *The Beat* via her encrypted mail server. Moments later, a chat request began blinking for her attention. Olivia accepted the request. A 3D chat window opened, like a little box holding her editor's head and a detail of *The Beat*'s London office.

"Livvie, you're back online. I was getting worried. Everything all right?"

"Not quite. A friend of mine got shot. Two friends, actually."

"Oh, God." Helen Fischer was in her late fifties, wore her hair short and silvered. She had great cheekbones.

"Brian's all right," Olivia said. "Not all right, but you know what I mean. He's hurt, but it's not as bad as it could have been. I haven't been able to track down Jodee, but he didn't look too bad off, either."

"Are *you* all right?"

"Sure."

"Why don't I believe you?"

"I'm fine, Helen. Really."

"I'm reading your piece as we speak, by the way. It's good, as usual. This one wraps up the series. What's next?"

Olivia stared at the chat box, her brain suddenly devoid of ideas. "Eh. I don't know?"

"That's a first."

"There's tons going on. I'm just tired. Have you heard anything about a bioweapon getting smuggled out of Aleppo?"

"No." Helen looked sharply interested. "What kind of bioweapon?"

"Weaponized anthrax, or something worse."

"This is a real thing?"

"I don't know. Some BBC people were talking."

"There's nothing trending. Something you want to look at?"

"Maybe. I'll ask around, see if there's anything there." She'd already asked around a bit, but it wouldn't hurt to look some more. "Helen? Can you advance me some money?"

"For the bioweapon story?"

"For anything. Yeah, the bioweapon story. Sure."

Helen removed her glasses and leaned forward, the tiny rendering of her head, no bigger than a mouse's head, seeming to come off the tablet. "Livvie, are you sure you're all right? You don't sound like yourself."

"I'm fine."

"You've been out there a long time."

By "out there" she meant the chaotic places. The Disaster. Olivia had seen a lot, experienced a lot. She had survived . . . but it was different now. Brian made it different. For the first time since childhood, Olivia might as well have FRAGILE stamped on her forehead in big red letters. Or HANDLE WITH CARE. That's probably what Helen was seeing, without knowing it. Maybe Olivia had always been one of the broken people, or one of the about-to-break people. But now she *felt* like one. And she didn't like it.

"I'm going to get some sleep, Helen."

"Take care of yourself. Wait. There. I just transferred your fee for exclusive rights to the bioweapon story."

"What if there *isn't* a bioweapon story?"

"Then a different story. I know you, Livvie. You'll scrounge up something."

❀

SHE COULDN'T SLEEP. IT WAS cooler at night, but not in this room, which was like an oven turned off but still holding heat from the human-casserole-baking temperature of midday. No longer hot enough to produce a nice crust, but plenty hot enough to baste Olivia in her own sweat.

Finally she gave up trying for natural sleep and dug out the Nytol, swallowed a tablet, and lay back down. A while later, rosy light trembled on her eyelids, rousing her . . . and she smelled smoke.

Olivia rolled off the bed and stumbled to the window. Fires burned as far as she could see, but it wasn't Aleppo. It was home: Seattle. Even the *sky* was burning in red and black striations of smoke and flame. It looked like the end of the world. Olivia opened her mouth to scream. Searing hot wind scorched her throat—

And she sat up in bed, choking and gasping.

A fucking dream. But so real, like a full-immersion movie.

She worked her parched mouth, trying to produce some spit. A water bottle sat on the dresser. She started to swing her legs off the bed—but stopped.

Someone was standing outside her door.

She saw the toes of his shoes in the gap at the bottom. Assuming it was a he.

Assuming it was Crazy Hair.

Was the door even locked? There was a key to turn from the inside, but had she done that? She couldn't remember. Slowly, she put her feet on the floor and stood up. The boards creaked. Instantly the shoes disappeared, and hurried footsteps retreated down the hall. Olivia grabbed her shirt and yanked the door open in time to catch a glimpse of a man hunching down the stairs, pursued by his own grotesque shadow.

In the morning, by the time she arrived at the hospital, Olivia had decided to leave Syria and go back to Seattle with Brian.

FIVE

EIGHT DAYS LATER, IN SEATTLE, Brian said, "Here I go." He looked like a man in custody: This way to the execution chamber. Or a man with bad news, the worst news: I'm sorry to tell you this, but we've found an inoperable mass. It's time to get your affairs in order.

Or a man going to meet his soon-to-be ex-girlfriend for coffee.

Time to get your affair *in order.*

Olivia sat on the sofa with a cold can of Interurban IPA, watching him. Brian had been on a walking cast and crutches for a week, but he hadn't yet walked out to see Ryleigh Magaw. Until yesterday, he hadn't even told the poor woman he was home. "The timing's not right," he kept saying. Meanwhile, Olivia found life in his cramped one-bedroom West Seattle apartment increasingly uncomfortable. It wasn't Brian's family pictures everywhere announcing he was a package deal, or his challenging decorative choices, such as the R2-D2–shaped waste can in the kitchen. It was Ryleigh: the unseen presence. Brian's not quite officially ex-girlfriend was like a third roommate, occupying her own space inside their heads. Sometimes (like practically every minute of the day) Olivia wondered what she was doing here.

"Nobody's forcing you to do this, you know." Olivia plucked at the beer can tab, making it buzz like an African thumb piano.

He smiled gloomily. "We both know I have to. It's already been too long, and it isn't fair to you or Ryleigh."

"It doesn't seem like you want to tell her."

"That's only normal."

"Look, if it's causing you so much pain . . ."

"Of *course* it's causing pain," Brian said. "What else could it do?"

Olivia slumped. "Maybe this whole thing was a bad idea."

"Quit looking for the exit, Liv." He sighed. "This stuff isn't free."

"What stuff?"

"This." He lifted one crutch and waved it around. "Us, being with each other. Besides, you've never even met Ryleigh. I'm the one dumping her. It sounded easier back in Aleppo."

"I know."

"And it *does* hurt."

"Bri, I know."

"Do you?"

Olivia stopped plucking at the beer can tab. "You think I don't?"

He looked away, as if he were listening to a secret advisor Olivia couldn't hear. Falling into Brian's arms had been easy, because Olivia had ample experience falling into men's arms—and falling right back out of them at her convenience. She should have stayed in Aleppo.

"Anyway," Brian said, "my Uber's waiting."

With other men it had been easy to avoid painful breakups. Step one: Don't start a serious relationship. Step two: See step one. Classic fear of abandonment. She *knew* that. Get out before you got hurt, before you had to feel even a dim approximation of the pain you felt when your parents left you. But with Brian, she had discarded her own cardinal rule: Stay free.

Now she hated the idea of losing him. And the idea was all the more sharply real after mistaking him for dead back in Aleppo.

"Hey, Bri?" He looked back at her. "I'm sorry. And I hope it's not too awful."

He nodded. "I'll call. Unless she kills me. Which she might." He looked closely at Olivia, as if sensing her inner turmoil. "What's wrong?"

In the torture cell she had covered his mouth with hers, desperately trying to blow life back into him. It was still the most vivid part of the alternate memory. Brian's lips, cold and lifeless as rubber. But what had started out as the "primary" memory was now submerged and secondary in her mind. The new memory line, the one in which Brian had not died, had taken over. But some of the worst parts of the other one still poked through.

"Liv?"

She hesitated to say what was occupying her thoughts. "It's just . . . that two-memory thing."

"It's still bothering you?"

She looked up. "Yes."

"Maybe you should see your doctor."

"I already saw him."

"What? When did you do that?"

"Last week."

"Why didn't you tell me?"

"I would have, if it had turned out to be anything." She didn't like feeling defensive, but . . . she felt defensive.

"So what did he tell you?"

"Nothing."

"Nothing?"

"Okay, not nothing. He said what I described feeling right after hitting my head sounded exactly like a concussion. Headache, nausea, confusion. Everything but the blackout. And I'm not even sure about that part. There was a moment when I thought I was going to faint. Maybe I did."

Brian nodded. "So there it is."

"No. There it *isn't*. A concussion doesn't give you two memories of the same thing."

"You just said you felt confused after you hit your head. Did you tell the doctor that?"

"Yeah."

"What did he say?"

"He said that made sense."

Brian looked at her, waiting.

"Look," Olivia said, "forget it. I was just confused, *am* confused. Whatever."

"Are you thinking about seeing someone else?"

"Like who?"

"Another doctor," Brian said. "A different kind of doctor."

"What, like a psychiatrist?"

He shrugged.

"Hell no," she said.

"Okay, then don't. Liv, you're all right. It's just some weird . . . *thing*. Some stress thing."

"Right."

Brian pushed his glasses up. "Anyway, I have to go get this Ryleigh business over with."

"Okay."

He planted his crutches and swung between them, heading for the door.

"Wait." Olivia jumped up, ran over, and hugged him awkwardly under his crutches. "Good luck."

"Thanks. Hey, you know in a couple more days I won't need these stupid crutches. Maybe I should wait."

"Good *luck*, Brian."

"Right. Here I go."

She stepped back. Did she want him to go dump Ryleigh, or did she want him to stay, let it hang on, so it would be easier for Olivia to dump *him?* That would have been her usual strategy in this situation. Except she would never have let herself get into this situation in the first place.

"Was there something else?" he said.

"Nope."

After he left, Olivia twanged the tab on her IPA, muttered "Happy days," and drank.

✹

TWO HOURS PASSED AND BRIAN didn't call or text. Coffee with the old girlfriend. Got it. Olivia's usual reaction would have been to help herself to another beer, shrug it off, pretend she didn't care. In the past, she hadn't needed to pretend. For the millionth time she checked her phone for messages. Nothing. In her mind, Brian and Ryleigh held hands across the table at Starbucks (the least cool coffee shop in West Seattle), exchanging soulful looks. Of *course* it's causing pain, he'd said before he left.

Olivia felt sick to her stomach. She wished she could feel something else, like anger. Or trust. Especially trust. She needed a stronger emotion, or a more positive one, to push aside the emotion that was making her feel abandoned. Anger was always good for that. But her anger tank was empty. And she was new to the idea of trusting people not to leave her when she desperately needed them to stay.

Enough. She stood up and grabbed her keys. Two hours and she was reduced to a level of emotional insecurity reserved for thirteen-year-olds. A walk around the block would clear her head.

On the coffee table her phone started bleeping and a chat request spun over the device like a silver coin. International chat request. Disappointed but curious, Olivia picked up the Gates-7 and finger-flicked the spinning icon. After a brief twinkle of instability, the spinning coin ballooned into a virtual bubble the size of a coaster. The bubble contained the image of Helen Fischer's head. She looked tired.

"Helen—"

"Hi," Helen said. "There's something going on. I need to ask you a question."

Olivia peered at the chat bubble. Helen looked exhausted. "What time is it over there in London?"

"Middle of the night. Never mind that. A few weeks ago you asked me if I had heard anything about a hot biological getting smuggled out of Aleppo. You remember that?"

"Sure."

"And you said you talked to a couple of BBC guys, correct?"

"Yes."

"Names?"

"They didn't know anything," Olivia said. "I mean, the one guy seemed freaked out, I guess. But he didn't *know* anything. It was all rumors. Everybody—"

"Livvie, do you remember the names or not? I'm trying to cover all possible angles, and I'm constrained."

Olivia noticed Helen was wearing a bathrobe. It was hard to see much detail in a chat bubble, but that was definitely a bathrobe. And Helen's hair was disheveled, her face drawn and pale. Olivia had never seen the editor of *The Beat,* live or in chat, look anything less than impeccably put together. *There's something going on.*

"I'll get my notebook," Olivia said.

From the bedroom closet shelf she pulled down her travel bag, which she had neglected to fully unpack after returning from Aleppo with Brian. Because she traveled so much, she had packing and unpacking down to a science, but since Aleppo, her life had gotten sloppy. Unpacking? In a way, she never unpacked. Olivia always kept a go-bag ready, since she never knew when the Disaster would call. Brian *hated* her go-bag. "It means you're never fully where you are," he said. Which was a valid point. But was the current state of her bag a positive sign or merely the reflection of her muddled feelings about commitment? It wasn't a go-bag, but it wasn't a stay-bag, either.

The black edge of her work journal poked out of a side pocket on the bag. She grabbed it and returned to the front room.

Helen's bubble-enclosed face was popping Tylenol or some other pill.

"Okay." Olivia flipped through pages to find the right date. "Toria Westby. Video reporter. The driver, all I've got for him is 'Mike.' But they were a team. He's the one who was so worried." But he didn't have any real information about a smuggled biological weapon—or hadn't appeared to. "Helen, are you all right? You don't look well."

"Fever, aches and pains. Probably the flu. Thanks for the names."

"Tell me what's happening."

Helen looked down for several moments. When she raised her head and peered out of the bubble again, her eyes were red. Was she *crying?* Sick or not, that wasn't something Helen Fischer would do, not while talking with a professional connection. Olivia held the phone up, the chat bubble suspended inches from her nose.

"We're breaking this tomorrow," Helen said. "We aren't the only ones. But you better believe we're going to be first."

"Breaking what tomorrow?"

"Contagion. In Europe, England, the Indian subcontinent, Australia, China. And the United States."

All the air seemed to go out of the room. It felt like the day Olivia's father died, just sitting there in his favorite chair, fifty-two years old and in good health, tennis twice a week, eating right, or right enough, and *boom*—a heart attack. Olivia, only seventeen at the time, had found him slumped over the arm of the chair, as if he'd dropped something on the rug. It was an antique Mughal rug he had imported himself. If you dropped something on it—a peanut, your house key, almost anything— it instantly vanished into the intricate pattern.

"You understand what that means, don't you?" Helen said. "That the disease turns up everywhere at about the same time?"

"It means it could be deliberate."

Helen nodded. "Otherwise we have patient zero on a world tour while exhibiting symptoms of a serious illness, infecting people as he goes. Not impossible, I suppose, but it doesn't feel right. Beyond that, the pattern of the outbreaks looks strategic."

"Jesus Christ. I haven't seen anything about this. How could I miss it?"

"Up to now, you'd have had to dig to see it, to connect the dots."

"And *The Beat* has been digging." Olivia felt left out, which was dumb. But she felt it. Left out of the latest disaster. Abandoned. Except this time it sounded like the whole world was the hot zone. The Disaster was coming to her. No need to pack.

Helen said, "Last week I started getting reports from CJs. Reports of people falling ill, disappearing from their homes. Distraught family members. Local law enforcement sealing apartments, houses. Crazy stuff."

"*Reliable* reports?" Olivia didn't trust so-called citizen journalists—a term that could be defined as anyone with a phone. They liked to see their names acknowledged on legitimate news blitzers, and were cool with not getting paid. Basically, amateurs with a jones for attention, or crusaders incapable of, or uninterested in, analyzing context. They made it harder to earn a living. Why pay for textured content when shallow info-bursts drew just as many eyeballs?

"These were independent reports," Helen said, "coming in from Paris, Warsaw, Mumbai, the Eastern Seaboard of the United States. Even right here in London. Taken individually, each local case is a minor mystery. But when you see it happening all over the place, it reveals a disturbing pattern."

"That's putting it mildly."

"Privately, I put the word out. I told reporters specifically what to look for. And guess what?"

"You got more mystery stories for the pattern. Helen, the World Health Organization must be seeing these patterns, too."

"I have no doubt of it."

"Then why hasn't an alert been issued? Why isn't the public being told?"

"Let me tell you about Perth. I think this answers your question. In Perth, they did ring vaccinations. Someone gets sick, and they stop the airborne spread by vaccinating everybody in a ring around the infection point, like digging a trench, a firebreak, to stop a forest fire."

"I know what ring vaccinations are."

"Good. But that's not the scary part."

"Then what is?"

"Perth was one of the earliest reports. But no one's doing ring vaccinations in any of the other locations. If there's something to vaccinate against, why wouldn't they be doing it everywhere?"

Cold fear rippled through Olivia. "Because the vaccine doesn't work."

"That's what I think. Guess what the Australian minister of health has to say about ring vaccinations. Not that I've actually talked to the minister. But her office responded. Eventually."

"Ah . . . they've never heard of any such thing?"

"Correct."

"There's still got to be a public health alert."

"It's coming, believe me. But what if they don't know what to say? What if they've been caught completely flat-footed and don't want to cause a panic?"

Olivia wanted to be skeptical. "What's the contagion?" She knew what they had used the ring vaccination strategy for back in the seventies, but she couldn't let her mind go there. Not yet.

"I don't know," Helen said.

"I want to work this."

"I thought you were taking yourself off assignment for a couple of months."

"I want to work."

"Give me the angle," Helen said.

Olivia thought for a moment. "In Aleppo, I can find out if there's anything to the rumors of a hot biological. But I have to be on the ground where I can get face time with my network."

"You have money?"

"I still owe you a story for the last advance, remember?"

"Then you are officially back on assignment."

"Thanks, Helen. I'll leave tomorrow."

TWENTY MINUTES LATER, BRIAN CAME through the door. "Well, that was fun."

"You didn't call," Olivia said from the bedroom, where she was packing.

"I was with Ryleigh practically the whole time." The refrigerator door opened, bottles rattling. "Then I needed some time to process."

"And how'd that go?"

Brian stumped down the hall and stood in the doorway, propped on his crutches, a can of IPA in his right hand. Olivia turned away from the bed where her bag lay open, half packed.

"Come on," Brian said. "Don't look at me like that."

"Like what?"

"Like I'm lying or something. She wouldn't stop trying to talk me out of it. I didn't want to be an asshole—I mean *more* of an asshole—so I listened. But I don't think dragging it out helped, either."

"Bri."

"She wanted to know how I could be so terrible. How I could *betray* her. And at first I didn't have an answer. The truth is, I *am* betraying her. All right, 'betray' is too strong. We weren't married, or even engaged. But she—"

"*Brian.*"

He leaned sideways, looking past her. "Hey, what's with the bag? Are you *packing?*"

"Now listen. Don't get nuts. I'm heading back to Syria."

He stared at her. "You're not really."

"I am."

"I can't believe this. *Why?* Because of Ryleigh?"

She told him. He listened. His expression changed like rapid phases of the moon. From disbelief, to confusion, to sharp interest, to full-moon worry. There was no anger phase. He swung through the doorway and sat on the bed beside her, propping his crutches against the wall. It was a small room, barely space for the bed, a dresser, and two unhappy people. Brian held her hand.

"What's the plan, exactly?" he said.

"I fly out tomorrow. I'll have to go to Turkey first, and there might be trouble at the border. God knows there usually is."

"I guess I can't talk you out of it."

"Bri, you know this isn't about you. About us, I mean."

"Yeah." He tilted the IPA to his lips. "That doesn't mean I think it's a good idea. You said you were going to listen to me the next time I said something wasn't a good idea, remember?"

"I remember."

And like that, she didn't want to go. She *would* go, but she didn't want to. When she'd closed the chat bubble with Helen, she had been filled with nervous, anticipatory energy—the same feeling she always got before an assignment. But she had known, of course, that there was also an element of escape. She reached for the IPA, he handed it to her, and she took a couple of swallows.

"So, Ryleigh was pissed?" she said.

"She was not happy."

"Aside from that, Mrs. Lincoln, how was lunch?"

"Oh, just really, *really* great. Can I have my beer back?"

"No." She put the can on the floor, shoved her half-packed bag off the bed, pushed Brian back, and straddled him. Nose to nose, looking into his eyes, she said, "I don't want to go. Isn't that weird? I *always* want to go."

"You're not going?"

"I didn't say that."

She kissed him, his living breath in her mouth.

In the morning, the world changed, but not in a good way.

SIX

HER FLIGHT DIDN'T LEAVE UNTIL later in the afternoon, so while Brian
was in the shower, Olivia ran out to grab a coffee and some breakfast treats. Morning commuter traffic on California Avenue was heavy.
She stood waiting for the WALK light across from Hotwire Espresso, her
thoughts tracking over the various difficulties she was likely to encounter at the Turkish border with Syria. Being massively jet-lagged wouldn't
help, but at least the war was over. The coalition was friendly toward
journalists, even if the remnant of Assad's power structure wasn't. It was
amazing Bashar al-Assad had remained president since 2000. Or maybe
not so amazing. His father held power for nearly thirty years. Tyrants
tended to assure their own longevity.

The light changed and Olivia started to cross. A man in an unbuttoned shirt, black T, and sunglasses came out of Hotwire, holding two
lidded disposable cups.

It was the man who had followed her in Aleppo — Crazy Hair. Except now his hair was cut short and neat. Olivia stopped in the middle
of the street. The man didn't seem to notice her. He turned and walked
down the sidewalk.

She followed him.

At the next block he stopped, waiting for the light. Olivia caught up.
It was just the two of them. Olivia's heart raced. "Hey," she said.

The man turned — and it wasn't him. Just some guy who looked like
him, a guy with a similar body type and cheekbones, two Olivias reflected in the silver lenses of his sunglasses.

"Yes?" he said.

"Nothing. I'm sorry, I thought you were someone else."

He smiled. "No problem."

Olivia walked back to Hotwire. The encounter disturbed her. She was still jumpy about what had happened when she'd stayed the night in the Baron Hotel. Jumpy enough to react strongly to a guy who, really, only somewhat resembled the man who had followed her and had stood across the street smoking—the man who had, she was sure, been standing outside her room in the middle of the night.

The line moved, and Olivia bought a double espresso, muddy. Living in the Middle East for so many months, she had acquired a taste for very strong, unadulterated java. She also grabbed some blueberry scones, one for her and one for Brian. As she turned from the counter, her phone began vibrating in her pocket. The woman behind her was staring at her own phone when a red holo-projected NewZalert exclamation mark jumped out of it and jiggled as if attached to a tiny spring. Everyone who wasn't already holding a phone reached for theirs, including Olivia. She finger-flicked the exclamation mark and the announcement of an emergency address by the president flashed up.

Olivia ran back to the apartment.

Brian stood in his boxer shorts, holding a cup of coffee. He looked both bleary and alarmed. His tablet lay on the back of the sofa, projecting a fifty-inch screen.

"Are you seeing this?" he said.

On the screen, the president of the United States spoke from the Oval Office. Paula Crawford looked serious as a heart attack as she read from a prepared text.

". . . all necessary measures to ensure public safety. The variola virus is highly contagious. Travel restrictions will remain in place so long as it is deemed prudent, until the virus is brought under control. For now, the CDC is coordinating with the World Health Organization. And I repeat: There is no need for panic at this time. We are doing what Americans have always done in the face of adversity. We are working the problem. For now, every citizen has a part to play. If you or someone you know is experiencing any of the following symptoms, I urge you to contact your healthcare provider immediately: fever, headache, severe back pain, vomiting. Especially if you notice the appearance of flat red spots on your face, hands, and forearms. If you do not have a healthcare provider, or if your healthcare provider is not available, a national toll-free number has been created to receive your report."

The number flashed under Crawford's face, which made her look like she was pitching a time-share in Belize.

"My fellow Americans," she continued, "do not hesitate. At this stage, we are dealing with a containable emergency. But if we are not vigilant, if we are not resolute, we as a nation together, and as members of the world community, may face the most serious consequences. Now I will turn you over to the surgeon general, who will amplify my remarks. Good morning, and God bless the United States of America."

The feed switched to the surgeon general, who restated what the president had just said, adding a further layer of urgency.

Olivia said, "Did she say *variola?*"

"Yeah."

"Holy shit. Variola is the smallpox virus."

"I know. But they didn't say smallpox. They definitely didn't use that word."

"No." Olivia was thinking about Helen Fischer. Contagion around the world. People falling ill and disappearing, their homes sealed by authorities. (And what would happen to anyone who dialed the number still flashing on the projection screen? Olivia wondered.) Helen herself not put together, sick, red-eyed.

"Didn't the WHO eradicate the virus back in the seventies or eighties?" Brian asked.

"Yes. The last known case was in 1977. If people were dying of smallpox today, we would know. You can't hide something like that. The presentation is too aggressive."

"Yeah?"

"Google it."

Brian already had his phone out, swiping with his thumb. He stopped, holding the screen up. "Oh, my *God.*"

"Yeah."

"Wait. Jesus. Listen to this. Smallpox killed over three hundred million people in the twentieth century. Three. Hundred. Million. How could they keep this under wraps?"

"They couldn't."

"'Eradicated' means all the virus was destroyed, right? I don't get this."

"The Russians and Americans kept some," Olivia said. "There was a big debate over that. I read a whole book about it. But it was supposed to be this tiny amount, tightly controlled. Later on, the Russians began secretly replicating variola, creating vaccine-resistant strains. They had *tons* of it. Of course, the book was written by an American. Probably the US has tons of it, too. Why not? Nukes aren't enough. We need disease, too. What the hell, throw in pestilence. Weaponize insects and rats."

"Anyway, sounds like you're not going to Turkey. Not with the travel ban in place."

"Doesn't look like it."

Brian said, "Nobody would do this."

There was real pain in Brian's eyes. Pain and fear. He'd handed out water in Aleppo after the hot war ended. He'd seen starving children, corpses, people whose bodies had been mutilated by barrel bombs, bullets, hellfire. But he probably didn't fully believe in the capital D that was the world Disaster that never stopped, that was always right here, under the surface, even in places like Seattle, while it was in your face in places like Aleppo. Seeing it dawn in Brian's eyes made Olivia ache. Gently, she said, "There are, Brian. There are people who would."

"You think the Russians would actually attack with this stuff?" He looked like he really wanted her to tell him. "Why would they do that? We're not at war with Russia."

"It doesn't have to be the Russians. A lot of stuff could have gone missing after the Soviet Union collapsed. It could be out there. It's plausible. Assad is Russia's man, right?"

"This is unbelievable." He looked ill.

"Maybe it's not variola major. I think there are lesser kinds." Even as she said it, Olivia was calling bullshit on herself. If this was a weaponized version of variola, it wouldn't be *less* virulent. If anything, it would be worse, more easily transmitted, more thoroughly deadly.

"Three hundred million."

"Bri."

"This could get so bad." The Disaster had just landed on Brian's head, right here in West Seattle, like Dorothy's house dropped out of a tornado spun up a world away.

Olivia touched his arm. "Let's take a breath. We don't know what's going on yet."

"Right, okay. I'm going to call my parents."

"Go ahead."

"Liv? You should call your mother, too."

"Stepmother. She doesn't need to hear from me."

Brian turned his anti-bullshit gaze on her. "You're always saying stuff like that."

"No, I'm not. Stuff like what?"

"Like she doesn't need to hear from you. Or you don't get along. Or it doesn't make any difference because you were never that close. Stuff like that."

"Brian, come on."

"I'm just saying, you know, if you're ever going to patch it up, now's a good time."

Olivia's stepmother had been born in Jaipur, and Rohana firmly inhabited her culture. During Olivia's teen years, Rohana wore saris and shopped every week at The Souk, a tiny shop in Pike Place Market that specialized in herbs and spices from her home country. She filled the cupboard with cumin seed, garam masala, and cardamom pods, among dozens of others—more than she would ever need, in Olivia's opinion. And she had redecorated the house. Slipcovers in burnt orange, ivory, and green. Knotted rugs, block-printed tablecloths, framed silks. Siddhartha in the dining room, and sandalwood vapors drifting from brass incense burners.

As a teenager, Olivia had found it off-putting. But maybe she had *needed* to find it off-putting. Otherwise, Rohana might have legitimately occupied the space left by Olivia's real mother. *Give her a chance,* her dad used to say. *She loves you.* Yeah, well . . .

"Okay. I'll call."

Brian rolled his eyes. "Don't act like it's me making you do it."

"It *is* you making me do it."

"Then don't call. Whatever."

He left the room with his phone in his hand.

Olivia felt like somebody was trying to force her to sit down when all she wanted to do was stand up and run as far away from the chair as she could get. Brian started talking in the next room, and Olivia picked up her phone.

It took a while to reach Rohana, who had moved back to India a couple of years ago to be near her family. Her *other* family. She now lived with her sister, Amala, in a suburb of Jaipur. The move had hurt, even after Olivia admitted to herself that she had abandoned her stepmother first, by keeping her at arm's length no matter how hard she'd tried to be present for Olivia.

"Of course everything is fine," Rohana said when she finally answered. There was no visual. Since returning to India, Rohana had retreated from the ubiquity of electronic society. She did not carry a phone but left it in one room of the house, as if it were an artifact from a previous century, a rotary black box hardwired into the wall.

"Rohana, is anyone sick around you?"

"You worry too much, Little Oh."

Olivia cringed. Rohana had always called her that, though Olivia had been fourteen when her father married her — only three years after Olivia's real mother died. Fourteen was too old for baby names, and forget about thirty. She couldn't argue with the accuracy of "little," though. Olivia had been five foot two until she got her growth spurt in high school and shot up to . . . five foot four. Also, Rohana had no children of her own and must have been blindsided by the self-obsessed melodrama of Olivia's adolescence. Olivia *knew* she could be difficult — then and now — but she felt helpless to do anything about it. Of course, defining her stubbornness as "helplessness" probably reinforced it. Olivia loathed self-analysis.

But she tried to keep these mitigating factors in mind, tried to be fair. Still, she hated the whole "Little Oh" thing.

"Not too much," Olivia said about the worrying. "But I do worry. Promise you'll stay inside as much as possible until this is over."

"I will promise no such thing."

"I just want you to be all right." Olivia closed her eyes. She hadn't known she was going to say that. She never said things like that to Rohana.

"I will be fine." Her stepmother sounded pleased. "Why don't you come and visit me?"

"There's an international travel ban, remember? I just told you."

"But there wasn't one last month, when your cousin Aanu married."

Olivia was glad there was no visual. She knew the guilt must be written all over her face. "I was in Syria."

"Not so far. And now you are in America, which is."

"I know." Olivia rubbed her eyes. "I don't plan very well."

"Little Oh, you don't plan *at all*."

Not true, Olivia thought, I always plan the exit strategy. But maybe not anymore. "Did I tell you I met someone? He's why I'm back in America."

"You know perfectly well you didn't tell me."

"I should have. I'm sorry."

"What is this person's name?"

"Brian. Brian Anker." She glanced up and saw Brian listening in the doorway. "He's a really nice guy."

Brian smiled.

"I'm so glad to hear it," Rohana said.

"Of course, he's not *perfect*," Olivia said, and Brian rolled his eyes.

"No one is, Little Oh."

✸

THEY MONITORED THE REPORTS ALL day and deep into the night. Olivia checked *The Beat*'s news feed. The story was there, posted minutes before the president's address. By now it was like one person waving her arms for attention in a crowd of people waving *their* arms. Every news source in the world was going crazy, and variola wasn't the catchword; smallpox was. Maybe the president would have given her speech this morning regardless, or maybe it would have been delayed another week — but it seemed clear that *The Beat,* and a few other news sources, had leveraged the government into the announcement. Olivia wasn't positive that was a good thing.

"Why not?" Brian said. "They have no right to keep vital information from the public."

They lay in Brian's bed, their muted phones projecting international news tickers, bright yellow-and-red ribbons of words unraveling in the air. It was almost midnight, the apartment dark except for the ribbons and a lamp on the bedside table. An empty bottle of Riesling and two glasses stood next to the lamp.

"What got me," Olivia said, "was the lack of information, vital or otherwise. I don't think they know how to deal with the contagion. If it's weaponized variola and there's no effective vaccine, what happens then?"

"People have to *know.*"

"But does knowing help them?"

"More information is always better, that's what you always say."

"Yeah. But if President Crawford had announced a vaccination protocol, something tangible to deal with variola, that would have been better.

Bri, without a vaccine there's going to be panic. You're not the only one Googling images of smallpox."

"I hate this." Brian picked up his phone and tapped off the news ticker. Then he reached for Olivia's phone, fumbled it, and the phone fell on the rug next to the bed. Brian had drunk more wine than Olivia.

"What are you doing?" she said.

"I just want a break from the blitz. It's nerve-racking. How do you stay sane right in the thick of it all day?"

Olivia didn't understand the question. "It's reality. I want to know what's happening."

"Can't we turn reality off for now?"

"All right."

She leaned over the edge of the bed and picked up her phone, the ticker still scrolling in the holo projection. Hanging off the bed, she started reading about a riot in Paris. Brian's fingers touched her hip, an invitation to vacate the blitz. She tapped off the feed and rolled over to face him.

"Reality is officially off-moded," she said.

Brian stretched past her and clicked off the lamp, too.

❁

THE CRUMP OF AN EXPLOSION jolted her out of her drifting edge-of-sleep thoughts. For an instant she was back in Aleppo, back in the war. A flicker of red firelight came through the window and played on the ceiling over the bed. Olivia remembered the disturbing dream she'd had in the Baron Hotel. She sat up and started reaching for her clothes.

Brian rolled over. "What's happening?"

"I'm going to see."

Sirens skirled up. There was a fire station less than a mile away. Aggressive get-out-of-the-way honking came on, like the charge of a Spielberg tyrannosaurus.

Still groggy, Brian picked up his phone and began swiping for the news he wanted to escape a little while ago. "Holy shit, Shadowland is burning." Shadowland was a bar only a block away. "They think it's a gas explosion."

"Where are you getting that?"

"West Seattle Blog." The WSB was constantly updated, it seemed, by people who never slept.

Standing at the window, Olivia pulled on her pants and buttoned the waistband. A shawl of flame whipped high above the roof of the building next door. "You can see it from here," Olivia said. "I'm going to run over, have a look."

Brian turned on the lamp. "Wait for me."

"The operative word was 'run.'"

"I just have to find my pants."

Olivia was already halfway to the door. "Be right back."

"Hey—"

"What?"

"You don't think this is something other than a fire, do you?"

"Like panic in the streets? No. It's too soon for that." She thought of the riot she'd just read about in Paris and wasn't so sure she believed her own words.

"Liv, be careful. If you could just wait two minutes."

"I'll be careful."

Outside, the smell of gas hung in the air. She walked toward the fire, passing a nondescript white van parked across from Brian's building. Behind the cab, the van had no windows. Though it was the middle of the night, people streamed toward Shadowland, eager for spectacle. Olivia arrived on the corner of Oregon and California. Fire hoses, gripped in wrestling holds by heavily clad men, crossed streams before billows of flame and surging smoke. Glass fragments glittered in the street. A barstool hung snagged in the branches of a tree, blown there by the explosion. Thank God the bar had been closed, she thought. The faces of bystanders glowed in reflected heat, witnesses to either a local emergency or the emergence of the Disaster in their midst.

Most of the first responders were too busy to answer Olivia's questions. She approached a Seattle police officer doing traffic control. At 3 a.m., there wasn't much traffic for her to redirect.

"I'm a reporter," Olivia said. "Do you know what happened?"

"Yes," the officer said. "The building caught on fire. I need you to not stand in the street, please."

Olivia retreated to the sidewalk. She asked a few civilians if they knew what had happened. No one did. Some of them looked scared. A young guy with a full beard who smelled like he'd been bathing in a tub full of beer, said, "Everything's going crazy."

"It's trending that way," Olivia said.

"Hey, you here with anyone? You want to hang out?"

Olivia left him and walked back to the apartment. The sidewalk was empty. By now everyone was on California, watching the show. A man stepped out from behind the van parked across from Brian's building. He wore a gray hoodie with a Nike swoosh over the left breast. He walked toward her with his head down and hands in the pockets of his hoodie. Olivia started to walk faster. She slipped her hand into her pocket and found her key, prepared to gouge somebody's eye if necessary. Behind her, shoes scuffed the pavement. She started to turn—

And a hand clamped over her mouth and an arm circled her waist, pulling her in tight, trapping her arms. The man in the hoodie dashed toward her. She glimpsed his face. He was a boy, no older than twenty. Olivia screamed against the hand. She drove her heel into the shin of the man holding her. He yelped but didn't let go. Then the boy was on her, grabbing her legs. They carried her to the open loading doors of the van.

A third man crouched inside. When Olivia saw the hypodermic needle, she fought her attackers with increased frenzy. She bit the finger of the hand covering her mouth, tasted blood, but he didn't let go, and she couldn't *breathe*. A stinging needle-jab penetrated her shoulder. She bucked and fought and tried to scream. They held her down on the metal floor of the van. The doors slammed shut and the engine started.

Olivia's strength and presence of mind began to desert her. She realized, vaguely, that the hand was no longer covering her mouth, but when she tried to make a sound, all that came out was a pathetic little squeak, the sound of a drowsy puppy.

Oblivion swallowed her.

SEVEN

THE METAL FLOOR BUMPED AND swayed. Olivia opened her eyes. Everything was blurry. She lay on her back, something soft tucked under her head. She worked her lips, craving water. Her head itched. She reached up to scratch it and discovered her wrists were zip-tied together with disposable flex cuffs. She remembered the struggle, the hand clamped over her mouth, the taste of blood. The needle.

Fear swept away the cobwebs.

She tried to get up. Flex cuffs around her ankles hobbled her, and she fell, landing hard on her shoulder. A wave of nausea rolled through her, probably, she thought, a residual effect of the drug. She groaned.

A man said, "Hey, be careful."

Another man, farther away, shouted over the engine and road noise, "What's going on back there?"

"Nothing's going on," the first man said. "She woke up."

"Do you need help?"

"No."

"Don't let her hurt herself."

"I know what my job is," the first man said. He sounded young and aggrieved.

Olivia looked up. A blurry figure leaned over her. She squirmed away. "Don't touch me."

"I'm not going to hurt you," the man said.

"That's comforting." Olivia squinted, trying to bring him into focus.

"Just lie still." He came closer, not touching her but lowering his voice. "If you make trouble, we *will* drug you again. I'm serious."

Olivia tried to control her fear. Once, in Damascus, Islamic separatists had taken her captive. For a while, kidnapping journalists had been everyone's favorite hobby. They'd held her for three days in a window-less room that contained a filthy gray mattress and a porcelain bowl. The bowl served as a bedpan. Once a day, a woman with a scarf covering her face brought her food and water, took the bowl away, and returned it empty. Like this blurry man here with her now, her kidnappers had been young. But unlike the blurry man and his cohorts, the separatists had seemed strangely uncommitted. One day, no one came for the pot. The ammonia smell of piss competed with the fried bulgur patties they fed her. She tried the door and found it unlocked, the house empty. She had been lucky. But she had also kept a cool head, which is what she needed to do now.

"There's something wrong with my eyes," she said.

"It's the drug. I think it'll clear up."

Think it will clear up.

"Who are you?" Olivia said.

"The Elders will tell you that."

"Who are the Elders?"

"Stop talking now."

Olivia didn't push. She dreaded the needle. Maybe these guys were organized, but she didn't trust them to know what they were doing with the drug. What if her vision never cleared up? What if they injected her again and it stopped her heart?

Stay cool.

The man withdrew and sat on a bench along the wall, like you'd find in a police van—though this seemed to be some sort of com-mercial vehicle. No side windows, just the metal walls. There was a big gray toolbox behind the driver's seat, and a pair of jumper cables under the bench, the red-handled clamps sticking out. That was it. Nothing to indicate who these guys were or what they wanted with her. Oli-via groped around and found the soft thing, which felt like a rolled-up sweatshirt. She lay back, resting her head on it. After a while, her vision began to clear.

"Can I have water?" she asked.

The young man grumbled. He hunkered beside her again and offered her a bottle of water. White gauze and tape were wrapped around the man's middle and ring fingers. His face came into focus. It was the guy she had confronted at the crosswalk down from Hotwire, the one she had thought looked like the man who followed her in Aleppo. She took the bottle, pulled the nipple up with her teeth, and sucked warm water.

"Are you the one I bit?"

"It doesn't matter."

"What's your name?"

"You don't need to know my name."

"Look," Olivia said, "you don't have to tell me your real name, just tell me what I should call you."

The driver turned around. "Just tell her your name. It doesn't matter, and you're scaring her."

The bench guy glared at Olivia. "I'm Emilio."

"Where are we going?"

Emilio took his bottle back and slapped the nipple down with the flat of his hand.

"I just want to know where we're going," Olivia said.

"You'll know when we get there."

Emilio went back to his bench. Olivia closed her eyes and tried, un-successfully, to relax. What was Brian doing right now? For that mat-ter, when *was* "right now"? Olivia had no idea how long she had been unconscious. At the thought of Brian, of the safety and intimacy of his West Seattle apartment, of his bed, her throat tightened with emo-tion she didn't want, and she couldn't easily swallow. She had started to think of Brian as "home." The salesman was through the door and he had his sample case open, selling her a life she wasn't yet ready to live. It didn't matter anyway. If Brian was "home," he might be a home she would never see again. It had happened before. One day you kissed your mother goodbye in the cancer ward and life as you knew it was over. One day you walked into the living room and your dad was slumped over the arm of his chair. This time it would be Olivia who left forever.

She craned her head around. Daylight came through the van's dirty windshield. From her low angle, all she could see was a washed-out blue sky. Something about the light made her think of open country. She couldn't see the face of the driver or of the guy riding in the passenger seat. The passenger was wearing a gray hoodie, though. He must be the guy who came at her on the sidewalk. Nike. And that meant the driver was probably the one who had injected her.

They rode in silence. Then, after what felt like an hour, the van pulled off the road and parked. Olivia had been drifting in and out. Now she sat up, tense.

"What's happening?"

Emilio shook his head. "*Shhh.*"

The engine switched off. The driver came into the back. He stooped over Olivia. Maybe forty years old and stocky, he had the air of someone in charge. She remembered him crouching in the back of the van with his hypo.

"We're gonna be here a few minutes," he said.

"I need the bathroom."

"Later," he said. "Do you want a cheeseburger?"

She stared at him.

"A cheeseburger," he repeated.

"No." Olivia was starving, but she was damned if she would take anything from these assholes. A tiny, pointless act of defiance.

"Suit yourself." The man started to turn away.

"Wait," Olivia said, changing her mind. What was the point in not eating? "I'll take one. But no cheese or onions. Or mustard."

No one said anything, then the driver laughed. "Is there anything else you'd like?"

"No, I'm good."

The man returned to the cab and reached for something under the seat. He tossed it back to Emilio. A roll of duct tape. Before Olivia could react, Emilio tore a piece off and slapped it over her mouth. Olivia shook her head, kicked out at him.

"You might as well calm down," the driver said. "The tape comes off once we're back on the road. I know it's uncomfortable, but it's temporary. You try to rip the tape off, these boys will stop you. We don't want to disrespect you any more than necessary." He pointed two fingers at her with thumb cocked. "I'll be right back. Brothers," he said to the other men, "be vigilant. And respectful."

"We will," Nike replied.

Olivia rested her back against the wall of the van. On the bench, Emilio produced his phone and started swiping on 2D mode. After the burger talk, she didn't feel quite as threatened, though she knew that was a false perception. Christ, they'd just taped her mouth shut.

From the passenger seat, Nike said, "Do you believe she's got it? I don't believe it."

Emilio concentrated on his phone and didn't look up. But Nike turned around, a big crooked-toothed grin on his face. "There's no *way* she's got it."

Emilio looked up. "Shut it."

"You're not the boss of me," Nike said.

Emilio shook his head and looked back at his phone. "Idiot."

Nike winked at Olivia. "He's very jealous of you."

Emilio stood up, lighted phone in his clenched hand, like he was getting ready to throw it at Nike's head. "Can you quit talking about stuff you're not supposed to talk about?"

Nike turned sullen. "I don't know why we can't. What difference does it make? She's never going to repeat it."

And like that, Olivia's fear roared back.

"Robbie's not going to like it," Emilio said.

"Hey, don't tell him. Come on. I didn't mean anything."

Everybody stopped talking, giving Olivia time to think. Was Robbie the older man who had drugged her? Or was it somebody they were going to meet later? The van must be parked near a burger joint, she thought. If she was going to scream, fight to get away, this might be her best chance. She started to reach for the tape. Emilio stared hard at her. She dropped her hands back in her lap. A few minutes later, the driver's door opened and the older man climbed in, preceded by the smell of hamburgers and french fries. Nike turned sideways on his seat and took the drink tray from him. The older man looked at Emilio and back at Nike.

"All right, what's going on with you two?"

Nike stared at the drink tray. "Nothing. Arguing about soccer."

"Soccer. Look at me, brother."

Nike raised his head slowly, flicking Emilio a worried glance before meeting Robbie's eyes. He opened his mouth to speak, but Emilio interrupted. "This dummy thinks the Sounders have a prayer."

Nike, visibly relieved, said, "They *do*, they absolutely do."

"You're ignorant," Emilio said with real heat.

The older man (Robbie?) didn't seem to be buying it. "Both of you keep your minds on what we're doing. You know how important this is."

"Yes, sir," Nike said.

Emilio nodded and sat down.

The older man tossed a Burger King bag to him. "We get rolling, you give her a hamburger if she wants it. The plain one's for her."

They pulled back onto the road. Olivia stripped the duct tape off her face. It felt like half her lips came off with it. Emilio dug a plain burger out of the bag and held it up like a question. Olivia nodded, and he flipped it into her lap.

She ate half the burger but felt too sick with anxiety to finish it. After about fifteen minutes, the driver pulled the van onto the side of the road and turned the engine off. He came back and hunched over, opening a big clasp knife. Olivia almost did scream. *What difference does it make? She's never going to repeat it.*

He lowered himself to his knees and cut the flex cuffs off her ankles but left the ones binding her wrists. Olivia didn't move. He folded his knife closed and shoved it in his pocket. "Bathroom break, okay?"

"Yes."

He threw open the loading door, hopped down, and extended his hand. Olivia let him help her. She blinked in the sunlight. The van was parked on the shoulder of a deserted stretch of two-lane road bordered by woodsy countryside.

"You're Robbie?" she asked.

He blinked. "Yes. Go that way." He pointed.

Olivia stumbled down a shallow embankment and into the woods, Robbie right behind her.

"Okay, this is good enough. You can go behind that cedar tree." He looked embarrassed. "Don't try anything foolish."

Behind the tree, which wasn't nearly wide enough, Olivia dropped her pants and underwear and squatted in the brush. It took forever to go. She peeked around the trunk. Robbie was half turned away. She finished and fixed her pants. "I'm done," she said.

He seemed to want to say something. Olivia waited. "All this," he said, "it's undignified. I know, and I'm sorry."

Olivia didn't know what to say.

"The fact is," Robbie continued, "you're a very special person."

That caught her off guard. "What do you mean?"

"It's not your fault—being a girl—but I'm just saying: If you *weren't* a girl, you'd be the most important person alive."

EIGHT

A COUPLE OF HOURS LATER, the van rocked to a halt. Above the windshield, a metal entrance sign hung between twenty-foot poles: SANCTUARY. Robbie rolled down his window and talked to somebody Olivia couldn't see.

"How'd it go?" the person—a woman—said.

"Stressful, but we have her."

"The back unlocked?"

"Yes," Robbie said.

A few moments later the loading door opened. A woman with a round face, wearing a military-green Castro cap, leaned in. She held an AR-15, which she kept pointed down and away.

"Hey, Emilio," she said in greeting, then: "That's her, huh?"

"That's her."

The guard studied Olivia. "She doesn't look special." Behind the woman, a narrow dirt road wound away into the woods.

"Dee, are you going to pass us through or not?"

"One sec."

She slammed shut the loading door. Then an electric motor began to grind, and there was the sound of chain-link rattling. Robbie rolled the van forward. They traveled a short distance and stopped again. This time Robbie killed the engine. He and Nike got out.

The loading door opened. A fat man wearing a denim shirt and red baseball cap said, "Come on out of there, miss." When he spoke, his big walrus mustache bobbed up and down, as if he were chewing the words before spitting them out.

Olivia crawled to the open doors, her wrists still flex-cuffed in front of her. The mustached man helped her down, breathing audibly through his mouth. Emilio slid out behind her and walked away without a word. The air felt cool and clean. They had gained some elevation. Nike and Emilio entered a big multigabled ranch house. The house sprawled, throwing wings off the main structure. It looked old and in need of paint. A wheelchair ramp slanted up to the porch. A couple of outbuildings stood between the ranch house and a barn. A six-foot woven-wire fence enclosed the property, topped with three strands of razor wire. Beyond the fence, a guy in a cowboy hat rode a brown horse along the tree line.

Olivia looked around, taking it all in. From where she stood, it was about forty yards to the fence. "Where is this? Why'd you bring me here?"

"This is Sanctuary," the fat man said, injecting solemnity into the word. "And from what I hear, you might have called it home, as much as any other honored tenant, except for the obvious problem."

"Are you in charge?"

He grinned and shook his head. "Oh, heck no. I just keep things organized around the ranch, is all. My name's Cranston. Here, let me see those cuffs."

Olivia held out her hands. Cranston produced a pair of yellow-handled wire cutters and snipped the flex cuffs off. Olivia rubbed her wrists, each bearing a red circlet where the cuffs had chafed the skin.

"If you're not in charge, who is?"

"You'll meet him pretty soon. Maybe tonight, if he's not too tired."

"Then what happens?"

Robbie ambled over with his thumbs hooked in his belt. "You don't have to concern yourself about that. You'll get the answers you're entitled to. For now, let's get you situated."

Cranston and Robbie started walking her toward one of the outbuildings, a slant-roofed structure not much larger than a garden shed. If they put her in there, she would be helpless again, just like she'd been in the back of the van. She couldn't let that happen.

Halfway to the shed, Olivia bolted.

She ran full-out for the fence, anticipating the bang of the AR-15 with every pounding footfall. But it didn't come.

"Hey, stop!" Robbie yelled. "Don't do that! Don't touch the fen—"

She made it to the fence and leaped at it, already picturing the scramble over the top, the razor wire slicing her, the sprint for the trees. If they shot her, they shot her. Anything was better than getting locked in that shed, where they could do whatever they wanted with her. But when Olivia's hands touched the woven wires, a powerful electric jolt surged into her and flung her backward. She landed hard on her back, the breath knocked out of her. Robbie and Cranston ran to her, Cranston winded by the exercise, wheezing and coughing. The rider loped his horse up to the fence, his hand resting on the butt of the pistol holstered on his hip. The woman in the Castro hat watched from the gate, but her long gun was still shoulder-slung.

"I wish you wouldn't hurt yourself, Miss Nikitas," Robbie said, helping her to her feet. He looked genuinely pained. "Take it slow now, let your breath catch up. That's six thousand volts you just tangled with."

Olivia pulled away from Robbie and hugged herself.

"Don't be so afraid," Robbie fretted.

When she recovered herself, Olivia said, "Stop saying that. I'm afraid, okay? Jesus, who *are* you people? What are you going to do to me?"

"That's up to the Elders," Cranston said. "And the sooner they decide, the better. We're running out of time to get this done."

Robbie said, "You have to calm down. You can see there's no way out of here, can't you?"

Olivia could see it. *What's he mean, running out of time? Running out of time for what?*

"Come on now," Robbie said. "You've had long, difficult day."

"*Please.*" Olivia hated the note of pleading in her voice.

"Please what, miss?"

"Don't lock me in that shed."

Robbie looked hurt. "You make it sound nasty, but it's very comfortable. Besides, it's for your own privacy as much as anything else."

"My privacy. Are you people *crazy?*"

"We like to think not," Cranston said.

They walked her back to the shed, and Cranston used a key to open the door. Inside was a built-in sofa bed. On a hinged desk sat a clock and battery-powered lamp. There was also a folding chair, a braided rug, a pellet stove, and a chemical toilet. The shed smelled of pine sap and the toilet.

"Someone will bring you food in a little while. Just make yourself at home."

Home.

They withdrew, Robbie pulling the door shut behind him. Olivia stood on the rug, listening to the key turn. After a minute she gripped the handle and pulled. She was locked in.

A skylight admitted sun. Olivia dragged the folding chair away from the desk and stood on it to look out the small fanlight window above the door. The chair wobbled. Except for the female guard, Dee, the property appeared empty. Everyone had gone inside the ranch house. Dee, who had a little shack of her own about the size of a small garden shed, looked in Olivia's direction and raised her open hand. Olivia climbed down.

Later, a key turned in the lock and Emilio entered with a tray of food. Breaded chicken breast, mashed potatoes, and green beans. Also a plastic bottle of Lipton iced tea. Olivia made no move to take the tray.

"Don't worry," Emilio said. "It's not poisoned or anything. It's good, even. Our women know how to cook." He set the tray on the desk and started to leave.

"Wait," Olivia said. He turned back to her, somehow belligerent without saying a word. "Tell me what's going on. What is it these Elders are deciding about me?"

"You'll know soon enough." He smiled, and it was cold as a codfish.

❋

IN THE NIGHT, OLIVIA CAME awake on the hard sofa bed. She'd heard a vehicle.

The clock said 10:15. The fanlight lit up. Shadows wheeled across the ceiling. Olivia rubbed the bad sleep out of her eyes, dragged the chair over to the wall again, and stepped up. A black SUV idled in front of the ranch house, throwing headlight glare on a dozen or so people. She recognized Nike, Emilio, Robbie, and Cranston. Two old men were front and center. The hawk-faced one leaned on a walker. The other sat in a wheelchair with a watch cap pulled over his ears. The Elders? A few other men, all of whom looked at least as young as Emilio, completed the all-male welcoming committee.

Behind them stood three women, all dressed similarly in jeans and pullovers. Somehow, they weren't part of the official group. Olivia thought of servants assembled for the arrival of the lord of the manor.

The guard—apparently the only woman on the ranch with a position of authority—wasn't present.

Someone turned off the SUV's engine. The headlamps went dark, the brake lights flashed once, and three doors opened. A couple of men got out of the front, and a much younger man emerged from the back seat. The front passenger wore a black duster and a slouch hat. Despite the clothes, his overall appearance was unmistakable. Olivia almost fell off the chair.

It was the old man who had seemingly come back to life under the madrassa in the Old City.

What the hell was going on here?

The man who got out of the back seat also looked familiar. Lanky, wild hair. The one who had stalked her in Aleppo. She was almost positive.

Oh, fuck.

The driver opened the hatch and lifted out several suitcases. A couple of the young men came off the porch to help.

The old man turned toward Olivia. She could feel his gaze.

He started walking toward the shed, moving stiffly. Olivia got off the chair. She retreated to the desk, switched on the cheap battery-powered lamp, and stood squarely facing the door.

A key scraped in the lock.

The door opened. The old man stood framed in a doorway too small for him to pass through without stooping. He looked tired, the skin under his eyes bruised and puffy. He held up his right hand, palm out, as if he were taking an oath. The hand looked big enough to unscrew her head like a lightbulb. "My name is Jacob."

He pulled his hat off and, ducking, stepped into the shed. One of the young men Olivia hadn't seen before slipped in behind him and stood to one side. Jacob made the shed feel even smaller than it was. He moved closer. Olivia wanted to back up but stood her ground. Looming over her, Jacob said, "I'm very glad to see you again. We last met in a dangerous place. You remember."

"We didn't exactly meet."

"Do you *remember?*"

"Yes."

"Tell me."

"You were there. You don't need me to tell you what happened."

He leaned in. Odors of travel sweat and tobacco and stale deodorant came off him.

"Tell me both memories."

Olivia stepped back. "I don't know what you're talking about."

"For all our sakes, I hope you're lying." He crowded her. "Tell me the truth."

Olivia backed up some more, far enough that her legs encountered the sofa bed, and so she sat to give herself a little distance from the man. Jacob stood over her, crushing the crown of his slouch hat in his huge blue-veined hand. Others pushed into the shed. Robbie. Cranston, breathing asthmatically through his mouth. These men, so much larger than Olivia, seemed to displace all the oxygen in the room.

"All right," she said. Olivia closed her eyes, deliberately turning her attention to a faded corner of her mind, where the old man who stood over her now instead lay dead on a table in a torture cell beneath a madrassa in the Old City. It wasn't a false memory, the result of shock or trauma. She wasn't somehow making it up for unconscious reasons she couldn't understand.

It was real.

"I remember seeing you dead," Olivia said.

Jacob stood up straighter. He appeared relieved. "What else?"

"They had tortured you, stabbed and electrocuted you. Burned you."

"Yes. What else?"

"My—my friend also . . . died." It hurt even to say it. Instinctively, Olivia knew Brian's death had also been real, as real as his recovery in the second memory stream, the memory stream that now predominated even as the other, darker events retreated into the shadow of the new reality. She found the first reality, where Brian died, difficult to contemplate. He died in that torture cell because of *her*. She couldn't get around that. Nor could she reconcile the existence of the two memories.

"And yet we are both alive," Jacob said.

"What's going to happen to me?"

"It will be resolved tomorrow." He started to turn away but stopped. "You men leave us," he said.

Cranston and Robbie looked at each other. The third, younger man appeared uncertain.

"Go on," Jacob said.

They withdrew, pulling the door shut behind them. Jacob sat on the chair with his hat in his lap. Even sitting, he seemed to fill the room. "To-morrow when you come before the Elders, questions and answers will be more formal. Before then I want you to understand the significance of what the Society does." He glanced at the door, lowered his voice. "In short, the choices we make assure the future."

Olivia said, "Choices like kidnapping me?"

He shook his head. "That was regrettably necessary. Miss Nikitas, I'm on your side in this situation."

"What *is* this situation?"

"I'm sorry." Jacob stood and put his hat on. He looked tired, his broad shoulders slumping.

Olivia stood up, too. "Whatever you're doing, it doesn't justify kid-napping me."

"I'm afraid it does, Miss Nikitas. The decisions the Society makes are sometimes very painful, but they serve the greater good. If I didn't be-lieve that, my whole life would be meaningless."

Olivia stepped closer. "Please. After tomorrow will you let me go?"

He held her gaze for several seconds. "Rest now," he said.

Jacob let himself out. A moment later, the lock turned.

NINE

NOW THAT SHE HAD LOOKED, she could not stop looking.

Olivia paced the confines of her shed, trying to walk away from what she could no longer ignore. In a corner of her mind, Brian lay dead.

But *was* it real?

She couldn't sleep. Watching from her unsteady perch, Olivia saw more vehicles arrive. The grass parking area in front of the ranch house filled with SUVs, sedans, even a couple of motorcycles. The riders wore gray ponytails and shirts with the sleeves hacked off, like aging hippie bikers. Olivia counted at least twenty people. Most—but not all—of them were male. They shook hands on the porch, pointed toward Olivia's shed.

Around 1 a.m., a silver Hyundai Santa Fe arrived. The guard in the Castro cap, Dee, opened the gate, checked the vehicle, and let it pass. It must have been the last one. After it rolled through, Dee secured the gate and walked to the ranch house. The Santa Fe parked among the other vehicles. Five men climbed out. Four were Japanese, all of them wearing suits. The driver, in chinos and a chambray shirt, looked like a ranch hand.

Several men, Robbie among them, had been smoking and talking on the porch. When the Hyundai pulled up, Robbie abandoned his chair and came down the steps, plugging his cigar in his mouth and offering his hand to the Japanese, shaking hands and doing a little awkward bow to each one in turn. Instead of going into the house, as everyone else had done, they spoke insistently to Robbie and kept pointing toward the shed. Olivia couldn't hear what they were saying. After a couple of minutes of discussion, Robbie brought them in her direction.

Olivia got off her chair and retreated to the sofa. Her heart beat faster. The door opened, admitting a whiff of Robbie's cigar smoke. He stood aside, and the four Japanese men pushed up to the doorway but did not enter. They stared at her, and she stared back. The silence became unnerving.

"Who are you?" Olivia said.

No one answered.

"You can't keep me here. You can't *do* this."

"Do not be agitated," one of them said.

"I *am* agitated."

"Enough?" Robbie asked.

"Yes," the man who had spoken replied.

They withdrew, and Robbie closed and locked the door again.

※

OLIVIA WOKE OUT OF FITFUL dreams. She rubbed her eyes. Dust motes drifted in a slanting shaft of sunlight. Something had awakened her, a noise.

The sound of a key.

The door opened as Olivia rolled off the sofa bed she hadn't bothered to open. She stood, groggy with bad sleep. Dee, the guard, entered. She wasn't armed. Others, all men, lingered outside.

"What now?" Olivia said.

"They're going to take some of your blood," Dee said.

She heard the words but almost couldn't process them. "What?"

"It's no big deal, but you've got to let them do it. No fighting."

"Nobody's sticking another needle in me."

"If you fight, it's going to get rough. So don't fight, okay?"

A rawboned man in a corduroy sport coat with patches on the elbows stepped into the shed, his thick white hair like a swoop of whipped cream. He held a black leather kit in his right hand. Two young men followed him inside. The white-haired man looked ill at ease. The younger guys looked eager.

They left the door open.

Olivia could see the gate in the distance behind them. There was no one attending it. Would it be electrified, too? Even if it were, the mechanism to open the gate was right there. If she could manage to get out of the shed, maybe she would have a chance to make a break for the woods. But even as the thought occurred to her, the hopelessness of it descended. Before that dread could smother her, she started to make her move —

But Dee moved first. Without knowing how it happened, Olivia found herself pinned to the floor, her right arm bent at an unnatural angle and the guard's knee pressing into the small of her back.

"Lie still," Dee said. "It's nothing but a blood draw. I promise."

Olivia struggled.

The young men started to move in.

Dee said, "Stay *back*. I've got this."

The young men looked at each other. One of them shrugged, and they remained where they were.

Dee dug her knee in, making it hurt.

Olivia stopped struggling. "Okay, all right."

The doctor, or whatever he was, opened his kit on the desk. He took out a syringe.

"He's not going to hurt you," Dee said. "You understand?"

Olivia gritted her teeth. Dee removed her knee from Olivia's back and helped her sit on the sofa bed. The doctor approached.

"Roll up your sleeve," he said.

Olivia complied. The doctor swabbed her skin at the crux of her elbow and drew two vials of blood. He held one up to the light and shook his head, as if he were put out by the absurdity of it all. He turned to leave. When Dee didn't follow the other three out the door, the doctor looked back.

"I'm going to stay with her, calm her down before it starts," Dee said.

He looked doubtful.

"It's all right," Dee said.

"I'll have to tell Cranston."

"Go ahead."

The doctor mumbled, unhappy. He pulled the door closed behind him but didn't lock it, since Dee had the key.

"Before what starts?" Olivia said, already thinking about overpowering the guard and making her escape. Which was a joke. She would have had as much chance overpowering a mountain lion.

Dee said, "I know you're thinking it's just you and me now, the boys are gone. Right? Don't try it."

"I wasn't thinking that."

"Yeah, of course not. Listen, I don't need the boys."

Olivia rubbed the small of her back. "So I noticed."

"I didn't mean to hurt you."

"You didn't?"

Dee grinned. "Well, not so it lasts."

"What's going to happen to me?"

"They're going to evaluate you. It's like a board of regents. They want to know whether you can perform, I think. I'm not positive how it works. Women are never allowed to see the inner-circle operations. Which is bullshit. We're all part of the Society."

"The Society? What the hell is that?" Olivia felt like a contestant on an un-reality TV show.

Dee glanced over her shoulder, as if someone might be listening at the door—the same thing Jacob had done. She dropped her voice. "You don't need to know that yet. I'm not supposed to talk about it. But we're doing something really, really important."

Olivia nodded at this crazy person. "Right. You 'assure the future.'"

Dee's mouth opened and her eyes got wide. "Who told you that?"

"Jacob."

Dee sighed, visibly relieved. "He shouldn't have, but I guess it doesn't matter. He's the Shepherd; he can do anything he wants. Listen. If you're accepted—and if what I've heard is true, I think they *have* to accept you—you will be the first woman Shepherd in the history of the Society."

Great, Olivia thought, I can't wait to put that on my résumé. "Why wasn't he supposed to tell me about assuring the future?"

"Some of the Elders think you should be vetted without any prep." She glanced at the door again. "There's some hostility about you and about the direction of the Society in general."

"Naturally. Look, what exactly are they—"

"I can't tell you anything else. Just answer their questions honestly. There will be a lot of them."

Olivia hoped the questions made more sense than this conversation did, but she wasn't hopeful. "If you've never seen the inner workings, how do you know how many questions?"

"I'm . . . friends with someone who knows. It's kind of a test. If you pass, it's going to be one of the greatest days. There's never been a woman before. I think it will make a difference. Some of us have wanted this to happen for a long time, so don't screw it up." Dee smiled reassuringly and touched Olivia's hand. "Just kidding. Since you're legit, you *can't* screw it up."

"What if I fail?"

"You won't fail."

"But if I do, will they let me go?"

"You won't fail."

"Thanks for the vote of confidence, I guess."

"You're going to be fine." Dee crossed to the door and opened it. "Here they come."

TEN

CRANSTON AND ROBBIE ESCORTED HER to the house. Dee walked behind them. Olivia felt small between the two large men, but she was used to that. She was also used to the whole testosterone effluvium that dominated men at war, or men at work, or, really, men everywhere — especially when they perceived their dominance under threat. What was strange in this situation was that Olivia, so far as she could see, presented exactly zero threat to the dominance of this man-group. Yet there it was: In some way she didn't yet understand, they feared and resented her. The older men showed her respect, but it was the phony, condescending respect of the boys' club for the female interloper.

On the porch, Robbie turned to Dee. "What you did was a breach. No one's supposed to be alone with her except Jacob."

"She was scared. I made a judgment call."

"That wasn't smart."

It was all Olivia heard, as Cranston took her by the arm and pulled her into the house. Wagon wheel chandeliers hung from exposed beams. Men sat on big, clunky chairs and sofas constructed of oak and buttery leather. There were no women, at least initially, but just then, one came out of the kitchen with a tray of coffee mugs. She was one of the small group of women who had stood on the porch, apart from the men, last night. Wives? Housekeepers?

When Olivia appeared, everyone stopped talking. They watched as Cranston led her through the room. Olivia felt on display, evaluated. These guys were sizing her up. Going by their dour looks, Olivia guessed she fell short of their expectations.

They walked down a hallway and entered a long wood-paneled room.

Cranston shut the heavy door, and it was suddenly very quiet, like shutting the door of a vault. Three old men sat behind a table at the end of the room: the man in the wheelchair, still wearing his watch cap; the hawk-faced man, whose scraggly white hair gave him a crypt-keeper appearance, his walker stowed in a corner; and sitting in the middle, Jacob.

Before each of the men sat a water glass. Two pitchers of ice water, lemon slices floating on top like small lily pads, anchored two corners of the table.

A fourth chair, to the left of the crypt-keeper, remained empty, although it had its own water glass.

Centered on the wall behind the old men hung a picture of Earth taken from deep space, an old photo from the Apollo program.

A gallery of portraits lined the other walls—three men enclosed in every frame. The most recent-looking picture was of the same men now sitting behind the table, only they were much younger, middle-aged, barely recognizable. In it, Jacob retained his beard, but it was black and trimmed, in the style of Ulysses S. Grant. The other portraits tracked back in time, color surrendering to black and white, regressing to daguerreotypes and down to pre-photographic eras. Some were done in oil, others were charcoal sketches. Near the end of the gallery three faces had been inscribed on a copper plate. But it was always three men, and they went back a long way.

A folding chair faced the three old men.

"Go ahead and sit." Cranston dropped his hand on her shoulder and pushed her down.

What now, she wondered, defend my dissertation?

Jacob cleared his throat. "Would you like water? We're waiting for—"

The door opened and somebody said, "Sorry." Olivia turned. Her Aleppo stalker, Crazy Hair, entered the room and closed the door behind him. He hurried to the front, sparing Olivia a glance, and sat next to the crypt-keeper. Again, Olivia was struck by the resemblance between Crazy Hair and Emilio. Were they brothers? Jacob frowned at him, cleared his throat again, and spoke. "Now that we are all assembled, we will begin."

"Wait a minute." Olivia pushed Cranston's hand off her shoulder. "I have some questions of my own. Who the hell are you people?"

The old men exchanged looks. The stalker pulled nervously at his lip.

"Don't speak unless you are asked a direct question." Cranston's hand landed on her shoulder again, heavy and firm. His big belly bumped against her. Olivia tried to shrug the hand off, but Cranston dug his fingers in. He reeked of Old Spice. She glared at him. "You don't have the right to do this. None of you."

"We have every right," the crypt-keeper said. "We have a duty."

"You don't have the right to kidnap me."

Jacob sighed. "Miss Nikitas, we are not having a conversation. There are two possible outcomes of this questioning. One is very disfavorable to you. Please be quiet."

Olivia stared at him but kept her mouth shut.

"Good. We will continue. I am Jacob. This"—he nodded to the man in the watch cap—"is Martin. And this"—nodding to the crypt-keeper —"is Andrew. My alternates. Our young friend sitting next to Andrew is Alvaro. The next in line."

"That's in dispute," Andrew said.

"This isn't the time," Jacob said.

"Emilio should be here. He's part of the argument."

"This isn't the *time*," Jacob said. "Martin? Begin."

Martin cleared his throat. It sounded like a garbage disposal clotted with gunk. He measured Olivia and asked, "What is the Parable of Two Cities?"

"I can speak now?" Olivia said.

Jacob inclined his head.

"Okay," Olivia said. "I don't know what you're talking about. What two cities?"

Martin scowled. He dug his pinkie into his ear and screwed it back and forth, as if he were tightening something.

"Andrew?" Jacob said.

The crypt-keeper pursed his lips. His chin puckered like a skin bag cinched closed. "I don't see the need to continue. She doesn't know the parable."

Olivia dropped her head, then looked up. "You at least have to tell me what we're talking about."

"What is the Parable of Two Cities?" Andrew repeated.

Olivia sighed. "I don't know it."

Jacob said, "It begins this way: 'A man left his home in the shining city and followed a crooked path.' What is the next sentence? Take your time." He nodded at her encouragingly.

"Helping her isn't allowed," Andrew said.

Olivia rolled her eyes. "I don't know it."

"I think that settles the matter." Andrew folded his liver-spotted hands under his chin. "Remove her, so we can discuss the order of transference. That's the only real issue."

Jacob lowered his eyes and nodded.

OUTSIDE, DEE SAT ON THE porch rail, with the two young men from before standing on either side of her.

"Take her back." Cranston released Olivia's arm and retreated into the house.

Dee pushed off the rail. "I got this."

The young men, both in khakis and polo shirts, looked doubtful.

"Seriously," Dee said.

She escorted Olivia off the porch, between the parked vehicles, and across the yard. The young men followed at a short distance.

"What happened in there?" Dee asked.

"I don't think I passed."

"Those old guys can be hard to read. You probably did better than you think."

"I didn't."

Dee glanced back at the men following, dropped her voice. "Tell me what happened."

"They asked me to recite a parable I'd never heard of, and when I didn't know it, they ended the meeting. At first I thought Jacob was in charge. But one of the other Elders, Andrew, he seemed to take over."

"That isn't good."

"It didn't seem like it, no."

"They only asked you one question, to repeat the parable?"

"Yes." Olivia stopped walking. "What are they going to do with me?"

"Keep walking."

"Tell me what they're going to do."

"Problem?" one of the polo-shirted guys said.

"No problem." Dee shoved Olivia, not hard. "Move," she said under her breath. "I'm already in trouble."

Olivia started walking again, taking the measured steps of a prisoner approaching the gallows. If they locked her in the shed again, she would be helpless. Right, she thought, as opposed to being helpless *outside* the shed.

"What's going to happen to me?"

"Nothing."

"I don't think I believe you."

They reached the shed. Dee produced her key.

"Help me," Olivia said.

"They won't hurt you," Dee said, but wouldn't look at her. She unlocked the door.

"Please. You know this is wrong."

Dee pushed her through the doorway.

"*Please,*" Olivia said.

Dee looked troubled. "I can't," she said, and pulled the door shut. Olivia heard the bolt clack into place.

THE DAY PASSED. NO ONE brought her food or picked up the tray from earlier. In the Damascus house, when the separatists stopped emptying the chamber pot, it meant that they had decided to run away and let her go. Olivia doubted a similar disruption of services meant the same thing at Sanctuary. Above the skylight, gray overcast interrupted the sun.

A vehicle's engine started, and the gate rattled open. Olivia dragged the chair across the floor and stood on it, nose pressed to the fanlight. Dee was back at her post. The silver Hyundai drove toward the trees, the gate rolling closed behind it. The Japanese contingent going home with Olivia's blood?

Olivia waited for the racket of the closing gate to cease, then rapped her knuckles on the window, hard enough, she hoped, to be heard across the yard. Dee looked over but otherwise didn't acknowledge her. She fiddled with something in the guard shack, then crossed to the house. Olivia rapped on the window and waved. Dee stopped with one foot on the porch and looked across the yard to Olivia's shed. The moment stretched out. Dee made a downward pushing gesture—a be-quiet gesture—and continued into the house.

Hours passed, and still no water or food. Still no communication. And no other vehicles had departed or arrived. Standing on the rickety chair,

Olivia watched people move past windows in the sprawling ranch house. Darkness descended, lights came on, and window blinds closed. Olivia turned on the lamp and lay on the sofa bed. She sensed that something bad was going to happen.

What was Brian doing, she wondered. By now he must have called the police, but they may or may not be looking for her. Olivia was a thirty-year-old woman, gone for less than two days. Even if they believed Brian when he told them her absence was suspicious, what could they do about it? If Brian had been watching from the window when the men took her, he would have called the police immediately, and the bastards would never have gotten her to Sanctuary.

No, the cavalry wasn't coming. Olivia was alone.

You are not alone, Rohana had said to her once when she came into Olivia's room and found her sobbing for her mother. She sat on Olivia's bed and stroked her hair. That one time, Olivia had allowed her stepmother to comfort her. It hadn't been a miracle. The whole relationship hadn't flipped. But it did change. For a while it was different. Now, lying alone in her little prison shed, Olivia could almost feel Rohana's hand. That memory was a good one, even if afterward Olivia had worried that her acceptance of comfort from Rohana had been a kind of betrayal of her real mother.

Her mouth was dry. Hunger gnawed at her, but she doubted she'd be able to keep anything down, even if they gave her food. She stood on the chair and probed the skylight, sliding her fingertips over the box frame. It was completely sealed, no nails or screw heads accessible — not that she had anything to use as a screwdriver, not even a dime in her pocket. Rain started. It pattered on the roof. Olivia's face looked back at her from the black mirror the skylight had become. Raindrops squiggled over her features. Frustrated, she jumped down, picked up the chair, and flung it at the skylight. It bounced off the frame and almost hit her on the rebound.

AROUND ELEVEN O'CLOCK, THINGS FINALLY started happening. She heard voices in the yard. From the fanlight she watched more than a dozen people, umbrellas in hand, cross the yard to the barn, where light now blazed every time the door opened. The doctor appeared on the porch of the ranch house. In his right hand he held his medical kit. Following the others to the barn, he moved haltingly, picking his steps carefully, probably worried about his shoes in the wet sod. He looked like a man crossing a minefield of dog shit.

Martin and Andrew emerged from the house wearing blue robes. The robes looked ceremonial. Olivia thought of death cults. "Oh, fuck me."

Jacob, though, did not appear.

The rain fell steadily, making the wheelchair and walker impractical, so two young men picked up Martin and carried him. A very large man with a long biker-beard carried Andrew in his arms like a troll with a wizened damsel. Others followed with the wheelchair and walker.

They all disappeared into the barn.

Olivia got down from her perch. She felt shaky and scared. There was nothing in the shed she could use as a weapon.

Wait.

Hinges anchored the desk surface to the wall and the two supporting legs folded in, to free up space. Olivia knelt in front of the desk and examined one of the folding supports. Only a sliding hinge held it to the underside of the desk. Olivia wrenched and twisted it. The support cracked partially free but refused to completely break off. She worked it aggressively, wrenching the support back and forth, twisting it.

"Fuck you," Olivia shouted at it. "*Fuck* you."

She climbed back on the chair to see if anything else was happening. A figure came walking toward the shed, head down in the rain.

Olivia jumped down and grabbed the support again, wrenched at it with crazy-person force—and it snapped free. She staggered back and crashed into the wall. The support was a hollow metal tube, disappointingly lightweight. She held it up. Use it as a club, or a spear? She touched the jagged end that had twisted free of the sliding hinge. Spear. Definitely spear.

A key scraped in the lock.

Olivia turned with her half-assed spear gripped in both hands, lips skinned back, feral and terrified in equal measure.

The door opened.

Dee said, "What are you doing?" She was alone and unarmed, holding nothing but the key she'd used to unlock the shed.

"What are *you* doing?"

"Helping you."

Olivia looked past her. The rain fell dark and steady. That was all. "Really?"

"Yeah. We're getting you out of here."

"We?"

"The friend I mentioned."

Olivia moved to the door, still gripping the table-leg spear, afraid of tricks. Not that they needed to trick her out of the shed. The men could simply drag her out to the barn. Even Dee could have dragged her.

"We have to hurry." Dee turned her back and walked away. Olivia stepped into the downpour, looking around in case there was someone waiting to club her over the head. The sod, saturated with rain, squelched around her shoes. Cold mud soaked her feet. She looked toward the barn. Light seeped from the hayloft. What were they getting ready to do in there, with their ceremonial robes and syringes?

The sound of a car door opening drew Olivia's attention. The passenger door of a little yellow Toyota pickup truck hung open.

"Get in," Dee said, her words strained and tight, and she ran off toward the gate.

Olivia approached the pickup and looked inside the cab. Her Aleppo stalker sat behind the wheel. Crazy Hair Alvaro. He said, "Please get in now. Before I change my mind about this."

The gate rattled to life, rolling on its track.

Olivia ducked into the cab, still holding her pathetic spear, and pulled the door shut. Alvaro started the engine. He worked the clutch and powered them in reverse, the light truck slewing, throwing clods of muddy turf past Olivia's window. She braced her hand on the dash and planted her feet. Alvaro slammed the clutch into first gear and churned them toward the open gate. They passed through and skidded to a stop.

The gate started rattling shut. Olivia got out and stood in the rain. Dee slipped through the closing gate. The barn doors opened. People and light flooded into the yard. Men ran toward the gate, shouting.

"I broke the key off in the power box," Dee said, "but it won't be that hard for them to open the gate. All they have to do is disengage the chain drive."

Olivia started toward the gate with her table-leg spear.

Dee pawed at her shirt sleeve. "We have to get out of here. What are you doing?"

"Making it harder." The gate finished closing. Olivia drove the flimsy spear into the chain drive and wrenched it.

"Good idea," Dee said.

Angry, shouting men had almost reached the gate.

"Get *in*." Dee pushed Olivia into the cab.

A gunshot rang out. Olivia stiffened, flashing back to the Old City. Dee piled into the cab next to her, shoving Olivia against Alvaro. He accelerated them up the dirt road, ramming the shifter into Olivia's hip.

"Goddamn it," Dee said. "I'm hit."

"What, what?" Alvaro sounded frantic.

"Keep driving," Dee said.

"Is it bad? Where are you shot?"

"It's not bad."

"There's a hospital in Idaho Falls."

"Forget it. We have to save the Shepherd."

"The Shepherd?" Olivia said. "I thought Jacob was the Shepherd."

"Not anymore," Dee said. "Now *you* are."

PART II

THE POWER

ELEVEN

THE TOYOTA PICKUP RACED AWAY from Sanctuary, Alvaro hugging the steering wheel. Wiper blades swiped the windshield, and the headlight beams followed the twisting road, veering between dense woods. With every turn, Olivia was squished between her rescuers.

Dee groaned, clutching her leg below the knee. "*Damn* it."

"Flashlight in the glove box," Alvaro said.

Olivia popped open the glove box, grabbed the flashlight, and thumbed it on. At calf level a dark stain spread around two holes in Dee's pants.

"I need to see the wound," Olivia said.

Dee pulled the pant leg up to her knee. Two neat holes drilled through the meat of her calf.

"It looks clean," Olivia said. "In and out."

Dee looked at her. "You know gunshot wounds?"

"I've seen a few."

The truck jolted over a pothole and Dee winced. "What's happening with your leg?" Alvaro said.

"In and out, like she said. Clean. But it hurts, and I'm bleeding all over your raggedy truck."

Alvaro said, "There's a first-aid kit behind the seat."

Olivia twisted around. The ranch house lights flickered between trees and, with the next sliding turn, disappeared. She rummaged behind the seat. Among the bungee cords, painter's tarp, cans of oil, and loose tools she found a white metal box with a green cross on the lid. She placed the kit on her lap, flipped open the latches, and raised the lid. The inventory was basic and depleted. Butterfly bandages, gauze, a few sterile wipes, roll of white tape, a small pair of scissors. "There's not much here," she said.

"Just bandage it." Dee sounded strained.

Olivia handed her the flashlight and started pawing through the med kit. The truck jolted and bounced. "Can't you slow down?"

"They can still stop us," Dee said.

Alvaro concentrated on the road. "This wasn't a good idea."

"You said yourself there's no choice," Dee said. "With Andrew in charge, we're on the wrong team."

"It's not supposed to be about *teams*. I shouldn't have left Jacob back there."

"If he's even alive."

"What a fucking mess," Alvaro said.

Olivia stripped open a packet of antiseptic wipes. She dabbed the bullet wound, and Dee jerked her leg away.

"*Shit*. That stings."

"Hold still." Olivia pressed a couple of square bandages over the entry and exit holes and wound gauze around Dee's calf, using the whole roll, and taped it off. "I think we should take you to a hospital."

Dee shook her head. "We can't chance it."

"Shit." Alvaro stood on the brakes and the truck skidded to a stop, throwing Olivia against the dashboard and Dee against Olivia.

A horse and rider blocked the road. The rider's rain poncho made him look vaguely like a figure out of time. He trained a pistol on them. The road was narrow and the woods marched right up to the edge on both sides. The truck's wipers clacked metronomically.

Alvaro said, "That's it."

Dee rolled down her window. "Caleb, is that you? Let us by."

"Can't do that," the rider called back. With his free hand he raised a walkie-talkie to his mouth and spoke into it.

"We have the new Shepherd," Dee said. "There isn't any reason for the ceremony. Andrew's wrong."

"Bullshit," Caleb said.

Alvaro tapped the steering wheel nervously. "They'll get that gate open pretty soon."

Dee reached over Olivia and squeezed his shoulder. "We're going to make it."

Alvaro shook his head. "We don't even have a weapon."

Olivia felt trapped between the two of them. "What were they going to do to me back there?"

"Kill you," Alvaro said. "They were going to kill you in the ceremony of transference."

It hit her like a punch in the mouth. "*Why?*"

"They don't want you to have the power," Dee said. "They want it for themselves."

"I don't have any power."

"You have all the power in the world," Alvaro said. He didn't sound thrilled about it.

"If all they want to do is kill me, why doesn't this guy on the horse shoot me right now?"

"He won't," Alvaro said. "He'd be afraid of disrupting the transfer."

"*What* power? What *transfer?* What the *fuck* are you guys talking about?"

Dee nodded. "Alvaro's right. He's afraid."

He's afraid? Olivia's mind raced. How the hell did she get here, trapped in a car with two lunatics? Sure, they helped her escape from some scarier lunatics, but still. One thing Olivia knew from years of covering chaotic situations, situations when the world stopped making sense, was that you had to figure out what the new rules were—because there were always rules. And the sooner you knew them, the greater your chance of survival.

"You're saying he won't shoot me here and now, *no matter what?*"

"No," Dee said.

"He definitely won't!" Alvaro said.

Olivia said, "Well, somebody shot *you*. That bullet could have hit me instead."

"Whoever fired that gun wasn't authorized. It wasn't security, trust me. And no one else at Sanctuary should have been armed."

Olivia decided to take a chance, since the alternative, clearly, was that they would haul her back to the ranch and kill her. "Do you have something sharp?"

"Why?"

"Never mind." The first-aid kit was still in her lap. Olivia raised the lid and rummaged until she found the scissors. "Open the door. Let me out."

"That's not a good idea," Alvaro said.

"You guys just said he won't shoot me."

Dee hesitated.

"Let me out," Olivia said. "I'm not running away. Where would I go?"

Dee opened her door and maneuvered around, giving Olivia room to climb past her. "What are you going to do?"

Olivia ignored her. The summer rain fell cool and steady, made a crackling sound in the woods. She held the scissors in her closed fist, only the tips sticking out. Walking toward the horse, the bright head-lights behind her, she kept her hand turned back, hiding the scissor tips. What if Dee and Alvaro had it all wrong? What if this guy decided to put a bullet in her? Trying to predict what a frightened man with a gun will or will not do was never a smart play.

"Now you stop right there," Caleb said.

"I want to give up. I want you to take me back." She moved closer. "Huh?"

"Those two"—Olivia nodded back at the truck—"they made me leave."

"I don't know anything about that." Caleb sounded uncertain. He pointed the gun away. They were right: He was afraid of her, or at least afraid to shoot.

Close enough now to make her move, she struck out with the scissors, driving the sharp tips into the horse's haunch. The animal reared, squeal-ing in pain. Caleb held on, just barely. The horse, scissors jiggling loosely in his haunch, charged into the woods.

Sorry, horse.

The pickup's engine revved. Olivia looked into the woods. It was pitch-black between the trees. If she ran, would she be able to get away? Doubtful. They were too close to the ranch and probably too far from any outside help. But she had been sitting in the back of the van when they brought her here and hadn't seen what lay beyond the woods.

This might be her only chance.

Alvaro got out of the pickup and stood watching her. "You have to come with us. We're miles from anywhere except the ranch. They would catch you before you could get out of the woods."

Olivia thought about the barn, the old men in their ceremonial robes. She walked back to the truck and climbed in, putting Dee in the middle. Alvaro dropped into the driver's seat and hit the gas. They roared out of the woods and fishtailed onto the county road. Alvaro punched it. The lights of a house twinkled in an otherwise dark and empty field.

"Who has a phone?" Olivia said.

"There's no connection out here," Alvaro said.

"Somebody give me a phone." She needed to talk to Brian. "Come on."

No one spoke.

Olivia snapped, "Give me a goddamn *phone.*"

"Alvaro?" Dee said.

He didn't take his eyes off the road. A muscle jumped in his jaw.

Dee produced a basic disposable unit, 2D function only, and handed it to Olivia, who pressed the on button. Zero bars appeared. She dialed Brian anyway. Nothing happened. After a couple more tries, she gave up —but kept the phone, clutching it in her lap. Sooner or later civilization would turn up again.

Alvaro glanced in the rearview mirror. "Nothing yet."

Olivia held the phone tightly.

Dee touched her hand. "You want to call your boyfriend."

"Yes."

"It's not a good idea," Alvaro said.

Fuck. You.

Dee said, "If you bring him into this, you'll put him in danger."

Olivia stared out the window.

"She won't listen to you," Alvaro said. "She's stubborn."

"You kidnapped me," Olivia said. "Now I'm supposed to just completely trust you?"

"We helped you escape." Alvaro's voice was flat, with barely contained impatience. "Dee got shot helping you. Yes, I expect you to trust us. At least for a little while."

Olivia studied his profile. "I've seen you before. In Aleppo. It was you following me from the hospital, wasn't it?"

"Yes."

"You were supposed to grab me in Syria, is that it? But you missed your chance, so you had to do it here?"

"No. I wanted to warn you. I was afraid of what Andrew and his people would do if they got to you first. Jacob told me what happened in the madrassa. I didn't believe him. How could the link have migrated to you, an outsider? A *woman*. It didn't make sense. I wanted to see for myself. But I couldn't do it. It wasn't that I didn't believe Jacob. It's that I didn't *want* to believe him. At night I came to your room, but when I heard you get up, I ran." He bit his lip. "I'm a coward sometimes."

"You aren't a coward," Dee said.

Alvaro grunted.

"Time is all that matters now," Dee said. "Olivia, give us a chance to make you understand. You've inherited a great power. If you don't use it to fix what you broke, the Society will take it away from you. And taking it away means you die."

"Her life doesn't matter," Alvaro said. "It's the world."

These people are crazy. "I have to tell Brian I'm all right. That's not negotiable. After that, you can try to convince me of . . . whatever it is you're talking about."

"That's fair," Dee said. "Alvaro, that's fair?"

He watched the road.

THE FIRST CHANCE SHE GOT, as soon as they were in a populated area, Olivia planned to run like hell.

The rain stopped. An hour later, the lights of a town appeared on the horizon. Olivia opened her hand. The phone had bars. It was almost 2 a.m. Her thumb hovered over the touch screen. 911? Alvaro was watching the road, but Dee had her eye on her. Olivia tapped redial and Brian's number connected. He picked up before the second ring.

"Hello?" He sounded wide awake.

"Bri, it's me."

"*Liv.*"

"I'm all right. Now listen—"

Alvaro tore the phone out of her hand and turned it off. Olivia grabbed for it. Alvaro elbowed her away. The truck swerved, juddered on the shoulder, swerved back onto the road.

"Goddamn it," Olivia said.

"You told him you were all right. That's what you wanted." Alvaro stuffed the phone in his pants pocket.

"Fuck you."

"This won't work," Alvaro said. "If she can't control her temper, how will she control the halo?"

"She can do it." Dee sounded certain.

Alvaro glanced over. "How bad is the leg?"

"Hurts like hell."

To Olivia's disappointment, they bypassed the town and continued into the wooded countryside. Alvaro guided them to Frank R. Gooding State Park. The headlights slipped over a sign prohibiting camping, hunting, and open fires. Nothing about kidnapping. The park closed at 9 p.m. A chain blocked the road. Alvaro turned off the engine but left the lights on. He got out, taking the keys, and retrieved bolt cutters from the back of the truck. He hunched over, bore down on the long handles of the cutters, severing the chain. Olivia, staring at his back, reached for the door handle.

"Don't," Dee said, grabbing Olivia's arm. "Whatever you think, we're not insane. This is about the future. Everyone's future. Hear us out."

Olivia pried Dee's fingers off her arm, but the opportunity was gone. Alvaro returned to the truck, slammed the door, started the engine, and drove into the park.

TWELVE

ON THE PARK ROAD, THE pickup wound between thick stands of pine. After ten minutes, Alvaro stopped and killed the engine. Olivia stared into the dark under the trees. This time she would get away. But before she could make a move, Alvaro reached under the seat and came up fast with something in his hand—more flex cuffs. Olivia yanked on the door handle, but Alvaro caught her left arm and zipped one side of the cuffs tight around her wrist. Dee slipped her right hand through the other loop.

"You assholes," Olivia said. "This is how I'm supposed to start trusting you?"

Alvaro got out of the truck, leaned back in. "You would run away as soon as I wasn't here to stop you. Am I wrong?"

"You have to give us a chance," Dee said. "I know this is scary."

Olivia looked into her eyes. "Tell me one thing. If you don't convince me about this power, whatever it is, are you going to let me go?"

Dee dropped her gaze.

"That's what I thought."

"Once you understand, you won't want to run away."

Alvaro lifted something out of the back of the truck, a large bundle. He hoisted it onto his shoulder and carried it into the woods. About twenty minutes later, he came back and opened the passenger door. "Ready."

They entered the woods, Alvaro supporting Dee, who had to hop on one foot. They came to a broad clearing drenched in moonlight. The blue nylon shell of a tent stood glowing from within. Beyond the clearing, a river made burbling sounds.

"Great," Olivia said. "Are we going to make s'mores?"

Dee pushed through the flap first, pulling Olivia after her. Alvaro ducked in behind them. The tent was big enough to sleep four. An electric lantern hung from the apex of the flexible rods supporting the shell. Alvaro bumped it with his head, and the tent filled with swooping shadows. Dee lay back, groaning from the pain in her leg, and Olivia sat down beside her. Clean wound or not, Olivia knew the woman should be in a hospital, not a tent. Sweat beaded Dee's round face.

Alvaro sat cross-legged in front of them and looked at Olivia. "You have a scar on the back of your neck."

"What?"

"You know what I'm talking about, but you don't know what made the scar."

"Some bug." She reached back and touched the ridge of scar tissue.

"You saw this 'bug'?"

"Yeah."

"So you know it wasn't an insect."

Olivia started to reply but stopped. In her mind's eye the thing squirmed out of Jacob's hair, its metallic-looking carapace shiny with blood. At first she had identified it as a beetle or some other insect. Later, she told herself it might have been a micro-drone similar to the flies she and other journalists sometimes deployed to capture video. But she had known it was neither of those things. Eventually other stuff crowded it out of her thoughts, mostly Brian and his impossible resurrection.

"You're saying, what, that it was man-made?"

"It's a link between the Shepherd's brain and a machine that can manipulate probability streams, change the course of reality from the point of change onward," Alvaro said. "We call them crisis points — crossroads events where the highest probability outcome threatens humanity. It used to be the threat of a cumulative effect, but since the mid-twentieth century, crisis points have become dangerously amplified. That was a crisis point under the madrassa in Aleppo, a single end point along the timeline that could threaten the odds of survival for the human race."

Olivia closed her eyes. She was in the hands of absolute lunatics. "Come on. Where would a thing like that even come from? Who could build it?"

Alvaro leaned in. "Do you remember when Andrew asked you to recite the Parable of Two Cities?"

"Something about a guy going for a walk. What does—"

Alvaro interrupted, reciting from memory: "A man left his home in the shining city and followed a crooked road. Along his journey he encountered many perils and obstructions, and many times lost his way. When he came to the final bend he found himself in a rude and primitive place. It was the same city from which he set out." Alvaro ran his hands through his hair. "Everyone in the Society knows the Parable of Two Cities. Our children are expected to memorize it."

Olivia stared at him. "That's great. It's more of a riddle, though, don't you think?"

Alvaro returned her stare. Did the man ever blink? "The parable is translated from the original Aramaic. It's part of the Society's ritual heritage. It comes down from the beginning, hundreds of years ago. But it's the truth behind the parable that matters. The probability machine was created by a future civilization. It's the mission of the Society to choose alternate probability outcomes at crisis points so the future that created it can exist."

Olivia nodded slowly, as if she were humoring a child. "Right . . ."

"The road symbolizes time," Alvaro said, plowing on doggedly, like a crackpot conspiracy theorist. No, that wasn't it. Alvaro didn't entirely believe what he was saying, or he was leaving something out, something he knew but couldn't say, and it was making him grouchy. "The perils and obstructions along the road are crisis points," he went on. "The primitive city and the shining city are the same, one in the future and one in the past. We know the shining city—the future—exists, because we have the probability machine. Otherwise, how could it be here? So we *have* to use the machine. Do you understand what I'm saying? It's deterministic, an unbroken loop. Now you're the Shepherd and you have to continue the mission. There isn't any other choice."

Olivia said, "Wait. The traveler is a *time* traveler?"

Alvaro pulled back. "You don't believe me, of course."

"Ah—"

"You have two diverging memories," Alvaro said. "In one, a dead man lies on a table. In the other, the man is alive. What's your explanation?"

Exasperated, Olivia said, "I don't need to have an explanation of my own to know yours is horseshit."

"Jacob used the probability machine to choose a path forward from the crisis point—the only path forward that preserved the future. The choice cost him his life. He knew it would, but he chose it anyway. And you reversed his sacrifice."

"A probability machine," Olivia said tonelessly.

"Yes."

"Those people back at the ranch, they wanted to cut this link thing out of me and put it back in Jacob?"

"It doesn't work like that. Cutting the link out would damage it and kill the Shepherd. That used to just be part of the traditional lore, too. But in modern times we've used magnetic resonance to image Jacob's brain, so we know for a fact that the link is too intricately woven into the brain. It only migrates when the Shepherd dies. The next Shepherd in line is supposed to be present at the time of death. There's a ceremony. But I wasn't there when Jacob died. *You* were, and the link migrated to you. No one thought that was possible—for it to migrate to someone like you."

"What he means is 'for it to migrate to a woman.' It's always a man." Dee propped herself on her elbow. "That's why, according to Andrew and his followers, you can't be legitimate."

"That's not the only reason," Alvaro said. "Andrew wanted my cousin Emilio to be the next in line." Olivia thought, Not brothers; cousins. "There are all kinds of reasons why that's a bad idea." Alvaro sighed heavily. "After what happened at the ranch tonight, we know Andrew's faction always planned for it to be Emilio, even though Jacob had rightfully chosen me. And, yes, some members of the Society believe the order of transference can only be male."

"They *all* believe it." Dee sounded pissed off. Or maybe the gunshot wound made her cranky, which would be understandable.

"Not everyone," Alvaro said.

Dee reached toward him and they touched fingertips. "I'm sorry. Obviously I didn't mean you."

They had their own vocabulary of touch. Olivia thought of Brian and felt her impatience and anger rise. "Isn't your Society kind of low rent, considering how much power this probability machine would give you? I mean, no offense, but that pickup we're rattling around in is a piece of junk."

For the first time, Alvaro smiled. "Hey, I love my truck."

Dee ignored him. "There's a big argument in the Society over how much to use the machine. Most think it should be kept as true to the original intent as possible."

"Strict crisis–point management," Alvaro said. "Whenever we've strayed from that path, it hasn't gone well. Andrew and his group want to stray. That's why it's important you keep the link."

Olivia sighed. "Okay, so . . . exactly what is it you want me to do? I mean right now."

Alvaro turned to Dee. She nodded, and Alvaro said: "I want to instruct you in how to use the link. I know you don't believe the things I've told you. And there's a lot more I haven't told you. For hundreds of years the Shepherds have guarded the future by choosing probability streams that steer the human race around crisis points. We're now living in the catastrophe Jacob tried to prevent. It's happening out in the world. I know that's a lot to take in. Don't worry about it right now. The first step is to make you believe."

"I have to tell you," Olivia said, "that's a big first step."

Alvaro pulled a nylon rucksack over and unzipped it. He reached in and withdrew a clear baggie of what looked like tea leaves. "I want you to chew these."

"What are they?"

"Jai ba leaves, indigenous to Thailand. They produce a mild opioid effect that interacts well with the link. It's to reduce your natural resistance."

"I don't think so."

"The effects are like smoking a joint."

"No drugs. Besides, you said I already linked with this machine, and I wasn't drugged then."

"I talked about that with Jacob. We think the circumstances had something to do with it. You had been in a firefight. Your friend had just died and you were alone in the dark. Your body was probably flooded with adrenaline, and your amygdala would have produced a large amount of glutamate. In other words, your brain chemistry was already altered even without the jai ba leaves. But unlike the jai ba effect, you would have been in an agitated state and liable to make reckless changes in the probability stream without knowing you were doing it."

Jesus Christ. Welcome to Crazy Town, Olivia thought.

Dee sat up. "Olivia, the sooner you do this, the sooner you get to see your friend again."

"It's the only way," Alvaro said.

Olivia raised her left arm, the one flex-cuffed to Dee. Dee's arm came up with hers. "Take these off and I'll try it."

"No."

"Look," Olivia said, "you want me to trust you. Okay. Show me I can, by demonstrating you trust me. I don't like being restrained against my will. Do you?"

"Alvaro," Dee said, "go ahead. She won't run."

Alvaro opened the bag and picked out a few of the green-brown leaves. "First chew these, but don't swallow. They'll make you sick if you do."

Olivia held her hand out. She sniffed the leaves. Dry and brittle, they smelled faintly of licorice. She pushed them into her mouth and started grinding them between her molars. They didn't taste like licorice; they tasted bitter and dusty. Still grinding, Olivia held up her cuffed hand again. Alvaro produced a key that looked more like a fish hook and used it to press the release tab. He unzipped the cuffs, freeing Olivia's wrist. She rubbed it, calculating her chances of getting out of the tent without Alvaro stopping her.

The chances were zero.

"Let yourself become aware of the link," Alvaro said.

"How do I do that?"

"By not trying."

"For fuck's sake."

"It's like not being able to see something because you're trying too hard."

"I don't even know what I'm supposed to be seeing." The dusty taste of the leaves made her a little nauseated.

"That's enough." Alvaro held his hand under her chin. "Spit them out."

She spat the pieces of leaf into his palm. Some bits stuck to her tongue, and she scraped them off with her fingernail.

"It's like a ring of light," Alvaro said. "We call it the halo."

"You've seen it? I thought only somebody with the bug could see it."

"I've seen the *actual* halo, the probability machine itself. Not inside my head, the way a Shepherd sees it."

Olivia was barely listening. She turned her head toward the tent fly. But the jai ba effect had already taken hold. Just turning her head had produced a trembling effect, as if her eyes were thimble cups overfilled with tears. Alvaro placed his hands on her shoulders and pushed her down on her back.

"Let the halo come up. It's there. The world is a vast chessboard. If you wanted, you could make a move. But for now you are simply looking at the board."

She wished he would shut up. Mild opioid, my ass. At this point, she doubted she could even *find* the tent fly, let alone crawl through it and run away. No wonder he was willing to uncuff her.

The electric lantern hung suspended above her like a mechanical moon, and then it *was* a moon, or a luminous door that opened wider and wider, expanding, not into a chessboard but a bright halo that, somehow, was inside and outside her head at the same time.

The halo encompassed the world.

Billions of lives swarmed within the light. She felt immense power . . . and didn't want it. Her body writhed as she attempted to retreat from the halo. She felt the stones and roots beneath the tent dig into her back, but it was almost as if it were somebody else's back; she was more in the halo than in the tent.

"What's wrong with her?" Dee said.

"She sees," Alvaro said.

Woozy and frightened, Olivia turned on her side and drew her legs up sharply, her knees encountering something that yelped in pain.

Dee.

"Ride it out," Alvaro said. Who was he talking to? Olivia peered through her watery, thimble-cup eyes. Dee sat up, rocking and clutching at her wounded leg. Olivia, empathizing, remembered all the other wounded: in Syria, in Iraq, in the killing fields of Kenya, all the wounded of the world, all the victims of the Disaster. Brian's warm blood bubbling between her fingers . . .

But Brian had recovered, Brian was alive. Instead, she focused on Dee, isolated her in the halo, just this one person, not the world's billions, not the overwhelming crush. If she could heal just this one wound . . .

A chain of events unfolded before her.

Men pour out of the barn at Sanctuary and run shouting across the muddy sod. Dee swings toward the passenger door of Alvaro's truck. One of the running

*men points a gun, a big revolver. He pulls the trigger. Muzzle flash. A bullet rips
through Dee's leg.*

No.

Olivia looked deeper.

*Now the same man is dressing alone in one of the ranch's wood-paneled bed-
rooms. The gun lay in a box on a neatly folded pile of undershirts in an open
dresser drawer.*

As he reached for the gun, Olivia tried to make him leave it, but she
couldn't. No part of his decision presented a chess piece she could move.

Olivia looked deeper — deeper and farther back, following a line of
probability choices like a single bright thread woven through an infi-
nitely intricate pattern.

*Now the man is packing a bag in a different bedroom, with yellow walls and
a vase of lilies on the dresser. He holds the revolver in his left hand, the one with
the heavy gold wedding band, weighing it like a question. A middle-aged woman
in wide-bottomed mom jeans says, "If you bring that thing, you'll have to check
the bag."*

Olivia pushed at the man, and this time it worked.

*"Yeah, you're right." The man sighs, returns the gun to its box, and places it
on a high shelf in the closet.*

A densely tangled road map of probability threads appeared before
her.

*Because the man isn't in the bag-check line at the airport, a woman who had
been waiting behind him is able to make her flight on time instead of missing it
and booking a later one. Her presence on her scheduled flight touches the lives of
several others. And her absence on the rebooked flight changes yet more probability threads, more than Olivia can follow, each winding into a world altered by her
seemingly inconsequential push in the yellow bedroom. It's overwhelming. Olivia
can follow any one of the threads, witness the consequences, lose herself in the altered lives of strangers. Instead, she slings herself out of the halo.*

"God." White stars whirled and pulsed before her eyes. Olivia moaned.
A steel wedge split her head. She could still feel the power of the halo.
She sat up and hung her head between her knees, sick to her stomach.

Someone touched her back.

"Are you okay?" Dee asked.

"I don't know. Those leaves. They did something to me."

"No," Alvaro said. "They only relaxed the part of your brain that
might have resisted the link."

Slowly, Olivia looked up. "I saw things."

"The halo."

"*Things*. People. People doing things. All of it through a ring of light. It was terrifying."

Alvaro licked his lips. He looked eager and . . . something else. Jealous? "Only Shepherds have taken the halo inside themselves and seen what you've seen."

"I never want to see it again."

"You have to rest," Dee said.

"I won't do it again." Olivia could still sense the causal effects, the untold consequences of one simple alteration. If it had been real—not simply a hallucination produced by the jai ba leaves—it was too much power, too much responsibility. How could anyone ever grasp it? It was like handing a hydrogen bomb to a toddler. Hallucination. It must have been. The leaves weren't a mild opiate but a powerful hallucinogenic. The kind of godlike power she'd experienced inside the halo could not exist.

"Here's water."

Dee stooped over her, holding out a bottle of Aquafina. Olivia reached for it, and gasped when she realized what was wrong.

Dee was standing on both feet.

The bullet wounds were gone.

THIRTEEN

DEE PULLED BACK. "WHAT'S WRONG?"

"Your leg."

"What about her leg?" Alvaro glanced at Dee's legs.

"That man shot her when we were leaving the ranch."

"What man?" Dee looked confused.

"Some guy that came out of the barn."

"Nobody fired a gun at us," Dee said.

"I saw the goddamn bullet holes in your leg. I *bandaged* you."

Dee and Alvaro looked at each other.

Olivia got up. She felt shaky. Alvaro stood up as well. The tent was too low for him to stand upright without stooping.

"He was heavyset," Olivia said. "Maybe he's one of those guys who's afraid to go anywhere unarmed. He shot you when you were about to get in the truck."

They stared at her.

"Come *on.*" Olivia backed away, rubbing her forehead where the steel wedge tapped in a little deeper. The lantern light hurt her eyes. "This is insane."

"*You changed something,*" Alvaro said.

"How can you not remember the gun?" Olivia shook her head. "This can't be happening." But she knew it was. The same thing had happened in the torture cell in the Old City. Brian bleeding out, and then Brian not bleeding out, wounded but not as severely.

Dead, not dead.

"This is a new probability," Alvaro said. "*I told you not to change anything.*"

"Why can't you guys see it?" Olivia said. "It *happened*."

"Only a Shepherd is aware of the changes, only someone who has hosted the link. That's how Jacob knew you'd changed his probability choice."

"So Dee getting shot is one of your crisis points?"

"No. It doesn't *have* to be a crisis point. That's just the discipline of the Society, to use the power only when it must be used."

"I can't breathe," Olivia said. "I need air." She turned, ducked through the flap, and almost walked into a tree. The clearing was gone; the tent now stood in the thick of the forest. What the hell? Though she clearly remembered stepping into a grassy moonlit clearing, that clearing had vanished, and moonlight barely penetrated the canopy. Disoriented, Olivia held herself still, her hand pressed to the craggy bark of the tree trunk. The night air was cool and damp and heavily scented with pine. She worked her lips and tongue, still tasting the bitter jai ba leaves.

Alvaro and Dee had followed her out of the tent. Dee set the lantern on a stump. Alvaro took Olivia's arm. She shook him off. A new memory scaffold was rising around her existing memory. Cutting the chain and driving into Gooding State Park—that memory was still there. But now there was also a memory of parking alongside a rural two-lane and leaving the pickup to tramp directly into the forest.

"You people are making me crazy." She pointed at Dee. "You were hurting and I wanted to help you, and it started happening. I could *see*."

Alvaro turned to Dee. "She's reckless."

"She doesn't understand how to use it. You can teach her."

"No," Olivia said. "No way. I want this thing out of my head." The thought of it squirming around like a grub in her brain intensified her nausea.

"I told you," Alvaro said. "There's only one way that happens. You would have to die."

"You said Jacob had it before me, and he's not dead."

"He was when the link migrated. Your probability choice brought him back along with your friend. From that point on, we've all been living in a different world. The *wrong* world."

Dee said, "Let Alvaro teach you."

"I don't want any part of this."

Alvaro clenched his fists so hard the tendons stood out on his arms.

"You *are* part of it. It doesn't matter that you didn't know what you were doing. Jacob made a choice that saved the world. You reversed the choice."

Olivia paced around, feeling trapped and crowded. "What are you even talking about? Save the world from *what?*"

"The epidemic," Alvaro said.

Olivia stopped pacing. "The variola outbreaks?"

"Yes."

"What's that got to do with me?"

"You brought your friend back to life in a new probability stream," Dee said. "Something you changed had consequences."

Olivia couldn't believe she was having this conversation. In her mind, she saw the infinite weave of probability threads. A man leaves his gun at home, and it alters the life paths of numberless strangers. There was a word for that, too. While gamely wading through articles about super-positions (a word that kept nagging at her even after she returned to the States), trying to get a clue as to what had happened to her in Aleppo, she had followed a hyperlink and arrived at a discussion of chaos theory. There she encountered the butterfly effect—basically the idea that small changes can cause large-scale repercussions. Large and not so large, too—like pitching your tent in a different location. That she could deal with, but she couldn't accept what Dee now seemed to be saying.

"You're pinning a fucking smallpox epidemic on *me?*" Olivia said.

"There's still time to choose Jacob's probability and stop it," Alvaro said. "I can teach you how to do it. But it has to be soon, before things spin out of control or something happens to you."

"The original probability, the one that means Brian and Jodee get killed?"

"And Jacob," Alvaro said.

"Forget it."

"Three lives," Alvaro said, "against millions. Perhaps billions."

"I don't think so. We have vaccines, the World Health Organization. Every country affected will pitch in."

Alvaro folded his arms. "Listen to yourself!"

"What?" she said, though she knew perfectly well that the WHO wasn't capable of stopping the outbreak. They didn't even have an effective vaccine.

"The World Health Organization?" Alvaro said. "Not billions dying, maybe only millions, or a few hundred thousand. If we're lucky. All that against *three* lives, and only one you really care about. People care about those other lives, too. But you're still wrong. The epidemic is a crisis event. That means it threatens the continuation of the entire human race. But you don't know what you're doing. You wanted to 'help' Dee. So you fixed her leg, but you don't have any idea what else you've done. Just like when you saved your friend in Aleppo."

Olivia rubbed her temples. "I just made it so she didn't get shot. How could that be bad?"

Alvaro shook his head. "You aren't listening. Everything's interconnected. Canceling the bullet wounds changed the world in a thousand ways we'll never know. Do you remember Elián González?"

Olivia sighed in exasperation. "What are you talking about?"

"Elián González. The Cuban child who got deported to Cuba back in 2000. It was a custody battle between the parents."

"I know who Elián González is," Olivia said.

"When federal agents came to get him out of the house where he was staying, there was a photographer present. One of his pictures won the Pulitzer Prize. An agent in tactical military gear pointing a weapon as the crying child is being ripped out of the arms of the fisherman who'd rescued him at sea and had been caring for him."

"I'm not following you." Olivia's head throbbed. "What's it got to do with Dee's bullet wound getting healed? What's it got to do with the epidemic?"

"That was an election year. The Cuban community in Florida was already mad at the Democrat running. But Gore might have won anyway, except for that photograph. It angered people. *Seeing* it angered them. The Republican won, but just barely, and only because the Supreme Court halted the incredibly close recount. After that, 9/11 happened, and after that, Bush invaded Afghanistan and then Iraq, and hundreds of thousands of people died who would not have died otherwise. The unintended consequences of one photograph."

The road map of probability threads. Olivia could have followed any one of them through an infinite landscape of causal connections. She could have lost herself.

"Every probability choice costs something," Alvaro said. "Here's what you don't know about Elián González. He was a crisis point. There was a probability before the one you're familiar with, one with a much higher likelihood of occurring. In that probability there was no photograph. Gore won the presidential election. And after 9/11 there was no invasion of Iraq."

"And that's *bad?*"

"Strangely enough, yes. Because without the disruption caused by the invasion, something far worse would have happened."

"But there were no WMDs in Iraq."

"No. But the invasion threw the region into chaos, which disrupted a complicated terror network that was preparing for something horrific involving a nuclear weapon, a suitcase bomb. The Iraq War cost hundreds of thousands of lives, but it saved millions. What you did in Aleppo saved your friends and Jacob, but at the cost of a smallpox epidemic. How does that balance out for you?"

Olivia turned away. "I need to think."

"Maybe you should lie down," Dee said. "Come back in the tent."

"I don't need to lie down." She didn't believe them. She *couldn't* believe them. Surely what happened when she chewed the jai ba leaves had more to do with her brain chemistry than it did with probability streams.

"You keep rubbing your temples," Alvaro said.

"My head hurts."

"It happens when a Shepherd chooses a lower probability end point over the highest. There's always a cost. Every crisis-point decision takes its toll on the Shepherd, sometimes a massive toll. Your headache is just a sample."

"I have to go." She backed away, stumbling in the undergrowth.

Alvaro moved closer. "I'm sorry, but you can't."

"Then we're going to have a problem."

Dee also stepped closer. "The crisis point—"

"I don't believe you," Olivia said.

Alvaro was close enough to grab her, but he didn't. Not yet. "You have to stay with us." He looked pained. "We're not your enemy."

Olivia bent over, holding her stomach. "Going to be sick."

Alvaro and Dee hesitated, and at that moment of hesitation—

Olivia bolted.

"Stop!" Alvaro yelled.

She got only a few yards before he overtook her and wrapped her in his arms, his weight and momentum taking them both down to the ground. Olivia fought, thrashing and twisting against his superior strength.

"Please," he said, "stop fighting."

She got one knee planted and tried to push him off. "Help! Somebody help me!"

Alvaro flipped her on her back and covered her mouth with his hand, pushed down hard. It was dark, but she could feel panic radiating off him, matching her own panic.

"Nobody can hear you. We're alone out here."

That was probably true, but Olivia screamed against his hand anyway. It forced him to keep one hand occupied. Even if there was no one to hear, her screaming obviously rattled him.

Over his shoulder, Alvaro yelled at Dee, "Get the cuffs. In the tent. And something to gag her with."

Olivia fought harder. He had her right arm pinned, but her left was free. She flailed at him. He turned his face aside, came off her hips, and bore down harder on her face. Olivia had taken self-defense classes. She had always known that if she ever found herself in a situation like this—being forcibly held down by a man—she would not surrender passively. Now she brought her knee up hard into Alvaro's groin. The angle wasn't perfect, but the maneuver proved effective. He made a sound between a cough and a gasp. Before he could recover, she drove the heel of her hand upward into his nose. Blood spurted and he fell back, both hands covering his face. Olivia rolled free and scrambled to her feet.

Dee stood in front of her, holding the flex cuffs. Olivia, panting, bared her teeth, ready to fight.

Dee dropped the cuffs and showed her empty hands. "This isn't what we want."

"I'm going home."

"If you do that, millions of people will die."

"I don't believe you. It's crazy!"

Alvaro stood up, one hand covering his bloody face, the other cupped over his groin. She could outrun him in his present condition, but what about Dee?

"Even if you make it home, the Society will catch up with you. With

Andrew in charge, they won't teach you to be a Shepherd. They'll execute you."

"Leave me alone."

Olivia ran.

Behind her, Dee crashed through the brush. It was too dark to run flat-out, but Olivia did it anyway. Branches and evergreen boughs whipped her. She ran with her arms raised, protecting her face. She fell, picked herself up, ran again—toward the sound of chattering water. Her feet tangled in dense brush and again she pitched onto the ground. Her stomach heaved. She threw up, her head pounding as she gasped for breath.

She listened.

Dee must have stopped or slowed down, because Olivia couldn't hear her anymore. She sat up, wiped her mouth, got on her feet. At the bottom of the slope, a creek glimmered in new moonlight. On the far side of the creek, the orange coal of a cigarette glowed bright, dimmed . . . then floated to the right. Probably not a cigarette but a joint. Now she could make out three dim figures. Olivia ran a hand through her hair, straightened her shirt, and walked down the slope.

She splashed through the creek, icy water soaking her shoes and socks. Three heads turned toward her. Boys getting high in the park. "Hey," one of them said when she stepped out of the creek and came toward them. Empty beer cans, some flattened, littered the ground. Three dirt bikes leaned on kickstands by a trail.

"Hi," Olivia said. "I got a little lost. Any of you guys have a phone I can use?"

The kid who had said "hey" stood up, holding the joint with a roach clip. He wore a brush cut and a band shirt. Olivia knew the band: Desperate Freeloaders, an underground English-language group out of Berlin. Two bass guitars and one accordion. Their specialty was antifa politics. Desperate Freeloaders swam in the same alternative-media pond that *The Beat* occupied. Idaho was maybe the last place on earth Olivia would have expected to encounter a Desperate Freeloaders fan.

"Phones don't work out here," he said.

The guy sitting next to him, a teenager with big puffy hair, reached for the roach, and the Desperate Freeloaders guy held it away from him. "Don't be a dick," the third boy said. Only the third boy wasn't a boy but a girl, probably a few years younger than the other two, which would make her fifteen or so. Her side-shaved head and baggy clothes had thrown Olivia off. Tattooed wings swept back from the girl's ears. Desperate Freeloaders shrugged and passed the roach to the sitting boy.

"How far is it to town?" Olivia asked.

"Far enough."

Olivia sighed inwardly. "How about a lift?" She nodded at the dirt bikes. "I can pay."

"Why should you? We're not bums. What are you doing here, anyway? This place is closed."

"I'm a journalist. I'm, uh, doing a piece about the, uh, resurgence of the wolf population."

The puffy-haired kid coughed, expelling pungent smoke. He looked around, as if the wolves might have been closing in this whole time.

"There's no wolves around here," Desperate Freeloaders said.

"They . . . only come out at night to hunt in packs," Olivia said unconvincingly, giving up on the stupid wolf story.

The girl laughed. "You're not a journalist!"

"I am. I really am. Do any of you guys read *The Beat*?"

Desperate Freeloaders gave her the side-eye. "You write for that rag?"

"Yeah. You read it?"

"What's your name?"

"Olivia Nikitas."

"No shit?" He stepped closer and squinted at her. "You do kinda look like her."

Olivia retrieved her wallet and showed him her driver's license, tilting it to catch the moonlight. Desperate Freeloaders grinned.

"You been over in Syria. That's badass."

"So how about that ride?"

"Yeah, okay. Your girlfriend coming, too?"

"My—?"

He pointed. At the top of the ridge on the other side of the creek, Dee stood watching them.

"That's nobody," Olivia said.

"Maybe she's a wolf that got lost from her night-hunting pack," the girl said.

"Yeah," Desperate Freeloaders said.

The puffy-haired kid sucked hard on the remaining scrap of the joint. "I told you guys I heard somebody yelling."

"Can we go?" Olivia said.

A few minutes later, she was straddling a dirt bike, her arms wrapped around Desperate Freeloaders's waist while he impressed the hell out of her with his talent for almost crashing on every turn of the trail. Desperate Freeloaders—what were the odds?

Everything was connected to everything else.

FOURTEEN

SHEFFIELD, IDAHO, AT THREE-THIRTY IN the morning was an empty movie set of a small town. A blinking traffic light hung above the biggest intersection. Puddles, lingering from earlier showers, absorbed yellow light. The unmufflered dirt bikes shredded the night, but there was no one around to care. Of course, all the businesses were closed. But many had CLOSED UNTIL FURTHER NOTICE signs in the windows. Desperate Freeloaders — who Olivia learned was named Stefan — tucked his bike into the curb and cut the engine. His friends, Doug and Angel, did the same.

Olivia swung off the seat. She felt like she'd been riding a paint mixer. The inside of her head was still jittering.

"You got somebody to call?" Stefan produced his wafer-thin Trinity model.

Olivia took the phone but didn't punch in Brian's number. The Society was hunting her; that much she did believe. What level of surveillance were they capable of? Maybe she was being paranoid, but she didn't want to take a chance on letting Emilio and company know where she was headed.

And if she called the police, what would she tell them? Could she even find her way back to Sanctuary? And if she did, what could she prove? Plus, all that would take time. Alvaro and Dee had spooked her with their running-out-of-time talk. Olivia didn't want to accept what they'd said about the pandemic, but what if it was true? What if only part of it was true? How much time could she afford to waste?

Stefan and his friends stood by their bikes, watching her. They looked like self-conscious musicians posing for a band photo. "Hey." Stefan walked over, his hand out. "If you're not going to use that thing . . ."

Olivia held on to the phone. "Uh, I need to get to Seattle."

"Bus comes through early."

"Greyhound?" Olivia started Googling the website.

"Not on my phone," Stefan said.

Olivia looked up. "How am I supposed to get a ticket?"

"You could buy one in the hardware store, but they're closed."

"Right," Olivia said. "It's almost four in the morning."

"They're closed all the time," Stefan said. "It's the epidemic. Everybody's scared. There's almost nothing in the whole town open since yesterday."

Less than forty-eight hours since the president's announcement. Fear spread faster than variola.

Angel, with the wing tattoos on the sides of her head, walked over. "If you wait by the road, the bus might come anyway. Sheffield's on the route, even if there's nobody around to sell you a ticket."

Olivia said to Stefan, "Look, buy the ticket on your phone and I'll pay you."

"No. I don't buy anything online. That shit is monitored." Stefan wiggled his fingers. Reluctantly, Olivia handed him the phone. He put it in his pocket. She looked at the others, but no one volunteered the use of theirs. "Hey," Stefan said, "you ever want to do a story about Sheffield, I can be your source."

Olivia shook her head. "Sorry? Why would I want to do a story about Sheffield?"

"Because all kinds of shit goes on around here. You know, massive political corruption."

"Massive, huh?"

"What you should do," Stefan said, "is give me your number."

"You can contact me through *The Beat*."

"I'll give you my number, then."

Angel said, "Give it *up,* Stefan."

"No, really." Stefan rattled off his number and followed it with a big grin. "Aren't you going to write it down?"

Olivia tapped her forehead. "I have near-perfect recall. Comes with the job. Where do I wait for the bus?"

"Walk that way, out to where Main Street meets the state highway. There's a bench. It'll come at like six, I think."

"Or it won't," the wing girl said.

"Thanks, you guys."

Stefan hooked his thumbs in his pockets. "Hey, we could hang with you, if you want. Until the bus comes."

"No, we can't," Angel said.

Olivia smiled. "I'm good, thanks." As she walked away, she heard Stefan say, "Bad-*ass.*"

"Whatever," Angel said. "That chick's never going to call you."

The dirt bikes kicked into life, making a window-rattling racket, though together the sound barely amounted to the noise of one real motorcycle. They ripped past her, two on the left, one on the right. Stefan popped a wheelie and raised his left fist. Yeah, fight the power, kid, fight Sheffield corruption. Three kids playing rebels in a small Idaho town, but without them Olivia might never have gotten out of the woods.

She found the bench where Main Street met Highway 51. Away from the town lights it was too dark to see much of anything else. Crickets chirruped. The moon played hide-and-seek in the clouds. At least it was summer. Every time a pair of headlights appeared, Olivia grew tense. What if it was someone from Sanctuary? Maybe Nike and Robbie and a few of the young guys hunting for her, huddled in the back of the van with hypos and handcuffs and gags.

Dawn came up, revealing two lanes of hard-used road split by a faded yellow line. Utility poles leaned like giant drunken stick figures. Soon the Greyhound arrived and its door swung open. The driver was wearing a filter mask of the type used in doctors' waiting rooms or in airports, or that covered the faces of Japanese tourists everywhere. He sold her a ticket to Seattle, the route's end point—an eleven-hour ride.

Olivia passed down the aisle to the back. The bus was about half full. Some of the passengers were wearing masks, too.

Those masks wouldn't stop variola.

Nothing would.

THE BUS REACHED THE SEATTLE Greyhound station at half past five in the afternoon. Olivia's headache had finally subsided. A lone yellow cab, remnant of massive herds hunted to near extinction by Uber, rolled slowly past the bus station. Olivia flagged it and took it straight to Brian's apartment in West Seattle.

She stood on the sidewalk under his window, looking up. The window was open. Why was she hesitating?

Because I'm afraid, she thought, observing the fact of her fear, barely moving her lips. Dee had said, *If you bring him into this, you'll put him in danger.*

"It's all bullshit," Olivia said out loud, but she didn't believe herself.

Shepherds, probability machines, insects burrowing into her brain — though she couldn't accept all the specifics, she knew *something* was going on. *I have seen the halo.* (*Hallelujah.*) And she had reached into it and erased Dee's gunshot wound, which no doubt had unleashed the dreaded González effect. But . . . probability machines? Was the only other explanation a psychotic break, a fugue state caused by bad brain chemicals and her experiences in the Disaster? Maybe she should have taken the cab to the nearest headshrinker instead of to Brian's apartment.

Olivia dug out her wallet and folded it open. She teased out the key tucked behind her driver's license. Brian had made her the key as soon as they got back from Syria. It was their version of an engagement ring. Except Olivia didn't want to be fully engaged. She closed the key in her fist, put her wallet away, and strode to the lobby door, which buzzed open when she punched in the code on the keypad.

She ran up the stairs to the third floor. Brian's door opened before she reached it.

"Liv?" He had his car keys in his hand. "*Liv?* Oh, my God."

"Bri." She started toward him. He barreled down the hallway and hugged her like he wanted to break her in half and put her away in a safe so she wouldn't disappear again. She hugged him hard, too, his tall, bony frame like a deep-planted anchor in the tornado of the world Disaster. Brian Anker: appropriate name.

"Where did you go, what happened?" he asked, his voice full of emotion. She recognized where it came from: a terror of abandonment. It was a terror she'd spent more than a decade very deliberately subverting in herself, ever since that day she walked into the living room and encountered her father's body slumped over the arm of his chair, his dead eyes searching the complex pattern of the rug for his lost life. But Brian wasn't one for subverting his emotions.

"I got a little sidetracked," she said.

"What? Jesus, you're lucky I love insane people."

"People? Not just me?"

"You're the finest representative of the type." He studied her eyes. "Wait. It's not just that you got sidetracked. Something bad happened to you." She could hear him struggling to keep his voice steady.

"I'm all right, Brian. I—I'm all right now that I'm back."

"What *happened?*"

"Let's go inside."

A deep scar in the hardwood entry pointed to the living room. The tan window blinds half lidded the view to the street. Every picture, every piece of furniture, every stain and scar and smell, added up to *home.* Though it had been only a short time, Brian's apartment had become more of a home than anyplace else she'd lived since she was a kid. This scared her more than a little bit. Home was the place that hurt you.

She looked back. Brian stood with his hands in his pockets, watching her, a deeply worried expression on his face. He waited for her to speak.

"This is going to be hard for you to believe," she said.

"I'll believe you."

"Brian. I mean *really hard.*"

He removed his glasses and wiped the lenses on his T-shirt. A thing he did, like a coach calling a time-out before the next play, a momentum-changing tactic. Not his momentum; hers. "I'm listening." He replaced his glasses and adjusted them on the bridge of his nose.

"Okay. But I want to call my stepmom first, make sure she's all right." Part of Olivia felt fragile, and that fragile part swung toward Rohana, her living connection to the past. She was thinking, what if the González effect did something to advance variola into Jaipur? "And I need—"

He shook his head. "First tell me where you've been." He shut the door. "And what was that phone call yesterday? You couldn't stay on the line even five minutes to tell me where you were? My God, I was starting to think you'd been abducted or something. It didn't make sense that you'd just leave. But I remembered what you told me, that you had trouble sticking around. Do you remember when you told me that?" He said it like a test question. "And do you remember what I said to you?"

She nodded. "You said I wouldn't do that with you."

"That's right. So I *knew* you hadn't run out on me two nights ago."

"Brian."

"I knew you wouldn't just check out, fly back to Syria or wherever. Back to the—the *Disaster,* as you call it. You didn't take your precious go-bag. You might think you're capable of that, but I don't—"

"*Brian.*"

"What?"

"I *was* abducted."

After a moment, he closed his mouth.

She told him everything, going back to the torture cell and connecting it with the abduction by the Society. Parts of the story sounded so crazy that she almost swallowed back the words before they could escape into the open, where Brian would use them to pity her or be afraid for her sanity. And he did flinch slightly when she started talking about the link-bug and Brian's resurrection. She'd brought up that part before. The two-memory problem. But he didn't interrupt, didn't object. And if he felt pity or feared for her sanity, he didn't allow those thoughts to creep into his eyes. She almost wished he would allow it to show. Brian's goodness sometimes felt like a fraud.

When she finished, all he said was "I need a drink."

He went into the kitchen. The refrigerator opened, rattling bottles. This was another time-out tactic.

He returned with two bottles of IPA, his limp barely noticeable.

"So you ditched your crutches," she said.

"Yeah, it's down to a dull ache. Look, you really believe everything you just told me is true? That thing where I died. That—whatever you called it."

"Probability."

"Yeah. I'm having trouble with that."

"It was real. I remember it. Only now the old probability feels more like something I read about or saw in a movie. It doesn't feel, I don't know, three-dimensional anymore."

"How can you be sure it ever was?"

Olivia sipped her beer. Taking *her* time-out. She'd anticipated this question and wanted to get her answer right, state it with the conviction she wished she felt. "Because I know what's real, even when it doesn't make sense that it could be. I trust what my brain tells me is true, and this is true."

"I believe you."

"Really?"

He bobbed his head. Sipped his beer. "I mean, I want to."

She raised her eyebrows.

"You know," he said, "I'm willing to. Trying to. I know you're telling the truth. At some level, I mean."

"At some level. Like I'm deluded?"

"No, I didn't say that. Liv? You said yourself this was going to be hard. Well, it's hard."

"At this stage, I guess that's the most I can hope for." She finished her beer and set the empty bottle on the end table. "Thanks for sort of believing me." She meant it. "Can I use your phone to call Rohana now?"

"Of course."

He gave it to her. The number rang through. Olivia's aunt Amala picked up and said that Olivia's stepmother was perfectly fine—and sound asleep, it being barely past 7 a.m. in Jaipur and Rohana being a late riser. Was it an emergency? Should she wake her? No, no, things are good here.

Olivia handed the phone back to Brian.

"Everything okay?" he asked.

"Yeah, I think so. Brian?"

"What?"

"If it were reversed, I doubt I could have met you even halfway, not without proof."

"You would have," he said.

"I really wouldn't have. If you ever told me a story like that, I'd think you'd lost your mind."

"You believe what your brain tells you. I believe what my heart tells me."

"Oh, my God, that's sappy."

He grinned. "I know. That's why I said it, since I knew it would get you to make that face."

"What face?"

Brian twisted his features into a rubber mask of revulsion.

Olivia said, "I have never in my life made a face like that."

"Sorry, but you have. Absolutely."

"Liar."

"You wanna fight about it?"

"Yeah." She pulled him in by the waist of his jeans, stood on her toes, and kissed his mouth. After a while, they separated. "My breath must be terrible," she said, smiling.

"It's a challenge."

"Hey—"

"Kidding! Or, not really kidding, but you know."

"Which way to the nearest toothbrush?"

"Meet me in the bedroom when you're done?"

"Sure, but Brian? I'm a little shook up, and I've been on the bus all day. Do you think we could just lie down? I'd like to sleep a little, but I want you near me."

"Of course. Jeez. You've been through a lot."

"Thank you. We can rumble later on, okay?"

"It's a date."

Her purple toothbrush was brush-down in a water glass, where she had left it two nights ago. Olivia realized she was looking for differences, subtle changes butterflied up by her halo choice.

She wandered back to the living room, scrubbing her teeth hard, her mouth filled with sudsy, peppermint-tasting toothpaste. The sound of Brian thumping around in the bedroom gave her a warm domestic feeling of comfort. But at the window she stopped cold, the toothbrush in her fist.

A white van was parked across the street.

She quickly rinsed her mouth and ducked her head into the bedroom. Brian, shirtless and shoeless, saw her face and stopped unzipping his pants.

"What?" he said.

"We have to get out. Now."

FIFTEEN

"WHY, WHAT'S HAPPENING?" BRIAN TUGGED his zipper up and grabbed his shirt.

"The Society. I'm so stupid to come here. It puts you in danger. It puts both of us in danger."

"Hold on. What happened? What'd you see?"

"Bri, they're parked across the street, just like before. We have to get *out*."

Brian pushed past her into the living room.

"Be careful," she said.

He stood beside the window, sneaking a look between the blinds. "I don't see anybody."

"The van. I told you—they grabbed me and put me in the white van."

He looked at her. "You didn't say the van belonged to a florist."

"What?" She joined him at the window. The words SEATTLE'S BLOOM-ING flowed in pink script across the side of the van.

"Liv?"

Olivia shook her head. "I didn't notice that, just saw the van and panicked." Olivia bit her lip hard. "I have to get a grip."

"You've been through a lot. Look, we're not being smart. We should have called the police as soon as you got here."

"It's a waste of time."

Brian frowned. "Why?"

"I've been thinking about it, Bri. There's no proof I was kidnapped."

"Why would you make it up, for God's sake?"

"I wouldn't. But the police don't know that. I'm a grown woman who disappeared from my boyfriend's apartment for a couple of days. That's not long enough to be considered a legitimate missing person, according to the law. Also, what do I tell the police? 'Excuse me, Officer. Could you help me out? See, I was kidnapped by a cult that believes they can change reality.' You really think I should tell them that?"

"Yes!"

"Even *you* don't believe me."

"I don't *dis*believe you."

Olivia rolled her eyes. "So do I tell them part of the story, leave a bunch out? Or tell it like Jacob and the rest of them were all crazy and I didn't know what they were talking about?"

"Something like that last part, yeah."

"My story wouldn't cohere, and the police would know that. They would know I wasn't telling them everything, and the more I do tell them, the more ridiculous the whole thing sounds."

"Let it sound ridiculous. What happened is the truth, right? Just say it without saying you believe in the ideas of the cult or whatever it is."

"But I *do* believe some of it. So I tell the truth, in which case I'm crazy. Or I tell a lie, in which case I'm a liar."

"You're saying we don't do anything?"

Olivia's shoulders slumped. "I don't know. All I can say is I have to get out of this apartment. The Society knows about this place. It makes sense they'll look for me here. I was stupid to—"

"Uh, you're not going anywhere without me. And stop saying that you're stupid."

"Brian. I know you want to be my big strong protector and everything, but come on. I can take care of myself, and I won't be responsible for putting you in danger. Also, I didn't say I was stupid; I said I did something that was stupid. What are you grinning at?"

"I just know you really well."

Olivia was annoyed and tried not to show it. "I suppose you know me better than I know myself?"

"No. But I do know you. Mostly because you told me stuff that you don't tell other people. That's what you said."

"Yeah. I hate it when I do that. So what is it I'm missing here?"

"You want to go. Just like you were ready to fly back to Syria before the variola outbreak made that impossible."

She tried to look blank, but she knew what he meant and she didn't want to admit it. "I don't want to leave. You know I don't." She sounded unconvincing, even to herself.

"You do. It's part of your makeup that you want to be . . . loose. Or that's not even it, not exactly. It's not something you want. It's something you *don't* want. You don't want to be connected."

"I have a request. Could you not psychoanalyze me?"

"Sorry." Brian touched her shoulder. "Look. If you want to go away by yourself, hide out in a cave or whatever, you can do it. *I'm* not kidnapping you. I'm just saying, don't use my vulnerability as the excuse, okay? I'm a grown-up, too. I don't need you to leave me for my own good. That's ridiculous, and kind of insulting when you think about it."

I'm a grown-up. Isn't that what he'd said after she got him shot in Aleppo?

Olivia rubbed her forehead. "See? This is why relationships suck."

"They only suck if you don't want to be in a relationship."

"Look, I'll make a deal. We stop talking about the relationship, and I'll tell the police my story. Does that make you happy?"

"Marginally."

Since they wouldn't be returning to the apartment for a while, they each packed a bag, locked up, and drove Brian's seven-year-old Ford hybrid to the Seattle Police Department's Southwest Precinct station, which was across the street from a giant Home Depot. The station looked like a DMV building. Tan brick façade, flat roof, glass doors. They got out and Brian pointed his key fob over his shoulder, making the car alarm chirp.

Across the street, pandemonium reigned in the Home Depot parking lot. Cars and trucks jammed every space. Men and women *ran* into the store. Others pushed carts loaded with purchases—power tools, sheets of plywood, home generators, all kinds of stuff. Horns honked. People argued loudly. Olivia had been in Louisiana to cover Hurricane Ike. That's what this reminded her of, the mad, last-minute rush to prepare for the storm. Except here almost everyone was wearing a filter mask.

Olivia shook her head. "Do they really think a particle mask is going to protect them from variola?"

"They're scared. It started right after you disappeared. Rumors are flying, and the government isn't doing much to put them down."

"What kind of rumors?"

"That the contagion is weaponized, that it's a bioattack."

"We already guessed that."

"Yeah," Brian said, "but it gets worse. It's all over the internet that the stockpiled vaccine doesn't work against this weaponized strain."

"If that's true, we're screwed."

"Liv, I think it's true."

Olivia looked at the chaos boiling through Home Depot's parking lot. A couple of guys had started shoving each other. A pregnant woman in a baseball cap dragged a big box with a picture of a gasoline genera- tor printed on the side. The shoving match seemed to be about the gen- erator. The pregnant woman dragged it toward the open hatchback of a Honda. A Buick sped out of the lot, clipping somebody's cart, scatter- ing hand tools, boxes of batteries, and two bags of cement mix. The bags burst open, expelling dusty clouds, like silent explosions.

"This is bad," Olivia said. "We're wasting our time with the police. I've been out of touch two days. I need news, I need information. Helen can fill us in about stuff not getting out to the general public."

"We're already here," Brian said. "Let's go in."

"It's pointless."

"Come on. What are you afraid of?"

"I'm not afraid, at least not of talking to the police."

"You're kind of acting like you are."

Maybe he was right, just a little bit. The police were unlikely to be as forgiving about the outlandish details as Brian had been, not that she was going to give them the most outlandish ones. And talking to the police could also be the first step in directly confronting her abductors—and Olivia *was* afraid of them, almost atavistically afraid.

"Let's get this over with," she said.

A uniformed officer took her report. He had a wide, florid face, what they could see of it around the filter mask. Olivia was unable to provide anyone's last name or a motive for the kidnapping. Despite everything she'd been through, her near-perfect recall delivered a couple of license plate numbers, but she doubted there would be any criminal records at- tached to the owners of the plates. She left Syria out of the report. The officer keyed in the other details, such as they were. His eyes kept flicking toward the door. Was he worried about Home Depot's chaos invading the station, or did he just want to finish and leave? "I need your phone number and address," he said.

"I don't have an address right now. I can give you his." She pointed her thumb at Brian.

"All right, what is it?"

Brian recited his address.

"We're not going to be there, though," Olivia said.

The officer gave her an up-from-under look.

"We're traveling," Olivia said.

"Phone number?"

"Mine?" Olivia said.

The officer waited.

Olivia rattled off her number. "But I don't have the phone. I mean, they took it."

"The ranchers took your phone?"

"The kidnappers. They just live on a ranch. I'm going to replace the phone, but it might not be today. Do you want his number?" She pointed at Brian again.

"Why not," the officer replied. When the report was finished, he told them someone would contact local law enforcement in Idaho and ask them to check out the ranch.

"Thanks," Brian said.

Once they were outside again, Olivia said, "See?"

Half a dozen SPD officers poured out of the station and circulated through the Home Depot parking lot, breaking up fights, writing citations, directing traffic, restoring order. At least they weren't wearing full tactical gear. Not yet. The woman who had failed to load the generator into her Honda sat under the open hatchback, weeping into her hands.

Olivia said, "Let's get the hell out of here."

They parked on a quiet residential street a mile from the precinct station. Brian reached for his phone. "I'm going to call some friends, find us a place to crash."

"Great." Olivia pulled her duffel bag into the front seat and extracted her tablet from a side pocket. "I'm going to get in touch with Helen."

Brian got out and walked away with his phone.

Olivia booted the tablet, which was wafer thin, flexible, and, until activated, transparent. This was her Samsung IsnGlas, much more expensive than the tablet she carried into the Disaster. She waved through a couple of projections and finger-flicked a blinking orange notification of waiting messages. The message from Helen Fischer was priority encrypted. Olivia flicked the alert symbol trembling above the IsnGlas. A fractal blur appeared and swiftly organized itself into Helen's face.

Olivia gasped.

Lesions covered Helen's face to the point of making her nearly unrecognizable. "I've been calling you, Livvie." She spoke haltingly, her words thick. The vid was a close-up. When Helen opened her mouth to speak, her tongue, pebbled with smallpox lesions, moved clumsily. Olivia closed her eyes. Tears seeped from under her lids.

Helen continued: "I have a new assignment for you. The assignment is to live. If you've already been infected, it's too late. Nothing can save you. What you're looking at right now, that's your future."

Ashamed of her weakness, Olivia opened her eyes.

"But if you're not infected," Helen said, "you still have a chance. A good chance. But first you have to know a couple of things. Whatever you hear from mainstream media, forget it. The epidemic is already a hundred times worse than anything officially acknowledged, and Big Info is complicit in confusing the issue, probably in the interest of forestalling mass panic, and good luck with that. Second, vaccine stockpiles are inadequate. But it doesn't matter, because existing vaccines are useless against the outbreak. Livvie, this is a global, full-scale bioterror attack, possibly state sponsored."

Helen paused, her breathing labored. Her head drooped. After a minute, she lifted her face to the camera again.

"There's a man," she said. "In America. About a thousand years ago we went to Oxford together. Najid Javadi, Iranian born but a naturalized US citizen. He liked me. The feeling was mutual." Helen coughed, turned away from the camera, turned back. "Najid contacted me. He has the vaccine. The real thing. He broke all kinds of laws to tell me about it. The dear man wanted to save me. Isn't that wonderful? Well, it's too late for me. But maybe not for you, Livvie. I made him promise to give you my dose, but you're going to have to hurry. Najid's gone into hiding, cut himself off completely after the one message to me. He stole the vaccine from the lab where he worked. Apparently, your government has been aware of the existence of the weaponized version of variola for some time, though they had not expected to see it deployed like this. Najid's vaccine is experimental and highly secret. If the authorities catch up with him, he's buggered." Helen recited the address of a house in suburban Chicago. "It's not his house. It belongs to someone out of the country, a friend of Najid's. Go there as fast as you can. Najid's gone offline, totally. He's afraid. You have one of those memories, Livvie, so remember everything I just told you. I have to go now. Things are pretty bad over here. You're one of the good ones. Go now, right now. And stay alive."

The window collapsed and the IsnGlas tablet turned vitreous.

Olivia immediately sent Helen a chat request. It blinked for a full minute, then disappeared unanswered. She set her tablet aside and stared out the windshield. Ornamental sycamores stood still in the August sun. Oscillating sprinklers cast lassos of bright water. Crows side-walked on power lines, as if mocking Brian, who paced up and down the sidewalk, speaking into his phone. The world presented its normal aspect, but Olivia knew it was on fire and that she had struck the match. Variola was loose in the world. The truth rushed at her. In some impossible way, she had chosen this.

She had done this to Helen.

Brian put his phone away and came back to the car. He dropped into the driver's seat. "We are about to become house sitters in Puyallup, of all places." The smile departed his lips. "What's wrong?"

"We're going to Chicago, and we're leaving right now."

SIXTEEN

ON THEIR WAY OUT OF Seattle, they hit a Safeway superstore. It was mobbed with filter-mask-wearing shoppers banging carts in aisles depleted of stock.

"Holy shit," Brian said.

"Let's split up. Grab a bunch of bottled water and some snacks. I'll get stuff in the deli and meet you at the checkout."

In the deli, Olivia reached for the last submarine sandwich. A large hand connected to a hairy wrist grabbed the other end of the sub. He wore an XXXL Seahawks jersey and looked like he could have used one more X to make a comfortable fit. If he were hollow, Olivia could have climbed inside, with room left for a twin sister, if she had one.

"Sorry," Olivia and the offensive lineman said at the same time, and they both let go of the sub. It fell back into the case.

"Go ahead," Seahawks said.

"No, it's okay."

The lineman rubbed his chin. "This place is nuts. I mean, it's always nuts on game day, but this is over the top."

Olivia said, "It's probably because of the outbreak, not the game."

"Oh, yeah." He looked around. "The main thing is, treat everybody respectfully, right?"

Before Olivia could respond, a woman shoved between them, grabbed the sub, and dumped it in her basket. Olivia and Seahawks shrugged at each other and moved on.

At the checkout line Brian held a couple of quart bottles of seltzer water and a bag of corn chips so crumpled that it looked like the Seahawks guy had been sitting on it.

"That isn't what I meant when I said grab a bunch of bottled water."

"All the regular water's gone already. This is all that's left."

"We should grab a couple more."

"Liv? This is *it*. These two bottles. There isn't any more."

"Shit. I didn't do any better." She held up a quart tub of German potato salad and a couple of egg salad sandwiches.

Back in the car, Brian said, "The weird thing is, there's nothing about variola in Washington State. Nothing on the news."

"It can show up anytime. People are stocking up for a long siege. Besides, you can't trust the news. Come on, let's go."

They picked up the 90 and sped east. If they rammed straight through, sharing the driving, they could cross seven states and arrive in the Chicago suburb of Elmhurst—where Helen's old Oxford classmate was hiding—in thirty hours or so. They stuck to that plan, avoiding population centers, stopping only for gas, drive-through-window coffee, and bathroom breaks. Except for big commercial haulers, the eastbound lanes of the interstate were ominously empty.

"Traffic's always light out here," Brian said, to justify the weirdness— hey, nothing to worry about!—but it came off like he was making up a fact he wanted to believe. The sun was setting behind them. So was Idaho.

"It's August," Olivia said. "Where are the families on vacation?"

"I don't know."

"I do. They're holed up, scared spitless. And they should be."

"I gotta pee," Brian said. "Going to hit this next rest stop."

"We should avoid people more than we already are. Everyone we talk to is a risk vector, especially the farther east we go."

"I still have to go to the bathroom."

"You can pee on the side of the road."

"Really?"

"Naw," Olivia said. "Do the rest stop. I've got to go, too."

"You could squat by the side of the road."

"It's not the apocalypse yet, buddy."

A few tractor-trailer rigs were parked on the commercial vehicles' side of the rest stop, but on the civilian side there was only a Subaru wagon that looked like it had detoured through perdition. Dust and dirt coated the car. A hubcap was missing. The Subaru looked tired, played out, like an old dog after a hard run. Olivia came out of the women's room and stood waiting for Brian. It was muggy. Clouds of pepper-speck insects swarmed the light standards.

There was someone sitting in the car.

He—or maybe she—slumped over the wheel. Olivia looked back at the concrete restroom structure. Still no sign of Brian. After a moment, she approached the Subaru. The driver was probably sleeping, she thought. Olivia stopped about twenty yards from the car. She had a bad feeling. Steadying herself, she crossed the remaining distance, got close to the dirty window. The driver, a middle-aged male, was not sleeping. Scabs covered his face and bald spot. Ticks probed for blood among the scabs. She stumbled back, almost tripping over her own feet. She no longer had to go to the other side of the world to find the Disaster.

The Disaster had found her.

When Brian came back from the men's room, Olivia was waiting in his Ford with the windows rolled up. "Variola's made it at least as far as Montana."

"Did you get an internet connection?"

"No. Guy in that Subaru told me."

"How does he know?"

"He has it. Come on, let's drive."

Brian looked at the Subaru. "We have to do something."

"Like what? He's dead, Bri."

"Call someone. There's probably an emergency phone at this rest stop. Or those truckers, they might have CBs. Do they still use CBs?"

"I don't know."

Brian started to get out of the car. Olivia grabbed his shirt sleeve. "Bri, we need to go."

"Just leave a dead body sitting there?"

"Yes. We don't know anything about this version of variola. If it's been weaponized, maybe it's contagious outside the usual cycle. Maybe there are microscopic particles floating around us right now."

"Then we're already exposed."

"Or we're not. But the next time we get out of the car, we could be. The point is, we don't know."

"I'm going to tell one of those truck drivers, at least."

"What if they're dead, too? Or infected? They could be contagious without showing any outward signs. Or what if the guy you walk up to has already seen the body in the Subaru and he's locked himself in his cab, afraid to either drive farther west or go back east? He could be sitting there with a road-warrior pistol-grip shotgun. Sees you waltzing up and panics. What if you've got it, he's thinking."

"That's a little paranoid, don't you think?"

"It's realistic."

"This doesn't feel right."

"I want us to get vaccinated. After that, we can be the good guys again. Right now we have to be the careful guys. Bri, please?"

Brian nodded, not looking happy. He took his hand off the door handle.

They got back on the highway, and a mile down the road they passed a pickup truck pulled onto the shoulder. Brian had walked the hybrid up to eighty-five miles an hour, and at that speed the pickup flashed by on Olivia's side of the car, and she didn't spare it a thought until much later, when it was too late.

They ate the deli sandwiches and split the bag of corn chips. The bag had been manhandled and crushed so badly that, basically, they poured corn chip gravel into their mouths and washed it down with seltzer water. All the salt and seltzer made Olivia feel bloated.

Whenever she wasn't driving and they happened to be passing close enough to a decent cellular signal, Olivia used Brian's phone to scour news sources and social media for information on the outbreak. It became obvious that Helen had been right: Official declarations about the situation, dutifully repeated by CNN, Fox, and other major news outlets, did not jibe with the reality as reported in social media and the alternative press, not even when you filtered out the obvious conspiracy-theory bullshit. Corporate-owned news was in the business of mitigating panic, while variola was scorching through populations on five continents. In Australia and eastern Europe people were burning the dead and burying the remains in mass graves. Militarized police forces had been deployed in a dozen American cities, including New York, Baltimore, Los Angeles, and Chicago. People begged for a vaccine, and the government promised it was coming. But for now, everyone was told to stay home.

Brian, who had fallen quiet in the last few hours, said, "I can't believe we're fewer than five days out from the president's speech."

"It's accelerated," Olivia said. "Normal incubation for smallpox is around twelve days, I think. A week, at minimum. This has to be a genetic modification designed for maximum spread of infection."

"A weapon, for Christ's sake. Why would anybody do this? It's evil."

"It's human."

Immediately she regretted saying it. Brian didn't argue the point, and that was out of character. It was now three o'clock in the afternoon, and they were just over the border into South Dakota. Brian looked drawn and haggard—an appearance manifesting on his features that Olivia could almost not credit. Even in Aleppo, in the thick of the Disaster, he had retained his boyish looks.

"You okay?" she asked.

"I'm all right."

"Want me to drive for a while."

"No. You should nap."

"I should." But she was unable to stop thinking about probability streams and altered realities. It was easier to believe in them out here in the empty spaces, with the road spacers thudding under the tires. Could she make it all right again? Did she really have that power? Or had it been some kind of drug-induced hallucination when she chewed the jai ba leaves? She turned inward, afraid but compelled, and searched for Jacob's crisis-point probability choice, the one that prevented the variola outbreak. It was there, cornered and dangerous—persistent.

For now it was still a world awaiting permission to overtake the one she had created to save Brian. Olivia sensed her power, the power to reach into the halo and touch it—reach in and *choose* it. She became frightened and withdrew abruptly, blinking, rubbing her eyes. Had she fallen asleep? Brian glanced at her.

"Nightmare?"

"Sort of."

He kept flicking his eyes to the rearview mirror. Olivia turned in her seat and looked out the back window. Far behind them, sunlight glinted on metal.

"You see him?" Brian asked.

"The car? What about it?"

"I think they're following us. I mean deliberately."

"Who's paranoid now?"

"I've tried slowing down, let him catch up, you know?"

"But he doesn't catch up?"

"No. Not even on the downgrade. I mean, people speed up on the downgrade, right?"

Olivia remembered the pickup truck, pulled off the highway a little past the rest stop in Montana. A beat-up yellow Toyota.

Like Alvaro's.

Brian chuckled, shook his head dismissively. "I'm just tired. It's easy to get spooked out here."

"No. It's *them*."

"Them who, the Society?"

"Dee and Alvaro."

Brian craned around to look out the back window, as if Dee and Alvaro might be riding the bumper, waving. His attention off the road, the Ford swerved into the breakdown lane. "Shit." He faced forward again and corrected the drift. "You really think it's them?"

"It's them. They knew I would go to you. I *told* them I would. They must have been following us since Seattle."

Brian looked in the rearview mirror. "What do we do?"

"Keep driving," Olivia said. "But we have to figure out how to ditch them before we get to Elmhurst."

❁

SIXTEEN HOURS LATER AND TWENTY miles outside Elmhurst, Olivia was behind the wheel. A ramp exited off the right lane and fed into State Highway 47. She stayed in the passing lane, as if intending to ride it all the way into Chicago. This close to the city, the traffic had gained some heft, though nothing compared to what it probably was under normal conditions. Olivia kept checking the mirror. The pickup had moved closer. There were two people in the cab.

"Hang on," Olivia said. "I'm going to do something."

"Okay." Brian braced himself.

She calculated the angle, waited for the last second, and gunned across three lanes to the exit. Horns blared, tires squealed, brake lights flashed. A BMW swerved out of the way, and Olivia accelerated behind it just in time to slam onto the ramp, cutting in front of somebody in an RV. The driver laid on the horn and shot her the finger.

Brian, both hands braced against the dash, said, "*Jesus Christ.*"

She looped back, headed north on 47, and exited again, this time into a shopping complex called the Huntley Outlet Center. Reebok sportswear, Banana Republic, et cetera. A few dozen vehicles were scattered around the vast parking lot. Olivia pulled in next to an F-350 truck, big enough to conceal them from anyone passing the outlet center on the highway. Olivia and Brian were both breathing hard. Olivia's heart raced on an adrenaline surge.

"Where'd you learn how to drive like that?" Brian said.

"I'm self-taught," she said, craning around to look out the back window.

They waited. The sunlight began to fail in a polluted haze. Gradually the parking lot cleared out, leaving them stranded amid twenty acres of asphalt.

"Let's find this guy," Brian said. "What's his name again?"

"Najid Javadi. Put the address into your GPS." Olivia delivered the address from memory, and Brian tapped it into his phone.

Half an hour later, they rolled onto East Sherman Avenue in suburban Elmhurst. Neat lawns, oak trees, a lot of middle-class homes. Javadi's address looked like 1950s construction — tan brick, big windows, slate roof. Olivia could almost see the TV antenna that must have been belted to the chimney seventy-odd years ago. A garden gnome with a pointy red hat stood on the porch. The house was dark, and there was no car in the driveway.

"What time is it?"

Brian looked at his phone. "Half past eight."

Olivia parked at the curb, turned off the engine, unbuckled her seat belt.

Brian said, "There's nobody home."

"He might be in there, in a back room or something."

At the front door she rang the bell, waited, rang it again. She could hear the bell tone inside the house, but no one came to the door. She returned to the car.

"Let's wait a while."

It was a quiet street, not even a barking dog, everyone huddled behind locked doors — waiting and praying. None of them knew what Olivia and Brian knew, that inside the house with the garden gnome was vaccine that could save them.

Brian racked his seat back and folded his arms. "Going to rest my eyes."

"Go ahead. I'll watch for Javadi."

An hour passed. Olivia's eyes grew heavy. They had been driving for more than thirty hours, catching ragged naps between turns at the wheel. She started to drift when something rapped against the driver's side window. Olivia startled awake. A man stood in the street pointing a flashlight into her eyes. She blinked, held her hand up. Her other hand reached for the ignition button but didn't press it.

Brian sat up, rubbed his eyes. "What's happening?"

"I don't know. Some guy out there." She lowered her window a few inches.

The man said, "Who are you, and what are you doing here?"

"Are you a cop?"

"No."

"Then please get that light out of my face."

The light moved aside. Olivia lowered her hand. The man holding the flashlight looked like a fit sixty-something, his white hair and mustache as neatly trimmed and edged as the lawns. "I'm the neighborhood watch captain," the man said. "That's my house over there." He pointed at a brick bungalow across the street. "You two have been sitting out here a long time."

"It's a free country," Brian said.

"Yes, and I'm free to ask what you're doing here, am I not?"

"We're waiting for a friend to get home."

"Is your friend supposed to live in that house?"

Supposed to? "Yes."

"Then you're going to have a long wait. That place is empty. Has been for weeks. The owners pay a lawn and garden service, but I don't think they're advertising for new tenants. It's the only rental on the block." He sniffed, like he'd caught a whiff of something rancid.

The bottom fell out of the little hope chest Olivia had carried halfway across the country. She turned to Brian. It looked like the bottom had fallen out of him, too.

SEVENTEEN

THEY'D DRIVEN AWAY FROM JAVADI'S (apparently empty) house and now sat in the car outside a pharmacy in an empty strip mall. Brian played with the screw top on an empty seltzer bottle. "What now?"

"I don't get it," Olivia said. "Helen wouldn't have given me bad information. That message was barely two days old."

"Maybe you misremembered the address."

"I didn't."

"So we're back to my last question. What now? I have an idea, if you want to hear it."

"Not really."

Brian looked hurt. "Why not?"

"Because it's going to be some version of giving up and turning around."

"You don't know me as well as you think you do."

"Okay, go ahead. What's your idea?"

Brian cleared his throat. "We go back. Stock up on supplies and go back."

"*Brian.*"

"It's not 'giving up.' It's practical—realistic, as you like to say. We go to my friend's house in Puyallup. He and Joyce are stuck in Paris because of the travel ban. I've been to their house. It's perfect, not in a development or anything, set back on a couple of acres. We go there and ride it out, ride out the epidemic and whatever else happens."

"Wait a minute," Olivia said, suddenly realizing: "He's *in there.*"

"What? Who's in where? You're not even listening to me."

"Javadi. He's in that house."

Brian tossed the bottle into the back seat. "For crying out loud. You heard the night watchman. The house is vacant."

"Neighborhood watch captain."

"Whatever."

"Javadi's hiding out, remember? He's scared. He wants to disappear. If he's seen going in and out of a house in Elmhurst, the neighbors are going to wonder who he is. So he doesn't go in and out."

"What, he sits around in the dark for weeks, or however long he's been there? Liv, we've got to get realistic. You said yourself, the longer we stay out in the open like this, the more exposed we are."

She turned to him, hiking her leg up on the seat. "Bri, he's in there. I know he is."

"Okay. Say he is. Say he's hunkered in a closet or something. What do you want to do, go up and ring the doorbell again? Obviously he's not going to come crawling out to answer the freaking *door*. We have to start being smart before we run out of options. I mean, come on."

Olivia grinned. "You're kind of cute when you get agitated."

Brian closed his mouth, probably to evaluate his next words. Finally, with forced lightness, he said, "Yeah, everybody tells me that."

"They do?"

"You know what I read one time?" Brian said. "I read that when couples fight, what makes it probable they will stick together in the long run is that if one of them offers an olive branch—makes a repair attempt, with some humor—and the other one accepts it, instead of clinging to their anger."

Olivia waved her hand in front of her face, as if warding off a swarm of gibberish. "That's great, Bri. I don't know what the hell you're talking about."

"What I'm saying is, when we have a fight, or one of us is mad, the other one always makes a repair attempt. Don't you think that's a positive sign?"

"Who's mad?"

"I am—I mean, I was. Because we were fighting about what to do next."

"That isn't fighting. That's disagreeing. Do you have a crowbar?"

"What?"

"Brian, for Christ's sake, do you have a crowbar or not? Like for changing tires or whatever."

"It's called a lug wrench. Aren't you going to thank me for accepting your repair attempt?"

"No. I'm going to get the *lug wrench* out of the trunk and we're going to go back to Javadi's house and break in."

⚜

OLIVIA PARKED THE CAR ONE block over, in case the watch captain was still keeping an eye out, then got out and approached the house on foot. The night was muggy. Brian slapped a mosquito on his neck. Olivia carried the lug wrench in her right hand, holding it along her thigh, trying to make it less conspicuous. Javadi's house was still dark, the driveway still empty.

"This is ridiculous," Brian said. "Somebody's going to call the cops on us."

"Keep it to a dull roar, okay?"

"You planning to put a silencer on the lug wrench?"

"Let's do the back door," Olivia said.

"Or let's not."

Olivia ignored him, walked quickly up the driveway, and slipped around the side of the house. Brian trotted after her. A six-foot-high board fence enclosed the yard, giving them cover from the neighbors. Brian approached the back door and peered through the window. Olivia's attention fastened on the tool shed. It looked like a typical prefabricated structure dummied up as a rustic barn, complete with red paint and miniature hayloft doors. But something about it felt wrong, besides the outdated taste.

"I can't see a damn thing in there." Brian turned to Olivia. "What are you doing?"

"Does that shed look funny to you?"

"No, just ridiculous," Brian said.

"It looks funny to me." She approached the shed and tried the door. It was locked and felt solid as a bank vault.

Behind her, Brian said, "I thought you wanted to break into the house."

"What I want is to find Javadi and get the vaccine."

"You think he's in there?"

"Let's find out."

She used the tapered end of the lug wrench to probe the space between the door and the jamb. The gap was narrow, almost nonexistent.

"If you use that thing, it's going to be loud," Brian said.

"Maybe I can sort of crack the wood and peel it away from the lock."

"Uh, sure."

A light tucked under the eaves of the shed came on and a man's voice came from a hidden speaker: "Stop that. This is private property."

Olivia stood back, bumping into Brian. "Mr. Javadi?"

"Leave now, or I summon the police."

"My name is Olivia Nikitas. I'm a friend of Helen Fischer's. She told you about me."

The voice went quiet. Olivia and Brian looked at each other. The voice spoke again: "Helen didn't say anything about there being two of you."

"She didn't know."

Silence. It went on for two full minutes.

"If you don't open up," Olivia said, "I'm going force the door. I know you won't call the police. Nobody knows you're here, and that's how you want to keep it, right?"

Nothing.

Olivia started working the tapered end of the lug wrench between the door and jamb. Brian grabbed hold and helped her.

"For God's sake, stop," the voice said.

"Let us in and we will."

After another silence, Javadi said, "I need proof you're who you say you are. Hold up some ID to the camera behind the light."

Olivia produced her driver's license and showed it to the camera.

"Not so close."

She pulled it back a little. A minute went by. "Well?"

"Please wait."

A few minutes passed. Inside the shed, something clanked, and clanked again. After another minute, the door buzzed, the sound of an electric lock disengaging. Olivia handed the lug wrench to Brian and pulled the door open. Inside was . . . another door. The second door was set in a standing metal box about the size of a construction site's chemical toilet. Dull amber light gleamed on steel plates lining the walls of the otherwise empty shed.

"This place was built to take a serious hit," Brian said.

"I think it's a bomb shelter. I mean underground, under our feet. That's why no one sees him coming or going. The shelter is probably well provisioned."

The second door presented a handle with no moving parts and with a key pad and biometric thumbprint reader. Olivia reached for the handle . . . and stopped. On the floor was a small box, like the box an expensive pen would come in. She picked it up, removed the top. Inside was a disposable syringe, already loaded, a sealed packet containing a sterile swab, and two Band-Aids.

"That the vaccine?" Brian said.

"It must be." She gripped the handle on the second door and pulled. The handle might as well have been welded to a wall. "Goddamn it."

"We've got the vaccine," Brian said. "Let's get out of here."

"Bri, there's only one syringe, one dose."

"Oh. Shit."

Olivia looked up. She didn't see another speaker grille, but she said, "Hello?"

The steel-lined walls absorbed her voice. She yanked the lug wrench out of Brian's hand and rapped on the metal door. "*Hello?*"

Brian pulled on her arm. "Too loud. Jesus."

"Bri, one dose means only one of us gets vaccinated."

"Yeah, I get it. I'm not as dumb as I look."

She looked at her feet and back up at him. "I'm sorry."

"We both need sleep."

"And vaccine." She stepped past him and out of the shed. He followed, and the door fell shut behind him. The lock engaged with a smart *clack*. "Hey." Olivia waved at the camera. "Mr. Javadi. There's two of us. We need two doses."

"I'm sorry, but I can't give you any more."

"Call Helen."

"I can't do that, either."

"Why not?"

"She's dead."

Olivia stopped breathing. Her strength deserted her and she wanted to lean on something. Brian was handy. Instead, she braced her hand against the wall.

"You didn't know," Javadi said.

"She left me a vid. I'm not—I'm not surprised."

After a moment, Javadi said, "I only have enough left for my brother and his wife. They're still in Charleston but are coming soon. I'd give you more if I could."

Next door, backyard floodlights came on.

"Let's go," Brian said.

"If you expose me," Javadi said, "it won't do you any good. You won't get any more vaccine. I promise you that."

Olivia chewed her lip, trying to think.

Javadi said, "Administer the shot intramuscularly. Do you know how to do that?"

"Yes."

"Use multiple pricks to administer. At least four."

"I understand."

"Goodbye, then."

Olivia looked at the box in her left hand.

"Liv?"

"All right, all right."

They skulked back through the neighborhood and managed to reach Brian's car unseen. Inside, Olivia removed the disposable syringe from the box. "We're doing this right now."

"Great," Brian said. "Where do I poke you?"

Olivia shook her head. "Nope. You're getting the shot."

"No."

"Bri—"

"It's not an option," Brian said.

"It's me that got you into this mess in the first place. We're not going to argue about it."

"You're right," Brian said. "We're not going to argue about it. *You're* taking the shot." She started to interrupt him, and he held his hand up. "Just listen, okay? For one minute?"

"Go ahead."

"What if it's all true, all that stuff about probability streams, everything you said that happened to you? You believe it, don't you?"

"You don't."

"But you *do.*"

"Brian, I don't know what I believe."

"Yes you do. And not wanting to believe something isn't the same as *not believing* it."

She didn't say anything.

"So if it's true, you have to take the shot. Because if I die, it's no big deal. I mean in the grand scheme of things. But if *you* die, it's bad for everybody on the planet. Right? So roll your sleeve up."

Olivia narrowed her eyes. "You just want to be a stud and save me. You think I hallucinated half the stuff I told you."

"So what? It's not what *I* believe, it's what *you* believe."

"Goddamn it, Bri."

"Well?"

"You don't get to talk me into sacrificing you."

Brian rolled his eyes. "God, you're stubborn." He reached over and grabbed the key fob. "But I am, too. We're not going anywhere until I give you the shot."

"That's infantile."

Brian stuffed the fob in his pocket. "So what?"

Olivia sighed. "All right. Okay. You're making sense, as much as I hate to admit it." She handed him the sealed packet. "Swab me first."

When he started to tear the packet open, Olivia yanked the sleeve of his T-shirt up to his shoulder and quickly jabbed the syringe four times into the thick deltoid muscle.

"Ow." Brian pulled away, rubbed his shoulder. "That wasn't fair."

"Neither is contracting variola. Give me the swab." He glared at her, and she plucked it out of his hand, wiped the four red dots on his arm, and covered them with a Band-Aid. As soon as she was done, Brian pulled his sleeve down like he wanted to rip it off.

"Seat belt," she said. "We're going."

"Going where?"

"To fix this mess."

✺

OLIVIA DROVE THEM OUT OF Elmhurst, into the urban sprawl.

Helen was dead.

Olivia had already known that was probably true, but having Javadi confirm it—that made the reality sink in. She had known Helen for years, worked closely with her, argued with her, respected her. And Helen, even while dying, had tried to save Olivia by sending her to the vaccine. Olivia wanted to believe the end had been swift and not too painful, but she knew it hadn't been. If reports and social media posts were reliable, this fully weaponized variola was hemorrhagic, with close to a one hundred percent fatality rate. Helen's death had likely been horrific.

Grief expanded against Olivia's barriers, like threatening floodwaters. She held it back, but there was seepage.

A 7-Eleven came into view. Olivia wiped her eyes and pulled into the parking lot.

"What now?" Brian asked, and she could hear how angry and hurt he was.

"Brian, I had to do that. I had to give you the shot."

"I don't see it that way."

"I'm not going to watch you die. I can't. I did once, but I can't again. It's not going to be my fault that you die twice. Do you understand?"

Brian took a deep breath, closed his eyes a moment, and opened them. "It doesn't matter if I understand. It's done. By the way, I'm not thrilled about watching you die, either." He pointed at the convenience store, but his face remained stony. "What are we doing here?"

"I need wine. Cannabis would be better, but we don't have time to find a shop."

"You want to get high? *Now?*"

"In the tent, Alvaro gave me these narcotic leaves to chew. It's part of the process for accessing the probability machine. Letting down natural barriers, something like that."

"Makes perfect sense."

She gave him a measuring look. "How long do you plan to be mad at me?"

"I'm not mad at you."

"You are. And if you're waiting for my repair attempt, forget it."

Brian made a sound that wasn't quite a laugh. "You're a lunatic."

"Anyway, I'll be right back." She started to climb out of the car.

Brian put his hand on her shoulder. "I'll get it. You need to stay away from people."

"All right."

He opened his door. "For the record, I'm *not* mad at you. I'm mad at myself for not taking the syringe away from you when I should have known you'd jab me with it." He got out, threw his door shut, entered the store. Taken it away from her? And he thought *she* was delusional.

Olivia drummed her fingers on the steering wheel. Brian returned to the car with two bottles of wine.

"I got one white and one red."

Olivia pushed the ignition button. "You're still mad at me, aren't you?"

"Maybe."

"Find us a motel, okay? I'm going to save the world."

Brian produced his phone and said, "Motels." Tiny glowing signs and logos sprouted like neon flowers in a palm-sized garden. He finger-flicked one. "Three Bells. About half a mile toward the city, right on this road."

Olivia cocked her elbow over the seat to look out the rear window and started to back up. Across the street, a battered Toyota pickup sat in front of a dollar store, grille facing the street, parking lights on. Olivia stepped on the brake.

Brian looked out the rear window to see what she saw. "What's wrong?"

"That pickup."

"Is it them?"

They both looked harder, trying to figure out if it was indeed Dee and Alvaro.

Traffic intervened. A metro bus lumbered between them and the dollar store, and when it passed, the Toyota was gone.

Olivia got off the main road and threaded through a series of back streets and alleys. She never caught another glimpse of the pickup.

"Are you sure it was them?" Brian asked.

"No, but I'm not taking chances."

Half of a red neon vacancy sign blinked in front of the Three Bells Motel: ANCY. A stone planter with some scraggly, weed-looking things sat in front of the office. Olivia parked and turned to Brian. "Classy." Across the street was Big Jones Tires. A giant cutout of Big Jones himself stood on the roof, his arms in a muscleman pose, truck tires hanging from his biceps.

"You didn't say anything about quality. Wait here. I'll check us in."

"Brian? I'm going to fix this."

He nodded. "You keep saying that."

A few minutes later, Brian came out of the office with another man, probably the manager. He was short and almost perfectly round, a beach ball with arms and legs, a pair of suspenders, and a scraggly beard. The manager looked at Olivia and turned to go back into the office. Brian shrugged and followed him. The next time he came out, he was alone and holding a key.

✸

TWIN BEDS WITH A NIGHTSTAND separating them. A Rorschach blot of indeterminate origin—coffee, blood, semen?—stained the bedspread on the mattress nearer the bathroom. Olivia looked at it and saw a squirrel. On the wall behind the beds hung a framed black-and-white photograph of a Chicago street scene out of the 1920s, everybody in the shot wearing a hat. Trapped under the glass of the cheap picture frame, a flattened bug looked like a cartoon bullet hole, its legs the radiating cracks.

"I need to call my parents," Brian said.

"Don't tell them where you are. I mean, not specifically."

"Why not?"

"In case somebody's listening."

Brian slipped his phone out. "You mean somebody besides the usual suspects, like Homeland Security?"

"Yes."

Brian stood by the dresser, turning the phone in his hands. "Maybe you should call your people, too."

She looked up. "My people?"

"I know you don't want to call Rohana, but you must have other relatives, cousins, aunts and uncles."

"There are some cousins. I haven't kept up."

"Where do they live?"

"Bri, I need to concentrate on what I'm about to do." Olivia didn't like being reminded of her fundamental disconnectedness from family. Rohana lived on the other side of the earth. It was so easy to make excuses for not seeing her that Olivia could fool herself into believing they weren't excuses at all. At least, she could fool herself some of the time. The cousins, the aunts and uncles on the East Coast—she simply ignored them. Most of them she hadn't seen since childhood, anyway. And she was so busy with the Disaster, who could expect her to maintain relationships with people she barely remembered?

"Sure," Brian said. "Okay."

Olivia retrieved a plastic cup from the bathroom and stripped away the clean-guarantee paper wrapper. Sitting on the bed nearest the window, she twisted the screw cap off the white wine and poured the plastic cup three-quarters full. Brian, still holding his phone, watched her. "Do you really need to get drunk first?"

"Not drunk. Loose. I'm trying for something like what those leaves did to me."

"Like a narcotic that messes with your brain?"

"Sort of."

He pointed at the bottle. "It's probably going to take something fancier than Barefoot Cellars Chardonnay."

"It's what I've got."

Olivia finished the wine in her cup and filled it again.

Brian shifted his feet restlessly, looking unhappy. "You want me to be quiet while you . . . fix things?"

"I don't know. Yes. It'll probably take a few minutes to get in the mode." She sipped her second cup of wine, looked at it, and put the cup down. "Maybe that's enough. Could you turn off that overhead light? But leave the lamp on."

Brian killed the overhead. Olivia lay back on the bed, folded her hands over her stomach, and closed her eyes. At once, despite her agitation, the exhaustion of more than thirty hours on the road swept through her. She yawned.

After a while, Brian said, "How are you doing?"

"Good, I'm good." She toed off her shoes. One of them thumped on the floor. She pushed the other shoe with her foot but never heard it drop. She was *so* tired. Olivia found herself drifting down, like a diver in dark water, toward a murky light. Power emanations rippled through her. Olivia's fear awoke, and she began to struggle, push back. But the light drew her down, grew sharper and more intense: a white ring of power.

The halo.

EIGHTEEN

LIGHT OVERWHELMED HER. BRILLIANT SPOKES radiated from a hub. The spokes glimmered, like a pre-migraine aura. She concentrated on Aleppo, the Old City, and saw the ancient buildings reduced to rubble by time and war. The crisis point. Olivia felt the power of the probability machine, the power of the halo. Besides being a crisis point, Aleppo was the epicenter of the world's everyday Disaster. What if she used the probability machine to fix that—to nullify the Disaster? Fix things so that there'd be no civil war, hundreds of thousands would live, untold numbers of children would not be orphaned, treasured artifacts of the ancient world would avoid wanton destruction.

Olivia trembled on the brink of godlike choices.

And she pulled back from the staggering complexity. Even tracing to its origin a single aspect of the war would be like attempting to trace a single thread through an intricate tapestry. The Disaster was too big for backtracking solutions. She could see that the Alvaro and Dee faction of the Society had this one aspect right: The power of the probability machine had to be restricted to immediate crisis points. As much as she might want to, she couldn't surrender to the impulse to tinker with the daily Disaster. One manipulation would trigger who knew how many unintended consequences. She could make the Disaster worse than it already was.

From the center of the halo, she concentrated: *variola*.

And the halo zeroed in, like the objective lens of a microscope focusing on a drop of pond water. Numberless lives squirmed in the drop, a city's population.

The focus grew tighter.

A dark, stone-walled room rose around her—the torture chamber beneath the madrassa in the Old City where Brian had died. But Brian wasn't present now. This was before. Kerosene lanterns lighted the room, two of the lanterns on the floor. A clean-shaven man in Western clothes, jeans and a blue work shirt, held a third lantern in his fist, illuminating the old man stretched out on the table. Three other men stood around the periphery, and on the walls, their shadows pantomimed a conference of grotesques. They were all young, early twenties, except for one; that one, a slightly older man, had a scar like a trend line bisecting his eyebrow. Very distinctly, the scarred man said, "I won't allow this." He spoke with authority, and the others paid attention.

Olivia knew the man with the scar. He had been kind to her one time when she was embedded with a group of rebel fighters. But in a nearer memory, he had intervened outside the madrassa, saved her life. And here he was again, intervening on behalf of the captive laid out on the table: Jacob, the previous Shepherd. The scarred man was the key—the linchpin. The difference between life and death in the torture cell. Olivia was certain of it.

I won't allow this.

The halo had brought her to the moment prior to Jacob's choosing of a new probability—one that had cost Jacob and Brian their lives, but somehow prevented the release of weaponized variola.

Olivia reached out. If she could trace the scarred man back, find some way of positioning his choices so that the variola release was prevented *and* Brian lived . . .

But like a wheel stuck in a deep rut, Olivia found she could only travel the scarred man's route to the destination that saved Brian. Something inside her, something fearful and desperate, wouldn't let her kill Brian, no matter what the greater good. There had to be a way of achieving both outcomes. There *had* to be.

Jacob's eyes slipped side to side and started to roll back. At this moment in the halo, the old man controlled the link. Olivia felt the shift coming through her. In the next moment, if she allowed it, a new probability stream would take over, the flow altering around the man with the scar, changing the fate of millions.

And, of course, killing Brian, Jodee, and Jacob.

Olivia wrenched herself away before it could happen.

Inside the halo, the spokes became like sharp needles, jabbing her, trying to force her back to the torture cell and Jacob's choice. Olivia endured the pain and turned deliberately away, seeking another point of influence.

Variola.

From a high perspective: An SUV—a tan Jeep Cherokee—pulled away from a checkpoint on Aleppo's outskirts and headed into the desert, wheels spinning up yellow dust. Behind it, a line of vehicles advanced and soldiers approached with weapons while whisper drones hovered like prehistoric insects.

Olivia didn't understand. What was she supposed to look at? Where was the scarred man? Had she been wrong about him?

It was becoming difficult to concentrate. Leaving the torture cell, rejecting the solution to the crisis point presented by the probability machines, looking for another way—it all created a tremendous strain.

Something pulled at her like a weak magnetic attraction. Olivia turned her full attention on the Jeep speeding away into the desert. She remembered crossing the city to Brian's hospital on the state-controlled side of Aleppo. It had taken forever because of all the checkpoints. At first she had assumed the extra level of security was the result of the brief, disorganized uprising. But those soldiers had been searching for something specific. Probably, she now knew, a hot biological.

Through increasing pain, Olivia rewound the probability. Back in line, the Jeep rolled forward. Soldiers on either side held their hands out: HALT. The kid behind the wheel braked. And he *was* a kid, no older than the boy with the amputated leg who had shared Brian's hospital room and offered Olivia his mother's chair. The driver used the back of his hand to wipe sweat off his forehead. He looked guilty as hell.

Olivia concentrated. Where was it? Where was the smuggled variola? Or was it some kind of key to access the biological? Was the boy himself the key? Whatever it was, it had to be in this vehicle. But she couldn't *see* it. And if she couldn't see it, how could she manipulate the probability choices of the soldiers searching for it?

She could practically feel the waves of fear and anxiety wafting off the boy. The soldiers had to pick up on it, she thought. But if they did, it wasn't enough to encourage them to aggressively dismantle the Jeep. Probably they had been here all day in the hot sun, inspecting hundreds of cars and trucks. She could see the boredom written on their faces. The soldier in charge, a middle-aged guy wearing a side-slanted military beret and a thick mustache, directed his men to search the Jeep in the usual manner, inspect the cargo hold, look under the seats, open any containers. But it wasn't enough. He was about to pass the Cherokee through.

The driver looked desperately nervous. He wanted to get away from the checkpoint—that was Olivia's point of influence. As the checkpoint commander approached the Jeep, Olivia pushed the boy toward a reckless probability end point. He panicked, keyed the ignition, and flattened the accelerator. The Cherokee jerked forward, sending one of the soldiers to the ground. The others shouldered their rifles and opened fire.

Whisper drones swarmed after the Jeep, pursued on the ground by their own shadows. One of the drones launched a miniature rocket. The rocket streaked over the vehicle and exploded directly in front of it, forcing the driver to swerve wildly. The right wheels canted off the road. The Jeep teetered and went over, sliding onto its side.

The soldiers double-timed out to it, weapons raised. The driver climbed out of the passenger window, his face bloody, and held his hands up. Gunfire ripped across his chest, and he fell forward, arms hanging down.

Olivia snapped out of the halo and came up gasping on the motel bed, her head throbbing. The lamplight spiked into her eyes and she rolled away, hiding her face. She could still see the boy's body jumping with the impact of automatic weapon fire and falling forward. Dead, where before he had lived.

Olivia had done that.

But if the boy had something to do with smuggling variola out of Aleppo, didn't that make him complicit in a crime against humanity? So why should it bother her? Because the truth was, she didn't know what the boy was doing, or indeed if he was doing *anything*. Olivia felt nauseated. She sat on the edge of the bed, her eyes barely open, and hung her head between her knees. "Bri," she said, before realizing she was alone in the room.

And that wasn't the only wrong thing.

She raised her head and looked around. The light hurt, but she forced herself to keep her eyes open. The standard motel two-beds-and-a-TV arrangement was the same, but it was as if elves had arrived while she was gone in the halo and . . . spruced things up. The furniture was better quality. Not a *lot* better, but better. There were no stains on the bedspreads. Maybe because they were different bedspreads. An art deco depiction of the Sears Tower replaced the plastic-framed photograph of old-time Chicago. A cork stuck out of a bottle of Chablis on the nightstand. Hadn't it been a screw cap, and hadn't the wine been Chardonnay? Olivia's head swam with nausea and a sense of dislocation.

She got up and stumbled to the bathroom, shielding her eyes from the lamp, her vision fragmented in a migraine shimmer. Dimly, she was aware that the bathroom was different, the shower curtain replaced with frosted glass. Where was Brian? She went to her knees and vomited into the toilet. Distantly, she heard the outside door open. She pushed herself up, feeling muzzy. Voices spoke in the next room.

Voices. Plural.

"Bri—" She came through the door and stopped.

Looking sullen, Brian stood between Alvaro and Dee. The Society apostates wore hospital-blue filter masks. N-95s, Olivia suddenly knew —an info fragment out of the new probability stream tumbling to the surface of her conscious awareness. N-95s offered ninety-five percent protection from airborne viruses and were the filter mask of choice for anyone who could get their hands on one.

She had failed. The epidemic wasn't over.

NINETEEN

"I'M SORRY," BRIAN SAID. "IT looked like you fell asleep. I didn't want to wake you, so I went outside to call my mom and dad." He shrugged. "These guys came out of nowhere."

Olivia tried to focus through the pain. "Are you all right?"

"He's fine," Dee said. The mask partially muffled her voice. Besides the mask, she still wore her Castro cap, and she still held her chin up, as if daring anyone or anything to take a poke at her and see where it got them.

Olivia leaned heavily on the bathroom door frame. A new memory scaffold had begun to rise around the old one. The room looked different because it was a different room in a different motel. Somehow the change she made at the Aleppo checkpoint caused a ripple (butterfly effect?) across the new probability stream.

"Hey—" Brian came across the room, and she sagged into his arms.

"What's wrong with her?" Alvaro said.

"How should I know? She was napping when I left the room."

"Wasn't napping," Olivia said. "I told you what I was going to do. Bri, I have to sit down. And either turn that lamp off or put something over it."

"She used the link," Alvaro said to Dee. "I told you she was reckless. It was a mistake to wait."

"You said we shouldn't spook them," Dee said.

The pain spiked. Olivia closed her eyes and pressed the heels of her hands against her temples.

Brian helped her to the only chair. She opened her eyes to slits, shaded them with her hand. Brian retrieved a bath towel and draped it over the bedside lamp. "Better?" he said.

Olivia made an unhelpful, noncommittal noise.

"What did you change?" Alvaro asked.

Dee nudged him. "Give her a minute. She looks sick."

"Some water?" Olivia said. "I need water."

Alvaro moved closer. "Tell me."

"Back off," Brian said.

Alvaro turned on him. "Do you even understand what's happening?"

"Yeah, I do. You're trying to bully my girlfriend. And I'm telling you to back off."

Olivia held her hand up. "It's all right, Bri." She looked at Alvaro and Dee. "I *tried* to fix it. I really did."

Alvaro craned his head back, his lower lip curled between his teeth, then looked at Olivia. "I know you probably tried, but you don't know what you're doing. Tell me what you changed, what you did in the halo."

"Brian," Olivia said, "I really need that water."

Brian disappeared into the bathroom and came back with a plastic cup of water.

"Thanks." Olivia drank the whole cup without pause. It hurt just to tilt her head back. "I didn't screw around this time."

"But you didn't stop the outbreak," Alvaro said.

She stared at Alvaro's filter mask. "I guess not."

"So you didn't go to the crisis point."

"I *did*."

"The crisis point is the torture cell. Jacob told me about it."

"I found a different way," Olivia said.

"It's not possible."

Olivia tried to stand. A wave of nausea rolled through her, and she fell back into the chair. Brian crouched beside her, worried.

"I need to know what's going on out there," she said. "I need the goddamn *news*."

But as she said it, the news rose inside her, part of the fresh memory scaffold lifting out of her brain fog, like the eternal haze of dust in Aleppo, to lie over the more present memory of a mostly uneventful cross-country drive from Seattle. The new memory presented a harrowing journey through a nation under martial law, a violation of travel restrictions that could have landed them in jail, or worse. Military-imposed curfews kept major population centers locked down.

Behind it all, a giant number, an almost unfathomable number: twenty-three million.

Olivia slumped. Her lips moved. "Twenty-three million infected." That was in the United States alone.

"Everybody knows the CDC lowballed that estimate." Dee sounded disgusted.

"It's probably that many dead," Alvaro said, "and twice as many infected. The weaponized smallpox develops fast. And there's no vaccine."

"I'm going to be sick again." Olivia leaned over, head between her knees. What had she done? Brian put his hand on her back. Bile percolated up her throat. She swallowed it back, sat up slowly, her head throbbing, and looked at Alvaro and Dee. "You followed us all the way from Seattle?"

"With a GPS tracker I attached to his car." Alvaro nodded at Brian. "We lost you a few times when the satellite connection dropped. But it always found you again."

Dee said, "We got to Seattle way ahead of you, Olivia. We knew where you would go. Eventually the Society would have figured that out, too. You're lucky Emilio didn't arrive before we did."

Olivia stood up, moving with the delicacy of someone balancing a bowl of hot soup on her head. "I want to look outside."

Alvaro made room for her to pass. At the window, she gripped the plastic pull-rod of the curtain and racked it aside. In addition to Brian's hybrid and Alvaro's ramshackle pickup, only a half-dozen vehicles occupied the parking lot. A fully lit declaration of VACANCY shone beneath the Skyline Motel sign, but the closed blinds in the office windows sent a mixed message. An overturned garbage can scattered trash across the walkway. No traffic moved on the main road. The lights of Chicago in the distance made the night sky glow. On the other side of the road stood a diner. In her mind, Olivia could still see the ghost of Big Jones Tires.

More memories of Olivia's disastrous probability surfaced. She and Brian trading turns behind the wheel while the other hunted for internet connections on the secondary roads they had resorted to using the nearer they approached populated areas and state borders. Variola attacks had plunged the world into barely restrained chaos. Almost as frightening as the millions dead were the reports out of Moscow indicating a much lower incidence of infection. A statistically impossible lower number. India and Pakistan, two of the less stable nuclear powers, openly hurled threats — India at Russia, Pakistan at India. How long would it be until they hurled something more lethal than threats? Russia, meanwhile, denied reports suggesting Russian immunity from the virus. A flat-out lie, easily contradicted by independent observations. Meanwhile, North Korea, always the wild card, had gone ominously silent.

"You made it all worse," Alvaro said. "I can see it in your face. What was it like before you manipulated the probability stream?"

"Bad, but not this bad. The mass deaths hadn't happened, at least not in the United States. And I don't think anyone was talking about Russian immunity." Olivia shook her head. "I screwed up, but I can still fix this."

Alvaro crowded her, his eyes flashing with anger. He looked road-tired and nerve-frayed, and not a little threatening.

Dee said, not to Alvaro, "You're good right there, partner."

Brian grunted. Dee had his arm turned up behind his back.

"Hey, let him go." Olivia tried to push past Alvaro, but he blocked her.

"Calm down," he said. "Both of you. We're on the same side. Listen to me: Olivia, Jacob's probability choice is still there. You can go back into the halo. You can choose it."

"I know that."

He gripped her shoulder and squeezed hard. "Then you have to *do* it."

"Hey." Olivia pulled away.

"Let *go*," Brian said, and Dee pushed him into the wall face-first and levered his arm. Brian made a weird, gasping scream that went right to Olivia's heart.

"*Settle down,*" Dee said. "We aren't here to hurt anybody."

"You're hurting *me* right now," Brian said through gritted teeth.

"Leave him alone," Olivia said. "I'll do it, for Christ's sake."

Alvaro, who hadn't shifted his attention off Olivia by a single millimeter, said, "You can't enter the halo again for at least a day. That's under normal circumstances. We know from past experience that the farther you veer from the crisis point, the more dangerous it becomes for the Shepherd. It's built in, like a fail-safe. If you go back in too soon, the link will fry your brain. It's happened before."

"She needs time," Dee said, "and we're not safe here."

Olivia took a deep breath. "I know where there's vaccine. Vaccine that's effective against this weaponized strain of variola. And it's not far from here."

Alvaro's eyes said it first. "Bullshit."

"She's telling the truth," Brian said.

"I am," Olivia said. "There's a house in Elmhurst."

"We tracked them to Elmhurst," Dee said. "That much is true."

Alvaro said, "When the right probability takes over, nobody will need vaccine."

"*If* it takes over," Olivia said. "What if I can't do what you want me to do? What if the link's already damaged and no good to anybody, including you? We might all have to survive in *this* probability."

"Only the Russians have vaccine," Alvaro said. "That's what everybody's saying."

"There's a guy hiding out in a bunker only a few miles from here. He worked in a government bioresearch lab where a test vaccine was developed. He stole some."

"How do you know about him?"

Olivia told him about Helen and Javadi. She found it increasingly difficult to concentrate. Her stomach roiled with fresh nausea. The aura effect intensified. It splintered light and created blank spots. Her head pulsing with the post-halo migraine, she gave up trying to read Alvaro's eyes. The room tilted, and she swayed forward. Brian yelled, and Olivia fell against Alvaro and into darkness.

TWENTY

OLIVIA EMERGED GRADUALLY FROM A swamp of surrealistic dreams: Jacob was nailed to a table in a stone room beneath the earth, a room ankle-deep in blood. Brian's face floated on the blood, a flimsy skin mask, eyeless, with straps attached to its ears like the straps on an N-95 filter mask. A starving child held a granola bar in one fist and a lantern in the other, while a cat slopped around her legs in the syrup-thick blood. "Qetta, qetta," the cat said.

Someone touched Olivia's shoulder. "Hey, how you doing?"

She tried to reply. But her lips and tongue had temporarily forgotten how to make meaningful noise together. She blinked. The migraine aura was gone. Brian's face hovered, a big white planet.

"You fainted." Planet Bri put his glasses back on.

"Uh-huh." Her head hurt, but not murderously so. She sniffed at a very bad smell and touched the front of her shirt, which was damp.

"You threw up," Brian said. "I cleaned it off with a wet towel."

"My hero." She rubbed her eyes, looked at him. He hadn't shaved since they departed Seattle. His lip was puffy, crusted with dried blood. She reached out, hovered her fingertips over the lip. "What happened?"

"I ran into a wall," Brian said. "She's right over there." He pointed.

Olivia carefully turned her head. Dee sat on the other bed, her back propped against the wall, holding a plastic cup of Chablis. Her filter mask lay on the bedside table, like one bra cup severed from its twin.

"Hey, no hard feelings," Dee said.

Brian touched his puffy lip and winced. "Easy for you to say."

In Aleppo, Olivia had gotten him killed. She had screwed up. Now she had a second chance, and she wouldn't screw up again. Next time she was in the halo, she would scrutinize all her moves, calculate the collateral repercussions—find a way to preserve the future *and* Brian. There had to be another way of heading off the variola attack. She knew the move existed because it *had* to exist.

Or did she know only that she *wanted* it to exist?

What's the first rule of relationship club? Don't let the salesman through the door.

A toilet flushed, the faucet ran, and Alvaro emerged from the bathroom. "Dee, you have to keep your mask on." His was still in place.

"These two aren't even sick."

"We don't know who's a carrier and who isn't. We don't know what's in the air around us right now." He gave Olivia an appraising look. "So, you're better?"

"Still shaky. But yes, I'm better."

Alvaro sat on the chair, glanced at his watch. "In the morning, you can try the link again. If that doesn't work, I want you to take us to this Javadi person and his bunker. We can't go anywhere tonight. There's a curfew."

Olivia pointed at the TV. "Can we have the news?"

"No."

Surprised, Olivia asked, "Why not?"

"It's pointless."

She laughed, which hurt her head, so she stopped. "That's your opinion. Your uninformed opinion."

Alvaro shrugged. "I don't watch the news, okay? It's endless talk and depressing video. Most of it isn't accurate, anyway."

The idea of someone, especially during a worldwide emergency, not wanting to see the news—Olivia couldn't begin to fathom it. Being cut off from the steady flow of information, for even these few days, was like denying her water, or air. "Turn the lights out and crawl under the covers?"

"Whatever they're saying, it doesn't matter. Tomorrow the crisis won't exist. And if it does, the media won't fix it. It's all lies, or it's information they want you to have, not the information that matters."

"Whatever. I'll get it on my IsnGlas."

Dee said, "Alvaro spent half his life at Sanctuary, since he was a kid. They isolate the future Shepherd so the world doesn't contaminate him."

"The world doesn't contaminate people," Brian said. "That's like saying the ocean contaminates fish."

Olivia picked up her tablet but didn't boot it. "The ocean *does* contaminate fish. Ever hear of mercury poisoning?"

"That's not what she's talking about."

"I got plenty of the world," Alvaro said, "before I went to Sanctuary. And it's not like the old days. Even when I was in Sanctuary, I got out, traveled. Jacob showed me the world I was eventually going to be responsible for."

Olivia put her tablet aside. "How old were you when they took you to the ranch?"

"Thirteen."

"Alvaro's family is a big deal in Society history." Dee sounded a little drunk. "Jacob was honoring that when he chose him. In 1943, Alvaro's grandfather saved the world." She toasted Alvaro with her plastic cup. He made an annoyed face and waved away the honor.

"Weird," Brian said. "I thought it was the Allies who kicked Hitler's butt. Assuming that's what you're talking about."

"Tell him," Dee said.

"Why bother?" Alvaro yawned, chin down, rubbing his eyes. "He doesn't believe us anyway."

Olivia adjusted to a more comfortable position on the bed. "Then tell *me*."

Alvaro lifted his head. After a moment, he said, "All right. First, what happened at Sanctuary, it has historical context. There has always been a struggle for dominance inside the Society. It's factional, and it goes back to the beginning." He paused, pulled off his filter mask. "I feel like a fool wearing this thing when nobody else is." He tossed it toward the bed. It landed on Dee's foot.

"And when was that?" Olivia asked. "The beginning."

"Third century AD. The first Shepherd was a Roman soldier named Decius. Unlike most of his class, he was educated and a follower of the Mithraic cult, at least until he broke away and started his own sect. We know about him because of the scroll record he left."

"What about the factions?" Olivia said.

"One believes the halo should only be used at crisis points, and then as minimally as possible—to limit the butterfly effect. It should be easy. The machine is *keyed* to crisis points. The other faction, it has a looser definition of 'crisis.' They believe it's all right to manipulate probability streams for other reasons. Material gain, for instance. Basically, in our time, Faction One is represented by Jacob and me, and Faction Two is represented by Andrew and Emilio."

Brian sat on the bed beside Olivia. "Wait a minute. Emilio's your cousin, so wouldn't it also honor your grandfather if he got picked to be the whatever-it-is?"

Dee snorted.

"Exactly the opposite," Alvaro said. "From the 1920s to 1944, a Shepherd named Ellis Beekman headed the Society. Back then, Sanctuary wasn't a rundown ranch in Idaho. It was a Teutonic compound in Prussia. It was luxurious. Beekman was known for making probability choices that financially benefited the Society, often at the expense of innocent bystanders. In the twentieth century, the consequences of self-serving probability choices became exaggerated."

"Because?" Olivia said.

"The interconnectedness of the world. And later, the big weapons, the world-destroying weapons. It was Beekman who manipulated the New York Stock Exchange in 1929 and caused a worldwide economic depression. He then used the Society's cash reserves to buy shares cheap and build a stock portfolio that later generated millions. A lot of people got hurt by the Depression, yes?"

"Yes."

"Well, that was nothing compared to what came next. Adolf Hitler gained power because of Shepherd Beekman. See, we needed another world war to bring the US out of the Depression and make all those stocks valuable again. The Society was also heavily invested in Krupp, the German arms manufacturer. You see how this works?"

"Sounds like a recipe for *creating* crisis points," Olivia said.

"Exactly. Beekman always thought he had it under control. But misusing the halo so much caused a terrific strain. A brain embolism killed him. My grandfather, who wasn't the official successor, was the only one present when Beekman died. The link migrated."

"And your granddad saved the world," Dee said.

Alvaro shrugged. "He made a probability choice that prevented Nazi scientists from completing their nuclear weapons program ahead of the Allies. A team of Norwegian saboteurs successfully attacked a fortress in Vemork, Norway, where the Germans were conducting heavy-water experiments. But in the most likely probability end point, the saboteurs failed, the weapons program continued uninterrupted, and Germany won the war."

"Tell her the other one," Dee said.

Olivia noticed that a skeptical grin had crept onto Brian's lips. He wasn't buying any of this. Of course, it all sounded ridiculous. But Olivia had seen the halo. Brian hadn't.

"Grandfather Abelard chose a probability that prevented nuclear war during the Cuban Missile Crisis. Khrushchev could have gone either way. Abelard nudged him, made sure the right person had his ear at the right time."

Brian made a noise that wasn't quite derisive. It could have been mistaken for a sniffle, some dust in the air.

"When Grandfather died there was a traditional ceremony, an orderly migration of the link to Jacob."

"And Jacob put the photographer in Elián González's bedroom," Olivia said.

"What?" Brian looked confused, like he'd missed an episode of a Netflix series. Confused . . . and maybe past his bullshit threshold.

"Apparently," Olivia said, "we needed the Iraq War."

"This is where I check out." Brian grabbed the Burgundy, uncorked it with the cheap corkscrew he'd purchased when he bought the wine. There were no more plastic cups, so he drank directly from the bottle. Judging by the face he pulled, he might have just swigged straight lemon juice. Brian wasn't a wine drinker, not even when the wine was good.

Olivia asked, "Who built the probability machine, and why?" She knew part of the answer from the previous probability stream, when Alvaro claimed the machine came from the future. She wanted to see if he gave the same answer now.

"I can't tell you that."

"Naturally," Brian said.

Alvaro shot him an annoyed look. "It's not an arbitrary decision. The Society started as a splinter cult, after it broke away from Mithraism, which had been around for hundreds of years all over the Roman Empire. The Society kept some of the Mithraic traditions—rituals and rites of initiation." He looked at Olivia. "The Elders wanted you to recite the parable—that's an example. The original members of the Society built their temple underground, beneath an existing religious structure, the same way Mithraic temples were sometimes built beneath Christian churches."

"And nobody has any idea where the machine came from," Brian said, like he was saying, *What a convenient load of horseshit.* Olivia decided sarcasm didn't suit him, though he was pretty good at it.

"*We* know," Alvaro said. "But you're an outsider. Olivia is an outsider, too. Anyway, besides the Shepherd, his successor, and the Elders, no one — even in the Society — knows the whole truth."

"Well, here's to you." Brian raised the wine to his lips, thought better of it, and put the bottle decisively on the floor. "Holy men, or men who think they're holy. That never works out."

Alvaro gave him another annoyed look. "No one said anything about holy men."

"You just said—"

"What I just said happened a long time ago. The Society evolved."

Olivia cleared her throat, "It *did* feel like a religious cult, except for the physics references, words like 'superposition' and 'end point.'"

"The Society isn't a cult anymore," Alvaro said. "And the machine is a real machine."

Brian frowned. "Probability streams, superpositions. The words are meaningless. You might as well call it magic."

"The words aren't meaningless. They're new words, mathematical words derived from chaos theory to describe old effects connected to the probability machine."

Brian goaded him. "So if it's not a religious cult, what's the right name for it?"

Olivia was less and less happy with this side of Brian. She said, "Anyway, it looked more like a demented Kiwanis meeting than a religious cult."

Dee laughed. "That's dead-on. Testosterone city."

Alvaro stood and paced over to the window. He pushed the curtain aside and looked at the parking lot. "You're head of ranch security. That's not a subservient role."

"The Elders like my military police background, and they're short on experienced security people. As soon as a man turns up who can do my job, he'll do it. Andrew and the others begrudge me the position. I guess it doesn't matter now, anyway."

Alvaro turned away from the window and looked at Dee with his sleep-deprived raccoon eyes. "Let's stop talking and get some rest."

"It's all bullshit anyway," Brian said.

Olivia sighed. "Bri, it's real. I don't know how, but the probability machine is real. I've seen it work. Before I made a choice in the halo, the world was different. Variola wasn't as widespread. Maybe there were deaths, but not in the millions. Martial law hadn't been imposed. Our whole drive from Seattle happened differently. Christ, we were even in a different motel. I have both memories in my head. I mean right now, as we're sitting here." Olivia closed her eyes briefly. "Please don't look at me like you wish you could give me a pill to make my bad thoughts go away."

Brian winced. "I wasn't thinking that."

"But?"

"But I only remember the drive one way. I only remember *everything* one way."

Alvaro said, "We all see the world one way. Olivia is linked, so she remembers more than one probability. Jacob, too — or at least he remembers the one previous probability, the one he chose himself."

Brian looked like he was about to get argumentative about it. Olivia squeezed his leg. "Bri, let it go. I need to sleep now."

"I'm sorry, sure."

She lay back and closed her eyes. Tomorrow she had to go again into the halo, and she dreaded it. Despite that, soon she fell into troubled sleep.

TWENTY-ONE

VOICES LURED OLIVIA OUT OF sleep. She sat up, rubbing her eyes. The room smelled like wine and road sweat. Which is what you got with four people, thirty hours in two cars, and one unused shower. Brian slept next to her, his shoes off and his legs drawn up. His glasses sat on the table next to Dee's filter mask. Brian did his not-quite-snoring thing, the sound of air whistling through a narrow passage. Alvaro and Dee lay on the other bed. The room was dark, but not dead-of-night dark. Daylight seeped around the heavy curtains. The voices came from outside.

Olivia quietly swung her legs off the bed and stood up. She felt a little unsteady but her headache was gone. The unsteady part was probably because she was so hungry. As for headaches, she needed to locate caffeine before her body remembered what it was missing. She stepped around the beds and pulled the curtain aside just enough to see out. The morning light hurt her eyes. Across the street, where traffic was moving again, Trigger's, a diner, was open for business.

A Volkswagen Current was parked in front of the motel office. A girl sat in the passenger seat. She had short blond hair and looked no older than twenty. She drew on a vapor pipe like an asthmatic sucking a medical inhaler. White mist hung around her face.

The voices came from two men standing outside the office. One of them Olivia recognized as part of her new memory scaffold: the motel's desk clerk, the same guy who had checked them into their room. She had seen him briefly yesterday, when he insisted she and Brian both sign the register. He was somewhere between thirty and fifty, wearing a red polo shirt, his hair like wispy corn silk teased across his scalp. The other man was probably a couple of inches over six feet, and middle-aged. He wore a shiny sport coat over a button-down shirt with the tails hanging out.

Both men wore filter masks.

"I already *told* you," the tall man said, "I don't have a credit card. I don't have cash. I don't have anything—because I don't have my fucking wallet." He looked like he wanted to kick the desk clerk across the parking lot.

The clerk replied, though Olivia couldn't hear what he said, and waved his hands at the tall guy in a shooing-away gesture. The tall man shook his head, disgusted, and returned to his car. The blond girl didn't look at him. The Volkswagen backed out angrily and joined the traffic heading into Chicago. The desk clerk remained in the doorway, looking in Olivia's direction. Not *at* Olivia, but in her direction. After a moment, he started to walk toward their room.

Behind her, Dee said, "What's going on out there?"

Olivia turned away from the window. "Some kind of argument."

Voices inside the room did what voices outside the room had failed to do. Alvaro woke so abruptly it was as if someone had poked him with a sharp stick. He half fell off the bed, looking around wildly. Focusing on Olivia, he said, "You're up."

"Uh-huh."

Brian rolled out of sleep and groped for his glasses, knocking them onto the floor. "What's happening?" He hung over the edge of the bed, retrieved his frames, and pushed them onto his face.

"Nothing," Olivia said. "We're going to breakfast."

Alvaro shook his head. Apparently he had a different idea about that. Right on cue, somebody knocked on the door, loudly, and Olivia snatched it open. The desk clerk stood in the frame. He looked past her.

"You got four people in there."

"Yes. Our friends showed up late."

"You can't have four people without paying for four people."

Olivia said over her shoulder, "Alvaro? The man needs money."

Alvaro, looking disheveled, pawed his wallet out of his hip pocket.

"Is that your pickup?" the manager asked.

"Yes."

"I almost had it towed."

Alvaro nodded. "Okay, thanks for not doing that. How much do I owe?"

"No, no, no. In the office."

Alvaro seemed confused.

"You have to register, which you should have done last night. Every-thing legal and up front. Way things are, my ducks have to be in a row. *Everybody's* ducks have to be in a row."

Olivia was already pulling on her shoes. "We'll meet you at the diner. Brian, let's go."

"Wait——" Alvaro was like somebody who'd let the dog's leash slip out of his hand.

Dee, standing up and appearing anything but confused, said, "I'll go with them."

It was as if someone had forgotten to turn Trigger's on. Half a dozen people sat scattered around the diner that could have accommodated twenty times as many. Most of them stared at phones and tablets. Little villages of projected news tickers and talking heads glimmered on table-tops while plates of food went ignored and cups of coffee gave up ghosts of cooling steam.

Olivia and company sat in a booth by the window. They ordered food and coffee, and the waitress left a silver carafe and four cups, one in front of the empty place next to Dee. The waitress wore a painter's can-ister mask, which made her appear to be a giant dishwater-blond mantis. Olivia drank her first cup and refilled it from the carafe. There seemed to be only two people working the diner. An old guy in a filter mask manned the grill on the other side of the pass-through. Periodically he came out in his grease-stained apron to collect dirty dishes, his stringy, old-man muscles flexing on his forearms when he lifted the plastic tubs. The waitress covered the tables and counter and took care of the register.

Olivia touched Brian's hand. "Did you get through to your parents?"

"No." Brian looked troubled about it. "It rang but nobody answered."

"They're probably all right."

"Yeah." Brian picked up his coffee. "How about you?"

"How about me what?"

"Are you going to call Rohana?"

"Later I will."

She waited for it: Brian's push for her to do something she knew she was supposed to do but resisted doing anyway.

This time, the push didn't come, and Olivia felt obscurely disap-pointed. Maybe part of her wanted to be pushed.

"Here comes Prince Charming," Brian said.

Alvaro entered the diner like he already wished he was exiting it—looking around impatiently, rubbing his hands on his pants. He crossed to the booth and stood there. "We're wasting time."

"I got you pancakes," Dee said. "They don't have waffles. The thing's broken. The waffle-making thing."

Alvaro said, "You're all crazy," but he looked hungry and slid into the booth beside Dee.

"I need food," Olivia said. "Before I try again."

Brian picked up the carafe and tilted it toward Alvaro's empty cup. "Coffee?"

"Yes." Alvaro leaned over the table and said to Olivia, "I have the jai ba leaves. The wine was a mistake. Alcohol muddles your brain."

Olivia sipped her second cup of coffee. "It got me to the halo."

"And no doubt impaired your judgment."

She slurped down more coffee.

"I've been thinking," Brian said, and they all looked at him. "About what you guys are calling a probability machine." He adjusted his glasses. "That's right, isn't it—probability machine?"

Alvaro affected a bored look. "What could you possibly know about it?"

"Nothing. But that's mostly because I don't believe it exists. A mechanical thing that can change destiny or something? I don't think so. But when you think about the whole concept of probability machines, and if you grant that people are a kind of biological machine, then you could say we—all of us—are little probability machines that go around choosing different probabilities every day, if not every minute. All choices change the local reality, right?"

Olivia topped off her cup. "Brian has a minor in philosophy from a not very good school."

"It's a *great* school." Brian placed his hand briefly on her shoulder, letting her know he wasn't seriously disagreeing with her, or God help them, starting an argument. Sometimes Brian was *too* nice.

"Except maybe not the philosophy department," she said.

"The probability machine is real," Alvaro said. "I've seen it."

"You said that before." Olivia put down her cup. "I thought you had to be linked to see the halo."

Alvaro, who still looked road-haggard even after sleeping, picked up his coffee cup. "Jacob is old. When the time for the migration nears, the current Shepherd escorts the next in line to the place under the Old City. Only the Shepherd and his chosen successor go. That's why we were in Aleppo by ourselves. We got separated, and Jacob was captured. They must have tortured him to find out what he was doing in that place where they found him."

"What place was it?" Olivia asked.

Alvaro shook his head. "Only the Shepherd and his successor can know that."

"*I'm* a Shepherd. That's what Dee called me."

Alvaro seemed to think about it, then he shook his head again. "Not the same thing. Sorry."

"But you saw the probability machine," Brian said.

"Yes."

"Well, what did it look like, what was it made out of? Did it have an on-and-off switch?"

Alvaro said, "You can be a very irritating person."

"But it was an actual machine?"

"Machine is not the right word, but it's all we have."

"Why isn't it the right word?" Olivia asked.

"I can't tell you any more. *Won't* tell you any more. But it's real. As real as this table." He rapped his knuckles on the tabletop.

The waitress arrived with food. While Olivia ate her eggs and hash browns, she took out her IsnGlas tablet and connected to Wi-Fi. IsnGlas security software paid granular attention to the incoming datastorm. Keeping the tablet on private 2D resolution, she accessed her message accounts. Helen's last urgently flagged message sat there like a bright red crime-scene marker. Scores of unread messages populated her in-box. Many friends and colleagues were still in the heart of the Disaster, though it was becoming difficult to distinguish where the "heart" was located anymore. Almost lost in the avalanche of messages was a new one from Olivia's stepmother.

Dear Olivia,

(You see? I use your grown-up name, since you are so unhappy when I call you Little Oh.)

I am writing to let you know that I am still alive and all is well. Yes, I realize the world is falling apart. But the world is always falling apart.

This is not something you learn from books or from your personal experience of very bad places, but from time. The cycle of tragedy is always with us. Of course, you think you know all about this truth and that I cannot tell you anything you haven't already decided for yourself. Well, trust me when I tell you, Olivia, that the world will always go on even though we will not. And for now I am going on nicely myself. When these foolish travel bans are lifted, I hope you will come visit me. If you do, I will take you to my favorite market with your auntie who you never see.

Love,
Rohana

Olivia clicked her tongue. Old resentments needled her from the inside, as if a puffer fish lived in her chest just waiting for Rohana to irritate it into puffing up and jabbing Olivia's heart with its poisonous spines. Olivia didn't *want* to be irritated, but she couldn't help it. Which is what she always told herself. Her stepmother had a real knack for getting to her with the truth. *You see? I use your grown-up name, since you are so unhappy when I call you Little Oh.*

Unhappy? If a fucking puffer fish had a right to protect itself, why didn't Olivia? "Little Oh" is what Rohana started calling her when Olivia desperately needed her mother—her *real* mother—who would never come back.

Alongside her inbox, news-crawl hyperlinks invited Olivia to read about the unchecked spread of variola across the globe (except parts of central Russia, where it appeared to be very much under control), civil unrest in Europe and, increasingly, the United States. And the escalating nuclear tensions on the South Asian subcontinent.

Olivia picked up her IsnGlas and stood.

Alvaro looked alarmed. "Where are you going?"

"Getting the check. We're wasting time."

✺

BACK IN THEIR MOTEL ROOM, Alvaro produced a baggie, opened it, picked out a few brittle jai ba leaves, and dropped them into Olivia's palm. They looked like tea leaves, or the veined wings of minute fairies. "You remember what to do?"

"Grind them between my teeth for a while and spit them out."

"Yes."

She started to put the leaves in her mouth. Alvaro stopped her with a hand on her wrist. "Wait. Once you link to the probability machine, if you remain passive, you will find yourself confronted with the original crisis point."

"I know. I've already been there, remember?"

"This time you absolutely must surrender to Jacob's probability. You must choose it, no matter what your personal resistance might tell you to do. You understand? Choose it, or allow *him* to choose it. However it works. Since it's not the highest end-point probability, it will cause you discomfort, but not at the level you've been experiencing it in your other choices when you deviated more wildly. But don't turn away."

"Yeah, I got that." Olivia felt impatient to get started. As much as she feared the power inside the halo, she was more frightened by the consequences of allowing the present situation to stand. At the same time, she was irked with Alvaro. *He* had never linked to the machine, had never felt the awesome power and responsibility.

Olivia looked at the jai ba leaves. "Let's get it over with." She put the leaves in her mouth and started grinding them between her molars, releasing the dusty, bitter taste. She sat on the bed nearest the bathroom. There were too many people in the room. "I can't do this with everyone standing around staring at me."

"Are you sure you should be eating those things?" Brian looked worried.

"I'm not eating them. Don't worry, I've done this before."

Dee crooked her finger at Brian. "Come on. Let's get some more coffee."

Brian shook his head. "I'm not leaving her alone this time."

"I will be here," Alvaro said.

"I meant not leaving her alone *with you*."

Olivia lay back on the bed. The jai ba was starting to numb her tongue and lips. "It's okay, Bri. He won't hurt me."

"This is stupid."

"Bri," Olivia said, "just go. Please." She felt drifty. There was some more talk, but she didn't follow it. Distantly, she heard the door open and close. Alvaro pulled the chair over beside the bed. The lamp clicked off.

"That's enough," he said. "Spit them out."

She opened gummy eyelids. Alvaro was a shadow. He held his hand under her chin. She turned her head and spat out the jai ba leaves. A few flakes stuck to her tongue. She scraped them off with her fingernail. The room was dim, but inside, deep down a well of consciousness, a bright ring burned like holy fire.

Olivia plunged toward it.

❀

HER MIND CLEARED. SHE OCCUPIED the white-fire center of the ring. Around her, the world's billions swarmed like clouds of minute fireflies. Brian had suggested that humans were, every one of them, little biological probability machines. And now Olivia was about to bypass all their personal choices and make a huge one on their behalf.

Variola.

She found herself in the torture cell. Jacob lay bound to the table. Kerosene lanterns hissed. Three men stood over Jacob. The man with the trend-line scar bisecting his eyebrow said, *I won't allow this.* Jacob's eyes rolled up, already seeking a different probability. This was the moment. Allow Jacob's choice to prevail. It would be so easy. Just . . . let go. Let it happen. It wouldn't even be as though she were actively doing it . . .

And open your eyes in a world where Brian is dead. Where Jodee is dead.

There had to be another way. She *knew* there had to be. It wasn't wishful thinking, and she wasn't a monster willing to sacrifice millions for the lives of one or two individuals she happened to know and care about personally. It didn't make sense for the probability machine to exist if all it required of the human link was a default decision the machine had already determined. Shepherd Beekman had manipulated probabilities for profit, which precipitated a worldwide depression and the rise of fascism. Maybe it was a matter of degree and intention. Dee wanted to believe probability manipulation could deliver a better world, one that didn't require crisis intervention. Beekman and Andrew's faction wanted the machine to arrange a dragon's vault of treasure. All Olivia wanted to do was to tweak the original crisis solution.

She tried to turn aside, to go seeking her alternate path. A nearly irresistible force compelled her to remain focused on Jacob and the scarred man. Olivia strained and pulled until she broke free, back into the halo.

TWENTY-TWO

AROUND OLIVIA, THE HALO GLIMMERED, and her perspective shifted. Like grinding gears clutching into the wrong slot. Resistance. And pain. Her deliberate turning away from the torture cell, the crisis point that the machine wanted her to focus on, created tremendous tension. Just as it became harder and harder to concentrate, the view through the halo cleared.

A tan Jeep Cherokee rattled up to a checkpoint on the western edge of Aleppo. Not this again. What was she missing? The kid driving the Jeep looked anxious. Sweat glistened on his face. The Cherokee advanced. Whisper drones hovered in. Armed soldiers held their hands out in a STOP gesture. The kid applied the brakes and waited. Olivia focused briefly on the license plate number. Normally, she would have no trouble recalling the numbers. But would memorizing something in the halo work the same way?

The commander, a middle-aged man wearing a side-slanting beret and thick mustache, directed his soldiers to search the truck.

What, *what* was she missing? Maybe nothing. This might not be the place. Then why did the halo present it to her as an alternative to Jacob in the torture cell? This checkpoint and this Jeep *had* to be significant, had to be connected to the crisis end point.

She swooped in like an invisible drone, a video fly tiny enough to go anywhere, see anything. Olivia minutely examined the Jeep while the soldiers, more clumsily, did the same. They failed to find anything, and so did she.

The pain of being in the wrong place, of abandoning the torture cell crisis point, intensified. This was it, her second chance, and once again she was failing. She could make the kid hit the gas pedal again, and the soldiers would stop him, but she knew that wouldn't change anything.

The soldiers completed their search. The beret-wearing checkpoint commander approached the vehicle. The driver flexed his hands on the steering wheel. Sweat poured off him. Even in this little tableau there were a thousand choices any of these human probability machines could make. But which one should Olivia make? Power and pain rippled through her. Why had she thought she could do this? There was no alternative but to allow the gravitational force of attraction slingshot her back to the torture cell.

Except ... no.

If she couldn't figure out this checkpoint, if stopping the kid *here* didn't work, she could stop him before he ever arrived at the checkpoint. She had done it with the guy who shot Dee back at Sanctuary. She'd found a decision point in his recent past and tweaked it to make him leave his gun at home — unarming him before he had the chance to pull the trigger and send a bullet ripping into Dee's leg.

She could do the same with this kid.

Using the checkpoint as the landing spot, Olivia traced a single probability thread backward and found the boy arguing with a woman who could be his mother. The argument took place in a kitchen filled with hot sunlight. The mother stood with her arms crossed, her lips a stern line.

The boy spoke, a pleading look on his face.

His mother, if that's who she was, shook her head and replied.

A key lay on the table, where two plates and two glasses attested to a breakfast recently consumed. The mother unfolded her arms, eyed the key, rubbing her thumb over her fingertips, hesitating. The boy wanted the key, too. He started to reach for it.

Olivia *pushed*.

The mother snatched up the key and put it in her pocket — to the boy's apparent outrage.

And Olivia fell back into the ring of white light, too strained to follow the consequences of her simple move, knowing only that the boy would not drive the Jeep through a particular checkpoint at a particular hour, and that this could make a crucial difference. How, she had no idea, since the variola had not been hidden in the vehicle.

A siren reeled her out of the halo and into a world of pain. A blizzard of white stars swirled behind her eyelids. Olivia's head felt like a pain balloon, swelling and contracting. She rolled onto her side. "I feel sick." The jai ba leaves left a bitter aftertaste on her tongue. The stars faded, and she opened her eyes to slits. Except for the daylight seeping around the edge of the curtain, the room was dark—just as she remembered it being before linking to the probability machine. But something was very, very wrong. The tip of a cigarette glowed, revealing Alvaro's face. She had seen him smoking in the alley across from her hotel in Aleppo, but not since. That detail bothered her.

"Well?" he said.

Olivia sat up and put her feet on the floor. It was hardwood, not the high-traffic industrial carpet of the motel room. "Sick . . ."

Alvaro leaned against the wall, watching her. The smell of his cigarette smoke added to her nausea. She was grateful for the dark. It offered some slight relief from her post-halo migraine. But it was unnerving, too. The changes were all around her and she urgently needed to know what they were. And why didn't someone shut off that goddamn siren? "What's happening?"

"You tell me." He sounded different, his voice rougher, exhausted in a way it hadn't been before she closed her eyes and descended into the halo. As painful as it was bound to be, she needed to *see*. Olivia reached for the lamp, which was on the wrong side of the bed, and almost knocked it off the table. She fumbled for the switch and pushed it. Nothing happened.

"It doesn't work," Alvaro said. "You know it doesn't work. Wait—you don't know, do you? Goddamn it."

Of course she knew. The knowledge was right there, part of the new memory scaffold rising out of the murk. The shock wave from the nuke had knocked out half the grid on the Eastern Seaboard, causing cascading failures deep into the Midwest and, for all she knew, all the way to the West Coast. Major cellular networks had crashed. Phones and tablets scanned uselessly for signals.

She pushed herself off the bed and stumbled across the darkened room. It had become an obstacle course of shadowy furniture that hadn't been there before she altered the probability stream. A million changes, small and large, might have flowed forward from the Aleppo crisis point. She reached the window. It wasn't a curtain covering it but a heavy blanket nailed to the wall. She yanked it loose from the top corner, ripping it down so it hung like a flap of animal hide. Daylight flooded the room. She put her hand up, shading her eyes. Woods crowded the back of the cabin — the cabin on Rock River, still a couple of hours out from Elmhurst and Najid Javadi's bunker.

Olivia turned away from the window to face Alvaro and a room heavy on the knotty pine and faux frontier furniture. "What day is this, what time is it?"

He told her.

Fewer than fifteen minutes had passed. Of course. This wasn't time travel, no matter how disoriented she felt. With a terrible sinking of spirit, Olivia realized that in this probability she and Brian had not made it to the house in Elmhurst — which meant Brian was not vaccinated.

She held her throbbing head.

"You made it worse." Alvaro hadn't moved.

"No."

"Why bother to lie? It's obvious."

She pushed through a door into the bathroom, flipped up the toilet seat, and vomited into the bowl. Now her head felt like it was splitting open. Yes, she had made it worse. Instead of averting the catastrophe, her probability choice had accelerated it. Again. Preventing the boy from driving his Jeep through the checkpoint had accomplished nothing; worse than nothing. New memories rose and formed around the previous realities. Brian had been behind the wheel when NORAD alerts sprang urgently from their phones and flashed for attention. They had just passed Newville, Wisconsin.

Standing at the sink, her throat raw, she splashed cold water on her face. The mirror framed a haggard stranger. Sweaty strands of hair stuck to Olivia's forehead. There was something wrong with her right eye. She leaned closer. Blood suffused the sclera: the strain of a bad probability choice.

Outside, the siren continued to wail.

Olivia smelled cigarette smoke and turned away from the mirror. Alvaro stood in the doorway. "What's that siren?" she asked, drying her face on her sleeve.

Alvaro shrugged. "Everything's crazy out there. Some fool's probably winding up an ancient civil-defense siren."

Crazy out there. No shit. The pain made it difficult to think coherently. One memory scaffold tangled with another. But a single word stood out like a bright red emergency beacon: *Escalation*. On every news platform, in every conversation, the word had constantly come up. Escalation. The Pakistan-India-Russia triangle of denials, threats, and counterthreats. The United States pressuring Russia to help *de*escalate while at the same time demanding an explanation for the lower incidence of variola in the Russian Federation. Open hostility on the floor of the UN General Assembly. Accusations of Russian responsibility for creating the weaponized variola, if not actually releasing it. Counteraccusations from Russian surrogates, no doubt desperate for the vaccine everyone assumed Russia possessed.

Escalation.

Until . . . North Korea's addled dictator, Kim Jong-un, seized the opportunity of international chaos and threw a sucker punch. Three Hwasong-16 intercontinental ballistic missiles carrying thermonuclear payloads aimed at targets in the midwestern and eastern United States. Brian, gripping the steering wheel as if it were the last thing preventing the Disaster from overwhelming all of them, said, *What do we do?* Get off the highway, Olivia had said. It was all she could think of. If one of those missiles hit Chicago . . .

Brian had swerved toward an exit ramp too close to make at the speed they were traveling and almost rolled the car. Olivia kept saying, "Take it easy. Brian, slow down." They accelerated over a county road. Suddenly Brian took a hard corner and the Ford slewed onto a rutted private road that wound and plunged steeply through silver aspen toward a river.

"Brian, *stop!*"

He stood on the brake, the Ford skidding into the brush. For a minute, he sat there holding on to the steering wheel with white-knuckled fists, breathing hard, as if he'd been running, not driving.

"Are you okay?" Olivia said.

Brian nodded. He looked scared and tried to smile through it. "I'm good." He opened his hands and flexed his fingers. "Sorry, I kind of panicked."

A late-model SUV came up the road and passed them, wing mirrors almost kissing. A man and a woman sat in the front seat, the man scowling intently behind the wheel. Three kids occupied the seat behind them. An unhappy-looking girl of twelve or so, with a blond ponytail, stared out the window as they passed.

"Let's find a place to turn around," Olivia said.

Brian pulled forward, followed the road. Soon it split three ways. Quaint wooden signs stood next to each of the three splits: *Cabin 1, Cabin 2,* and *Cabin 3.* The Cabin 1 sign was knocked cockeyed, a fresh gouge taken out of it. There was enough room for a turn, and Brian started to do that.

Olivia said, "Wait. We better stay off the road for now. Let's take a look at Cabin One."

The gravel parking area in front of the cabin was empty. They sat in the car watching news reports. One of North Korea's missiles malfunctioned and broke apart over the North Pacific without detonating. NORAD defense systems tracked the remaining two and managed to intercept one.

But the third got through.

It landed short of its intended target, sparing Washington, DC. The warhead exploded over West Virginia, vaporizing its capital, Charleston. The firestorm also swept scores of small towns out of existence and left the George Washington and Jefferson National Forest seething in a radioactive conflagration. Now everybody was waiting to see if China would back Kim Jong-un's play. That was the news. And then the grid went down.

They had sat in Brian's car, stunned, speechless, frightened. Finally Olivia turned to Brian and said, "I have to fix this." The cabin was locked and unoccupied, but they found an open window. Unwashed dishes were piled in the sink; empty wine bottles and soda cans sat on the counters. On the dining table was a folder containing a copy of somebody's rental agreement. New people were due in a couple of days, but it was unlikely anyone was thinking of a relaxing weekend on the river. "I need something," Olivia had said. "Pot or alcohol."

Brian had looked at her as if she'd lost her mind. "You want to get high?" he said, his words a spot-on echo from the previous probability. For Olivia it was like watching a memory externalized and seeing how she had gotten it wrong.

"No. I have to go back into the halo, and I need something to replace the jai ba leaves they gave me after we escaped from Sanctuary."

They had barely started hunting through the cabinets when the sound of a fossil-burner became audible, and then tires crunched the gravel out front. Olivia and Brian had looked at each other and gone to the window in time to see Alvaro's ramshackle pickup truck come to a stop.

Now Alvaro stood in the bathroom doorway, his cigarette burning between the middle fingers of his right hand. "What was it this time, before you linked?"

She groaned. The new memory scaffold stood before her. Olivia's knees unhinged and she crumpled to the floor. Stricken, she drew her legs up, her body trembling.

"Had there even been a missile attack?"

She started to shake her head, but it hurt too much. "Not when I went into the halo from the motel."

"What motel?"

"Near Chicago. You were there. I chewed the leaves, the whole thing. But when I came up, we were here. My memory is getting confused. The headache . . ."

"You're making too many choices at the same crisis point. The pain is like a fail-safe mechanism. You have to stay directly on the crisis point, not deviate. The farther you move off point, the bigger the strain on you."

Olivia tried to pull herself together. She pushed herself to a sitting position and leaned against the wall. "Leave me alone."

Outside, at last, the siren stopped.

"You really fucked it up," Alvaro said.

She hated him for saying it, but his words hurt because they were true: She really *had* fucked it up. Again.

Olivia struggled to get back on her feet. Alvaro flicked his cigarette into the toilet and helped her. He wasn't rough about it. She glanced into his eyes and thought she saw a dim reflection of empathy.

"I'll fix it," she said.

"That's what I keep hoping. But you can't do anything for at least a day—longer, to be safe. You're putting a huge strain on yourself. We'll wait here as long as we can, then you can try again."

"No." Empathy for her pain or not, Olivia didn't trust Alvaro not to force the link to migrate. And could she blame him? Things were getting desperate, and she'd willfully failed twice already. She had brought them all to the brink.

"Why not?" Alvaro said.

"I know where there's a vaccine, effective vaccine."

Alvaro's eyes said it all: bullshit. Olivia had seen that look before, in the previous reality.

"It's true," she said. "There's a house in Elmhurst, outside of Chicago. That's where we were headed. In the last probability stream we made it and got the vaccine." She explained how she knew about Javadi, annoyed at being forced to convince the same man twice, in two probabilities.

"Nobody needs vaccine once you pick the right probability."

"Unless that's impossible now."

Alvaro went quiet.

"You said it yourself," Olivia continued. "Overlapping all these crisis-point choices is hurting me. What if they're hurting the link, too? What if I can't make another choice? What if no one can? Variola's everywhere. We need Javadi's vaccine."

"The link won't be damaged." He scratched his stubbled cheek. "But *you* might be."

The outside door opened. More than one person entered the cabin. Brian's voice came from the other room. "Liv?"

"In here."

Brian appeared, followed by Dee. All of them now crowded into the bedroom. Alvaro let go of Olivia's arm, and Brian held his open. "You look like shit." Olivia let him pull her in, where it was impossible to escape her traitor's thoughts. *I'll fix it.* This time she understood she had no choice. And "fixing it" translated to "goodbye Brian." A horrible memory had pursued her across all the probabilities since the first one: Brian's lips, cold and rubbery against hers.

Dee looked confused, then scared. "You did it, you linked?"

Alvaro said, "She tried to save Brian again."

Olivia, her face buried in Brian's shoulder, got angry. She pulled away from Brian and faced Alvaro. "I didn't *ask* for any of this."

It sounded childish even to her. Did anyone ever ask for any of the bad stuff that happened to them? The hard look was back in Alvaro's eyes. Was he weighing his options, calculating the risk of forcing the link to migrate to him? The moment passed.

"Let's go," Alvaro said.

Dee said, "Go where?"

"Olivia says there's vaccine in a place near Chicago."

Dee looked doubtful.

"It's true," Brian said. "This guy Javadi lives in Elmhurst."

"That's right," Olivia said. "He's in a bomb shelter that nobody knows about. At least I don't think they do."

Brian gave her a weird look. In this probability stream they hadn't yet been to the Elmhurst house. "How do you know that?"

"Take your shirt off," Olivia said.

"What? What for?"

"Just take it off."

Brian unbuttoned his shirt and pulled it off. Olivia stretched the short sleeve of his T-shirt over his shoulder. The Band-Aid was gone, his skin smooth, no sign of needle pokes. Now they were all looking at Olivia. She said, "I know because I've already been there. Both of us have been. But all that's erased now."

And she prayed Javadi was still in the shelter with his hoard of vaccine. The stream changed only from the point of probability choice forward. There was a chance.

If they could get to him before anything else happened.

✳

THEY LEFT THE PICKUP BEHIND and all piled into Brian's hybrid. Traffic on the 90 was heavy in both directions. After an hour they pulled off at Rockford to look for gas. There might be a run on it later, and if the power stayed down, the charging stations for the Ford's powerful batts would be useless. They quickly found a BP station on the rundown east side of town. The line stretched out of the station and down the street. They waited. When it was their turn, Brian handled the pump and Olivia stood on the other side of the car, looking at the sky. Her headache was bad but not debilitating. It was midmorning, the overcast feathery gray, like ash. The light was strange, or did she only imagine it was? Five hundred miles southeast, the country burned.

"Liv?" Brian said over the top of the car. "Liv, come on. Get in."

She lowered herself into the front passenger seat, her post-halo migraine like a vise squeezing her head. Dee and Alvaro sat in the back. Brian pushed the start button and the electric assist rippled up. The main road was clogged with cars. He pulled into the alley behind the gas station, wove through back streets, braking hard, making sharp, sudden turns, hunting a clear path to the interstate.

Broken glass glittered dully on the sidewalk in front of an electronics store, the iron security gate pulled out of the window frame like the rib bones of a mammoth, one end of a heavy chain still attached to the gate, and the other end to a trailer hitch bolted to the back of a beat-to-shit Escalade. Brian slowed down. A guy hunkering by the bumper, working on detaching the chain, raised his head.

"What the hell is happening?" Brian said. "Where are the fucking police?"

"Keep going," Dee said.

The chain guy stood and pulled his shirt up, revealing a handgun tucked in the waist of his jeans.

Dee slapped the driver's seat headrest. "*Punch* it, man."

Brian crushed the accelerator.

Ninety minutes later, they finally rolled onto East Sherman Avenue in suburban Elmhurst.

Four men stood in front of Javadi's house. They all turned toward the approaching car.

TWENTY-THREE

"IT'S THE NIGHT WATCHMAN," BRIAN said.

"In the middle of the morning?" Dee said.

Olivia rubbed her temples. "Neighborhood watch captain."

Alvaro leaned between the front seats. "We don't care about these guys. Where's the bomb shelter?"

"The guys we don't care about are standing in front of Javadi's house," Olivia said.

"Keep going. We'll circle back when the street clears."

"And what if the street doesn't clear?" Olivia said. "How long do we wait? Every minute in the open we're vulnerable to variola, or the next attack. Brian, pull up to them."

Alvaro poked Brian's shoulder. "Don't do that."

"Sorry." Brian rolled up to the men and stopped.

Olivia rolled down her window.

"What do you want?" The watch captain studied her.

"What's going on?" One of the other men stepped up to the car. He was stockier than the watch captain and losing his hair. He clutched a hammer in his right hand. The hammer bothered Olivia. Hammers made good weapons if you wanted to inflict some serious blunt-force trauma. When Olivia told a cop friend of hers that she didn't like guns, the cop suggested she keep a hammer beside her bed to discourage intruders with assault on their mind. The next day, she bought one at Ace Hardware, weighing it in her hand like a warrior choosing a weapon for close combat. She picked a twenty-four-ounce framing hammer. Too heavy to take overseas into the Disaster, but at home she kept it beside the bed. She used to wonder whether she would have the will to swing it into the head of a would-be rapist. No, that wasn't true. She knew she possessed the will. What she wondered was how it would sound and feel when the steel head punched through the bastard's skull, and how hard it would be to forget that sound.

"Roy, come on," the balding guy said. His hammer didn't look as hefty as Olivia's, probably only a sixteen-ouncer. "What are we waiting for? Who are these people?"

"I don't know. I don't know who they are." Roy did not take his eyes off Olivia. Was there a glimmer of recognition? Could memory artifacts slip across narrow probability changes and create something like a déjà vu effect?

"Who are you?" Roy said.

"Friends of the people who own this house. We left some stuff in storage. All we want to do is get it and leave."

The watch captain — Roy — wasn't buying it. "Friends of the owners. And who might they be?"

Olivia had no idea. Helen hadn't told her that.

"So I guess we're back to our original question," Roy said.

The other men, the ones who hadn't approached the car, looked nervously at each other. Two guys in typical suburban Levi's and short-sleeved button shirts. Neither of them had brought their tools, no rip-saws or rattail files or anything.

The guy with the hammer said, "Let's quit wasting time."

"They know about the shelter," Roy said.

"What? They do?"

"Oh, I'm pretty sure they do. That's why they're really here. But what they don't understand is that the shelter belongs to us. This is *our* neighborhood. We watched the Stevensons build the thing. You understand what I'm saying to you, lady?"

"Whatever," Olivia said. "I don't know what you're talking about."

Roy grabbed the hammer out of the other guy's hand and swung it into the hybrid's windshield. Olivia jumped and let out a yelp of surprise. The impact made a popping-crunch sound. The hammer's steel head punched through the safety glass. A spiderweb crackled around it. Roy pulled the hammer free. Before he could swing it again, if that's what he intended, Brian stepped on the accelerator and smoked down the street. "Holy shit. Are you all right, Liv? Holy shit." He tucked into the curb a few blocks from Javadi's house and turned to put his arms around Olivia.

She held him off. "Bri, give me a little space."

He backed up, then looked out the driver's window, like there was something super-interesting on the sidewalk—but not before she saw the hurt in his eyes. It was going to hurt a lot more to die in the torture cell in Aleppo. Any way you cut it, Olivia was responsible for Brian not making it. How could she let *him* comfort *her*?

Alvaro said, "This is the end of human civilization."

Brian turned back to Olivia. "And I thought *you* were gloomy. There's duct tape in the glove box."

Olivia squinted at him. "What?"

"Duct tape. For the hole that guy put in my windshield."

Somehow he had vanquished all traces of hurt feelings. He was so good at that. Was it an admirable trait or a deceptive one? Probably it depended on who was hiding which feelings from whom and for what reason. By now, Olivia should have been the world's leading expert on hiding feelings. Sometimes she wondered if she was hiding them or if she simply didn't have any. No, she had them all right. They were like a wound that you could ignore unless you touched it. Olivia had bumped her wound against Brian and was astonished when, instead of hurting, some kind of healing had begun. Now it hurt all over again, and worse than ever. Sooner or later, caring meant hurting. How had she forgotten that?

She managed a weak smile. "Ah. You came prepared for the apocalypse." She retrieved the duct tape, tore off a couple of strips, and covered Roy's handiwork with a big X.

"What do we do now?" Dee asked.

"Those guys back there," Olivia said, "I didn't count on them knowing about the bomb shelter. I should have. It was a dumb mistake. Anyway, they won't be able to break into it. It's like a bank vault. And Javadi isn't going to open the door for them, either. Assuming he's even in there during this probability."

From the back seat Alvaro said, "We have to try for the ranch. I can keep you alive there until you link again."

"Or you could kill me and see if the link migrates."

"Liv!" Brian looked appalled and at the same time like he was ready to fight whoever needed fighting.

Alvaro said, "I'm not a murderer."

"How the hell am I supposed to know what you are? Just a sec."

Olivia opened her door and puked on the street. "God, my head. It's worse than the other times." She slammed the door. "I'm not going back to Sanctuary."

"That's right," Brian said. "No way."

"You only saw part of Sanctuary," Dee said. "The part that was above-ground."

Alvaro said, "The ranch was designed to function even when the rest of the world is going to hell. There are underground shelters, well provi-sioned and capable of withstanding almost anything. If there's one place where anyone could survive, it's there. Except for whatever doomsday options the government has, I mean. But no one will survive for long. No bomb shelter will protect us if the Aleppo crisis point isn't repaired."

"You don't know that for certain," Olivia said.

The car got very quiet. Olivia could still taste the vomit. And the jai ba leaves. Then everyone started talking at once. Dee stuck two fingers in her mouth and cut loose with a game-stopping whistle. Olivia winced, holding her head. The whistle was like a hot needle shoved into the mid-dle of her migraine.

But everyone stopped arguing.

"We have to protect you," Dee said, "until you can link to the prob-ability machine again."

"That's great. Could you protect me a little more quietly?"

Alvaro said, "We're back where we started."

Olivia hiked herself around on her seat to look back at him. "No. We still might be able to get into Javadi's shelter, or at least get the vaccine. We talked to him before, in the other probability. He only gave us one dose, because he was saving the rest for his own people."

"So?" Alvaro fidgeted.

Olivia had known plenty of guys like Alvaro. Always impatient, always wanting to *do* something instead of thinking it through first. That wasn't necessarily a bad way to be. But in the Disaster it could easily get you killed. And now the whole world was the Disaster.

"His people," Olivia said, "were in West Virginia."

For a minute, no one spoke. Then Alvaro said, "So they must be dead."

"I don't know about 'must be,' but it's probably a fair assumption, es-pecially if they were on the road when the nuke hit. That guy's down in his hole all by himself and the world is falling to pieces on top of him."

Alvaro sat forward again. "So you think he *will* let us in?"

"He might. There's at least a chance. His complete isolation might make him change his mind. We should at least try before we drive all the way to Idaho."

Dee said, "Alvaro? It does make sense."

"I guess it does. But what about the neighbors?"

"They'll give up soon enough," Olivia said. "Javadi won't let them in, and they aren't going to break in with a hammer."

Brian faced forward again and started the engine. "Let's get supplies, in case this doesn't work and we have to cross the country. That should give those assholes time to give up on breaking into the shelter."

The parking lot of the Elmhurst Whole Foods was full. Brian double-parked and started to climb out. "Come on, Liv."

Olivia, head still throbbing, opened her door.

"No," Alvaro said. "You don't leave my sight."

"If he goes in there by himself, he'll come back with potato chips and tonic water."

"I'll go with him," Dee said.

Brian shook his head. "Nope. I'm not leaving Liv alone with him again. Sorry."

"For God's sake," Alvaro said. "We'll all go."

Olivia threw open her door and started walking toward the store. Car doors opened and slammed behind her, footsteps ran to catch up. Brian touched her shoulder to let her know he was there, and the other two fell into step.

"And now we are four," Olivia said. Marching into a crowded store. Why don't we just beg for variola to find us?

They prowled the aisles of Whole Foods, which weren't as depleted as the Safeway's were back in Seattle. Maybe Midwesterners were made of sterner stuff and didn't panic as easily. With the grid down, generators powered the cold cases and about half the lights. The store was shadowy but bustling, and almost everyone wore a filter mask. Large handwritten signs warned: CASH ONLY. No credit or debit purchases could be processed. Brian metaphorically raised his half-full glass to the cheese display. "This isn't so bad."

They walked toward the back of the store. A middle-aged woman with a small child, a boy about five years old, stood in front of the frozen dessert cabinet. The boy wore a filter mask but the woman didn't. The boy's mask had big Chicklet teeth drawn on it with thick black marker.

The mother stood there crying without making a sound. The boy stared at her, his eyes big and expressive over the cartoon teeth. Brian approached the woman. "Are you all right?"

She gave him a stricken look that hurt Olivia's heart. "There's a cloud," the woman said. "A radioactive cloud. I heard it on my wind-up radio. Do you think that's true?"

Brian looked at a loss. "I don't know."

In a low, urgent voice, Alvaro said, "We need to speed this up."

Olivia tapped Brian's arm. "Bri, come on."

At the checkout people were talking.

I heard North Korea is gone. We just fucking unloaded on them.

It was the Russians. A sneak attack.

Are we at war with Russia? Who are we at war with?

The smallpox is worse. I heard a hundred million dead and no way to stop it.

Variola, the whole thing's a government hoax. Keep the masses scared and begging for Big Daddy to keep them safe. We might as well kiss all our civil liberties goodbye. Anybody who didn't see this coming is an idiot.

This last from a guy in hunter's camo and a holstered sidearm riding his hip.

DOZENS OF PEOPLE STOOD ON lawns across the street from Javadi's house. The oak trees on East Sherman Avenue looked tired in the August heat. Brian parked around the corner, out of sight. "Do you think that woman was right about the radioactive cloud?"

"Don't worry about radiation," Alvaro said. "That takes time. Variola is a bigger danger."

Olivia opened her door. "Let's go."

Everybody piled out of the Ford. They walked one block over, intending to approach the house from the back. Olivia wanted to avoid another confrontation with the neighborhood watch.

Brian kept looking at the overcast sky.

"Brian?" Olivia said.

"The sky looks weird."

Did it? A low, purple overcast. Nothing special about it. But she felt the weirdness, too. On 9/11 people talked about the stillness of the sky after all air traffic had been grounded. But it had been more than an absence of airplanes. It was the stillness of something broken, broken so badly that though it might eventually be fixed, it would never be wholly right again. The stillness of this sky felt like that. Maybe their minds added the extra element of sorrow, but that didn't make it any less real. The purple overcast pulled across the sky like a shroud. The world was broken, and Olivia had broken it.

"Here?" Dee said.

"Yes."

They stood before a ranch house with an ornamental maple planted in the sloping front lawn, a birdhouse hanging from one of the branches. They would have to slip behind the ranch house and climb the common fence dividing the two backyards. Olivia rubbed her forehead, tried to organize her thoughts. It would be better if she did it alone. She was the one who had to talk to Javadi. And it would be less conspicuous if she trespassed by herself.

"Hey," Dee said, "there's somebody in the window looking at us."

"There is?"

The sky was reflected in the ranch house's big picture window. You had to gaze past the reflection to see the figure of a man.

"What do we do?" Brian asked. "This isn't—"

An explosion behind the ranch house sent debris flying into the air, the concussive force shattering the picture window out of its frame. Olivia instinctively crouched and ducked her head, her ears ringing. Her first thought was: IED. She'd heard dozens of roadside bombs in the Disaster. Her body reacted with a chemical dump: fight or flight. Her heart raced. Debris rained from the sky. A jagged board, barn red, clattered to the street behind them, and a dirty gray-and-black cloud drifted over the roofline of the ranch house.

Brian picked up the hunk of charred red-painted wood. "Jesus Christ."

"They're trying to blow their way into the bomb shelter," Olivia said.

TWENTY-FOUR

THE DOOR OF THE RANCH house burst open. A heavyset man wearing a white T-shirt and holding a hunting rifle came out. His head was bleeding. "What are you doing here?" he yelled.

"Whoa." Brian held his open hands up. "Take it easy."

The heavyset man aimed his hunting rifle at them. "We're not children!" he yelled. "You can't just come here."

A woman in a green housedress appeared on the porch behind the man. She held a butcher knife in her fist.

"Maybe they're nobody," the woman said.

Could Olivia be hearing this correctly? She cupped her hands over her ears and opened her mouth wide, trying to made the ringing stop.

"Get out of here," the man with the rifle said. "Get out of here *now*."

He pointed the rifle in the air and pulled the trigger.

The four of them took off running. Crossing East Sherman Avenue, Olivia looked toward the Javadi house. People filled the street. The explosion had blown out windows up and down the block. Glass glinted like ice crystals in suburban lawns.

"Do you think they breached the shelter?" Dee asked.

"I doubt it. And they're going to be pissed. We need to beat it out of here."

Back at the Ford hybrid, Brian got behind the wheel and Olivia started to get in the front passenger seat.

Alvaro said, "I want the front. I get motion sickness riding in the back seat too long. I need to look out the windshield." His eyes met hers briefly and looked away, embarrassed.

"Go ahead," Olivia said.

Once they were all in the car, Brian said, "Where to?"

Sounding exasperated, Alvaro said, "Sanctuary. We already talked about it."

Brian looked over his shoulder. "Liv?"

"Get on the 90 and go back the way we came. Between here and there, we can figure out if we really want to try the ranch. Meanwhile, we're headed in the right direction—away from the blast zone and any radiation. We'll stay on the road, avoid populated areas where it's more likely we'll run into variola, or the National Guard. Just like we did on the way here."

Alvaro said, "As soon as you can access the probability machine, you have to do it, even if we're still on the road."

"How do I know if I can do it, without actually doing it?"

"When all the pain is gone from the last time. Just tell me. I have the jai ba." He held up the baggie of dried leaves and shook it.

"All right."

"Good." Alvaro tossed the baggie on the dash.

Dee, who was looking out the back window, said, "Guys. The welcoming committee is coming this way."

Everyone turned. Half a dozen men, some of them armed, marched toward the car.

"Go already," Dee said.

Brian thumbed the start button, the engine powered up, and they accelerated away. The men stopped in the middle of the street. One man pointed a rifle at them but didn't fire. A few minutes later, Brian found the interstate ramp and they were on their way west.

✺

A COUPLE OF HOURS OUT of Chicagoland, the Ford's satellite radio came back online. Terrifying news, like toxic gas, filled the car. Variola burned out of control through populations on five continents. The CDC denied rumors that an effective vaccine had been produced and was being kept from the public while it crawled through endless safety protocols.

"The rumors are unequivocally false," a spokesperson said.

"Is it possible the CDC doesn't know about Javadi's vaccine?" Brian asked.

"I doubt it." But a darker possibility occurred to Olivia. What if they *did* know about the vaccine and had determined it too dangerous or ineffective? Olivia knew nothing about Javadi except that he had been Helen's friend. What if he was mistaken about the efficacy of his own vaccine? Not that it mattered; she still had to choose Jacob's probability. The one that kills Brian. Olivia felt heavy enough to sink right through the car seat.

"The whole thing's insane," Brian said.

In other news: North Korea still existed, despite tremendous pressure to pound it into atomic dust. But the prospect of unleashing hydrogen bombs on the Korean Peninsula made Japan very unhappy—not to mention South Korea, China, and Russia. China, the big dog, claimed the nuclear strike against the United States had been carried out by a "rogue general" in North Korea, not the official government. And there was some US intel to support the claim. Meanwhile, the rogue general had already been neutralized by agents of the Chinese. So problem solved. Except for the millions killed in West Virginia.

Americans wanted—no, demanded—a counterstrike. South Korea and Japan begged for restraint. The situation was no more stable on the Indian subcontinent, where the rattle of nuclear sabers between Pakistan and India had grown deafening.

In one short week the world had become a vast room filled with explosive fumes just waiting for someone to strike a match. Or, rather, *another* match.

"For God's sake, turn it off," Alvaro said.

Brian reached for the button.

"Not off," Dee said. "Music. Something, anything that isn't terrible."

"Yes." After an hour of news, even Olivia had had enough. At least for now.

Brian discovered a jazz station and locked it in. The road noise and the music made it possible to have a semiprivate conversation in the back seat. Olivia's head still hurt, but the post-halo migraine had backed off considerably. Which meant it was time to obsess about what was coming and what she was going to have to do. She almost wished the pain hadn't backed off. She almost wished it never would. In the front seat Alvaro started snoring.

"Dee? Tell me about Sanctuary, about the underground shelters. Is it really the way Alvaro says?"

"Yes."

"Do you believe it would be safe for us to go back there?"

"Safe? Hell no. Andrew and his people would sacrifice you immediately and make sure the link migrated to Emilio. Me and Alvaro couldn't stop it, even with Jacob on our side. And Jacob disappeared before Andrew announced the ceremony of transference. Alvaro doesn't want to believe it, but I think Andrew had Jacob killed. Or, best case, locked up."

"Then I don't understand. Why do you two want to go there?"

"There are five separate underground shelters at the ranch, all but one interconnected by tunnels. The one not connected is actually outside the gate, in the woods. We call it the foxhole, and it's there in case someone is caught in the open without time to code their way through the gate and get underground. The foxhole's intended for security people, mostly. We're the only ones likely to be outside the fence when a disaster big enough to need a bomb shelter is coming. Anyway, the thing is fortified and autonomous. I think I could get us in there and lock it down. You'd be safe from bombs, radiation, Andrew's faction, and anyone else. At least for a while. Long enough for you to recover and select the right probability choice. But if you do it while we're still on the road, it doesn't matter. How's your head?"

"Not good." Olivia hoped she sounded worse than she felt. She didn't want to be forced into linking to the probability machine any sooner than she had to.

"It'll get better," Dee said.

"Yeah."

Dee opened a bag of pretzels and watched the scenery go by. Olivia turned to her own window but looked inward, deep down, where she saw it—yes, the cornered, waiting memory of a very bad day in Aleppo.

IN THE MIDDLE OF THE night, in the middle of South Dakota, Alvaro, who was driving now, said, "We have to stop. Get fuel and charge the batteries."

Olivia heard the words through a veil of exhaustion. She had been dozing, half dreaming, half remembering her father. Her mother had long ago stopped making appearances in her dreams, at least the dreams she remembered. But her father and her stepmother still turned up. In the dreams with Rohana, Olivia was never unhappy. It was as if a deeper part of her mind understood something that was beyond her conscious grasp. Either that, or dreams were just weird.

She blinked, rubbed her eyes, still in the grip of complicated feelings of loss and regret. It was too dark to see much of anything beyond the edge of the road. The car slid onto an exit ramp, swung around, and a truck stop came into view. An oasis of light stranded in the prairie. There were a couple of semis and a few civilian vehicles parked around the diner/office/store.

"Too many people," Olivia said.

"No choice."

Alvaro brought them alongside a fuel pump. A hand-printed sign attached to the pump announced cash-only transactions. So way out here, too, the credit processing infrastructure was compromised, though they had electricity. The battery-charging station stood separate.

Brian unbuckled. "I'll go in and pay."

"Charging station, too," Alvaro said.

Olivia didn't like it. "Wear this." She found a filter mask and passed it to him.

Brian pulled the mask over his mouth and nose. "Don't look at me that way. I'll be right back."

"Just hurry."

They should have *no* contact with the potentially infected. But who was she kidding? Weaponized variola was airborne. She watched Brian cross the tarmac and enter the building. A beefy man in a yellow-and-black plaid shirt with the sleeves rolled above his elbows moved behind the counter. The man wore a shoulder rig, the handle of a big-ass gun sticking out from under his arm. Brian talked to him and slipped his wallet out of his hip pocket. After a minute, Brian turned and gave a thumbs-up, and Alvaro unhooked the pump nozzle, inserted it in the Ford's fuel port, and started filling the tank. Olivia kept her eyes on Brian. Instead of coming back immediately, he wandered out of sight.

"What's he doing?"

Dee said, "He's fine."

Nowhere in this picture was anything fine.

"Come on," Dee said, "let's stretch our legs."

They got out of the car. It was a warm night, quiet and windless. Maybe she was overreacting. The feeling was the same as what she experienced whenever she entered the Disaster. A sense of hyperalertness, the strain of nerves constantly on edge. Ceaseless fear. Now the Disaster was everywhere. And Brian, a human probability machine, had chosen to follow a dangerous thread into the unknown superpositional probabilities of this truck stop.

Finally Brian emerged and walked toward them. Something about his body language, the way he looked back at the diner, signaled something was wrong. Olivia's chest felt tight. Halfway across the tarmac, Brian stopped. As if someone had called to him, his chin came up.

"Bri?" She stepped toward him, and, shockingly, he stepped back. "What are you doing, what's wrong?"

Before he could answer, far to the east a brilliant white light silently detonated. Like a mini-sun hiding below the horizon. For one fleeting moment, the prairie became visible, shadows stuttering forth. Olivia blinked, and the world beyond the truck stop went black again.

"Oh—" Dee sounded like someone had slugged her.

With trembling fingers, Olivia touched her lips. Brian pulled his filter mask down. He looked as frightened as she had ever seen him, more frightened even than he had been after getting shot in front of the madrassa in Aleppo.

"Was that—?" Brian asked.

Olivia held her hand up. "Wait."

Deep rumbling thunder rolled out of the prairie. A tectonically *big* sound. The sound of giant stone wheels grinding out the last hours of humanity. Almost imperceptibly, the tarmac shuddered. A push broom leaning against the wall next to the truck stop's door fell over with a clatter.

Alvaro started shouting: "Get back in the car, everybody get back in the car now!"

The man in the plaid shirt blundered out of the office, his holstered handgun swinging under his armpit.

"What happened? What's going on?"

He sounded angry, but it was fear. Olivia had seen it countless times, experienced it in herself—waiting for the crack of a sniper's rifle, or huddled in a bombed-out building with a ragged assortment of rebel fighters while Russian planes dropped heavy ordnance indiscriminately all around them, killing children and every other living thing. Wanting to scream at the pilots. Wanting to *kill* them. So angry.

So terrified.

The truck stop guy's hand kept straying to the grip of his revolver. A big, long-barreled weapon. A *Dirty Harry* gun. Plenty of stopping power, but not enough to stop what was now unleashed. He looked directly, pleadingly, at Olivia. Despite his stubbled jowls and drinker's nose, fear had erased the adult and left a confused and frightened boy.

"It's coming" is all Olivia said.

An unsatisfactory response. The man licked his lips, looked around helplessly.

"Will you two get in the fucking car," Alvaro said.

Brian took another step back, a look on his face that made Olivia feel queasier than she already felt.

"Bri, come on."

He just stood there.

"*Brian.*"

"That truck stop," Brian said, "it was full of sick people."

"What?"

"After I gave that guy a couple of twenties for the fill-up and charge, I wandered into the diner to look for coffee. There were people slumped in the booths. They had serious lesions, and there was a god-awful smell."

"We have to get moving now."

"I was *exposed*. That place must have been thick with variola. I can't get back in the car with you guys."

"Bri, if it was in the diner, it's probably all over, including the air we're breathing right now."

He didn't say anything.

"You can't stay here," Olivia said.

"Does it really matter?"

She grabbed his arm and pulled him toward the car. "It *matters.*"

TWENTY-FIVE

ALVARO RACED PAST THE BATTERY-CHARGING station and back onto I-90 and headed west. In the back seat, Olivia fumbled with her lap belt. Dee knelt on the seat, facing the rear window. Olivia craned her head around. The truck stop rapidly receded, an island of light in a black sea.

"Goddamn it," Dee said. "Where do you think it came down?"

"Pretty far away," Olivia said.

"It's really happening." Dee sounded stunned.

The car strayed onto the shoulder. Gravel pinged the undercarriage, and Alvaro swerved them back onto the road.

Olivia nudged Dee. "Better put your seat belt on."

Dee sat down and buckled up.

Brian was quiet, staring out the windshield. To save them, he would have stayed behind at the truck stop, waiting for whatever hell got served up next. Would Olivia have been willing to do the same? He was tougher than she'd given him credit for back in Syria. A full-fledged member of the hard-nosed fraternity.

Olivia wanted to touch him. Comfort him in his obvious distress, using the tools he had taught her, simple human empathy and touch. But she couldn't make herself reach out, not when she knew what she would soon have to do. How do you reset a relationship to "safe-distance" mode? She needed the distance, so when she killed him it wouldn't hurt as much as she knew it was going to.

"I shouldn't have gotten in the car," Brian said.

"It doesn't matter," Alvaro said. "It's begun. The end. No one will survive. Hydrogen bombs or smallpox, take your pick. Even if you're a carrier, none of us will get sick immediately. We have another day or two. I

doubt we ever had more than a few days left, anyway. It's all up to *you*."
In the rearview mirror, he stared hard at Olivia, taking his eyes off the
road for an uncomfortably long time. "Link to the machine, fix this, and
all of us can go on."

Not all *of us*. Olivia sat back and looked out the passenger window,
through her own reflection and into the black. She felt sleepy, and her
thoughts drifted across the seemingly unbridgeable gulf. She was fourteen. Her mother had been dead for three years, but grief always circled
beneath the surface, a hungry shark waiting for her to drop her guard
and trail a hand or foot in the water. Her dad had just married Rohana,
and Olivia felt betrayed by both of them—betrayed and isolated.

On her way home from school one day, Olivia had a loud, hurtful
argument with her boyfriend, who had told her she was too "touchy,"
whatever that meant. When Olivia banged through the kitchen door,
Rohana had said, *You're late*. It wasn't a scolding remark but simply an
observation, delivered in Rohana's bluntly declarative tone. But that's
all it took. Rohana was cooking, and the house smelled of curry. The
house always smelled of curry. Why did she have to turn the house into
a Mumbai café with weird spices permeating everybody's clothes and
hair? Olivia winced at her teenage self's attitude, which now seemed
akin to some sort of racist reaction, though she certainly hadn't thought
of it in those terms at the time.

Olivia had blown up, slammed her books down, yelled *Why can't we be
normal around here!,* and stormed off to her bedroom—where she stayed,
determined to punish everyone by lying miserable and alone in the dark.
Her dad came home. She heard them talking. After a few minutes he
opened Olivia's door and told her she should come out now for dinner.
Olivia had replied, *I don't want any. It smells bad.* And her father had gotten angry, which was rare. *You need to grow up,* he'd said, then pulled her
door shut, not quite slamming it, like he was closing it to keep his own
temper contained.

Olivia felt worse and worse. Even back then, she hated self-pity. But
she was drowning in black, shark-infested waters. When her bedroom
door opened again, she was sure it was her dad, and she tried to steel
herself, pretend she didn't need him. Instead, she burst into fresh tears.

But it wasn't her dad; it was Rohana.

Olivia buried her face in her pillow. *Go away,* she sobbed. *I'm alone.*
Not: I want to be alone. *I'm alone.*

There was no soft-shoe retreat. The door did not close. After a few moments Rohana sat on the bed beside her and stroked her hair. *Little Oh, you are not alone,* she said. *You are not alone.* And Olivia couldn't stop crying. It wasn't until years later that Olivia started resenting Rohana for this small act of kindness that had begun Olivia's journey back to vulnerability. And where had that journey led? To her dad slumped over the arm of his chair.

And to Brian.

In the car, teetering on the edge of sleep, Olivia could almost feel Rohana's hand stroking her hair.

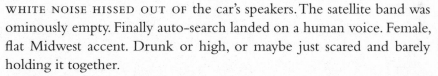

WHITE NOISE HISSED OUT OF the car's speakers. The satellite band was ominously empty. Finally auto-search landed on a human voice. Female, flat Midwest accent. Drunk or high, or maybe just scared and barely holding it together.

Things don't look good, neighbors. I think we could all use us some Willie Nelson about now.

Willie Nelson's voice warbled out, the recording sounding shakier than usual.

Olivia, who had been trying to find a connection for her IsnGlas, gave up and slid the flexible, wafer-thin tablet back into her pack.

In the front seat, Brian said, "Whoa—"

Olivia looked up. What could have been especially bright heat lightning suddenly lit up the northwestern sky. Could have been—but wasn't.

The Ford slowed down until it was coasting to a stop in the middle of Interstate 90.

"This is bad," Alvaro said.

Another flash occurred, followed by a series of three, all of them more laterally north.

God's Morse code: Dear children of Earth, you are hereby and forever doomed.

The radio crackled and went back to white noise.

The night returned to black.

"Maybe it's not what we think." Dee sounded like she wanted to convince herself.

Olivia had once done a piece for *Slate* about the history of the

START treaties. "They're going after our Minuteman silos in Montana and North Dakota. Trying to take out our strategic response capabilities. It won't help them unless they get the rest of our subs and bombers."

"That's *bullshit.*" Dee's voice quavered like Willie Nelson's. "You can't know that."

"I researched the nuclear triad for a story." Olivia lowered her window. Grinding thunder rolled out of the prairie. Except it wasn't thunder.

"Fucking North Korea doesn't have that capability," Dee said.

"I can think of a few other countries that do." It came out in a whisper. Olivia couldn't find her breath. It was as if the oxygen had been siphoned out of the car. She remembered walking into a public square in Raqqa and encountering a man hanging by the neck from a construction crane, naked from the waist down, shit running down his legs. Her reaction then was like her reaction now: This can't be real.

The car shuddered, like something big had tunneled under the road, making it buckle.

"Let's keep moving," Olivia said.

Alvaro began to accelerate.

Brian yelled, "Jesus Christ, look, look over there!"

Invisible claws scratched fire in climbing arcs across a black slate — missiles streaking away at incredible speed.

"We're launching," Olivia said numbly.

In a voice on the edge of sobbing, Dee said, "God help us."

✳

THE SUN NEVER APPEARED.

Darkness merely seeped away, leaving a pale, smoky dawn. The eternal overcast hung low, the sky like a compactor crushing the world. They came up on Bozeman, Montana, all of them exhausted after twenty hours on the road. Dee was driving. Traffic thickened in a confused flow. Some vehicles passed the interchange at high speed, others barely moving at all, as if the drivers knew they had to go somewhere but had no idea where. They passed a big Ram pickup loaded with furniture and boxes and roped down like a *Beverly Hillbillies* jalopy. All it needed was Granny tied on top in her rocking chair. Wind-smudged pillars of smoke marked multiple fires in the city. An overturned semi blocked the exit ramp.

"Anything on the radio? Anybody got any bars?" Alvaro asked.

Dee switched on the radio. White noise hissed at them.

"No bars." Brian put his phone back in his pocket.

"Try to stop here and gas up?" Dee said.

Olivia rubbed the sleep out of her eyes. "Exit's blocked. We'd have to get off farther down the road and backtrack."

"No." Alvaro sounded grim. "Keep going."

Dee looked around at everyone. "Yeah?"

Olivia nodded. "Let's push on to Clewson. It's only a hundred miles, and it's a lot smaller. Less chance of exposure."

AN HOUR LATER, TRAFFIC CLOTTED in front of a multiple-vehicle wreck blocking all the westbound lanes. A state police car, lights flashing and siren whooping, edged around them to reach the accident.

"No getting through that," Dee said.

Some drivers whipped their cars around and crossed the median strip to the eastbound lanes and headed back toward Bozeman. One guy in a Land Rover, determined to keep going west, went jolting over the scrub on the right side of the highway, plowed through a low wire fence, turned onto an empty road, and roared away.

"That's Highway 2," Olivia said. She'd noticed the sign miles back. "It can take us to Clewson."

"Right."

Dee backed up, swung into the scrub, and bucketed over to the road.

Highway 2 was a twisty snake of a road. It seemed to retreat a quarter mile for every mile west it gained. The extra distance sucked fuel. The Ford's engine quit a mile outside Clewson. By then they had been running on the depleted batteries for almost twenty minutes. Dee started cursing.

"I should have stopped in Bozeman."

Olivia held her head, the post-halo pain persistent but not agonizing. Could she link now? Part of her really didn't want to know. "I forgot about the batts. We left that truck stop in South Dakota without charging them."

They coasted until the momentum ran out on the shallow grade, and Dee guided the Ford onto the shoulder and set the brake. "Now what?"

"Here comes something," Brian said, looking out the back window.

Everyone turned. A tractor-trailer rig clutched down, air brakes hissing. Sleek and modern, painted white and blue. Its flashers started blinking, and it came to a stop maybe thirty yards behind them. The truck was big as a whale. A figure moved behind the cab's tall windows. The driver's door opened. A sturdy-looking woman with high cheekbones and wearing a green baseball cap climbed down. A shiny black braid, as long as her torso, swung between her shoulder blades. She stood by her rig, a pistol in her right hand, appraising them from a distance, the gun pointed down with her finger outside the trigger guard.

"You folks need help?"

Alvaro reached for his door.

"Let me," Olivia said. "You tend to scare people or piss them off, and you don't want to do either of those things to someone holding a gun."

Alvaro sat back. "Go ahead."

Olivia climbed out. Six-foot-tall letters on the trailer's side panel spelled WALMART. The air smelled of smoke and something else. Fried ozone? She waved at the driver.

"Hi. We ran out of gas."

"Gotchya." The driver tucked the gun under her belt. "Sorry about the piece. Things have gone a little south, and you've got to be careful. My name's Astina—that's Cree. It means 'hope,' but don't count on it. I can give you a ride into Clewson, you want. You can probably getchyou a can of gas and walk it back. It's not far. Or you could push your car over the crest and coast right on down. Can't push you with my rig. Too tall. I'd high-end you. There's a gas station practically right on the bottom of the other side. I bet you could roll your vehicle right up to the pump."

"Thanks. We'll push it."

"Good on you. My work here is done. Hate to see folks in trouble. I almost drove on by, then asked myself: Would you have stopped before the shit hit the fan? Answer was a straight-up yes, ma'am."

She turned and took hold of the grab bar to haul herself back up to the cab.

"Wait." Olivia stepped closer. "Have you heard anything? On the CB. I mean, if trucks still have CBs."

Astina let go of the grab bar. "You wouldn't believe how many people ask if we still use citizens band radios. And they ask it like they're asking their grandfather if he still has a rotary dial phone." She grinned. "Sure, it's ancient technology, but it's reliable and has its advantages. My cab's loaded with the latest electronics, computers, GPS, all that. And since yesterday it's all about as useful as two tin cans with a piece of string between them. CB's got a short range, but it's unaffected by the bombed communication infrastructure. So, yeah, I've heard stuff, even stuff from far off and out of range. You ever see that *Lord of the Rings* movie? That part where they light the fires as a relay signal? Each fire, you can only see it from a short distance. But as a relay, the signal gets all the way across Middle-earth."

This truck driver *really* liked to talk.

"What's the news?" Olivia asked.

Like a dimmer switch dialing the light down, Astina became at least as glum as Olivia felt. "The news is bad. They hit us on both coasts and kicked us in the bread basket, took out a bunch of our silos before we got any missiles off. Don't know about the subs and bombers."

"Who's 'they'?"

"That one's up for grabs. First hit was probably North Korea. What some people think is the Russians saw a chance and jumped on it, since the whole world was turning on them about the smallpox. Or maybe a coordinated attack, China and Russia. Course, they'll turn on each other next, if they haven't already. I don't know. It's all confused and not going to get any sharper in the near future, or any other future, I guess. There's millions dead in the US. Millions and millions, and going to be more from the radiation. Nobody's got an answer for the smallpox, either. Remember only a week ago, that was the worst thing in forever?"

"I remember."

"I guess it was just the fuse."

"Is the government doing anything? What about—"

"I don't know. Maybe there isn't any government anymore. You know, I'm not picking up CNN on the CB. It's just guys talking, telling each other what they've heard. Gossip, mostly. Once in a while you get word from someone in a zone where a piece of the internet is still functional, or they say it is. But you know what, it's mostly guys babbling about the End Times and reading Bible verses, or cursing out the Muslims. You get that? Who ever said the Muslims had *anything* to do with this mess? Anyway, I got to go."

"Wait. What about India and Pakistan? Have you heard anything?"

"Nope."

"Do you think it's the End Times?"

"Sure. But not like it's in the Bible. That's horseshit. If it is the end, it's because we made it that way. Us humans, not God. That's how everything is, and that's what people always do. Blame somebody else, and when they run out of somebody elses, they blame God. Which is like blaming Santa Claus for the crummy present your uncle gave you."

Astina hauled herself up and into the cab and pulled the door shut. Olivia turned back to the Ford. Astina rolled down the window and stuck her head out.

"Hey."

Olivia looked back.

"Don't hang around Clewson. Get in and get the hell out as fast as you can. The thing about the End Times is there's a lot of people who think that means it's okay to do all the bad shit they never hardly thought about doing before. I've seen some of what they do, and this mess just started."

"Are you stopping in Clewson?"

"Long enough to unload at the superstore, like I was gonna do anyway before the bugs and bombs started flying. Finish my job. After that, I'm heading to Portland."

"Good luck."

"You too."

TWENTY-SIX

THEY PUSHED THE FORD UP the shallow grade—Alvaro, Dee, and Brian putting their backs into it while Olivia steered. The Walmart truck growled past them, up and over the hill, Astina giving them a short, encouraging blast of the air horn. They crested the hill, everyone piled back in, and they coasted down into Clewson, running out of forward momentum just a few yards short of an Exxon station. They got out to push it up to the pump. The door of the mini-mart opened and a thickly bearded guy in a red T-shirt marched toward them waving his hands.

"No gas, sorry. Power's out and my generator just ran dry. Those pumps is dead."

"Whose pumps *aren't* dead?" Alvaro said.

"Power's out all over town, so I don't know. Depends on who's got a working generator. That guy don't." He pointed at a 7-Eleven across the street. "You go to the other side of town, could be the Conoco is running. But like I said, I don't know. Phones don't work neither, so you can't call and find out. Phones quitting—that's bad, ain't it? How do they make the cell phones quit? What I can do is if you're willing to leave a twenty-dollar deposit, I can loan you a gallon can. You find a working pump somewhere, come back with the gas and you're in business."

"It's a plan." Brian looked at the others. "Do we all go?"

"Miss?" The Exxon guy was looking at Olivia. "You look under the weather."

"I'm all right."

"You want, you can sit down inside while your friends go on a gas hunt. I got one of those battery-operated fans and some water bottles on ice that ain't all melted yet."

"Your head," Alvaro said to Olivia. "How's your head?"

"Bad."

"How bad?"

"I need more time," Olivia said.

"I think we're running out of that."

Exxon looked from Olivia to Alvaro and back, worked his lips like he was chewing something he wished he wasn't. "Anyway, I'll get that can. You can push your car over there next to the building." He turned and walked back to the store.

Olivia felt shaky. When the car was parked, she hugged the steering wheel and closed her eyes.

"I'll stay with Olivia," Dee said. "You two go."

A deep rumble came out of the sky. God's stone wheels grinding it out. Grinding it out exceedingly fine.

Olivia lifted her head. Everyone looked east. The attendant appeared, a red gas can in his fist. He stopped in midstride, looking east like everyone else.

The rumble subsided. It might have been a distant thunderstorm.

The Exxon guy approached them. He looked distracted in the way people get after they've received a cancer diagnosis.

"Twenty dollars."

"She and I are staying," Dee said. "If you could spare us some of that cold water."

"It ain't exactly cold at this point, but sure."

Alvaro said, "How do we find that Conoco station?"

Exxon focused on him. "Basically, walk straight down Harrison. You come to the Walmart, you know you're almost there."

"Thanks." Brian produced his wallet and handed the man a twenty-dollar bill, then he walked over to Olivia. "You going to be okay?"

"I'm good. Be careful yourself."

Brian looked like he didn't want to leave — or like he wanted to leave but for a different destination. He scuffed his shoe on the asphalt.

"Bri?"

"I'm worried about my parents. They're not that young, and my mom's got diabetes. Her legs are screwed up. I should be there."

"They're probably all right for now."

"Very optimistic. What are you basing that on?"

"Nothing."

Alvaro said, "Let's get going already."

Brian glanced back at him. "The boss is calling."

"I thought I was your boss." She grinned, trying to lighten the mood.

"You are. Absolutely."

He hugged her. Olivia patted his back. "Bri, really be careful."

"I will."

She watched him and Alvaro walk away down Harrison Avenue, the red gas can swinging in Alvaro's hand.

Exxon shook his head. "God damn everything that's going on." He turned to Dee and Olivia. "This way, ladies. My name's Chuck, by the way."

He led them into the store and behind the counter to the break room, a cubby space with a couple of chairs, a card table, and a few stacks of cardboard boxes printed with logos like LAYS and HOSTESS. Anemic daylight straggled through the dirty skylight. Chuck switched on the battery-operated fan perched on top of a box and aimed it at Olivia. The blades pushed the stultifying air around to not much effect. Chuck fished out a couple of plastic water bottles bobbing in a bucket of water and handed them, dripping, to Olivia and Dee.

"On the house."

Olivia accepted her water bottle. "Thank you. Do you have aspirin?"

"I do. Hold on."

He left and came back with a bottle of Bayer aspirin still sealed in its box. "Seven ninety-five."

Olivia couldn't tell if he really wanted the money. She decided it was best to err on the side of a normal transaction and handed him a ten-dollar bill.

"I'll get your change."

They twisted the caps off the water bottles. Dee said, "Tell me."

Olivia blinked. "Tell you what?"

"Your head. It's better now. Isn't it." Not a question.

"Yes."

Dee held her eyes. "You could go in. You could link."

"I don't know."

"Okay." Dee brought the water bottle to her mouth and tilted her head back, drank a third of the water and wiped her lips.

"Not cold," she said.

Olivia opened the Bayer and shook three tablets into her hand. She popped them in her mouth and chased them down with the not-cold water. Chuck brought her change and left them alone, pausing only to say, "I'll keep an eye out for your men."

Olivia used her sleeve to blot sweat off her forehead. "It's hotter in here than it is outside."

Dee was quiet. After a few minutes she said, "What's funny is I thought if only a woman were given a chance, she could use the probability machine to improve the world, maybe improve it a lot. Like stop people from starving, make different probabilities with better outcomes. You know, not just save us from the big crisis points. Make the world *work*."

"It doesn't have anything to do with being a woman."

"Yeah, I know. I just hoped with a woman it might be different. Instead, it's no better. It's kind of depressing."

"I'm sorry."

"Listen," Dee said. "You really have to do it this time. I know it's terrible, but you have to do it. Let Jacob's probability choice take over."

"I know."

"It's bigger than you and Brian."

"I *know*."

A sound like firecrackers came through the propped-open skylight. And in that moment, Olivia felt cold and hot at the same time, frightened for Brian. The same as when she'd waited for him and Jodee at Habib's Café in Aleppo and heard the ominous crack of sniper fire and knew her friends might be targets.

"That's gunfire," Dee said.

"Yes."

Outside, Chuck stood in the shade with his hands on his hips. "Somebody's shooting."

"We heard it."

"This ain't Chicago. But things start coming apart when the glue dissolves."

Olivia walked away from the store.

Dee caught up. "Where are you going?"

"To find Brian."

Chuck called after them: "You ladies should stay here. It's safer. Your men will be back soon. Just my opinion."

Olivia kept walking, and Dee stayed with her. The shooting stopped. No police sirens wound up. The streets remained disturbingly quiet. A big kid on a bicycle pedaled out of an alley and came toward them. Not a kid — a man, easily past thirty.

She waved at him. "Hey, excuse me."

He coasted up to them and stopped, planting his feet flat on the ground, straddling the kid-sized bike.

"Do you know what that shooting was about?" Olivia asked.

"Guy climbed onto the roof of the Rite Aid and started firing. Who knows why? Everything's fucked up."

Dee said, "Anybody hit?"

"Don't think he was shooting *at* anybody. Just shooting. Took out some car windows is all. But I wouldn't go that way if I were you."

He stood on the pedals and rode off.

Olivia started walking again, determined. Inaction — waiting — it killed her. She did so much of it in the Disaster. Waiting for word on whether someone she knew was dead or wounded. Waiting for the shooting to stop, or to start. Waiting for a cease-fire, a new offensive, the sound of helicopters, the word from a source on where to find an insurgency leader to be interviewed. Waiting.

Olivia was *done* waiting.

They came to the Walmart. Astina's blue-and-white semi, or one exactly like it, idled at the side of the building. No, it was Astina's all right. She stepped into view holding a clipboard, talking to a guy in a skinny black tie and white shirt. Astina's long black braid was unmistakable.

Two more gunshots popped off.

Olivia turned in the direction of the shots. A man came running down Harrison Street. It was Brian. He saw them and veered over, arriving out of breath.

"*Bri.*"

"I'm okay. There's a guy shooting."

Dee said, "Where's Alvaro?"

"I don't know. The shooter, he didn't seem to be aiming at people. And then he was. A bullet chipped off the street right in front of us. A little piece of concrete jumped up and nicked Alvaro under the eye. We both took off running in different directions."

Brian was having trouble catching his breath.

"*Shit.*" Dee looked like she needed to fight something *right now.* "I have to find him. We'll meet you two back at the Exxon station. *Be there.*"

"Stay off the main street," Brian said. "Go around."

Dee took off running. Brian shook his head. "Christ, this is just like—"

Olivia pulled his arm. "Come on."

"What?"

"Come *on*. If you want to see your parents, we need to ditch Dee and Alvaro."

They reached Astina right when the guy in the white shirt turned and walked away. Astina looked pissed off.

"Astina," Olivia said.

"Hey. You guys still hanging around?"

"With the power out, nobody can pump gas."

"Sucks, right?"

"What about you? That guy didn't look happy."

"Yeah. Store manager won't take delivery. Says he doesn't have the staff to unload the truck. Is that my problem? Wants me to hang around town, see if anybody shows up for work. That isn't happening."

"There's somebody taking potshots from the roof of the Rite Aid."

"Yeah, I heard it. Doesn't surprise me."

"You got enough fuel to make Portland?"

"Sure."

Olivia looked back down the street. Dee and Alvaro could show up at any moment.

"Trouble?" Astina said.

"We need a ride to Portland."

Astina shook her head. "Against the rules to carry passengers. Besides, I couldn't fit four in the cab."

"Two, not four."

"Still against the rules. What's he shaking his head about?" She nodded at Brian.

"He thinks it's funny you're worried about Walmart rules, considering what's going on."

Astina shrugged. "Rules are rules. Besides, it's Teamsters, not Walmart."

"How far is Portland?" Brian asked.

"Nine, ten hours."

"That's under normal circumstances, right?"

"We could help you," Olivia said. "You don't know what you're going to run into on the road."

Astina pulled on the end of her nose. She didn't look convinced.

"I——" Brian started to say something but stopped.

Astina waited.

"Look," Brian said. "I want to see my mom and dad one more time. They live in Portland, where you said you were going anyway. If you don't take us, I'll never see them again. I know I won't. Please."

Astina sighed heavily. "You guys don't play fair." She looked at the lowering sky. "You can't get in right here. I don't want that manager to see. Yeah, I know it probably doesn't matter anymore. All I can say is rules matter to me. Go a block back the way you came and cut over another block west. We're pulling out of here the back way. I don't want to give that prick with the rifle a big target."

"Thank you," Olivia said.

"Really," Brian said.

"Don't thank me. You said it yourself: We don't know what we're going to run into between here and there. Maybe you'll wish you stayed in Clewson."

Half running to get off Harrison Street before Alvaro and Dee turned up, Olivia faltered and Brian took her arm to keep her on her feet.

"You all right?"

"A little dizzy."

A few minutes later, waiting for Astina, Olivia said, "That thing about your mom and dad. You know it's not the last time, right? Back there I just meant Dee and Alvaro would drag us to Sanctuary."

He held his hand up. "Can we not talk about this anymore?"

"Bri. You don't even believe it."

"Liv, I know what you have to do. I just want to get home first, okay?"

TWENTY-SEVEN

PUSHING WEST INTO THE AFTERNOON, Olivia could almost believe it was a normal day. Traffic moved on the interstate. Random livestock grazed in the fields. A man changed his Hyundai's flat tire while a woman and young boy stood watching, the woman's skirt billowing in the wind. Approaching Spokane, the low overcast lifted and blue sky appeared like a promise.

But other things drove home the absolute not-normalness of the new world. Military aircraft crisscrossed the blue sky, leaving an apocalyptic tic-tac-toe of contrails. Troop carriers and heavily armored vehicles periodically took over the road, forcing Astina to clutch down and pull over to let them pass. And even once they got near Spokane, the internet remained dark and cellular service dead. Far to the west, streaks of coal-black cloud reached toward them like the fingers of an immense Reaper. Western Washington was burning.

The truck's cab was practically a self-contained studio apartment, complete with a sleeping area behind the seats, a mini-fridge, OLED screen, and other amenities. The truck itself was fitted to self-drive, so Astina could cross the country with no stopovers if necessary. But with global positioning inoperative, she had to do all the driving manually. Olivia, riding shotgun, wondered if Astina was up to it. Her face had grown flush. Sweat beaded on her forehead. She drank a lot of water, and she kept rolling her shoulders and taking one hand then the other off the wheel to flex her fingers and rotate her wrists. Aches, fever.

Early symptoms of smallpox.

"Do you feel all right?" Olivia asked.

"I'm okay."

"Astina?"

She turned to Olivia and their eyes met. Astina had the look Helen had worn the last time Olivia had spoken with her friend and editor.

Astina faced forward again, holding the big steering wheel with both hands, resting forearms on the rim.

"I know what you're thinking, but I don't have it."

"You could have it and not know."

"I'd know. If you're worried, I can let you out wherever."

Brian's voice came from the back: "No."

Olivia said, "We need to get to Portland."

Astina reached under her seat and came up with an N-95 filter mask and pulled it over her mouth and nose.

"Just in case," she said.

A pointless gesture, but Olivia said, "Thanks." If Astina was contagious, they were already exposed and beyond the ability of prophylactic measures to make a difference.

They drove on, departing the 90 at Ritzville and heading southwest on US 395. Astina picked up her mic and switched on the CB.

"Breaker one-niner. Big Tuna south on 395, Portland bound."

The radio hissed and crackled. After a few moments a male voice spoke: "Copy, Big Tuna. What can I do you for?"

"You been to Portland?"

"Yes, ma'am. Be advised, we got a checkpoint about three miles south of Kennewick on the Oregon border."

"Smokey? Come back."

"US military. National Guard, anyway."

"What are they checkpointing *for?*" Brian asked.

Astina keyed the mic. "What's the guard want with me?"

"Border stop. They're looking for bad guys and infected. Keep Oregon"—he pronounced it exaggerated, like *Or-a-gone*—"pure. Not possible, but things are nuts out here."

"Roger that."

"Big Tuna, you get to Portland, you'd best stay there."

"Why's that? Come back."

"Seattle is a radioactive cow pie. Ditto Los Angeles. Least that's what I hear. Nobody's coming out of them places to tell the story, and roadblocks are in full force. You hunker down now."

"Ten-four."

"Good luck."

"Back at you."

The radio went quiet.

A few miles north of the Columbia River, Astina pulled over, set the brake, and turned to Olivia.

"Look," Astina said. "I'm tired. I've been driving for days with no auto-assist. I've got bad allergies — germs aren't the only thing in the air, you know. I'm not sick, but I *look* sick."

"We believe you," Olivia said, not believing her at all but knowing Astina needed to believe she hadn't contracted smallpox.

"Great. But the boys and girls at that Oregon checkpoint might not. Have either one of you driven anything bigger than that little Ford hybrid?"

"I have," Olivia said.

"How much bigger?"

"Like a thirty-foot moving van. Drove it from Trenton to Charlotte. I mean — I shared the driving with a friend who was moving."

Astina nodded. "It'll have to do. I'm gonna show you the basics. Then me and your boyfriend are gonna get in the back with all the Walmart stuff, in case there's somebody at that checkpoint who's smart enough to know you should be driving alone."

"What if they want to see my license? Obviously I'm not certified to drive this thing."

Astina got out her wallet and removed the license from its sleeve. She handed it to Olivia. "We're about the same size, more or less. You're a little shorter and I'm a little darker, but we'll just have to chance it."

"They could make me open the trailer."

"They could."

"Then what?"

"Then I don't know. Maybe they won't care."

The lesson was brief. Astina and Olivia traded seats. Astina had her drive a mile running the clutch up and down the tree, especially had her clutch up smoothly from a dead stop ("So you don't look like an amateur pulling out of the checkpoint"), and pronounced her adequate. Olivia did not feel this was an accurate appraisal.

"This thing's scary big."

"You'll be all right. Here, put this on." She removed her baseball cap and handed it to Olivia. "Kind of stuff your hair up under it."

Olivia did it. "Is there another filter mask?"

"Good idea, and yes, I'll get it for you."

Netted crates and cardboard boxes filled the semi's trailer. Olivia stood by the bumper watching Brian and Astina climb over the cargo and squeeze down out of sight near the front. Astina's head bobbed up.

"This stuff is secured, but that doesn't mean it can't shift. Don't overdo it with the brakes. Pay attention. Give yourself plenty of stopping distance."

"I will."

Olivia swung the heavy door shut and secured it. She climbed back into the cab, buckled up, and took a minute to organize herself. Thank God her migraine had backed off, but she still didn't feel a hundred percent. Her drawn face regarded her from the side mirror. *I look as sick as Astina.* It was the aftermath of making the wrong decisions in the halo. It was the strain of what was happening now and what was coming.

She pulled an N-95 mask over her face and adjusted it so the stretchy bands weren't tugging on her hair every time she moved her head. In the mirror, Olivia was gone, replaced by a slightly closer approximation of Big Tuna.

THE WALMART TRACTOR-TRAILER WAS THE biggest vehicle in line at the Oregon checkpoint. From her high position in the cab Olivia commanded a view over the tops of the carbon-guzzlers, hybrids, and full-electrics inching forward. A pair of desert-colored lightly armored military trucks bracketed the highway. Four guardsmen, armed with assault rifles and wearing elaborate double-canister gas masks, examined the civilian vehicles and passed them through. Whisper drones hovered over the scene. The Columbia River sparkled just beyond, marking the border between Washington and Oregon.

Except for the Pacific Northwest landscape, Olivia could have been approaching a checkpoint in Aleppo. The Disaster had landed. Of course, it had always been here, cleverly disguised as virtuous civilization. But the human disaster was everywhere, the chaos boiling just under the surface. Maybe it was the awareness of that chaos that drove people to build civilization in the first place, pushed them to make meaningful connections, form relationships.

Olivia had spent her grown-up life guarding her own borders, keeping as much of the personal chaos out as possible. But borders not only kept the chaos out but everything else, too. Since her father's death, only Brian had passed through her personal checkpoint. Rohana was still waiting for clearance. Sorry, your papers are not in order. Only it wasn't Rohana's papers that needed ordering.

The line moved and she muscled the clutch, jerking the big rig forward. Two guardsmen approached. In their masks they looked like giant bipedal insects. Olivia lowered her window.

"What's your destination?" The guardsman sounded young, trying to cover his fear with an unconvincing tone of authority.

"Portland."

"Are you alone?"

"Yes, sir."

"Go ahead." He waved her through.

Olivia almost couldn't believe it. For all this kid knew, the trailer was loaded with pox-riddled corpses. She knew she should just go, but she had to know something that this guardsman might be able to tell her.

"Is it as bad as I've heard?"

"It's bad."

"Does—"

"Move your vehicle."

Olivia raised her window and hauled the trailer into Oregon. On the other side of the river she pulled into a crowded truck stop. Either Oregon had a functioning grid or the Crossroads truck stop came prepared with heavy-duty generators. Still no cellular service, though, Olivia saw. She wondered if the destruction of communications had been the result of cascading failures or because the cellular networks had been deliberately targeted. Not that it mattered at this point.

She parked the truck without even trying to make it look good. Muscling the tractor-trailer around was stressful. Olivia set the brake and turned the engine off. She could smell her own nervous sweat. Dark stains had bloomed under her arms, despite the AC.

She unbuckled, shouldered the door open, and jumped down. There was no one in the parking lot behind the building, nobody to see her let Astina and Brian out of the trailer. She unlocked the bar, swung it up, and opened the door. Brian, sitting on top of the cargo, waved. Her chest tightened with the kind of emotion she'd held at bay for years, guarding her checkpoints with lethal force.

※

BRIAN'S PARENTS LIVED IN SOUTHEAST Portland, in a neighborhood called Belmont. Astina let them off a few blocks away. "I'm not taking this thing down those narrow-ass streets," she said.

Olivia offered her hand. "Thanks for giving us a lift."

Astina looked at the hand, her eyes burning with fever, took it, and gave it a firm shake.

"Right," Brian said. "We wouldn't have gotten here without you."

"I don't know if that's true. You two seem pretty determined. But you're welcome."

Olivia opened the passenger door and climbed down. Brian folded the seat forward and clambered out of the sleeping space and down to the street.

Looking up into the cab, Olivia said, "Where are you going from here?"

"First off, I need fuel." Astina was sweating hard. It seemed unlikely she could bank many more miles. "I got a house of my own in Portland, but I think I better go see the folks. They're up in Centralia. If I can get across the border into Washington, that's where I'll go. I don't think the National Guard is stopping anybody from *leaving* Oregon."

"Stupid to waste them on the border at all," Brian said.

Astina grunted. "Good luck, you two."

Olivia stepped back and Brian threw the door shut. The big truck growled and huffed and slowly ground forward, blinkers on to reenter the sporadic traffic.

Unexpectedly, a deep tide of loneliness swept through Olivia. In her mind she saw the semis parked behind that rest stop in Idaho, and she remembered her fear that those high cabs held terrified truckers—or variola victims, like the one in the Subaru parked in front.

How much time was left to make the world right again?

TWENTY-EIGHT

QUIET LAY OVER TREE-LINED STREETS as Olivia and Brian walked into the residential neighborhood. Craftsman homes, some dating back to the early 1900s, stood silent and lightless, like funereal boxes. An old man in a sleeveless T-shirt and what looked like a World War One gas mask sat on the porch of a rundown house, one of the few in need of fresh paint and a new roof. He watched them as they passed on the sidewalk, his hand covering the pistol on his thigh.

A block farther, a large dog stood in the middle of the street. Its drooping head swung listlessly left and right, as if looking for something. It held clenched in its jaws a piece of yellow rope about eighteen inches long, one end of it tied in a knot as big as a baby's fist. The dog, a retriever mix, sniffed hopefully at them.

"Poor guy," Brian said. "Nobody to play with."

The dog followed them. Stopped when they stopped, walked when they walked.

"Go on home," Brian said.

But home seemed to be the pavement a yard or so behind their heels.

A flowering shade tree with purple buds reached protectively over the front porch of Brian's parents' house. Another Craftsman home, this one gabled and ornamented with architectural details and beveled windows. They mounted the porch. A man's bucket cap with a red-and-blue band sat on the glider. Olivia picked it up.

"Your dad like to golf?"

"He likes to sit out here and drink beer and *talk* about golf."

Brian knocked on the door. The dog that had followed them started barking. Olivia dropped the hat on the glider and turned. The dog sat at the bottom of the porch steps, the rope on the ground by its forepaws, jaws parted in that way dogs had that made them look like they were smiling.

The door opened, and Olivia turned back. If you put Brian Anker into a machine that bleached his hair, dragged his shoulders down like a wrestler's, and stamped his face with a wrinkle press, you'd have the man standing in the doorway.

"Brian! Thank God!"

The men embraced. Brian had a couple of inches on his father. "I'm sorry I didn't call, Dad. The phones don't work."

"Of course they don't. It's all part of it." He looked over Brian's shoulder at Olivia, his eyebrows elevating. "You're Liv?"

Olivia said, "I am." She hadn't thought that Brian had mentioned her to his father. But naturally he would have. Bri didn't live in a guarded fortress the way she did.

Brian and his dad stopped hugging and the older man held out his hand. "John Anker. Glad to meet you."

"Olivia Nikitas. Likewise."

"I've heard, well, not a *lot* about you. But that I've heard anything about you at all speaks volumes. Brian can be less than forthcoming, at least when it comes to who he's dating."

Olivia smiled, not recognizing Bri by that description. Brian was the most forthcoming person she'd ever met. "I guess he plays it close to the vest."

"Not really," John said. "He just likes to be sure, when it matters. This time I think he is."

Olivia's smile felt like a grimace.

Brian said, "Where's Mom?"

"Resting. Got a summer cold."

Olivia exchanged a look with Brian.

John turned away. "Come in and I'll make us something to eat. Nothing fresh, I'm afraid. The power's been out since it all started. Since the big attack. Frozen stuff made a hell of a mess."

They followed him into the house. It was as beautifully maintained as the exterior. The inlaid hardwood floor gleamed; the plants looked healthy. Family pictures occupied the top of the upright piano, and a portrait of Pope Benedict XVII peeked out from behind a schefflera plant, as if the pontiff was curious but shy about meeting strangers.

"You two look tired," John said over his shoulder.

"We've been on the road," Brian said.

"Pretty bad out there?"

"Yeah."

"Well, thank God you're home. There's beer. Not cold."

"I'd like to look in on Mom."

"I told you, she's resting."

"Dad—"

"Leave her be," he said, a little short, but then his face immediately shifted to make clear he didn't mean anything by it. "She'll come down when she feels better."

They ate lunch in the dining nook off the kitchen—peanut butter sandwiches, Ritz crackers, and warm Kona Big Wave Golden Ale.

"I'm not much of a cook," John said. "Karen would have made you something decent."

"How long has she been down with the . . . cold?" Olivia asked.

John looked sharply at her, but it passed in a moment, and his gaze became soft and ruminative. "A few days, I think. Yes. Three days."

"I hope she feels better soon."

"Where are your folks?" John asked. "Are they here in Oregon?"

"No. My mother and father died a long time ago, and my stepmother lives in India, in Jaipur. Is there any news about that part of the world?"

"Before the blackout, it didn't look good. Those two countries threatening each other like kids in the schoolyard. It's been days, though. Things might have calmed down."

"Or gotten worse." Olivia felt sick.

John said, "You two are acting scared."

"Things are pretty bad," Brian said.

"You have to keep your head up, son."

"I know."

John turned to Olivia. "He's always been the optimist."

"I'm just tired," Brian said.

"That I understand. When this mess gets straightened out, we can all go on vacation."

"Sure, Dad."

John stood. "If you don't mind, I'm going to lie down for a few minutes. I was up all night looking after Karen."

Olivia put her bottle down. "Of course."

"Make yourselves at home."

He walked out of the room and up the stairs. The quiet stretched out. Olivia broke it: "Bri, your mother—"

His eyes said, *Don't go there.* "She's always gotten sick a lot. When I was a kid, Dad used to say she was lucky because she got a *little* sick all the time so she would never get *really* sick."

"Okay."

He got up and left the room. She followed him to the porch. The dog was still moping around on the sidewalk with his piece of yellow rope. He lifted his head hopefully when they appeared.

"Go home," Brian said.

The dog stared at him, tongue lolling.

"Maybe there's nobody at home," Olivia said.

"Nobody alive, you mean?"

"I don't know."

"Buster just likes to follow people and hope they'll play with him. Everything isn't a tragedy even when everything could be."

"Buster?" Olivia said. "I didn't know you two knew each other."

"Sure. Buster lives a block over."

Brian leaned on the porch rail and dug the heel of his hand into the small of his back. Olivia knew she was supposed to touch him, but held back and hated herself for it. It was coming, the terrible thing she had to do.

"Is it real?" Brian said.

Olivia didn't reply.

He turned. "Is it *really* real? The goddamn probability machine."

"Brian, I think I can still fix everything. I'm strong enough now to try." It was true. The post-halo headache had all but vanished. She knew she could use the link again whenever she was ready. She could have done it sooner, maybe back in Clewson.

Brian smiled sadly and shook his head.

"What?" she said.

"Nobody can fix everything, Liv. All us grown-ups know that."

"Then I'm not a grown-up." She winced inwardly as soon as the words passed her lips.

Brian said, "I love you, you know."

"I love you, too." Olivia's words sounded perfunctory, but she didn't feel that way. She *did* love Brian. Why couldn't she say it with conviction, even now?

"I know you do," he said. "I'm going to go up and see my mom now."

"I don't think your dad wants you to."

"No, he doesn't."

Brian hugged her. Olivia's arms hung at her sides. "Bri."

"It's okay. I'll be right back."

He walked into the house, and Olivia stood there. Buster shook his yellow rope at her.

"Go *home*," Olivia said more harshly than she intended. The dog stared at her.

Olivia went back into the house, where she did not want to go. She walked around the empty rooms that somehow didn't feel empty. She remembered her own family home outside Seattle. In the long-lost days before her mother died, Olivia had never felt alone, not even when she was by herself. Later, she felt alone all the time, right up to this very minute.

She grimaced, a stab of loneliness plunging deeper than usual. Her own father had been born in New Jersey and moved to Washington State before she was born. Olivia's grandparents on his side of the family had both died before Olivia had grown old enough to be aware of them, except as the senders of spectacularly uninspiring Christmas gifts. Breast cancer got her grandmother, just as it later got Olivia's own mother. Her grandfather died a few years later, of a bad, or maybe broken, heart. Although Olivia never let herself romanticize that stuff. Hearts didn't break from grief; they failed because the grieving (usually) man fails to take care of his health once his wife is gone. That's what she told herself.

Rohana, of course, now lived in Jaipur.

If Jaipur still existed. And at that moment, in a rush of pessimism, Olivia was certain that it didn't, was certain Rohana was gone. She tried to push the thought out of her head. But it stuck like a poisonous thorn. If Rohana was gone, it was the end of repair attempts.

Brian came down the stairs looking like he weighed two hundred pounds more than he had when he went up.

"Mom's got it."

There was no question what "it" was.

"Oh, God."

"Dad looked up when I opened the door, but he didn't say anything. He's lying on the bed next to her."

Olivia wanted to say she could fix it, or she wanted to be someplace else, anywhere else—even back in the Disaster, when the Disaster seemed contained in another part of the world. All that was a lie, though, a lie she'd told herself.

"My parents didn't ask for this," Brian said.

"Of course not."

"But I went into the Old City on purpose. You told me not to come, but I did. I'm an adult and I made a choice."

"Brian, please don't."

"In real life you don't get do-overs."

Olivia couldn't speak.

"In real life you take chances, solve your own problems, or fail to solve them. It's not fair to make other people pay for your own mistakes. You agree?"

"Brian." Her voice trembled. "Quit it. You're too young to lecture me about life."

"I'm not talking about your mistake," he said, ignoring her. "Look, I'm not sure I believe in the probability machine. But if it's real, and it all happened the way you say it did, then it's not your fault. You didn't know what you were doing. You just wanted me to live. That's natural. I'm talking about *my* mistake."

"Goddamn it, Bri, I told you not to come with me that day. I *told* you."

He stepped closer. "Liv, you see that I can't let everybody else pay for my mistake. You see that, don't you?"

"Getting involved with me in the first place was a mistake."

He moved closer and put his hands on her shoulders. "That's just you feeling sorry for yourself."

"Come on."

"It's okay. I get it."

"You can be pretty smug." She didn't mean it . . . or maybe she did a little.

"You're right. I'm working on it." He reached into his pocket and withdrew four or five dried jai ba leaves. "I filched these a couple of nights ago on the road, when Alvaro was sleeping."

A trapdoor opened under Olivia's feet, but like a cartoon character she didn't have the sense to fall through it yet.

"Come on," Brian said. "Don't make me responsible for all this."

✦

BRIAN'S PARENTS HAD CONVERTED HIS old bedroom into a combination study/guest room. It was a sunny space with friendly blue walls, a white pine desk, and a matching bed and dresser. It wasn't a memorial room, the way some parents treat a kid's bedroom after he's grown up and moved away, with mementos and pictures everywhere. Olivia pulled the shade, took her shoes off, and sat on the bed. Brian handed her the jai ba leaves. She looked up at him. "I don't want to do this."

"Yeah, I get that."

"It isn't fair," Olivia said.

"You're the one who used to tell me life wasn't fair."

"Bri, there *has* to be another way."

"There isn't. You know there isn't. You already tried the other ways, and they all made things worse." His fingertips brushed her cheek. "I love you."

"Goddamn it."

"That's not the traditional response. I'm going downstairs now, so you can concentrate."

Olivia blinked away tears, but more replaced them. She couldn't bring herself to hold him one last time. Reaching for him would only validate the reality she rejected. It was like being paralyzed. What was the point, anyway? What was the point of trying to hold on to something you knew was going to disappear?

"I'm a coward," she said.

"Who isn't? Hey, don't sweat it. There's probably no probability machine anyway."

She watched him go out the door, turn, nod at her, and pull the door shut.

Olivia wiped her eyes roughly. She put the leaves in her mouth and began to grind them between her molars, releasing the bitter taste. She lay back, trying to hold off emotion but drowning in it anyway. She used to be so good at holding off emotion.

Her lips and tongue became numb, and she spat out the leaves. Swiftly, her sense of her physical surroundings retreated, and she became aware of the link. Deep down, the glimmering spokes of the probability halo drew her—

And just like that, she was back in the torture cell. She could turn away from it, as she had done before, but she didn't. Not this time. She ached with all her heart to reject it, to try another way. But it was too late for that and, finally, she knew it.

Her resistance gone, Olivia reached out . . .

✸

SOMETIME LATER, SHE OPENED HER eyes. The world gathered into her senses. Brian's room in the family house, the shade drawn. Just the way she remembered it. Olivia felt disoriented, not ready to get up and face the new reality. Right now she existed in a world of possibilities, if not probabilities.

But there was only one present truth.

She sensed it rising, a memory scaffold lifting out of the fog. In the hall outside the bedroom door, the floorboards creaked. The doorknob moved hesitatingly, a metallic rasp—the knob turning in its loose collar. The door opened, and Brian came through.

"Brian!" She sat up, almost blind with relief. But something was wrong.

"It's all right," John Anker said. "You must have had a bad dream."

PART III

THE DISASTER

TWENTY-NINE

A BAD DREAM.

One that she wasn't ever going to wake up from.

Grief overwhelmed her. She fell back on the bed, sandbagged. She was no different from anyone else. All disasters were personal, and her personal disaster had blinded her. Whatever she'd told herself every time she entered the halo and failed to choose Jacob's probability, the truth was simple and obvious. She had wanted Brian to live.

Brian's father stood in the doorway, looking enough like his son that for a moment Olivia had thought . . .

But no.

Brian was dead. Mission accomplished.

"I'm sorry," John Anker said. "I heard you cry out. Can I get you anything? Karen went to the store, but she'll be back soon."

"I'm all right. Thanks, Mr. Anker." Memories tangled in Olivia's mind. She tried to sort them. Without Brian, what was she doing in his parents' house?

"John. Please call me John."

Olivia tried to smile. It felt wooden.

"Well," John said, "I'll let you rest."

He withdrew, pulling the door shut. Olivia stared at it, and a new memory scaffold began to rise.

Brian died under the madrassa in Aleppo's Old City, his blood bubbling and spurting around her fingers. Jodee Abadi was also dead, shot through the chest by Kalashnikov rounds. Those two sacrifices so that Jacob could die, too, and the release of variola could be stopped.

On the other side of the balance sheet, millions who had lost their lives in Olivia's probability choices now lived. The smallpox attacks never oc-curred. The nukes never flew. The positive side of the world's ledger pre-vailed—for now. But *only* for now. Olivia thought of the González effect —"Apparently we needed the Iraq War"—and her stomach clenched. Since the mid-twentieth century, the Shepherds had been in the business of creating crises to avoid crisis points. And that included the *good* Shep-herds. If Andrew's faction ever regained possession of the link, it would be much worse. Olivia could see only one winner: the Disaster.

She sat up and put her feet on the floor. The post-halo headache was mild compared to her previous experiences. Of course it was; this time she had chosen an end point much closer to the most probable one, the end point that saved the world. The man with the scarred face was never in the torture cell, was never there to save Jacob. She touched the back of her neck, felt the seam of raised flesh. Whatever else had changed, the link remained securely zipped inside her head. She hated knowing it was there.

More of the memory scaffold revealed itself. Olivia saw the path she had taken to arrive at this house. After Brian died, Olivia had remained in Aleppo another ten days or so, but she couldn't concentrate on her job. She knew she was avoiding something she had no right to avoid. She was a witness, and Brian's parents deserved her firsthand account. Before he died, Olivia had promised Brian she would deliver it.

She departed the Middle East and traveled straight to Oregon.

While other probability choices had resulted in a change of location when she emerged from the halo, this one hadn't. Perhaps because there was only one destination possible. Still, it was odd that nothing else had changed.

She had shown up at their door, travel-beaten. And despite their own grief, they had welcomed her into their home and consoled *her*. Olivia could almost not fathom that level of empathy. She thought of her own lost home, her estrangement from her stepmother, and tears had threat-ened a second Great Flood.

And that's how she came to be in Brian's old bedroom, where Karen and John Anker had insisted she lie down and rest. Olivia had protested, but it hadn't gotten her anywhere. Besides, she'd been about to fall over.

Olivia put on her shoes and stood up. She stopped by the desk, her heart clenching. Here was one change: a childhood picture of Brian. He looked about five years old, sitting on a rocking horse, all cowboyed up with his hat and six-shooters. Had someone sat in here weeping over this memory?

She found the bathroom down the hall, splashed cold water on her face, combed her fingers through her dirty hair. A haunted, dripping face gazed back at her. She drank water from the tap, patted her face dry with a hand towel, straightened her blouse. She could smell her own sweat and felt embarrassed. All she wanted to do now was leave.

"My wife will be back soon," John Anker said. "I wish you'd stay for dinner."

"I'm sorry, I can't." Olivia could almost see Brian shaking his head. Always one foot out the door, right?

"At least wait for Karen to come home. She'll want to say goodbye."

Olivia made herself agree to wait, although every ounce of her wanted nothing more than to get out of there and lose herself in the oblivion of the road.

"Can I get you anything while we wait?" John asked.

How about a bottle of gin and a motel room?

"No thanks."

"I want to ask you something. It's a favor, I'm afraid."

"Go ahead, John."

"It's about, well . . . Brian's body."

Olivia kept her expression neutral, though inside, her new, fragile barriers were collapsing like walls made of matchsticks.

"They have him over there. We want to bring him home. That's all we want. But the government—theirs *and* ours—makes it so complicated, it's, well . . . it's overwhelming. Karen and I, we thought since you've been there you might know what to do."

"I'm sorry, John. I don't have a clue. I'll try to find out something and call you, okay?"

John Anker nodded once, tight-lipped, his own interior barriers in ruins. "Thank you," he said.

SHE SAT BEHIND THE WHEEL of her rental, the engine purring, her phone in her hand with Rohana's profile active. A single touch and Olivia could be talking to her stepmother. Only hours ago she had thought Rohana might be out of reach forever, gone in the nuclear flash of Olivia's bad choices—the opportunity for reconciliation obliterated. Now she had another chance, and she couldn't bring herself to take it. The biggest thing on her mind was Brian. If she brought him up with Rohana—"A friend of mine died"—Olivia wouldn't be able to contain the ferocious pain straining to get out. And she was afraid that Rohana would comfort her again. That was really it. That was all it ever was. She was afraid. If Brian had lived to see his mother restored to life, he would have been ecstatic, and he would have shown it. All Olivia did was retreat; what the hell was she so afraid of? It wasn't a fair comparison, though. Her personal disaster balance sheet was deep in negative territory. Brian and Jodee were dead, and would stay that way.

Olivia dropped her phone into the cup holder.

The plan was simply to drive. Destination irrelevant. So it was weird when she found herself catching the ramp to I-5 northbound, headed for a very definite place—Brian's apartment in West Seattle. The "home" she'd never been to, not in this probability stream. A place without witnesses to her vulnerability. She knew where Brian's spare key was hidden, in a little plastic box in the garden plot in front of his building. At least she hoped that was still true in the current probability stream. A tractor-trailer blasted past her before she could merge. The rental shuddered, and she thought of Astina, alive again in the world, another check on the positive side of the balance sheet.

❁

OLIVIA FILLED THE APARTMENT WITH voices and alcohol. She was avoiding the other thing she knew she had to do but was afraid to. News unwound in every room, projecting out of every device—and none of it was sufficiently distracting. Then grief performed a reverse miracle, turning gin into water. After a long day and a pint of Hendrick's she found herself stark staring sober and no closer to sleep than she had been two hours ago. This despite being barely able to keep her eyes open during the drive from Portland.

Olivia pushed herself off the sofa, ice clicking in her tumbler, and shuffled toward the kitchen. Her slippers slapped her bare feet as she passed through a BBC America projection streaming from her IsnGlas tablet. A reporter interviewed a weeping man. In the background, a child in a headscarf stood dwarfed by the ruined landscape while a cat circulated around her legs. Olivia stopped and turned back. A montage of images cycled past, some kind of historical retrospective of Western interventions in the Middle East. Night vision shock and awe. Saddam's statue came down. A crowd cheered, and the dead added up. Olivia thought, Because Jacob allowed a photographer to take a picture. The González effect.

Olivia fingered the ridge of scar tissue on the back of her neck. She could hide out with all the gin in the world and it wouldn't make any difference. She couldn't ignore her responsibility. Olivia would never deliberately access the probability machine again. But the machine continued to grind away, or whatever it did, under Aleppo. Waiting for the next Shepherd to enter the halo and shuffle reality. If not Olivia, then someone else. She could spend the rest of her life ignoring her responsibility. But when she died, the link would migrate. And she couldn't be certain she herself wouldn't use it again. The first time she linked, she had done so unconsciously, and it had created a chain of events that brought the world to its knees. What if, lost in a resurrection dream, she did it again? No. She couldn't risk it.

If Alvaro had been right and the existence of the probability machine proved the human race survives, then why did anyone have to actually use the machine? In the twentieth and twenty-first centuries, hadn't probability manipulation become a zero-sum game? Drop ninety thousand tons of bombs on Iraq to prevent a suitcase nuke from exploding in the West?

In a crisis-point superposition any number of probability end points existed. The most likely one produced the humanity-threatening crisis. But it didn't *have* to be the most likely one that collapsed the wave function. And there was always a cost. Ultimately, the probability machine was a cheat, a shortcut. Human beings had to learn to make better choices. And they would—

After Olivia destroyed the probability machine.

Olivia knew what she had to do, even if all she *wanted* to do was wallow in grief. Luckily, an old lesson, hard learned, reared up. This lesson was so fundamental, she had first learned it as a nine-year-old, then gradually forgot it in the new home diligently and lovingly reconstructed by her father and stepmother. When her father died, she learned the lesson all over again, and this time it had stuck.

Death + grief ÷ anger = relief.

Olivia needed that anger now. She needed it to help her focus.

In the street in front of the apartment, a motorcycle engine woke up with a window-rattling roar. Olivia crossed the room and looked out. A guy in leathers and black helmet goosed the throttle of a big Honda 750. A girl in blue jeans swung onto the saddle behind him, rapped her knuckles on the driver's helmet. He kicked the bike into gear.

And Olivia remembered Stefan.

The dirt bike guy who had given her a ride into a town back in Idaho, when she ran into the woods to get away from Alvaro and Dee. Back in another probability.

And with Stefan's name came a phone number. She had committed it to memory a probability or two ago. It was a habit, to automatically store away potentially useful information. The number bled across realities.

She returned to the bedroom and rummaged her phone out of her bag, pulled her thoughts together, and punched in the digits. Stefan wouldn't remember her, of course. The events that threw them together hadn't occurred in the present probability stream. This wasn't going to be easy.

The call rang eight times, then stopped. No voicemail box. Olivia re-dialed, with the same result. She kept at it. On the fourth round, somebody answered: "Who the fuck is this?"

"Is this Stefan?"

"I know who I am. Who the fuck are you and why do you keep calling? You got a fucking wrong number, is that fucking clear?"

"This is Olivia Nikitas."

Silence.

"I write for *The Beat.*"

More silence.

"What the fuck is this?" Stefan said.

"I'm a writer, a journalist, and—"

"I know who fucking Olivia Nikitas is. Why are you saying you're her?"

"I *am* her. Me."

"Fuck off."

"Wait, don't hang up. I can prove it. Google my picture, then accept my video request."

Stefan went quiet for a few seconds. "Anybody can look like somebody else."

Olivia rolled her eyes. "That's idiotic. Just do it."

"Why should I? What if this is some kind of hack?"

"Do it. I'm not trying to hack you. I promise. Besides, how does answering a video call make you any more vulnerable than a regular call?"

"Hold on."

A minute later, Olivia's phone started blinking at her with a video request. She accepted. Stefan's face materialized in a chat bubble floating over her phone. She nodded to him.

"You look like shit," he said.

"I've got reasons to look like shit. But I look like me, right?"

"I don't *get* this. You can't be her. It doesn't make sense."

Olivia clenched her teeth. "Okay. You know my Twitter handle?"

"Yeah. I follow her."

Her. Cute.

"I'm going to post something. Go look."

She swapped to her Twitter account, typed *Stefan, get your head out of your ass,* and swapped back to the call.

He was grinning.

"You believe now, right?"

"Is it because I commented? It's because I commented. Wow."

"What?"

"That story you did about rebels in Syria, that one where you were in bed with them? I posted a comment."

"Embedded—not 'in bed.' Jesus."

"Right, that's what I meant."

"Stefan? I need a favor."

"What do you mean?"

"I want you to do something for me, something near where you live."

"You know where I *live?*"

"Calm down. The, uh, *The Beat* sees where all the comments originate. It's just a cookie thing. It tells us where our readership is. Yours stuck out, because we don't have that many readers in Idaho."

"Holy shit. Yeah, it's the fucking wasteland out here, right?"

"Yeah."

"But if I knew you guys spied on everybody, I wouldn't have commented. I mean, that's US government shit."

"Stefan? Can I ask my favor now?"

"Whatever."

"There's a ranch outside of your town. It's called Sanctuary. I can't give you specific directions, but—"

"I know where it is."

That stopped her. "You do?"

"Everybody knows. We call it the Kook Farm."

"That sounds right."

"What's the favor?"

"I want you to go up to the Kook Farm and give a message to the woman at the gate. She's the security person. Don't give it to anybody else, just her. Her name's Dee."

"How do I know it's her and not somebody else?"

"She's the only woman guard."

"Why don't you do it yourself?"

"Because I'm out of the country, and besides, I want a local person's take on what you see when you go up there."

"Like I'm a source?"

"Sure. Yeah."

"I don't know."

Olivia closed her eyes briefly. "Stefan, this is so important. I really need you."

"Yeah?" He grinned. "What's the message?"

"Write this down. Ready?"

He looked down and away. She heard a drawer slide open. He was going to do it. Stefan held up a pen. "Go ahead."

THIRTY

A DAY LATER, OLIVIA SAT behind the wheel of Brian's Ford in the parking lot of a shopping mall in Idaho Falls. People wandered in and out of Sears. The lot was about half full. She sipped the coffee she'd bought at McDonald's and waited. When a ramshackle pickup truck rattled into view, she put the coffee down in the cup holder. The pickup, very familiar to Olivia, crept around the parked cars. The driver wore a Castro cap, and she was alone. Of course, there could be others—Society security goons already positioned in the parking lot—watching and waiting. Olivia had taken a risk sending her message. Now it was time to find out if the risk had been worth it. She inhaled, opened the door, and climbed out.

The pickup stopped. Dee, behind the wheel, studied Olivia from two rows away. Olivia guessed she was making up her mind, weighing her own risk factors. After a minute, she swung the truck into a parking space, got out, and walked over.

"I don't know you," she said.

"No. Not this time."

Dee narrowed her eyes. "Your message said not to tell Alvaro I was coming here. You know Alvaro?"

Olivia shook her head. "Again, not this time. But I *know* him. And you."

"I don't like games." Dee looked uneasy.

"I'm not playing one," Olivia said.

"Your message said, 'A woman can link.'"

"Yes."

"You're saying you've done it?"

"Yes."

"I don't believe you."

"You believed me enough to come here."

Dee opened her mouth and closed it again. She removed her cap, scratched her scalp, and replaced the cap, tugging it smartly down by the bill. "Who was that kid, the one who brought your message to the gate?"

"In a different probability stream, he helped me get away from you and Alvaro."

Dee chewed her lip, seemed to consider this. Olivia could see she wanted to believe—she was counting on Dee's desire for a change in the Society. At Sanctuary, Dee had said more than once how excited she was that a woman had finally been given a chance at being a Shepherd, even if it did happen accidentally. It broke the Society's tradition of male-only transference of power.

Dee looked directly into Olivia's eyes. "Why would you need to get away from us?"

"You guys rescued me out of Sanctuary. Later on I tried to ditch you, and you tried to stop me. I don't blame you. The link had migrated to me, and I was ignorant and might have done some real damage. Eventually that's exactly what happened."

"Back up. You were at the ranch?"

"Yeah. Andrew was going to kill me so the link would migrate to Emilio. It was some kind of power grab."

"Andrew and Emilio. We've been worried about something like that happening."

"Well, it did."

Dee studied her. "Let me see the back of your neck."

"I was wondering when you'd ask." Olivia turned and lifted her hair, exposing the nape of her neck. She felt Dee's finger trace the scar.

"Tell me," Dee said. "All of it."

They sat in the Ford and Olivia laid out the whole thing. The torture cell in Aleppo, the link, her accidental swapping of probability streams to save Brian, her kidnapping by the Society and the drama at Sanctuary, the variola and nuke attacks, and finally her decision to choose Jacob's original probability end point.

"And your guy died." Dee no longer sounded doubtful.

Olivia nodded.

"Jesus."

"There wasn't any other way. Somehow, saving Brian also saved Jacob. Their lives were connected by a common factor. It was the difference between variola escaping or not escaping."

"And you did that, let your friend die. That's strong."

"Most people would say it was an easy decision. One person or the whole world. I almost blew everything, trying to save him."

"But you didn't." Dee gave her a sideways look. "Most people wouldn't think it was an easy decision. They'd think it was the hardest decision ever."

"I didn't mean it like that." Olivia barely knew how she meant it. Her pre-Brian self, the way she had been before opening the door—that's the self who would have regarded the decision as easy. Everything's easier from a distance.

Olivia wanted to stop talking about Brian. With Dee, a relative stranger, she could appear dispassionate. It would be different if she ever told Rohana. Olivia couldn't imagine it. Even telling Dee, there was a cost. A painful knot tightened under her breastbone. The only way to loosen the knot was to stop talking about Brian and stop *thinking* about him, too. She couldn't do that second thing, of course. She doubted she would ever be able to do that. And it wasn't only Brian. He was like the gateway drug to the heroin of empathy and its consequential pain. (And rewards, Brian would have said. People didn't shoot heroin because they wanted to suffer.)

Dee touched her shoulder. "Are you all right?"

Olivia pulled back. "I'm fine."

"This is so weird," Dee said.

"Weird is putting it mildly."

"I mean, we're sitting here. I just met you. And all I know is what I remember. But you know all this other stuff. You've been in a different probability. You know two of me."

"There's only one of you," Olivia said.

"Yeah, but you know me in a situation I've never been in. I mean, one that I won't ever remember."

"Yes."

Dee obviously wanted to ask something, but she was hesitating.

"Go ahead," Olivia said.

"Huh?"

"You want to know something."

Dee straightened her shoulders. "How did I behave? When it was all coming down. Was I afraid?"

A black SUV pulled into a slot next to Dee's pickup. The driver did not get out. Two more men, young and wearing jeans, polo shirts, and sunglasses, stood talking and smoking under a light standard. It was hard to tell, because of the glasses, but Olivia thought one of them kept looking over at the Ford. Welcome to Paranoidville.

"Everybody was afraid," Olivia said. With the engine off, the August sun had really heated up the Ford's interior. Even with the windows down, it was baking hot. Olivia wiped sweat from her upper lip.

"But did I *act* afraid?"

"You were steady."

"How steady?"

"Listen," Olivia said. "I'm a journalist. I cover war zones. Hurricane aftermaths. Ethnic cleansings. Famines. All the places in the world where the seams are coming apart. So I've hung with a lot of people in the worst situations. Other journalists, soldiers, rebel fighters, civilians caught in the middle. Everybody's afraid. Some keep their equilibrium, some don't. That's what you did in the other probability. You kept your equilibrium. A lot of people didn't, but you did." *And so did Brian.*

Dee looked relieved. "That's something."

"It's a lot. Trust me."

The guy in the black SUV finally climbed out and walked toward Sears. The smoking men remained planted.

"You're a Shepherd," Dee said, shaking her head.

"Yeah." Olivia pulled her blouse away from her bra, letting some air in.

"The Society, the Elders—all of them, except Jacob—they said a woman couldn't do it," Dee said. "Not that women weren't allowed to do it, but *couldn't.*"

"It's a shit job anyway."

Dee looked out the windshield a moment, then back at Olivia. "The whole reason for the Society is to preserve the future. That's not a shit job."

"Unless the way you preserve the future is by putting it in jeopardy."

"What are you talking about?"

"Ellis Beekman ring any bells?"

A car pulled in behind them. Olivia looked at the rearview mirror. A woman sat behind the wheel, rummaging through her purse.

"Let me guess," Dee said. "We told you about Shepherd Beekman in the other probability."

"Yes," Olivia said.

"Then we must have also told you that Alvaro's grandfather took over after Beekman died, and then Jacob after him. The Beekman situation was a tragedy. The Society won't let something like that happen again."

"Won't they? What about the Andrew faction? What about Emilio? I just told you what happened in the other probability."

"It's not going to happen in this one." Dee sounded less than positive about that.

"Why not?" Olivia said. "Besides, even a good Shepherd does almost as much harm as a bad one. Close your window. I'm going to run the AC." Olivia started the engine and cranked the air conditioning. She adjusted the vents. Soon, cool air was blowing into her face. As soon as the engine started, one of the smoking men had dropped his cigarette and turned toward them, while the second man continued to smoke and barely glanced in their direction.

Dee shifted on her seat. "That's ridiculous, what you just said about good Shepherds doing as much harm as a bad one."

"Jacob was a good Shepherd?"

"Of course."

"But he created the González effect."

Dee looked uncomfortable, and it couldn't be the heat. "There were reasons for that."

"I know," Olivia said. "Sometimes you need to rain down carnage in one place to prevent it from raining down in another. Right?"

"Something like that." Dee sounded grumpy. "Look, I don't completely disagree. But I think the problem isn't that we use the machine too much. It's that we don't use it enough."

"Beekman—"

"Was wrong. The other Shepherds before him who tried to use it for personal gain were wrong, too. That's not what I'm talking about. What if a Shepherd found probabilities that improved the world for the sake of improving it? Eventually there might not *be* any more crisis points."

Olivia sighed. "Won't work."

"You don't know that."

"I *do* know it." Now it was too cold in the car. Olivia turned the blowers down. "I've been in the halo. It's too complicated. All I did was try to save the life of one person, and I couldn't do it without creating a catastrophe."

"You didn't know what you were doing. You could be trained. Shepherds are brought up in the Society. By the time the migration happens, they're ready. You're raw, but your heart is in the right place. I can see it is."

Olivia raised her eyebrows. "In this probability, you've known me for, what, an hour?"

"I'm not naïve. You aren't like the others. Your mind hasn't been poisoned with tradition. I can see that much."

"It's not tradition that makes it impossible. It's human limitations. Maybe the probability machine used to work before the twentieth century. Back when a wrong choice was unlikely to have global consequences. But I've *been in the halo.* It's impossible for one mind to trace all the probability threads that result from even a benign choice. Did Beekman know he was going to create the Holocaust when he allowed Hitler's rise to power? Did Jacob foresee the scope of the suffering his González effect would create?"

One of the men under the light standard wasn't there anymore — the one who had dropped his cigarette. Olivia scanned the parking lot and didn't see him. She twisted around and looked out the back window. The woman with the purse looked back at her, then dropped her gaze.

"What the hell is going on with you?" Dee said.

"Look at the guy over there smoking a cigarette by that light pole."

Dee turned, looked, turned back. "What about him?"

"Do you know him?"

"Know him?" She looked again. "Never seen him before."

"He's not from the ranch?"

Dee shook her head. "You're being paranoid."

"Probably." Olivia pulled her seat belt down and buckled in. "Let's go for a drive. Are you okay with that?"

"If it makes you happy." Dee buckled up.

Olivia rolled out of the parking lot, constantly scanning for other cars moving on them. None did. She got on the perimeter road and relaxed a little.

Dee said, "The González effect tormented Jacob until the day he died."

"Dee, listen to me. The probability machine can't be used anymore. It's too dangerous. Even when it's used correctly, to avert a crisis, it does it by creating other crises. And that doesn't take into account the deliberate misuse of the power for personal gain—to enrich the Society, for instance."

"You talk like there's an alternative."

Olivia pulled over and put the car in park. "There is."

Dee looked puzzled—and then shocked. "No."

Olivia looked intently at Dee. "The probability machine is like a magic credit card. We've been using it for a long time to bail us out of bad situations, and now it's become a bad situation itself. It's time to cut up the card . . . to turn the machine off."

The blood rushed out of Dee's face. She appeared shaken, then angry. "That's insane. Why are you telling me this?"

"Because I need your help. Yours and Alvaro's."

"Alvaro?"

"He knows where to find the probability machine."

Dee's face looked like a closed door. "He wouldn't tell you where it is. He wouldn't even tell me."

"I'm a Shepherd. Doesn't he have to tell me?"

"I don't know. None of this is the way it's supposed to be."

If Olivia were more like Brian, this would be the time to touch Dee's shoulder, to make a small physical connection. She tried. With an unreadable expression, Dee looked at her hand, and Olivia withdrew it. "Alvaro will listen to you, Dee. I know he will."

"He listens to me, but it doesn't matter. Alvaro is missing."

"Missing where?"

Dee sighed. "He never came back from Aleppo. Jacob's body is still there, too—and nobody knows where the link is. The Society is frantic. Emilio is over there right now, looking for Alvaro. Everyone thinks he must have the link. Wonder what they'd think if they knew it was right here, just a few miles from the ranch, and that a woman had it."

Suddenly Olivia was on full alert. "Are you going to tell them?"

Dee took a long minute before she answered. "No."

"Why not?"

Dee looked out the windshield. A couple of cars whooshed by. "Damn it. Because I know you're right. If Andrew knew you had the link, he'd sacrifice you in a heartbeat to see power migrate to Emilio. And Emilio having the link is nothing but bad news."

"Then come with me to Syria and help me find Alvaro."

"Come to . . . *me?*"

"Either we get to him first, or Emilio does."

Dee shook her head. "I hate all of this."

"I need your help."

"I'll *think* about it. This is hard to get my head around. I need to go back now. I've been gone too long."

"While you're thinking about it, think about this. The existence of the probability machine proves the future exists. You people always believed that meant you had to use the machine. Alvaro said it was deterministic. But how do you know I'm not part of that determinism? I showed up at the right time and place because I'm the one who's supposed to turn the thing off now that it's time to turn it off. No one in the Society would even consider doing that. You're all too invested."

Dee looked thoughtful and extremely uncomfortable. "I have to go."

Olivia put the Ford in gear and drove them back to the parking lot. Dee opened the door and started to climb out. Hot air rushed in, displacing the cool.

"Take my number," Olivia said.

"Tell me. Don't write it down."

Olivia recited her phone number.

Standing by the open door, Dee said, "You know what? When I read your message, when you said a woman can link—it made me think you knew something about Alvaro. That's why I met you." She slammed the door and walked back to her car.

❀

BACK IN SEATTLE, IN THE middle of the night, Olivia startled awake in Brian's bed. For several moments she didn't know where she was, and she was frightened. A chat alert spun in the dark like a mystic coin, each twirl in sync with the trill of the alert. She reached out and finger-flicked the projection. It stopped spinning and plumped into a bubble containing a blurry face. No, it wasn't the face that was blurry. With the heels of her hands, Olivia tried to grind the sleep out of her eyes.

"When do we leave?" the face in the bubble said.

"What?" Olivia blinked, and Dee's features resolved. "Dee."

"Yeah."

A vivid bruise discolored Dee's jaw.

Olivia winced. "What happened to you?"

"The guy I put on the gate while I went to meet you, he was around yesterday when that boy delivered your message. He got suspicious when I drove away in the middle of the afternoon, so he ratted me out to Andrew. They got rough with me." She touched her bruised jaw. "I didn't tell them about you. The fucking coup was on this whole time, and I didn't even know it."

THIRTY-ONE

OLIVIA ALMOST STARTED CRYING WHEN Helen Fischer's unscarred face appeared in the chat bubble projected from Olivia's IsnGlas tablet. The last time she had talked to her London-based editor at *The Beat,* Helen had been sick, already in the aggressive early stages of variola infection. In the last images of Helen, preserved in a recorded message, the older woman's face had presented a hideous battleground of smallpox lesions. By the time Olivia had read that message, Helen had probably been dead two days. Now she was back, restored to life, her blue eyes behind glasses as sharp and inquiring as ever, her ugly death a lost shade known only to Olivia.

"Livvie," Helen said. "This is a surprise."

Olivia wiped her eyes. "Hi, Helen. I need to go back to Syria."

Helen pursed her lips. "You just left Syria."

"I know."

"What's going on?"

"A story. And I need to do this fast."

Helen removed her glasses and leaned forward, peering closely at Olivia's image projected on the other side of the world.

"Are you all right?" Helen said.

"I'm fine."

"May I be honest? You don't look fine."

Good old Helen. Abrupt, to the point. No different than she'd been every other time Olivia talked to her. Absurdly, Olivia had to hold back tears again. Once the barricades were down they were really down. She had to get it together and keep it that way.

"I'm okay, really."

Helen put her glasses back on. "What do you need?"

"Border crossing and a safe, fast route into Aleppo. I know you have people in-country."

"And you want me to arrange this."

"Yes."

"The civil war is over. You can arrange public transport, if nothing else. What am I missing?"

"I won't be alone. And the person coming with me might not have a visa."

Helen sat back in her office chair. "You want me to help you smuggle someone over the border? Livvie, what the *hell* is going on? Why can't this unnamed person obtain a visa?"

"It would take weeks, with no guarantee she'd get it, and we don't have weeks. There are rumors of a bioweapon and a plan to smuggle it out of Aleppo. I told you about it before—before I decided to come home."

Helen looked skeptical. Olivia knew from past experience that that was a bad sign.

"You said yourself while you were still in-country that you didn't have anything to work on. You were pretty out of it when we talked."

Olivia had called after Brian died, compelled to connect with some-one. She knew people in Aleppo, of course. But Helen was conveniently far away and a kind of mother figure.

"A lead on the bioweapon has come up since I got home."

"Okay. What do you have exactly?"

"I can't tell you, not yet."

"Then I'm going to say no," Helen said.

"What? Come on."

"There's something off about this," Helen said. "I don't believe you're all right. Livvie, that was a hard blow you took, your friend dying. When you called and told me you were finished with Syria, I believed you. That was, what, four days ago? Now this."

Olivia took a moment, then: "I need to *work*. That's what's off, and that's all that's off. I've got a lead on the bioweapon story, and I need this woman because of who she knows in Aleppo. But if we have to wait for the endless processing of her visa, that lead might disappear. And trust me, none of us wants it to disappear. Helen, help me do my job. Please. Trust me."

After almost a minute, Helen said, "I'm still going to say no. And I'm sorry, Livvie. I think you should stay home for now and recover until you can make a more rational decision."

"I am rational."

"Then I wish you'd tell me the truth. Because you're not doing that. And that troubles me very much. It isn't like you."

"Thanks for the advice, but I'm going in."

"I'm sorry. And I wish you wouldn't."

"I'm sorry, too."

Olivia broke the connection. It wasn't going to be easy. But she knew she could find another way.

She knew it because she had to.

❋

THE KARKAMIŞ REFUGEE CAMP, ON the Turkish side of the border with Syria, looked like a carnival of nightmares. Hundreds of dingy white tents intermingled with shanty-like structures thrown together out of scrap wood and sheet metal. In the twilight, a constellation of cook fires burned red, like scattershot perforations between Earth and the Under-world. Barking dogs and the cries of children reached Olivia and Dee on the low hill overlooking the camp. So did an ugly smell, a ripe effluvium of rotting garbage, sewage, and burning meat.

"Welcome to the Disaster," Olivia said.

"God," Dee said.

"This camp isn't even official," Olivia said. "When the war ended, a lot of people returned to Syria, and they shut down the worst of the camps. Like this one. The remaining, official camps, like the one in Kilis, are a lot bigger and almost tolerable, with electricity, security, container dwellings, all kinds of amenities."

"What're container dwellings?"

"Shipping containers turned into apartments. They aren't as bad as they sound." Olivia removed her soft cap and mopped the sweat off her forehead. Before leaving the States she'd cut her hair boyishly short. Some kind of stupid leaving-the-past-behind gesture. Now she felt self-conscious about it.

"So what are all these people doing here?" Dee looked a little over-whelmed.

"The war stopped, but it's not safe in Syria. Not by any stretch. The homes and businesses these people left during the bombing, a lot of them don't exist anymore. It's going to take years to rebuild a humanitarian infrastructure that can bring everyone home. In the meantime, believe it or not, a place like this is a better option. For some people. At least, that's what they think." She gestured at the camp, at the visible piece of the world Disaster. Olivia's stomach was in knots. Had she always felt this way in the Disaster? She couldn't remember.

Getting to Turkey had not been a problem. Olivia, of course, had come here many times, and her credentials were in order. Dee possessed a passport, and the e-visa was approved in a single day.

Syria was another matter.

The international coalition occupying the country was not strictly defined as an occupying force. Assad's ruling party never fell during the long civil war. The Americans wanted Assad out—they had always wanted him out—yet he was still there, sick and wheelchair-bound but still the head of his government. Visas had to be obtained through the regime, and those wheels did not turn swiftly, and sometimes not at all.

But there was another way.

"Come on. We have to find a guy." Olivia hitched up her backpack and hooked her thumbs under the straps. They walked down into the camp.

During his employment with the NGO Oregon Helps, Brian had spent a lot of time in refugee camps, some worse than this one. Olivia had seen worse, too. But she had maintained a semipermeable barrier between herself and the human suffering. She had gone to those camps to get a story, tap an interview subject, follow a trail, research background. She had stood outside the Disaster even as she navigated through it.

Until Brian.

People ignored Olivia and Dee, or merely glanced up as they passed: haggard faces, old and young, in firelight. But a dog started following at their heels as soon as they stepped between the first row of tents. The mongrel looked like it had missed a few meals, but it wasn't the skinniest dog Olivia had ever seen. In Aleppo, she had once observed a dog—no more than a skeleton with a thin layer of mangy fur stretched over its bones—prowl through rubble, tracking the scent of crushed and buried human corpses. By comparison, this pooch was more like Buster and his piece of yellow rope back in Portland.

"Go home," Olivia said. The dog ignored her.

"How do we find this guy?" Dee kept her voice low, as if it mattered.

"My contact said someone would find us, once we reached the camp."

"Uh, seems we have a parade," Dee said.

"What?"

Dee nodded over her right shoulder. Olivia turned. Now, besides the dog, six children followed them, a couple of girls and four boys. They hung back a respectable distance, except for a girl in a red shirt and rubber-tire sandals. She was almost as close as the dog. Surprisingly, she reached out and grabbed the dog's tail.

"Bibi, la-a."

"What'd she say?" Dee asked.

"She said 'No.' The dog's name is Bibi, I guess. Bibi, no."

Bibi stopped following the women, and the child let go. The dog chased around to nip at its own tail. Olivia bent forward, left hand propped on her thigh, and waved for the girl, who looked about nine years old, to come closer. She did, her fingers clutching Bibi's neck fur, holding the dog against her hip.

"What's your name?" Olivia asked in Arabic.

The girl stared at her.

"We're looking for someone," Olivia said. "Can you help?"

The girl shrugged.

"A man named Jameel Antar. Can you show me where he is?"

In Arabic, the girl said, "Yes. Follow me."

Olivia stood up straight. "Really?"

Dee nudged her. "What'd the girl say?"

"She wants us to follow her."

"Should we?"

"I don't know. Yes."

Dee looked around the camp like she was in an iffy inner-city neighborhood. "Where's this kid's parents?"

"She might not have any," Olivia said.

"God, this place. You're right, it's a disaster."

The child spoke up in a mixture of English and Arabic. "La, mach *disaster*. Baytayy."

Olivia felt a stab of embarrassment. "I'm sorry," she said to the girl.

"What's going on?" Dee said. "What'd she say?"

"She said this is not a disaster, it's her home."

"Jesus. I'm an idiot."

The child walked past them with her dog. When Olivia and Dee didn't move, the girl called back, "Attabie fatatan."

Follow a girl.

They looked at each other and followed the girl.

She led them to a bearded man wearing jeans, a long-faded Lady Gaga tour shirt, and Adidas sneakers. He sat on a pillow under a make-shift lean-to made of tent fabric and wooden poles. A black cigarette jutted from the corner of his mouth. His eyes looked heavy, but when Olivia and Dee approached with the child, he stood with alacrity and greeted them.

"I am Jameel. Not my true name, of course."

"Of course," Olivia said. "We're—"

Jameel held up his hand. "I know who you are. Did you bring the payment?"

"Yes." Olivia started to reach for a zippered pocket on her pants.

Jameel waved his hand. "No, no. Not here. Sit down and have a drink."

"When do we cross?" Olivia asked, unshouldering her backpack.

"One hour. You are later than you said you would be."

Olivia and Dee sat on pillows under the lean-to. The tent fabric caught the pungent smoke rising from Jameel's cigarette and hovered it over them in a thin, noxious cloud.

The little girl and her dog stood facing them, waiting.

"She requires payment," Jameel said.

"How much?"

Jameel named a modest sum. Olivia produced a pair of coins and handed them to the child, who closed her grubby fist around them and ran away, the dog at her heels.

Jameel removed the cigarette from his lips and blew smoke. "I told the kids to watch for you."

"And whoever found us got paid," Dee said.

"They are all paid, but Akilah brought you to me, so she is paid a little more. Do you want smoke?" He held out a pack of Turkish cigarettes. On the front was the obligatory photo of the country's president, a hard-looking man wearing sunglasses. Turkey's version of Joe Camel.

Olivia shook her head. "No, thanks." She looked across to a dilapi-dated shack made of scavenged plywood and plastic sheeting. A man and a woman stood talking in voices too soft to hear. The woman wore a yellow hijab. A little boy poked his head out of the shack, and the man playfully gave him a tap on his crown. "Boop!" the man said. The boy pulled his head back into the shelter, and the woman laughed, covering her lips with a pair of fingers, as if she couldn't decide whether to stop laughing or blow a kiss.

La disaster. *Baytayy.*

A couple of hours later, they piled into a junky fossil-burner and drove from the camp to the small border town of Karkamiş. The wing mirror's plastic mounts had broken, and the mirror dangled by the cable meant to adjust the angle of view. It twisted and knocked against the door, like it wanted to get into the car with them. In Karkamiş the buildings stood dark in the moonlight.

"Power rationing," Jameel said. "The end of war has improved nothing." He parked on a deserted street and killed the engine. "Payment now."

Olivia dug out the money and handed it over. American currency.

Jameel pointed to the end of the street. The vague outlines of a gate were visible, and the tip of a cigarette glowed and dimmed periodically. "This crossing is no more official. Go on. The guard will let you through."

"You're coming to the gate with us, right?" Dee said.

"The guard has been paid."

"I don't like it," Dee said.

"Come with us," Olivia said.

Jameel chuckled. "You Americans are babies." He didn't say it meanly, but like it was an amusing and universally acknowledged fact.

They all got out of the car and walked to the gate. Olivia felt exposed on the open street, though there was no reason to think snipers might be lurking on the rooftops. It was the habit of fear; they weren't even in Syria yet. A ten-foot-high border fence stretched for miles, interrupted here and there by other, active gates. The endless Syrian diaspora had forced Turkey to erect barriers. They opened gates like water taps to measure the flow of refugees, or to cut it off altogether.

The guard dropped his cigarette and crushed it under the toe of his boot. A sidearm hung low on his hip, dragging his pants down and leaving his police tunic untucked on one side. Jameel embraced him. They slapped each other's backs like fraternity brothers, stood apart, and spoke to each other in Arabic. Olivia caught only a few words. They seemed to be talking about their families.

The guard turned to Olivia and Dee. In English, he said, "Welcome. Probably you think I am a corrupt official. You are right. But I am corrupt for the sake of the children. Not all foreign aid goes where it should. Yours will. Which of you is Dee?"

Dee raised her hand.

"Take this." The guard handed her an authentic-looking visa and passport, already stamped for Syria.

"Thanks," Dee said.

"Hide your true credentials. Two passports are not good."

"We'll handle it," Olivia said.

The guard nodded, opened the gate, and ushered them through.

Olivia and Dee walked down the road, the moonlight making little pale shadows before them. The gate closed with an iron *clank*.

"Give me your real passport," Olivia said.

Dee handed it over, and Olivia slipped it inside her boot sock. "Sorry, it's going to smell like my foot when you get it back."

They walked for almost an hour. The stars were so thick they were like a diamond crust.

"How far is it?" Dee asked.

"I don't know. Someone's picking us up."

"Good. When?"

A pair of headlights appeared in the distance. "Now, I think."

The women stopped walking. The lights drew closer. The sound of an engine became audible, along with muffled music. Soon a van stopped in front of them, road dust making a haze in the headlamps. Olivia blinked and waved her hand in front of her face. The headlamps shut off, leaving amber parking lights. Inside the van, the music stopped. Dee sneezed.

One person sat behind the windshield, a woman, her red curls wild in the dashboard light. The window rolled down and the woman stuck her head out. In a British accent, she said, "You Nikitas?"

"Yes," Olivia said. "Dee, this is Toria Westby."

"Hey," Dee said.

"Hey yourself. Get in, you two. It's better if we're moving."

"Where's your partner?" Olivia asked. "The guy who likes cigars."

Toria gave her an odd look. In the current probability, Olivia had never taken that first ride across Aleppo with Toria and her BBC cameraman, the cigar-chewing Cockney who sort of knew what a superposition was. As far as Toria was concerned, this was the first time she had ever laid eyes on Olivia in person. But Olivia remembered Toria, and it had been relatively easy to track down her number and arrange this pickup—once she identified herself, said Toria had come recommended by her editor, and promised a major lead on the rumored bioweapon story.

"Mikey," Toria said. "Mike's dead."

THIRTY-TWO

THE VAN SMELLED LIKE SUNSCREEN, hot batteries, and sweat. Olivia took the shotgun seat and Dee clambered into the back, where she stumbled in the dark and banged against the wall.

"What's all this crap?"

"That's my gear," Toria said. "Don't step on it, please."

"Sorry."

Toria swung the van around and popped the headlights back on.

"Thanks for picking us up," Olivia said.

Toria pushed the hair off her forehead. She smiled in the dash light. "You're going to make it up to me, I hope, with information."

"Sorry about your partner," Olivia said. "What happened?"

Toria glanced at her. "Did you know Mike?"

"In a way that's too complicated to explain right now, yes. A little."

"Right. We all stray out of the pasture sometimes."

Stray out of the pasture?

"Mikey was on his second marriage and it wasn't going great."

Ah. "We didn't have an affair. It's not that kind of complicated."

"Your business, not mine."

"What happened to him?"

"We were covering the mini-uprising. Mikey was getting some great footage, American gunships booming over the Old City. Real *Apocalypse Now* stuff. I'm in the frame, doing my thing, giving context, and a light tactical vehicle runs into Mikey. Camera goes flying. I'm standing there like a dummy."

"He got run over."

"Yeah. He was a good guy. *Fuck.* Such a stupid way to die, especially here. He could've got run over in Whitechapel, for fuck's sake. Anyway, BBC coughed up a new cameraman. I left him in Aleppo for this taxi run." Toria un-Velcroed a pocket on her pants, slipped out her phone —a sturdy Nexus 2D model—and woke it up and handed it to Olivia. "First five faces in the gallery, one of them's your guy. Those are the checkpoint commanders on the western routes out of the city."

When Olivia had tried to use the probability machine to subvert the escape of weaponized variola out of Aleppo and still allow Brian to live, the halo had repeatedly presented the vision of a checkpoint on the western edge of the city: *A kid in an ancient Jeep Cherokee approaches. The kid is nervous as hell. The checkpoint commander steps up. Repeat.* The halo refused to pinpoint the key, and though Olivia had "seen" the boy in his mother's kitchen and had manipulated the probability to prevent him from passing through the checkpoint, variola had nevertheless escaped —and the crisis had actually accelerated. The lesson? Good intentions aren't good enough, and nobody should have this power. Not her, not Jacob, certainly not Emilio.

Now, swiping through the pictures on Toria's phone, Olivia recognized a face she had seen in the halo on two occasions: a middle-aged guy with a thick mustache, wearing a side-slanting beret—the checkpoint commander who stopped the kid in the Jeep.

"This one, this is him." She turned the phone to Toria.

Toria glanced at it. "Baki Abboud. He's corrupt as they come, which is saying something in this place."

"What about the kid?"

Olivia had given Toria the Jeep's license plate number. Even though preventing him from driving out of the city that day hadn't forestalled the apocalypse, he was somehow a player. He had knowledge. Maybe something that connected him to Baki Abboud.

"Yeah," Toria said. "I've got his address. Lives with his mother. Father killed in the war. You want to talk to him first? He'll be easier to approach than Abboud. I can take you to him tomorrow."

"Maybe."

"Maybe?" Toria looked at her and back at the road. "You've got something more important to do?"

"Yes. And we're doing it tonight." Olivia looked back at Dee, who was kneeling, with her hands on the backs of the driver and passenger seats. "Address." Dee reached for a notepad and read off a street address.

The Society maintained safe houses in the eastern, formerly rebel-contested, half of Aleppo. But this wasn't one of them. This was a place only Jacob and Alvaro had known about. Per tradition, Jacob had arranged it for them privately, a place for them to stay before and after Jacob brought Alvaro to see the probability machine. Why not use one of the Society's safe houses? Olivia had asked before they left the States. "It's like a pilgrimage," Dee had replied. "The Shepherd and his successor make their own way. The old Shepherd reveals secret knowledge and then takes the new Shepherd to see the machine. After that there's a period of fasting. The Society is full of rituals."

"Toria, can you find that address without GPS?" Eastern Aleppo was still largely an internet dead zone.

"What's there?" Toria said.

"A man we have to talk to."

"Which man? And talk about what? He's got something to do with the bioweapon?"

"It's all related," Olivia said truthfully.

An hour later, they rolled into the Salah ad-Deen neighborhood on the southwest outskirts of the city. Part of the 1070 Apartment Project, the residential area had been heavily pounded and fought over during the war. Blocks of five-story buildings, hollowed out and devastated, stood like vertically organized abstract sculptures. The BBC van jolted and rocked over debris-strewn streets and finally turned onto a cleared avenue. Construction lamps cabled to poles directed their harsh glare over the pocked faces of still-inhabited apartment structures. Civilians circulated among makeshift cafés. Multiple generators made a racket like lawnmowers.

"Here," Toria said, tucking the van into the curb in front of a bleak façade checkerboarded with candlelit windows. A couple of young men sat on the sidewalk, backs against the building, smoking and talking. They looked over when the van stopped.

Dee pulled herself up between the seats. "I better go in alone."

"We go together," Olivia said.

"I'm staying with my stuff." Toria eyed the smoking men. "But you're going to share whatever you get, right?"

Olivia pushed open the passenger door. "Right."

On the sidewalk, Olivia found herself breathing the familiar dust-sifted air of Aleppo. This was, of course, only one Aleppo out of who knew how many possible iterations. She had seen how even tiny, localized shifts in the probability stream could have far-reaching influence. The González effect, for example. Had Dee been right when she suggested the probability machine could be used to arrange an improved world? Maybe in another timeline the Arab Spring uprising toppled Bashar al-Assad, as it did the leaders of Egypt and Tunisia. Or maybe an alternate probability existed where Assad was removed before his bloody war stretched into its second decade. Somewhere in the infinite probability choices could Aleppo have shone in the sun of art and culture and history, fulfilling its "shining city" parable? Or was its destruction inevitable, always arriving somewhere along the city's timeline?

Olivia shook off the doubt. That was just another danger of the power: It could seduce you into trying it again, with all good intentions. But if she knew anything about the probability machine, she knew intentions had nothing to do with outcomes.

They entered the building. Oil lamps burned in the lobby, wearing dusty auras. Their boots crunched over fine grit. Part of a wall had caved in, exposing a tangle of rebar. The stairwell was dark. Olivia and Dee produced flashlights. They crossed hazy beams as they ascended to the second floor.

"If only Jacob and Alvaro are supposed to know about this place, how'd you get the address?"

"Alvaro called me the night before Jacob took him to see the machine. He was excited and wanted to talk."

"Didn't that break tradition?"

"Alvaro and I have our own traditions."

The hallway was surprisingly clean, the floor swept. The window at the end of the hall bore the streaks of a squeegee. Street light projected a distorted window frame on the ceiling.

"This one," Dee said, pointing at a door. She kept her voice low. "Maybe hang back? If he's here, it's because he doesn't want to be found. Let's not spook him." Dee put her flashlight away. Olivia nodded and stepped back, extinguishing her own light, so she wouldn't be immediately visible when the door opened.

Dee knocked softly, waited, knocked again. "Alvaro?"

Nothing.

Down in the street, someone shouted angrily, then laughed.

Dee reached for the doorknob. Before her fingers touched it, the knob rattled and turned. Olivia tensed. Dee stepped back.

The door opened and a man said, "Who's that?"

Dee said, "Emilio?"

The door opened wider. Emilio, in a black T-shirt and jeans, leaned into the hall, his right hand behind his back.

"What are you doing here?" he said. "And who's *she?*"

"A friend who knows the country," Dee said. "Emilio, what are *you* doing here? Nobody's supposed to know this place."

"And yet you know it."

"I'm just trying to find Alvaro."

"We are all trying to do that." Emilio's hand came out from behind his back. It was holding a pistol. "You better come in here. Both of you."

He stepped fully into the hall, directed them through the door with his gun, and followed after them, pulling the door shut behind him. The room was small and smelled of tobacco and mildew. The furniture was old and lumpy, the sofa almost like the bloated carcass of an animal. The rug was threadbare, worn through to the floorboards in places. Many candles lighted the room.

"I know about you," Emilio said. "Andrew called and said you couldn't be trusted anymore. You're going to tell me what's going on."

Olivia stepped forward. "There's nothing going on. Why don't you stop waving that gun around? We all want to find Alvaro. Why don't we work together?" She barely knew what she was saying. Olivia just wanted Emilio to put the gun down, so they'd have a chance of getting out of this room.

But Emilio was having none of it. "You sit in that chair. *Do it.*"

Olivia turned her head to see what chair he meant—and Emilio gasped. "Now I see."

A scuffle started. Olivia turned. Dee had caught Emilio's wrist and twisted it expertly. The gun dropped to the floor. Dee kicked it away, at the same time pulling him down and around, following him like Muhammad Ali followed George Foreman to the mat. Olivia grabbed the gun.

"We're leaving," Dee said.

Emilio glared at her. "Traitor." He spat on her shoe.

Dee pushed him back on his ass and released his wrist. She stuck out her hand and said to Olivia, "Give me that."

Olivia handed over the gun.

Dee pointed it at Emilio. "We're leaving. Don't try to follow us."

Sitting on the floor, massaging his wrist, Emilio sneered. "They should have kept you in the kitchen."

Dee snorted. "Let's go." In the hall she tucked the gun into the waist of her pants and covered it with her shirt.

Outside, the smoking men were gone. Olivia said, "You're handy to have around."

"Just tell me what plan B is."

"We're still on plan A: Find Alvaro."

"That room up there? It's all I had. So we need plan B."

"Then we have to find the probability machine ourselves."

"How?"

"I'll figure something out."

"Well, you better figure it out quick. Emilio saw your scar," Dee said, causing Olivia to immediately cup her hand over the back of her neck. "He knows you have the link."

THIRTY-THREE

THE NEXT MORNING, AFTER FIVE hours of murderous jet lag and two of bad sleep, Olivia opened her eyes and still didn't know how to find Alvaro or the probability machine. She quickly put herself together and headed downstairs. They had spent the night in the Beit Wakil. Before the war, it had been a four-star hotel in eastern Aleppo. Now the most you could say for it was that it was open and, for the most part, structurally sound, not to mention cheap. And they had coffee, strong coffee, which Dee was drinking in the dining room when Olivia walked in. Foreigners occupied about half the tables, a few men in suits, others in safari shirts. Olivia spotted Dee, sat down, and poured a cup of mud.

Priority one was to find the probability machine, with or without Alvaro's help. If that wasn't possible, the backup plan was to track down the possible path of weaponized variola out of Aleppo. Jacob's original probability had prevented the escape, but Olivia worried that it was a temporary measure. Variola was still here *somewhere,* a potential, maybe even an inevitable threat. And there'd be no magic halos this time. They had to be on *top* of it.

"What's the plan?" Dee looked as bleary-eyed as Olivia felt.

"It's still gelling."

Dee nodded, slurped her coffee.

Olivia looked at her over the rim of her own coffee cup. "Look, I have some private business to take care of."

"You can do that while gelling?"

"Yeah." Olivia's coffee was hot enough to burn her tongue, but she didn't care.

"What's the personal business?"

"My friend—his body is still in Aleppo." She hated referring to Brian as a body. "His parents are having trouble getting him processed out. I said I'd try to help."

"Oh, sorry."

Olivia produced her phone. Three bars. In eastern Aleppo's patchwork cell coverage, the Beit Wakil stood a few blocks from a tower in the western half of the city. She tried the number of a Marine captain in her "reliable sources: military" directory.

"Who are you calling?" Dee asked.

"This captain I know. He might be able to help."

The call rang in weird fits and starts. Olivia was about to kill the sketchy connection and try again when a man's voice said:

"Burnley."

"Hey, it's me, Liv."

"I thought you went home."

"I did, but I'm back. Ted, I need your help."

"Of course you do," the captain said.

Olivia liked Burnley, and he liked her—but not in the same way. Hers was professional and his aspired to be more personal. When she first met him, the possibility of a personal connection hadn't been out of the question. Then she met Brian, and he got his foot in her door. Probably Olivia should have found a different Marine to help her track the body. But Ted Burnley was so *good*. If there was red tape, he had the scissors. But Olivia never stopped beating herself up for using the captain's attraction to keep him interested in helping her with stuff like expediting corpses out of Syria.

"This one is painless," Olivia said. "I hope."

She quickly outlined the problem.

"I'll make some calls and get back to you. Give me a half hour."

"Thanks, Ted."

They drank coffee and ate breakfast while they waited. Cucumbers, goat's milk yogurt, and khubz—a round Arabic bread, very chewy.

It was closer to an hour before Captain Burnley called back. "You're gonna have to go to the morgue."

"Shit." Olivia closed her eyes, rubbed her temple.

"So the deal is: face-to-face and have your bribe money ready. Only way to get anything done in this place. Anyhow, I greased the skids, but they still want you to personally ID the corpse."

The world grayed out a little, and black spots floated across her vision. For a few moments she couldn't speak. Dee looked worried.

"You still with me?" Burnley said.

Olivia pulled it together. "Yeah."

"Goddamn phones around here, you never know."

"Why do I have to identify him?" She didn't want to say Brian's name. "Don't they already know it's him?"

"It's an excuse. Some hospital bureaucrat wants you to hand him money. They might not make you actually look at your friend."

Olivia drank some coffee. Her throat felt almost too tight to swallow. "Which morgue?"

"There's only one," Burnley said. "This goddamn war, both sides bombed the hell out of each other's hospitals. Never saw anything like it. Now, your boy's an American citizen. That's the only reason he's got a cold locker." He gave her the hospital's name and address.

"Thanks, Ted."

"You going to be in-country for a while?"

"Possibly."

"Give me a call."

"Sure. Thanks again." She hung up and reached for her coffee. Noticing the tremor in her hand, she made a fist and clenched it tightly.

"What's going on?" Dee asked.

"I have to go look at my friend's body and bribe somebody. I mean, maybe I won't have to look at it. I don't know."

Dee studied her. "Are you up for that?"

"I don't know. Yes. I have to be."

"I'll come with you."

"You don't have to do that."

"I'm coming. You look like you could use some moral support."

✳

AS ARRANGED THE PREVIOUS NIGHT, Toria pulled up in the BBC van at 9 a.m. Olivia and Dee got in.

"You guys still look like shit," Toria said.

Olivia smiled briefly, woodenly. "Thanks. Lousy sleep."

"The kid's place is about twenty minutes from here."

"Uh, we need to go someplace else first."

Toria looked at the ceiling, as if beseeching the gods for succor. "You're not going to believe this, but I have a job I'm supposed to be doing."

"This is part of it. The bioweapon story. This side trip is just something personal I have to do first."

Toria tapped the steering wheel with her nails, which were red and chipped. "Okay, where are the Three Musketeers going this morning?"

"The morgue."

AN HOUR AFTER TALKING TO Captain Burnley from the dining room of the Beit Wakil, Olivia and Dee were following a harried orderly, or at least an orderly who affected being harried, into a large, starkly lit room lined with green tiles. Human meat lockers filled one whole wall, maybe thirty in all. A gurney with an empty body bag hanging sloppily over the edge stood in the middle of the room. There was a strong, almost overpowering smell of industrial disinfectant.

"We are very busy here," the orderly said, clearly put out by having to escort two foreigners.

"We understand," Olivia said. "Thank you for taking the time."

Unmollified, the orderly said, "I have a busy job."

"Why don't you try doing it with a little less talking," Dee said.

"Do not disrespect." The orderly consulted his tablet, scrolled. "Okay, this one." He strode to a locker, opened it, and slid out the tray, the casters rolling loudly in their steel channels. Green sheeting covered the body

"Brian Anker," the orderly said. He folded back the sheeting. "Miss?"

Olivia hadn't wanted to look at Brian's body, but suddenly she needed to.

Dee squeezed her arm. "You want to be alone?"

"Yes."

"No alone in this room," the orderly said.

"For fuck's sake," Dee said.

"Rules."

"Okay. There's a body I want to see," Dee said. "A different body. Another American. This is where the Americans are, right?"

"What body?"

"Jacob Shaw."

Making a big show of being put out, the orderly consulted his tablet again. "Over here."

He led Dee to a locker on the other side of the room. "Why you wish to see this body, I have no understanding. It will be necessary to update the log. Very expensive."

"What a surprise." Dee reached for her wallet. "How expensive?"

Olivia approached the open drawer containing Brian. Of course, she had seen many dead bodies, some the bodies of people she knew well, friends and colleagues. And she had seen Brian's body in the torture cell under the madrassa. But that time was part of an entanglement of memory scaffolds, like overlapping dreams.

What lay in that drawer was the final reality.

Brian's face seemed carved in wax. She whispered, barely able to get the words out. "Bri, I'm so sorry."

"Hey!"

Olivia looked up. Dee waved her over.

"You're not going to believe this," Dee said.

"Believe what?"

Olivia walked over to the other drawer. Dee stood beside it, looking outraged. The orderly stood at the foot of the tray, holding his tablet. Jacob's body was covered with green sheeting, just like Brian's. But above the shoulders, the sheeting lay flat.

Someone had taken his head.

Olivia rubbed her eyes. God, she was tired. "Are we sure this is Jacob's body?"

The orderly waved his tablet. "It says here. Please respect our efficiency."

Both women glanced at him, then walked away from the drawer, out of earshot, if they kept their voices low.

"Somebody thought Jacob might still have the link," Dee said. "Emilio?"

"Maybe. You said the Society was desperate to find it. If the link hadn't been able to migrate to anyone, it's logical to think it might have stayed in Jacob's head."

"I've never heard of that."

"When they took me out of the torture cell, Jacob's head was still attached. Something happened between there and the morgue. We need to establish provenance."

"Is it important? *We* know where the link is. So does Emilio."

"It might be important. We won't know until we find out what happened."

She dug out her phone. No bars.

"Hey." She raised her voice to the orderly. "Is there a landline in this hospital I can use?"

"First there is payment for the log work."

"Naturally."

A few minutes later, at a nurses' station, Olivia dialed Captain Burnley's Green Zone landline. A subordinate answered. Olivia identified herself and left a message. She wanted to talk to whoever it was who had taken Jacob's body out of the torture cell. It wasn't a sure bet that Burnley would know who that person was, but Olivia didn't know who else to ask. The subordinate said he would relay the message.

"Okay," Olivia said, handing the phone back to the nurse, "let's go talk to this kid Toria found."

✳

AT FIRST, THE BOY'S MOTHER was suspicious.

"What has Rashid done?" Her English was excellent.

For the third time, Olivia said, "He hasn't done anything. I just want to ask him a couple of questions."

"But why? He's only a boy. He's a good son."

"I promise he won't get in any trouble for talking to me."

Should she promise that? It didn't matter; she just *did* promise it. Olivia looked around the kitchen. Peeling linoleum floor, clean counters, neatly organized cabinets without doors. The inevitable dust of Syrian destruction filmed the windowpanes. This widow and her "good son" lived in the heart of the Disaster. War had eaten her husband, the boy's father. But they still made a home. A more typical disaster had eaten Olivia's mother and father. Olivia had responded by constructing barricades and declaring that disasters did not affect her anymore. Shayma's kitchen still felt like a home. All Olivia had was a dead man's apartment on the other side of the world and a stepmother who had tried to be a real mother even after Olivia had placed her firmly on the other side of her barricades.

The door opened and a mop-haired boy of fifteen or so walked in with a cloth bag of groceries. Olivia recognized him instantly. He saw

Olivia and stopped dead, though there was no way he could possibly know her.

"This woman wants to ask you questions," Shayma said. "She is a reporter."

Rashid put the grocery bag on the counter. Without looking at either of them, he said, "Okay."

"I will make tea." Shayma turned and filled the kettle with tap water.

Olivia cleared her throat. "Rashid, do you know a military man named Baki Abboud?"

Shayma dropped the kettle in the sink, making a loud noise. Without a word, she picked the kettle up and resumed filling it.

Rashid said, "No."

"A few days ago," Olivia said, "you were going to drive through Abboud's checkpoint out of the city. Can you tell me why?"

Mother and son turned toward Olivia, as if their heads were attached to synchronized swivels. Shayma looked scared. Rashid looked like he wanted to be someplace else.

"It's not true. How do you know this?" Shayma said.

If it wasn't true, what was there to know? Olivia reached for every reporter's magic card: "I have a source. Anonymous. Rashid, you aren't in trouble. But I need to know why you decided to leave by that checkpoint."

"He's a good son," Shayma said.

"I know," Olivia said, knowing no such thing, though she suspected he was. Didn't he just go out into the Disaster to buy groceries for his mother? What would Shayma think if she knew that in another probability Olivia had directed her son's death?

"A man told me to go," Rashid said.

Shayma said, "What? Who, what man?"

Rashid shrugged. "Just a man, someone I know."

"That's no answer," Shayma said.

Rashid looked at the floor.

Olivia said, "It's important." She tried to think of something to threaten the boy with, immediately felt shame, and was glad when nothing occurred to her. "Please, Rashid. It will save lives. And no one will know you told me. I promise. You won't be implicated."

"What is 'implicated'?" Shayma asked.

"Associated," Olivia said, "maybe criminally associated."

Shayma put the kettle down like she was using it to squash a scorpion. "You can go. My son has nothing more to say."

"Many lives," Olivia said to the boy. "Very many lives."

The boy crossed his arms tightly, as if he was holding the secret against his chest.

"Well." Olivia turned to the door. "Thank you for talking to—"

Rashid's chin came up. "Mahdi. That's all I know. Mahdi."

"This man. Mahdi. Does he have a scar, here?" Olivia pointed at her eyebrow and traced a crooked line upward. "A jagged scar?"

Rashid nodded.

It fell into place. Mahdi was the linchpin of the crisis point. He had been there when the shooting started outside the madrassa, when Brian and Jodee were hit, and he had stopped the gunman from shooting Olivia. That's why he couldn't be in the torture cell earlier to intervene with Jacob, not until Olivia placed him there in her alternate probability stream when she wanted to bring Brian back. In that altered probability, the kid who fired on the French peacekeepers and Olivia's party was alone. He wounded Brian and Jodee, but not critically, and the soldiers took him down before he could kill Olivia. Mahdi wasn't there that time, in Olivia's probability. But he was in *Jacob's*—he was there to be killed by one of the wounded soldiers, and therefore prevented from later playing a part in the smuggling of variola.

"What did Mahdi tell you?" Olivia asked. "Specifically."

"Only that I should drive out of the city and that I must go by the Omar ibn al-Khattab road."

Shayma, sounding disappointed, said, "Last week you told me you wished to visit Mansura."

"Mansura is a destination I made up by myself. I lied, Mother. I'm sorry." He looked at his shoes.

"Oh, Rash." Shayma pulled him in and hugged him. "Why did you do this thing?"

"I don't know. Mahdi is a hero. A hero asks me to do something, I have to do it."

"Mahdi is not a hero," Shayma said. "He fought in a confusing time and lived. Others did not live. And now he is dead, too."

"I know. But it didn't seem like a bad thing to do. Mahdi only wanted me to drive into the desert. It wasn't hard to say yes."

Olivia said, "He didn't say anything about what to do after you got out of the city?"

"No. Only that I must go by way of Omar ibn al-Khattab."

Yes, Olivia thought. The way that would force Rashid to pass through Baki Abboud's checkpoint.

Mother stood apart from son, her hands on his shoulders. "Look at me."

He raised his chin, but it was plain he didn't want to, that he was ashamed.

"Tell this woman the truth," Shayma said.

"I did. It's—"

"All of the truth, Rash."

Jesus. Olivia was glad Shayma wasn't prosecuting her in a courtroom.

Rashid sighed. "I was to drive two kilometers and stop. Someone was to approach me."

"Who?" Olivia said.

"I don't know. It doesn't matter. Mahdi was supposed to give me the final word to go, but he got killed and never did it. So I did not go."

This time, she believed him.

THIRTY-FOUR

A BLOCK AWAY, DEE AND Toria waited in the shade of a crumbling wall next to the BBC van, drinking bottles of water.

Toria saw Olivia approaching and stepped away from the wall. "What happened?"

"Water." Olivia reached out, and Toria handed her the Arwa bottle. The heat was brutal. Olivia wondered how she had endured it for so long. In the cauldron of the Disaster, she had been like a slow-cooking crab. Well, she was done. Almost.

She tilted her head back, chugged the warm water, and wiped her lips. "Baki Abboud."

Toria said, "What about him?"

"During the uprising, he tried to use a civilian to transport something out of the city. Not the biological itself, but something connected, maybe some kind of code or instruction. I don't know. Something."

"You mean the kid you just talked to?"

"Rashid. Yes. But I don't think the boy knew what was going on. Whatever it was must have been time-sensitive. It couldn't wait for the new checkpoints to come down, and Abboud wasn't willing to expose himself. This guy Mahdi, he recruits Rashid to drive through a particular checkpoint and out of the city. When the vehicle is searched, there's nothing to find, because the commander planned to plant whatever it is *after* the vehicle had been examined."

"Plant what?" Toria asked.

"I don't know. But somebody was going to stop the kid once he got away from the city, so this could still go down. We could be on the brink again next month, or tomorrow."

Toria looked at her strangely. "What do you mean, on the brink *again*? Tell me what's going on."

Olivia said, "I can't tell you anything else right now."

"You know what?" Toria said. "You're a real tosser sometimes."

"I know. I'm sorry. Look into Baki Abboud, the checkpoint commander. He's dirty and dangerous. If we can bring it to the attention of the coalition authority, maybe that will help."

"You want to go see this guy now, this Abboud?"

"No." Olivia handed back the water bottle. "You do that. It's a major story, trust me. You just have to dig a little."

"You're *giving* it to me? Why?"

"Dee and I have something else to do. Can you drop us at the Green Zone?"

"HOW CAN I HELP YOU, ma'am?" Private First Class Christopher Choshi stood with his hands clasped behind his back and his cover tucked under his arm. Beads of sweat glistened on his bald head. Olivia, Dee, and the private stood in sweltering shade under a fly in the Green Zone compound.

"You were in charge of bringing out the bodies from under the madrassa?"

"My detail was tasked with securing and identification of the deceased. The one on the table was pretty messed up."

"I know. Where did you take him, the messed-up one?" Olivia was trying hard to not think about Brian. Trying and failing.

"Well, ma'am, the body had identification, a passport, so we knew it belonged to an American. Automatically, that meant we had to preserve it until positive identification and next of kin could be notified. In this heat, they don't last long. The bodies. We bagged it, brought it to the Zone, and iced it. Later it got transported to a civilian morgue until arrangements to return it home could be made. But I didn't have anything to do with that."

"Private, what I'm trying to figure out is when the body lost its head."

"Ma'am?"

"I want to know who decapitated that corpse. It doesn't seem plausible it could have happened while in military custody, so—"

"No, ma'am. It happened in that room under the school—under the madrassa."

Olivia and Dee looked at each other. "What are you talking about?" Olivia said to the private.

"The body was decapitated in that room where we found it." He looked uncomfortable. Olivia didn't think he was lying, but what else could it be?

"I was in that room myself," she said.

"Yes, ma'am, I know."

"Then you know the body was intact when you found us."

"Yes."

"Are you saying someone slipped in and sawed the head off while we were all standing around right outside?"

"That isn't possible, ma'am. They would have had to penetrate our security perimeter. There's no way."

"I'm not understanding this," Olivia said.

For the first time, PFC Christopher Choshi looked not merely uncomfortable but uncertain. In fact, he looked troubled. Olivia felt a prickling sensation on her back.

"It's kind of crazy," the private said.

"What is?"

"We brought you up, and it was like a half hour before I went back down with my detail to bag and tag the bodies. Nobody went down before us. I guarantee that. The building was secure. But that guy's head was gone, and that's just flat-out weird. Maybe it was already gone and we were all mixed up. The heat does funny things to your brain."

Not *that* funny, Olivia thought. "There must be another way into the torture cell," she said.

Choshi shook his head. "No, ma'am, there isn't. I checked it myself."

"It doesn't make sense."

"Not a bit, ma'am."

"You missed something," Dee said.

He turned a cold stare on her. "What did I miss?"

"Somebody got past your security."

"Negative." He turned back to Olivia, clearly annoyed and ready to end the conversation. "Is there anything else?"

THE SOUND OF HEAVY MACHINERY rumbled through the Old City. In the square where Brian had been shot and where Jodee and Mahdi died, a backhoe's giant robotic arm pulled at the unstable wall of a shattered mosque. The clawed bucket scrabbled almost daintily at ancient brick. Golden dust hazed the air. Olivia tried to rub the sleep out of her eyes. A slight tremor caused by the movement of heavy equipment communicated through the earth to Olivia's body, exaggerating her nervousness.

The big green copper door of the madrassa was locked, but she had found a local man to let them in, a friend of Jodee's from before the war, when he worked as a guide to historical sites. Fawaz was an old man with good English. Stooped, wearing a white dishdashah, he had a bad hip and walked with a pronounced limp. He wore a dust mask that reminded Olivia of the filter masks everyone wore in the America of her aborted probability choices.

She had told him the truth, up to a point—that she had been in the cell under the madrassa when Marines rescued her, and that she wanted to see the place again for an article she was writing. Which could have been true, even if, strictly speaking, it wasn't. Olivia had no intention of ever writing anything about what had happened to her.

"It's all very bad." Fawaz fumbled with keys. He didn't need to specify what was very bad. All of it was.

The big padlock came away, and he hauled the door open. Inside, Fawaz said, "Wait." He shuffled over to a chair on which sat a crude power box. Wires ran from the box to the black cedar door frame of the stairwell, passed through an eyebolt, and continued down. Olivia recognized the box. Assad's men had used it to shock Jacob and who knew how many other victims. Now, when Fawaz touched a pair of twisted wires to a second, naked lead on the power box, a lightbulb flickered in the stairwell.

"Please go ahead," Fawaz said, gesturing toward the doorway.

Olivia and Dee descended the stairs. A single low-wattage CFL bulb lighted the way. They moved carefully. The narrow stone steps seemed to sag under the weight of time. Only days ago, Olivia had helped Brian struggle down these same steps.

Fawaz followed them, breathing heavily through his filter mask. The madrassa wasn't a school in the Western sense of the word. It was also a religious structure, dating back to the earliest architectural expressions of Levantine civilization. According to Fawaz, the Prophet had preserved this madrassa, while all around it history fell to war and destruction. Maybe he was right.

Olivia had to stop halfway down. A rank smell wanted to drive her back up the stairs and out into the dusty light of day. The smell of human suffering, old feces, dried urine, blood. The thick, stone-walled sleeve of the stairwell seemed to press in on her.

Dee tapped her shoulder. "Are you okay?"

"I'm good." Olivia forced herself to continue.

Three more bulbs, hanging from clips attached to the low ceiling, barely illuminated the cell. In the dimness Olivia's eyes were drawn to the place where Brian had died.

There was nothing much to see. Most of Brian's bleeding had been internal, like Olivia's grief.

"Holy shit." Dee stood by the table where Jacob had been tied down and tortured. "Look at this."

Olivia walked over. On the table, where Jacob's head would have rested, a dark glaze of blood gleamed. More dried blood stained the floor.

Fawaz shuffled over, his soft shoes scuffing the stones, his breathing labored through the dust mask. "All bad," he said. "A desecration."

Olivia turned to him. "Is there some other way into this room, different from the stairs we just came down?"

"Another way?" He looked confused. "There is only the one."

"There's nothing behind the walls?"

"Dirt. Rocks."

Olivia produced a silver cartridge the size of a pen. She twisted it and produced a brilliant light. By twisting the cartridge one way or the other she could fan the light or reduce it to a narrow beam. Fanning increased the coverage but scaled down the brightness. She adjusted it somewhere between a pencil's diameter and the broadest, dimmest setting.

Fawaz retreated across the room, visibly uncomfortable. "Many bad things have happened in this place. Such things leave a . . . stain of their own. I think it is time to go."

Olivia directed her light at the floor.

"We must go now," Fawaz said.

"Just a minute."

Olivia stepped away from the table, following the blood. On the floor near the wall a substantial pool had accumulated and dried.

"That's interesting," Dee said. "But I guess Private Choshi didn't think so."

"Or he saw it but it didn't lead him anywhere."

"That wall looks pretty solid."

"If you please," Fawaz said from the foot of the stairs.

Dee glanced toward Fawaz, dropped her voice. "You think he knows anything?"

"No."

"You must come now," Fawaz said.

Outside, they left Fawaz to secure the door of the madrassa.

"Seriously," Dee said, "what the hell—"

Olivia looked back at the madrassa. Fawaz had finished fastening the chain. He gave the big padlock a tug and turned to walk away, taking careful, shuffling steps, favoring his right hip.

"I think I know what it means," Olivia said. "The missing head. The blood."

"What?"

"We've found the probability machine."

THIRTY-FIVE

OLIVIA KNEW A GUY. SHE always knew a guy.

Covering the Syrian civil war, she had taken pains to foster friendly relations with people on all sides of the conflict. That included members of Assad's regular army, rebel fighters representing all the major factions, foreign jihadists, American advisors, and — when the coalition forces finally arrived — representatives from all participating member states. She exploited her credentials and reputation to get what she wanted when she wanted it — usually interviews with key people or an embedded position in the thick of the fight.

The day after visiting the madrassa with Dee and Fawaz, what she needed was a satchel bomb.

For that, you didn't approach Captain Ted Burnley or any other coalition military man or woman; you approached their enemy counterpart. For that, you called in all the favors you were ever owed just to arrange a meeting with the obese man who presently sat opposite her, sweating heavily through his white linen jacket. "And why do you want this thing?" He picked up his cup with the plump fingertips of both hands and brought the steaming black coffee to his lips. This café on the edge of eastern Aleppo was dark and underpopulated, which suited the nature of the conversation. Dee was back at the hotel, waiting — something she did not do well. One of the legs of Olivia's chair was shorter than the others. Every time she moved, it tipped a little. A small thing, but it made her feel off-balance in the negotiation.

"I can't tell you what I'm going to do with it," she said. "But nobody is going to get hurt. I promise you that."

There she went again, making a promise she was far from certain she could keep. On the plus side, if anyone *did* get hurt, it was likely to be only her.

The man, whose name was Ashraf, drank some coffee and set down the cup. "Let me tell you about such a thing. I could, if so inclined, locate an M183 demolition charge assembly. That is twenty pounds of C-4 plastic explosive, sufficient to blow up almost any armored vehicle, breach almost any barrier, and kill a large number of people. It is a very dangerous item. Since you are not an expert in handling explosives, one must assume a high possibility, if not probability, of injuries. Such an explosion will bring down a medium-sized building. Such an explosion detonated in any populous area will cause many deaths."

Olivia sipped warm water from a plastic bottle.

Ashraf saw her determination. "Perhaps a single brick of C-4, about one pound, will be sufficient?"

Olivia shook her head. "I need the satchel explosive, all twenty pounds. With a timed detonator." In her mind, Olivia saw the madrassa imploding into a burning crater. Not the ultimate goal — but she didn't know what it would take to destroy the probability machine, which *was*.

Ashraf studied her. The silence stretched out. "Again. For what do you want this?"

"I have to break into a place."

"Unless it is three feet of solid steel, twenty pounds of C-4 you do not need."

"Nobody will be hurt."

"Girls should not play with explosives."

Olivia forced herself to not reply.

A smile appeared briefly on Ashraf's face. "I only say such things because I know you American women hate being told you are girls."

Olivia waited.

Ashraf shifted in his chair, made uncomfortable by either her silence or his girth. "A remote detonator is safer than a timer."

"No doubt."

"But you prefer the timer, of course."

"Yes."

Assuming the machine was underground, a radio-controlled detonation might not work. And she couldn't count on having enough time to reel out a hardwired detonation. Olivia didn't know what the circumstances would be, but she was pretty sure she would be in a hurry.

"And you say your intent is to not hurt anyone?" Ashraf said.

"Yes."

"I should hope not." Ashraf finished his coffee and stood. "Come back in two hours. Bring the money."

✤

MIDNIGHT. THERE WAS A KNOCK on Olivia's door.

"Dee?"

"Yeah."

Olivia opened up.

Dee noticed the satchel. "Is that what I think it is?"

"C-4."

"Oh, fuck."

"It's going to be all right."

"How much do you have?" Dee asked.

"Twenty pounds."

"Are you kidding? You'll kill us both and bring the whole building down. You know that, right?"

"We don't know what to expect. I want to be prepared."

Dee looked unhappy.

"You don't have to come," Olivia said.

"I'm coming."

"It might be better if you don't. If things go bad, I don't want to be responsible for you."

"There's a better chance of getting this done if there's two of us," Dee said.

"I know."

Dee threw her hands up. "Then let's quit fucking around and do it already."

✤

A WHITE RIND OF MOON tilted over the dome of the madrassa. Olivia and Dee stood in the narrow alley across the square. All was quiet.

Dee carried the 9 mm pistol she'd taken from Emilio. Olivia had the satchel bomb strapped to her back and held a heavy iron pry bar she had liberated from the trunk of an abandoned vehicle.

After ten minutes of no one passing within sight, Olivia said, "Let's go."

They ran across the square. All the heavy, leaded glass had long ago been blown out of the madrassa's window casements; iron frameworks covered the openings. Dee watched to make sure no one was coming, and Olivia jammed the tapered end of the pry bar between the grate and the cracked stone.

Dee elbowed her. "Wait."

Olivia turned around. "What?"

"*Shhh.*"

The square remained quiet. The coalition-imposed curfew was in full force. If Olivia and Dee were caught outside, they'd be in trouble. Never mind the gun, never mind the breaking and entering of a historic structure. Never mind trespassing on a crime scene. Never mind the fucking *satchel bomb*.

"What is it?" Olivia whispered.

Dee had the 9 mm in her hand. "I thought I saw someone."

"*Thought* you saw, or *saw?*"

"Hold on."

Dee walked toward the alley they'd just left. She stopped in the middle of the square, listening. Olivia held the pry bar in both hands, flexing her grip, tense.

Dee produced a Maglite and pointed it along the barrel of her gun, which was aimed at the alley. The light slipped around in the dark making hectic shadows, revealing nothing. She turned the light off and joined Olivia again. "Never mind. Let's do this."

Olivia turned back to the window. Again she worked the tapered end of the pry bar between the framework and the stone.

"This is going to be loud."

She got both hands on the bar and pushed, putting her whole body into it, levering the grate out of the crumbling stone with a cracking sound that made Olivia grimace, even though she had been expecting it. She stopped and looked around the square, listening.

Nothing.

"Help me," Olivia said.

Dee got her hands on the framework above where Olivia now gripped it. Together, they wrenched it out of the wall. Olivia stumbled back, holding the heavy iron, which almost overbalanced her and put her on her ass. She set the grate down, leaning it against the wall. When she looked up, Dee was already climbing through the window.

Inside, Dee switched on her Maglite, shading the beam with her hand. They crossed the debris-strewn floor and huddled over the power box. Olivia attached the loose wires to the lead, and the bulb flickered to life in the stairwell, too dim and buried to be seen from outside the madrassa.

"Come on," Olivia said.

They passed into the stairwell, Olivia leading the way. The fetid smell of the torture cell rose up the stone sleeve. Again, a part of her wanted to stop, retreat to open air. But she held that part of herself in check and kept moving down.

Three bulbs illuminated the underground room. Immediately, Olivia crossed to the far corner, where the blood had puddled next to the wall. She pressed her hands to one of the stone blocks, big as a steamer trunk, and pushed. It did not give. She brushed her hands over the adjoining blocks, pausing to give each an experimental shove. Dee stood behind her with the flashlight.

"Anything?" Dee said.

"No. Damn it." She planted her feet and put her shoulder into it, grunting and pushing against the wall with all her strength. Nothing. She stood back.

"It's just a wall," Dee said. "If it was anything else, someone would have discovered it before now."

"Like the Society?"

"The Society wouldn't have needed to discover it. The Shepherds have always known where to find the probability machine. Maybe you were wrong—maybe it's not down here."

Frustrated, Olivia lowered herself to her knees and shoved again on the stone block that formed a right angle with the floor. It didn't budge.

"Look," Dee said. "It was a good guess, but I think we should get the hell out of here before somebody finds us."

"Wait." Olivia stood. "I'm probably doing it wrong. Those blocks are heavy. It would take some serious leverage to move them. Some kind of mechanism."

"Okay. So how do you activate it?"

Olivia turned back to the wall and started sliding her hands over the blocks, feeling for anything, a stud, a disguised pedal. Dee held her Maglite in her teeth and did the same. They moved in opposite directions, away from the dried puddle of blood. After a couple of minutes, Olivia stopped again.

"It wouldn't be so easy," she said. "It wouldn't be something you could stumble on accidentally."

She reached in her pocket and withdrew her cartridge light, twisted it on, and swept the beam over the wall. Dee did the same with her Maglite.

"There's nothing," Dee said.

"Wait."

Olivia craned her head back and pointed her light at the ceiling. It was low, but still too high for her to touch without something to stand on. Hundreds, if not thousands, of bricks, each roughly the size of a shoebox, comprised the ceiling. She crossed the room to the table, moving slowly, keeping her head back. Her light slid over the inverted terrain of rough bricks until it fell on a maroon handprint, barely visible, dried on a brick directly above the table.

"*Got it.*"

"What?" Dee said.

"It's there, *right there.*"

Dee joined her and looked up. "What?"

"The discoloration on that one brick—does that look like a handprint to you?"

Dee stood on her toes, as if getting a couple of inches closer might make all the difference. "No way."

"You see it?"

"Yeah."

Olivia put her light away and climbed onto the table. She reached up and put her hand on the brick, covering the handprint of the last person to touch it.

She pushed.

The brick did not move.

She pushed harder. This time, the brick shifted slightly, and fine, powdery grit sifted onto her face. She spat, and blinked it out of her eyes, braced her legs, and shoved with all her strength. Suddenly the brick moved, retracting into the ceiling with an audible *clunk.* Across the room, behind the wall, something big and heavy started grinding. After a moment, the large block near the bloodstain scraped back—

Revealing a tunnel.

Dee said, "Holy shit."

"Un–fucking–believable."

After a few seconds, the grinding sound behind the wall resumed, and the block slowly scraped back into place, as if it had never moved. Olivia looked up. The brick, which had retracted into the ceiling, had now returned to its flush position with the others.

"That was fast," Dee said.

"They wouldn't want to leave the tunnel exposed," Olivia said. "Alvaro must have moved the block from the other side. He comes into the chamber, and the passage closes behind him."

"Yeah. After the Marines took you out of here but before they came back for the bodies."

"He hears them upstairs and he doesn't know what's going on. Jacob is dead. Alvaro has to know if the link has migrated. Maybe he tries to move the body to the tunnel, but it's tied down. Anyway, the block only stays open less than a minute. There isn't time. Somebody could find him. So he uses something the torturers left behind. He cuts Jacob's head off, climbs on the table, opens the passage."

"That sounds right."

A man's voice. Both women turned, Olivia still standing on the table. Emilio, leveling a gun, stepped off the bottom step into the chamber. Two men followed. They looked vaguely familiar. Olivia had seen them at Sanctuary.

"Neither one of you move," Emilio said.

Dee pulled the gun she'd taken off Emilio the night before and pointed it at him.

"Drop your weapon," she said.

"We both want the same thing." Emilio didn't drop or lower his gun. "We want to protect the Society."

"I thought the goal was to save the future," Dee said.

The other men moved in opposite directions, away from Emilio, circling around, advancing on Olivia and Dee.

Dee kept her gun trained on Emilio, who was the only other person armed. "You two stop. Douglas, Kevin. Don't move."

They kept moving.

"She has the link," Emilio said. "You know it's wrong for her to have it."

"Just *back off*," Dee said.

"There's a new order of succession," Emilio said.

"According to you."

"Yes."

Emilio fired, the report painfully loud, banging off the walls and low ceiling. Even as she fell back, Dee returned fire, squeezing off three wild rounds. Emilio retreated up the stairs, and the other men froze.

Dee staggered against the wall and slid down it. The gun dropped from her hand. For one suspended moment, time seemed to halt.

Then Olivia jumped off the table and grabbed the gun. "You two get the hell out of here." She waved the gun.

The two men retreated to the stairs and stood there.

"Out!" Olivia fired twice, aiming wide. She didn't want to kill anyone; she just wanted them to leave.

They ran up the stairs.

Olivia dropped the clip and counted rounds. Seven left. She slapped the clip back in place, jacked a round into the chamber, put the gun down, and turned to Dee. Blood soaked through her shirt, high on the left side of her chest. "Oh, Jesus Christ." Olivia pressed her hand to the wound, applying pressure. Add another victim to her personal accounts ledger.

"Get out of here," Dee said. "You were right. They'll kill you to get the link."

"Hang on," Olivia said.

Dee clenched her teeth and nodded. "Just go."

Olivia picked up the gun. She returned to the table, climbed up.

Dee shouted, "Look out."

Olivia turned.

Emilio leaned out of the stairwell and fired. He was no marksman. Olivia shoved the pressure-switch brick into the ceiling and jumped off the table, and the stone block began to scrape back into the wall, revealing the passage. Olivia got off two more rounds, then dropped through the opening into the tunnel.

THIRTY-SIX

THE AIR WAS DRY AND stiflingly hot. Niches in the walls held bowls of oil and floating wicks that fluttered when Olivia passed by. She wasn't the only one down here. The tunnel wound unevenly through the earth, like the sinuously excavated route of a rock-and-earth-devouring creature. She listened for the sound of the stone block grinding and scraping aside. Had Emilio seen her push the pressure-switch brick into the ceiling? Did he know how to follow her? Eventually the tunnel split into branches. She paused, then followed the branch on her right.

Her footfalls thudded. Her breath rasped, and sweat stung her eyes. Some of the oil lamps had gone out, leaving the path before her in darkness. She almost turned back but decided to press on a little farther. The heat and silence enclosed her like a fist. She tucked the pistol into the waist of her pants and dug out her cylinder light, twisting it in the middle. The light came on—and she caught her breath. Shadows slid in the gaping eye sockets of a human skull. She moved the light. An entire skeleton lay in a stone bed carved into the wall, the bones tangled with scraps of ancient leather. Latin words were chiseled into the rock above the bed. She stood on her toes, blew dust out of the letters. NOS-TRUM PASTORIS. Her Latin was rusty, but she thought it could mean "Our Shepherd."

Olivia moved her light along the wall, revealing more remains, the leather scraps giving way to shreds of cloth. A catacomb, sealed off from the outside world for God knew how long, and that same phrase had been chiseled over every bed of bones.

She continued down the narrow passageway. Olivia had visited catacombs in Paris and Rome; by comparison, this was tiny, the remains of just a dozen or so people. For a while, she kept her light on the floor, looking for tripping hazards. The next time she redirected her light it found, not a skeleton, but the mummified remains of a man dressed in a robe similar to the ones she'd seen the Elders wearing at Sanctuary. Tomb of the Shepherds. Is this where they would have laid Jacob? Would *her* bones eventually have been left here? Maybe, if they'd ever accepted her legitimacy.

The next stone bed was empty. No, not empty. Her light discovered Jacob's severed head—blood clotted in the beard, the top of the skull hacked off.

"*Fuck.*" Olivia recoiled—but kept moving.

At a sharp bend, the tunnel branched again. Across the passage, through a crude archway, wavering lamplight cast shadows on a fresco. Olivia turned her light off and, passing under the arch, entered a long, narrow chamber with stone benches raised on either side. A dozen oil lamps lined the benches, six to a side. The fresco was painted on the far wall, inside a recessed vault. She approached it.

Time and streaks of soot had rendered the figures almost unrecognizable, but it seemed to depict three men enclosed by a ring of light. Olivia thought of the gallery of portraits in the conference room at Sanctuary. She wiped the sweat out of her eyes. On a step climbing into the vault, she saw Jacob's scooped-out brains lying in a messy lump like oatmeal. She'd almost stepped in them. "Gah." She stumbled back.

A scuffing sound behind her. "Who are *you?*"

Olivia whirled. Alvaro stood in the doorway, shirtless, his body glistening with sweat. He held a long-bladed weapon, something between a machete and a scimitar, and he looked gaunt, tired, hollow-eyed. Blotchy rust-colored stains covered his hands. Dried blood? How long had he been down here?

"My name's Olivia." She kept her voice steady and backed up.

"How did you get in here? You can't be here."

She tried not to stare at the machete. "I came through the wall of the madrassa, from that room where Jacob died."

Alvaro's eyes got wide. "You knew Jacob?"

"Yes."

"You're lying. I've never seen you before."

"I'm not lying."

"Jacob would not have brought you here."

"Who said Jacob brought me?" Olivia met his defiant glare straight on. "I came on my own."

"That's impossible."

"I'm a Shepherd," Olivia said. "The last one."

She might as well have clouted him with a bag of rocks. His mouth opened, closed. "But you're a woman." Like he was saying *But you're a duck* to one that happened to waddle into a shareholders' meeting.

"Right. And I knew Jacob *and* you. And Dee. I was in the torture cell when Jacob died. The link migrated to me. I didn't know what was going on, but I accidentally created a probability that let Jacob and my friends live but killed the rest of the world. Eventually I fixed that by going back to Jacob's original choice. That's what we're living in now."

Alvaro gaped at her. "Show me your neck."

"Put the machete down first."

He raised the blade, blinked innocently. "You think I'd hurt you?"

Olivia waited.

"I'm not a killer."

Olivia pulled the 9 mm from her waist and pointed it at him.

He took a step back. "I wouldn't hurt you. I've never hurt anybody in my life."

"That's great. You're not getting the link. Drop the machete. Now."

Alvaro laughed. "I never wanted the damn thing." He tossed the machete aside. It clanged on the floor.

"Oh?" She flicked her eyes to his bloodstained hands.

"I needed to know if the link was still in Jacob," he said. "That it hadn't migrated to a civilian. I guess it did?"

"Here." Olivia turned aside and tucked her chin down, exposing the back her neck, awkwardly keeping the gun pointed at him. She could only see him in her periphery. Alvaro stepped nearer.

"That's close enough," she said.

After a few moments, he said, "My God, it's true."

She faced him again. "You've been down here by yourself all this time?"

"Since Jacob brought me, yes. It's part of the ritual. In this chamber he revealed the true history of the probability machine. Then he left me, and I was supposed to follow his directions to the machine and witness it for myself, in solitude. But something went wrong. Jacob should have come back after a day, and then we'd complete a ten-day fast together before returning to the outside world."

"But he didn't come back," Olivia said.

"I waited, but I was worried. What if Jacob had a heart attack or had gotten injured? Aleppo is unstable, dangerous. I had to be near him for the migration. So even though I wasn't supposed to leave the tunnels until after the fasting period, I decided I had to. That's when I found him. I . . . did what I had to do and came back to the Mithraeum. After that, I didn't know what to do."

"So you did nothing." Olivia felt agitated and impatient.

Alvaro shrugged. "I completed my fast. I would have come out in another day or two. The water is almost gone. And I didn't know who had the link—if anyone did. Nothing like this has ever happened before. Sorry, I have to sit. I haven't eaten in a long time." He settled on a stone bench. There was a pleading look in his eyes, or maybe it was simply hunger. "Please," he said. "Tell me everything."

"It's a long story."

"I'm listening."

"Show me the probability machine first. I'm a Shepherd. I have a right to see it."

She was worried about Emilio. He might already be in the tunnels.

Alvaro hesitated. "If you're a Shepherd, you do have that right."

"You just saw the scar."

"But I can't show you the machine until you know what it is."

"I already know what it is."

"All you know is what you've experienced and what, if anything, you've been told. The Parable of Two Cities, how the Society exists to guarantee the future?"

"You're saying that isn't true?"

"It's partly true. And this is the only place where you would hear the rest of it—just as I heard it from Jacob. There's an order to follow. The ancient knowledge is passed to the new Shepherd. It's done here, in the Mithraeum."

"Okay already." She just wanted to get on with it, do what she came here to do. "What is it, then? What is the probability machine?"

"It's a weapon of war."

That stopped her. "*What* war?"

"One that hasn't happened yet. A war in the far future. The probability machine is the ultimate weapon. If you want to wipe your enemy off the face of the earth, go find crisis points that might result in that outcome, then push them hard. That's why the machine is keyed to crisis points—not to avert them, but to make them worse. One side or the other decided to hide the machine in the deep past. A technician—or maybe it was a military man, someone linked to the machine—came with it. But something went wrong and he got stuck in the third century with the weapon."

"Time travel." Olivia said. "You brought that up before, in a different probability."

"Even Einstein said time was an illusion," Alvaro said, "that there wasn't any real dividing line between the past, present, and future. The probability machine exists across all times and probabilities, from here to the 'shining city' of the parable."

"So it's a weapon. Yet another fucking weapon."

Alvaro nodded. "Originally, yes. But the Society repurposed it. Back in 235 AD, a Roman soldier, a deserter named Decius, found the time traveler down here. Decius was the leader of a small cult that had broken away from Mithraism."

Olivia kept looking toward the archway out of the Mithraeum. Was Emilio out there in the tunnels right now? Even if he had seen how she entered, his own superstitions about the Society's ritual order might stop him from entering a place only Shepherds were supposed to enter. No, she thought. She couldn't count on that. Emilio considered himself heir to the power.

"How far is it to the machine?"

"It's a ways."

"Come on," she said. "We have to go."

Alvaro stood up slowly. "I've been down here more than a week. Can't you tell me what's happening out there?"

"You're stalling." Olivia waved the gun. "We can talk on the way."

"That's blood on your hands, your shirt. At least tell me whose it is."

She hesitated. "Emilio shot . . . somebody."

Alvaro looked shocked. "What? Why would he—?"

"Later. Take me to the machine now."

It was time to turn it off.

THIRTY-SEVEN

THEY FOLLOWED A TWISTING TUNNEL that plunged them deeper and deeper into the earth. Oil lamps flickered in niches. With each step, the air became hotter. Frequently they had to duck to avoid hitting their heads on the low ceiling. The rising heat wanted to drive them back. Olivia used her sleeve to mop sweat off her forehead and clear her eyes.

"These tunnels are Roman?" she asked.

"They predate the empire."

"Tell me about that soldier, that deserter. Decius. You mentioned him once in another probability, too."

Olivia wanted to keep Alvaro talking, keep him distracted until they reached the machine.

"We must have known each other pretty well in that other probability," he said.

"We did some traveling together."

"I see. All right." Alvaro cleared his throat. "The man from the future befriended Decius, and when the man died, Decius was there. By then he knew about the probability machine and he knew the link would migrate. Of course, the scroll record isn't so precise, and educated or not, Decius was a man of his century. In his writings he calls the man from the future Viatorem. The Traveler. And he refers to the halo as a 'god power.'"

"Which he immediately started using," Olivia said. "Naturally. So it never was about protecting the future."

Alvaro stopped walking and leaned against the wall. He looked genuinely surprised at what she had said. "Of course it was. But Decius acted recklessly. His first time in the halo, he caused the emperor Severus to be assassinated by his own army. In history books the incident is actually called the Crisis of the Third Century. That changed everything—accelerated the downfall of the Roman Empire. Think of the ripple effects. The Society grew from Decius's own cult, as a corrective body. The future isn't guaranteed anymore, because it isn't the same future that produced the probability machine."

Olivia shook her head. "If the machine is here, that proves the future exists."

"No. The future exists because the *Society* is here."

"You sound like you're trying to convince yourself, not me."

"I know what I know."

Olivia thought: It doesn't change anything. She still had to destroy the damn machine. The fact that it existed right now did prove the future survived. Or, she thought, it proved she was about to fail at destroying the probability machine—or, rather, the probability *weapon*.

They continued walking until a weird silvery glimmer, like a migraine aura, appeared in the distance, reflecting on the walls.

Alvaro stopped and turned to her. "What you're going to see, only a small number of people have ever seen."

"Let's keep moving."

He pointed at her 9 mm. "The gun isn't necessary."

"I'm relieved to hear that."

Behind them, footfalls came rushing down the tunnel. Before Alvaro could react, Olivia shoved him aside and ran toward the glimmer of silver light, encountering waves of almost unbearable heat. It baked against her face, drew sweat streaming out of her body, as if she were melting through her clothes. Behind her, Emilio shouted, "Stop her!"

"Keep back!" Olivia fired into the tunnel behind her, the reports, slapping off the rock walls, painfully loud. She aimed high, not wanting to hit Alvaro. A pointless consideration, in light of what she was about to do. The explosion would probably kill them all. She dropped the now-empty gun and kept running.

The tunnel turned and dipped suddenly. She lost her footing and went sprawling, sliding into a high-ceilinged cavern, like a base runner trying to steal home. She pushed herself to her knees. A buzzing vibration in the air made her skin tingle. The silver-white light and buzzing sound emanated from a pit sunk in the middle of the cavern. Olivia scrambled to her feet, approached the edge, and peered over. Twenty feet down, a halo, like a ring of burning white magnesium, encircled a globe the size of a wrecking ball. The probability machine was a finely detailed miniature of planet Earth wrapped in clouds, with oceans and continents visible beneath. An artifact from the future somehow floating here beneath the ancient city. Olivia stared, open-mouthed.

A myriad of spokes glimmered between the halo and the Earth. So many spokes they became uncountable. The link stirred in sympathy, tingling inside her mind, and Olivia knew that here, contained in this fantastic machine, all the decision end points of all the human probability machines across time still existed—including the Shepherd choices Jacob had made over a lifetime of apocalyptic brinkmanship.

Including Olivia's own broken alternative worlds.

Below the machine, like an optical illusion, the native rock walls of the pit blurred into the shimmering walls of a shaft plunging to infinity. Olivia felt dizzy, and caught herself swaying at the edge, overwhelmed by the heat and the unreal quality of what she was seeing.

The halo distorted the atmosphere in rising waves of heat. Spokes glimmered with uncounted probability choices. The heat throbbed and burned. Through the link, the buzz resolved to granular detail—billions of voices speaking in billions of minor and major variations of lives lived and lost and lived again across countless probabilities. If she destroyed it, what would happen? The Society could be right: Destroying the machine might undo the world. She could be standing at the brink of her biggest mistake yet.

Olivia backed away from the edge, the twenty pounds of C-4 weighing heavily on her shoulders.

She heard them coming, Alvaro and Emilio, their voices arguing, getting closer.

Olivia shrugged the satchel bomb off her shoulders. Without knowing why, she said, "I'm sorry," and then she ripped a Velcro flap open and clocked back the delay timer to three seconds.

Emilio was the first one out of the tunnel, coming at her with his pistol leveled, yelling.

Olivia toggled the detonator and flung the satchel into the pit.

THIRTY-EIGHT

THE FIRST TIME OLIVIA HAD ever witnessed, close up, the explosion of a barrel bomb, a shock wave had torn through her body, lifted her off her feet, and dropped her flat on her back. She had blinked grit out of her eyes while a yellow cloud drifted across the sun, depositing a hissing rain of dust. She hadn't really been close up, of course. Any closer than fifty yards and she would have been obliterated by shrapnel, burning oil, and flying debris.

Terry Simms, a *New York Times* reporter who had been escorting her to a hotel in eastern Aleppo where journalists gathered, had bent over her. "Are you all right?" he'd shouted. Shouting was necessary or else she would not have been able to hear him through the ringing. "Yes," she had said, and he pulled her to her feet and hastily brushed the dust off her clothes. Later he had admitted he had just been trying to cop a feel, and Olivia hadn't known whether he'd been joking. It probably didn't matter, since by then they were in bed. But out there in the aftermath of Olivia's first big explosion, shouting through the dust and ringing bells, Terry Simms had said, "Things go boom around here a lot. You'll get used to it."

She had been in Aleppo less than three hours.

Terry had been half right. Things did go boom a lot, but no, she did not get used to it; she only pretended to. The same way she pretended to be immune to the small "d" disasters in her own life.

But no barrel bomb, missile strike, or IED had prepared her for what happened when twenty pounds of C-4 plastic explosive went boom not twenty feet from where she stood.

The pit roared and the ground shuddered in violent upheaval. Olivia threw her arms in front of her face. Scorching heat crackled her skin . . . and then abruptly withdrew. Silence filled the vacuum. At first she thought the explosion must have blown out her eardrums. Then she resumed breathing and heard the rasp and drag of air in and out of her lungs. Why wasn't she dead?

Olivia lowered her arms. Invisible fingers plucked at her shirt, mussed her hair. Dust whooshed by her and joined the rubble churning in white light, held contained by some force, and funneling back into the pit—an explosion do-over. It was like watching a perfect 3D projection run in reverse. Olivia forgot about Emilio and Alvaro, forgot about everything but the spectacle before her. They all should have been blown to pieces. Instead, this. Feeling drawn to it, she stepped closer, and the invisible fingers seized her hard—the same force that was calling back the explosive power of the C-4 now yanked her off her feet. She hit the ground face-down, and the force dragged her toward the funneling debris.

Olivia planted her hands and tried to shove herself back, but the force was too strong. The rough stone scraped the skin from the heels of her hands. She shouted, "*No!*" Someone grabbed her ankle. She looked back. It was Emilio, and behind him Alvaro held on to Emilio's arm, hauling back, jaw clenched, his hair flying around his face. It was as if a pressurized cabin had been breached and they were all being sucked toward the hole.

Olivia's head and arms crossed over the edge of the pit. Emilio's fingers dug painfully into her leg, holding on. Maybe all he wanted to save was the link, but if he could see what she now saw, he would know that possessing the link had become pointless.

Like water down a drain, the pulverized debris swirled into the shaft. The probability machine, a fractured globe bleeding light, was caught in the middle of the swirl. The machine plunged into the depths, falling until it winked out like a blue spark. The force of depressurization, or whatever it was, released Olivia. Her arms dangling into the pit, she watched the infinity shaft flicker and collapse into itself.

And then everything went dark.

Not simply dark, but the utter, seamless blackness of an underground cavern. In the next moment a deep rumbling surge came up from beneath the bedrock. It sounded like a charging herd of elephants.

Behind her, Emilio said, "Oh, my God." He released her ankle. Olivia pushed herself away from the pit and started to stand up. The ground shuddered, and a great rolling quake knocked her down again. She shouted, "*Fuck.*" The solid rock bucked and rolled and bounced her. With a sharp cracking of stone breaking away from stone, pieces of the cavern thudded down all around her. She covered her head with her arms, tried to draw her knees up to her chest, even while the quake bounced her violently. It went on and on, the way all disasters seemed to when you found yourself in the middle of one. A man—she couldn't tell if it was Emilio or Alvaro—screamed, and then the scream cut off abruptly. After that, the shaking finally stopped.

The dry sound of grit sifting down.

With trembling hands, Olivia dug out her cartridge light and twisted it on. A slender bar struck through the haze of suspended dust. She took a deep shuddering breath, coughed, spat, and stood up unsteadily. She twisted the cartridge, fanning the light, and swept it over the pit, which now bottomed out after twenty feet. The shaft, the corridor between past and future—if that's what it had been—was gone.

Olivia turned away from the pit. The earthquake had largely deconstructed the cavern. Massive chunks of rock lay all around her. She worked her mouth, tasting the gritty dust on her tongue. Her light fell on a man's foot. She moved the beam along the leg, the torso, and arrived at a jagged puzzle-piece of rock where the man's head should have been.

Somebody coughed. Olivia swung her light. Alvaro blinked and held up his hand. His hair had gone gray with dust. He looked stunned.

"Alvaro. Are you all right?"

"What happened?" He sounded dazed.

"Earthquake," Olivia said. "A big one. We're lucky the whole cave didn't come down on us."

"No," Alvaro said. "What *happened?*"

"I destroyed the probability machine."

He stared. "It's gone?"

"Yes. But we're still here, and we need to get out of this place."

"Wait." Alvaro knelt beside his cousin's body. He lifted his limp hand and held it. "I knew him his whole life."

"I'm sorry." She gave him a moment, then said, "But we have to go. Now."

She was worried about her cartridge light. If the battery ran down, they'd be lost—maybe permanently.

Alvaro looked up. "Go?"

"Yes. Go—back to the surface."

"I don't see the point." Alvaro sounded hopeless.

"Come on. We can't help your cousin, but we can help ourselves."

"It isn't about Emilio. You've destroyed the probability machine." Anguish had crept into his voice. "There's nothing waiting for us up there but the end."

Olivia wanted to shake him. "You have to get up. *Now.*"

He didn't say anything. He had gone back to dazed and defeated. Slowly, he got to his feet.

They scuffed and shuffled through the dark, led onward by Olivia's light striking through the haze. For every yard of forward progress, they lost half a yard. The earthquake had destroyed large sections of the tunnel network. With each step, Olivia feared the aftershock that could bring tons of rock and earth down on them. Hours dragged by without any sign of hope. Their field of vision was so narrow, and what they could see did not look familiar. The cartridge light began to dim. When it was gone, they would be finished.

Olivia stepped on something hard that rolled under her shoe. She stopped and redirected her light. A long bone, yellow with age. A human tibia.

"Wait." Olivia moved her light until it found the bed carved into the rock wall. She reached up. Her fingers trembled over the chiseled Latin. NOSTRUM PASTORIS. "I know where we are."

Alvaro grunted. He'd barely spoken since they left the cavern where the probability machine had been. Olivia put her hand on his shoulder.

"Come on," she said gently. "It isn't much farther."

At last they came to the passage into the madrassa. The stone block that had moved aside when Olivia pressed the brick pressure switch into the ceiling had detached from its rail and fallen inward, barricading entry into the chamber. Daylight shone through the gap, which meant the ceiling had tumbled down, and probably the madrassa's dome, as well.

"Help me," Olivia said.

Together they got their hands on the stone block and tried to muscle it aside, to widen the gap. It scraped a few inches but no more. Olivia let go and dusted her hands off on her pants. She worked her lips, her tongue coated with gritty dust. Her throat burned for water. She crawled onto the block and wriggled through the gap, emerging into a hazy shaft of hot sunlight. She knew the hardest part for Alvaro was coming up. She had left Dee wounded and incapacitated. If the bullets hadn't killed her, odds were high that the earthquake had. Olivia crawled, blinking and squinting, into the chamber and stood up.

Dee was gone.

"Hey."

Olivia turned. Alvaro was stuck halfway through the gap. She bent over, grabbed his forearms, and pulled. He came through, and she stumbled back, almost landing on her butt. Alvaro stood, derelict, head craned back, in the burning shaft of sunlight.

"This way," Olivia said, following a blood trail to the stairs.

Large, irregular sections of the madrassa's dome had broken off and fallen into the school, crushing desks and chairs. Olivia and Alvaro pushed through the green copper door. Outside, a civilian vehicle, a big Suburban, was parked in the square, a red cross fixed to the hood and the rear passenger door. Two men carefully loaded a woman, her left arm supported by a sling, into the back: Dee. She saw Alvaro and called out. It seemed to snap him out of his gloomy stupor, and he ran to her. Olivia's chest tightened with sympathetic emotion. She tried to push thoughts of Brian out of her head, but they had nowhere else to go. After some pleading, the medics let Alvaro climb into the back of the Suburban with Dee. Olivia was still standing in front of the madrassa, feeling a little stunned herself, when the vehicle drove away.

"Êtes-vous bien, mademoiselle?"

Olivia turned.

The woman, dressed in khaki, wearing dark glasses and a safari hat, regarded her. The round lens on the left side of her glasses possessed a polychromatic shimmer, indicating personal technology. She also wore a concerned look.

"Yes," Olivia said. "I'm fine."

"Pardon me," the woman said, switching to English. "You don't look fine. Is that blood? Would you like some water?"

"Water, yes."

"My name is Adriel." The woman unclipped a water bottle from her light utility belt. "What's your name?"

"Olivia." She took the bottle, filled her mouth, swished it around, and spat it out, then drank half the remaining water before returning the bottle and wiping her lips on the back of her hand. "Are you Red Cross?"

"No." Adriel pointed at the patch sewn onto her blouse: *APC.* "Aleppo Preservation Corps. My partner and I are assessing the earthquake damage to historical sites. As if the war damage wasn't bad enough. Are you quite sure you're all right?"

"Yes."

Adriel pointed at a man dressed similarly to her, including the same personal-tech sunglasses. Olivia hadn't noticed him until now. "My partner can get us transport if you need to see medical."

Olivia didn't reply. She was staring at the man. It was Jodee Abadi. He was alive, despite having died in Jacob's original probability choice, the one Olivia had reluctantly deferred to. Jodee was *alive.* What did that mean? If Jodee were alive, then Brian . . .

"Jodee!" Olivia ran toward him, waving. "Jodee, it's me!"

She stopped, as if she'd run into a zone of zero atmospheric pressure that deflated her lungs. The man had turned toward her and removed his glasses. He wasn't Jodee. The resemblance was only superficial. Olivia had filled in the physical contradictions with wishful thinking. It wasn't the first time.

"I'm sorry?" the man said.

"Never mind." She felt wrung out.

The man looked puzzled.

"I thought you were somebody else," Olivia said.

"Ah." The man looked to Adriel, who had joined them.

"She's a little rattled by the quake," Adriel said.

"Oh?" The man looked at Olivia with concern. "Were you inside when it hit?"

"Yes." She nodded at the madrassa. "I was in there."

"Then you are fortunate to be alive."

"Yes, I'm very fortunate," Olivia said, not sounding so. Her contradictory tone drew a probing look from the man. To forestall any further questions, Olivia asked, "Did the quake cause much damage?"

"Very much," Adriel said.

"With that on top of the war, how do you keep going?" Olivia asked the question perfunctorily, wanting only to be on her way now, out of the city, out of the Disaster, and this time for good.

"In Aleppo," the man said, "we have a proverb. I made it up myself. 'The act of destruction is the beginning of restoration.'"

✴

OLIVIA WAS AT THE ATATÜRK airport in Istanbul when her phone began trilling like a baby bird trapped in her pocket. She took the phone out. An incoming call notification sprang free, a blue neon holo of Toria Westby's name. Olivia almost turned it off and put the phone away. She was in no mood for conversation. But after a moment's hesitation she flicked the notification and brought the phone to her ear. "Toria?"

"Olivia! I've been trying to get in touch for days."

"Sorry. I've been a little out of it." In fact, she had spent two days making arrangements to have Brian's body returned to Oregon, and another week holed up with all her devices turned off in a tiny hotel room on the western side of Aleppo, enjoying an extended dark night of the soul. Once during that week she had started to call Captain Burnley, and a feeling of self-loathing came over her. The part of Olivia that might have taken any shred of comfort out of the captain's arrival was dead.

"I wanted to tell you about Baki Abboud," Toria said.

Olivia drew a blank. "Who?"

"The checkpoint commander, the one you put me on to."

"Oh, God," Olivia said. "I must be more out of it than I thought. What about him?"

"He checked out. Just like you said. Abboud was communicating with a terror group. He was going to help them obtain a biological weapon."

"What weapon?" Olivia already knew the answer.

"Smallpox. Weaponized variola. And get this. The canisters are serialized and traceable back to Russia. It's stuff that went missing after the collapse of the Soviet Union. Some of it wound up in Syria. This is so big, Olivia. I got my bosses to agree to hire you temporarily. We can write this together. You're freelance, correct?"

"Yes."

After a long pause, Toria said, "You don't sound very excited."

"I'm just really tired."

"Of course, I understand. That's one for the good guys, hey? Could have turned into a nasty business."

"We'll just have to keep on top of things," Olivia said. "Send me what you have. Encrypted. I'm waiting for my flight right now. When I get home we'll talk, all right?"

"Yes," she said. "Olivia, are you well?"

"I am."

"Right, then."

Olivia hung up and put her phone away. *When I get home.* And when would that be? Olivia was afraid, but not of the Disaster, not of variola or barrel bombs or torture states. She was afraid of what might come through the door that Brian had left propped open on his way out. She was afraid she would never get that door closed again, and how was she supposed to live when it was so easy for someone to just walk in?

Across from Olivia, a middle-aged woman in a hijab and long skirt sat next to a girl about twelve years old, who looked like she might be her daughter. The girl wore skinny jeans and a white T-shirt with big pink letters on the front that spelled DREAM, and she looked scared. To fly? To leave home? To arrive somewhere strange? The girl leaned against her mother, who stroked her hair and spoke comforting words Olivia couldn't quite hear. She watched the mother and daughter until the public address called Olivia's flight, then she picked up her bag and got in line.

EPILOGUE

FIVE MONTHS LATER.

Three flights, eleven hours in the air, plus another six in a disorient-ing series of international airports. Her traveling companion was a ghost; she should have been making this trip with Brian. By the time the self-driving cab pulled away from the curb at the Jaipur airport, Olivia was seventy percent zombie and thirty percent neurotic mess. The screen on the back of the front passenger seat displayed a wobbly 3D montage of tourist attractions. Looking at it made Olivia feel a little wobbly herself. Embracing her inner zombie, she closed her eyes and tried to go dead for the duration of the ride. Mostly, she failed.

The cab jostled her, bumping over deteriorated transportation in-frastructure. The world was neither the paradise Dee had desperately wanted nor the black pit of ruin they had all, to some degree or another, feared. For most of her life, Olivia had moved through the Disaster as if it were the only part of life that was real. Maybe the alternative prob-abilities weren't as likely as the Disaster, but they were real, too. At least, Olivia hoped they were. And it was possible to choose them, even if it caused her pain.

After an hour, the cab said, "We have arrived at your destination."

Olivia opened her eyes.

A modern duplex, well maintained, on a street of similar dwellings. A small khejri tree cast dappled shade over the entry. She opened the car door but sat a moment longer, not quite ready. Would she ever be? A long time ago Rohana had comforted her. *Little Oh, you are not alone.* But I am, Olivia thought, I am. She felt the breeze on her face. January in Jaipur, midfifties Fahrenheit—not unlike Seattle. Not unlike home.

Behind a window, a fluffy white cat with orange markings sat curled on the back of a sofa. The cat yawned and began grooming itself.

Olivia got out of the cab, shouldered her duffel bag, and followed the sound of voices. She came through a gate into a winter garden. Terracotta pots stood off the ground on ceramic feet. Thorny vines coiled over the fence like barbed wire. Sunbursts of marigolds proliferated. Two women stood talking by the fence — arguing, actually, but without heat. They wore sturdy-looking trousers and quilted jackets printed in floral patterns. One of the women was Rohana, the other Olivia's aunt Amala, whose garden this was.

"Olivia?" Her stepmother looked surprised, delighted, and cranky all at once. "You promised to call from the airport."

"I know. I'm sorry."

"You look so tired."

"It's a long flight."

The older woman tugged off canvas gardening gloves. "So. Come inside and eat."

"That's okay. I had something on the plane."

"I can imagine. Something inedible. Amala's soup is on the stove. Rasam. Fresh lentils." Rohana looked closely at Olivia. "What's wrong?"

"Nothing. I'm just really tired."

The moment stretched out. "Well," Rohana said, "if you don't want to tell me."

As her stepmother started to turn away, something caught in Olivia's throat. "I . . ." Rohana looked at her, waited. "A friend of mine died," Olivia said. "Last summer, in Aleppo. He was a really good friend. His name was Brian."

"Oh." Rohana's eyes softened and she stepped closer, as did Aunt Amala, the older women touching her, comforting her. And because she really had no choice, Olivia welcomed them inside.

"There," Rohana said, "there."

ACKNOWLEDGMENTS

No one writes a novel alone. I absolutely never used to believe this. But as another well-worn adage points out: *Experience is a great teacher.* So I would like to thank a few people. First and foremost, my brilliant wife, Nancy Kress. She read various drafts of this book and always had useful advice and ideas for improvements. The novel, and my life, are immeasurably improved by her presence. Good friends and good writers Daryl Gregory and Ted Kosmatka read drafts of the novel and provided useful insights as well. Thanks, guys.

Additionally, I'd like to say thank you to Patrick Swenson — writer, publisher, friend, and master of the Rainforest Writers Retreat, where I worked on the first draft of this book. And Kate Konigisor, who has an eagle eye. Also a tip of the hat to Elizabeth Bourne, who was always up for a cup of coffee at "The Foam," or a glass of gin at West 5. It's nice to have a friend in the neighborhood.

And I want to offer my appreciation to Dr. Maura Glynn-Thami for helping me get my medical details straight and for assisting me with some of the Middle Eastern cultural references and language issues.

I would also like to express my heartfelt gratitude to my editor, John Joseph Adams. John's excellent editorial advice and encouragement made *The Chaos Function* a better book and made the road to publication a stress-free experience. Thanks, man.

Finally, special acknowledgment goes to the resident canine, Cosette. If not for her constant poodling, this novel would have taken half as long to write.

Behind a window, a fluffy white cat with orange markings sat curled on the back of a sofa. The cat yawned and began grooming itself.

Olivia got out of the cab, shouldered her duffel bag, and followed the sound of voices. She came through a gate into a winter garden. Terra-cotta pots stood off the ground on ceramic feet. Thorny vines coiled over the fence like barbed wire. Sunbursts of marigolds proliferated. Two women stood talking by the fence—arguing, actually, but without heat. They wore sturdy-looking trousers and quilted jackets printed in floral patterns. One of the women was Rohana, the other Olivia's aunt Amala, whose garden this was.

"Olivia?" Her stepmother looked surprised, delighted, and cranky all at once. "You promised to call from the airport."

"I know. I'm sorry."

"You look so tired."

"It's a long flight."

The older woman tugged off canvas gardening gloves. "So. Come inside and eat."

"That's okay. I had something on the plane."

"I can imagine. Something inedible. Amala's soup is on the stove. Rasam. Fresh lentils." Rohana looked closely at Olivia. "What's wrong?"

"Nothing. I'm just really tired."

The moment stretched out. "Well," Rohana said, "if you don't want to tell me."

As her stepmother started to turn away, something caught in Olivia's throat. "I . . ." Rohana looked at her, waited. "A friend of mine died," Olivia said. "Last summer, in Aleppo. He was a really good friend. His name was Brian."

"Oh." Rohana's eyes softened and she stepped closer, as did Aunt Amala, the older women touching her, comforting her. And because she really had no choice, Olivia welcomed them inside.

"There," Rohana said, "there."